John Henry Overton

William Law, Nonjuror and Mystic

a sketch of his life, character, and opinions

John Henry Overton

William Law, Nonjuror and Mystic
a sketch of his life, character, and opinions

ISBN/EAN: 9783337369422

Printed in Europe, USA, Canada, Australia, Japan

Cover: Foto ©Andreas Hilbeck / pixelio.de

More available books at **www.hansebooks.com**

WILLIAM LAW,

NONJUROR AND MYSTIC:

AUTHOR OF 'A SERIOUS CALL TO A DEVOUT AND HOLY LIFE' &c.

FORMERLY FELLOW OF EMMANUEL COLLEGE, CAMBRIDGE.

A SKETCH of HIS LIFE, CHARACTER, and OPINIONS.

BY

J. H. OVERTON, M.A.

VICAR OF LEGBOURNE, NON-RESIDENTIARY CANON OF LINCOLN CATHEDRAL ;

FORMERLY SCHOLAR OF LINCOLN COLLEGE, OXFORD ;

AND JOINT-AUTHOR OF 'THE ENGLISH CHURCH IN THE EIGHTEENTH CENTURY.'

LONDON:
LONGMANS, GREEN, AND CO.
1881.

PREFACE.

A HUNDRED AND TWENTY YEARS have elapsed since the death of Mr. LAW; but happily there are still living several of his name and lineage, without whose sanction and assistance this work could never have been written. I desire, therefore, to express my thanks to Mr. and Mrs. Thomas Law, of the Hall Yard, King's Cliffe, to Miss Law, also of King's Cliffe, and to Mr. Farmery Law, of Stamford, all lineal descendants of Mr. George Law, the eldest brother of the subject of the present biography; to the Rev. Henry Law, Vicar of Clacton-on-Sea, a lineal descendant of Mr. Thomas Law, second brother of the same: in a word, to all the Law family, to whom I am indebted, not only for valuable information, but also for full permission to make use of all the private documents which bear upon my subject; also to the Rev. Richard Massey, Curate in sole charge of King's Cliffe, who has helped me in various ways in my researches at Cliffe; also to the Master (Dr. Phear) and the Librarian (Dr. Pearson) of Emmanuel College, Cambridge; also to my late colleague, the Rev. Charles John Abbey, who might fairly have claimed my subject as his own, inasmuch as William Law fell mainly to his province in our joint work on the Eighteenth Century, but who, with the courtesy and generosity which he has always shown, at once gave up the subject to me when I told him that I desired to write upon it. I have referred in my foot-notes to the late Mr. Walton's 'Notes and Materials for an adequate Biography of the celebrated Divine, William Law,' whenever I have made use of that most industriously compiled work; but my obligations to the writer are so great that they require a special acknowledgment. I am still more indebted to the Chetham Society, whose useful labours have rendered accessible our best sources of information respecting Mr. Law's personal habits and conversation.

CONTENTS.

LIFE

REV. WILLIAM LAW, M A.

— —◦•◦•◦◦— —

CHAPTER I.

INTRODUCTORY.

THE name of William Law is so unfamiliar to the present generation that it may be necessary to give some reasons why his life should be written at all. That he was one of the ablest of theological writers in a period remarkably fertile in theological literature ; that he lived a pure and conscientious life of Christian self-denial, at a time of great spiritual deadness ; that he influenced the generation in which he lived, indirectly but very really, as much or more than any man of his day ; that his whole character, moral, intellectual, and social, was a singularly taking one ; that he was, in his later years, almost the only notable representative in England of a phase of Christianity which has attracted and helped to form many saintly characters ;—these in themselves might be insufficient reasons for introducing an almost forgotten man of genius to a public which is perhaps already bewildered by the multitude of claimants upon its attention.

But the life and writings of William Law are of so striking and suggestive a character that they really ought

B

not to be allowed to pass into oblivion. He would have
been a remarkable man in any age, but he was doubly remarkable when we think of him as belonging to an age
which took its philosophy from Locke, its theology from
Tillotson, and its politics from Walpole : an age which had
hardly any sympathy with any of the phases of his character. For he stood singularly apart from his contemporaries,
though he influenced them so deeply. His Churchmanship
differed from that of the typical Churchman of his day as
light does from darkness ; it was not even like that of his
non-juring contemporaries, who were as much concerned
with politics as with theology. The life which he recommended in his practical treatises, and lived himself to the
very letter, was about as different as one can conceive from
the easy-going life of the eighteenth century ; while even
those who were stirred to the inmost depths of their spiritual
nature by the 'Serious Call,' did not, as a rule, become
like-minded with the author. What in him took the form
of a benevolent tranquillity, in them took the form of a
benevolent activity. His later phase of so-called mysticism
aroused, outside a very small coterie, an almost universal
feeling of unmitigated disgust. In fact, Law was as one
born out of due time ; he may be regarded as a relic of the
past, or as an anticipation of the future, but of his own
present he was an utterly abnormal specimen. To come
across such a man in the midst of his surroundings is, to
borrow the admirable simile of a writer of our own day,[1] like
coming across an old Gothic cathedral with its air of calm
grandeur and mellowed beauty in the midst of the staring
red-brick buildings of a brand-new manufacturing town ;
and, it may be added, the feeling with which he was regarded by many of his contemporaries was something like
that with which some *nouveau riche* might regard such a

---

[1] Miss Julia Wedgwood.

building, grudging it the space it occupied, which, in his view, might be more advantageously occupied by a manufactory or a Mechanics' Institute.

The present work has been undertaken, partly because the writer thinks that such a character as that of William Law will find more sympathisers now than it did in his own day ; but chiefly because he believes that Law's life and writings possess more than a mere historical interest. Law anticipated many of the difficulties which weigh upon the minds of thoughtful people nowadays, and answered them, if not always satisfactorily, yet always in a way that deserves and will command the most careful attention. And his character is just such a one as it is important in the interests of Christianity to bring into prominence. When Christianity is represented by some as adapted only for minds of the second order (except for the temporal advantages it may bring), it will be well to call attention to one whose intellect was undeniably of the highest order, and whose intense conviction of the truth of Christianity was obviously stimulated by no interested motive. When religion is assumed by others to be the special province of women and children, a Christian character of a singularly robust and masculine type may be a useful study.

It is strange that no adequate biography of so eminent a man as Law should have been written in the generation after his death. But it is by no means to be regretted that none was written ; for it could hardly have failed to be unsatisfactory. Law was one of those men of strong opinions and independent character who call forth vehement sympathy and vehement antipathy. It would have been all but impossible for a contemporary, or one who was nearly a contemporary, to take a calm and dispassionate estimate of such a man. Even if the writer's own views were not distorted by prejudice on one side or the other, he would have found it difficult to obtain sufficient information from unbiassed sources to enable him to form a fair estimate of the real value of the man and his work. The time has now arrived, however, when Law can be viewed in the dry light of history ; when we ought to be misled neither by the glamour with which his friends surrounded him, nor by the prejudices which prevented his opponents from doing him justice ; when, in short, we ought to be able to take him for what he was—a thorough man, full of human infirmities, but a grand specimen of humanity, and a noble monument of the power of divine grace in the soul. If the following sketch of one of the finest minds and most interesting characters of the eighteenth century fail to prove both attractive and instructive, the fault will lie, not in the subject, but in the biographer.

CHAPTER II.

LAW'S EARLY YEARS.

WILLIAM LAW was born, in 1686, at King's Cliffe, a large village in the north of Northamptonshire, about seven miles from Stamford. His father, Thomas Law, was a grocer; but his social standing was different from that of an ordinary village tradesman in the present day.[1] The Laws are a family of high respectability and of good means. We find the head of the family, so far back as three generations earlier than the subject of this biography, technically described as 'George Law, Gentleman.' Thomas Law married Margaret Farmery, a Lincolnshire lady. The name of Farmery was evidently much thought of in the Law family, for it reappears over and over again as a Christian name of various members. Eight sons and three daughters were the issue of this marriage, viz., George, Thomas, Giles, *William*, Nathaniel, Benjamin, Farmery, Christopher, Isabel, Margaret, and Ann. If there be any truth in the tradition that the 'Paternus' of the 'Serious Call' was William Law's own father, and the 'Eusebia' his widowed mother, he must have been singularly blessed in his parents. At any rate, it is plain that they brought up their large family well, for none of them appear to have given their

---

[1] Professor Fowler, in his *Life of Locke* ('English Men of Letters') rightly remarks that there was not so marked a distinction between the lesser gentry and the tradesmen in the seventeenth century as there is at the present day.

parents any trouble. William Law tells us himself that up
to the time of his leaving Cambridge, he 'had hitherto enjoyed a large share of happiness,' and in a short account of
his life prefixed to an American edition of the 'Serious
Call' we are told that 'his education and early years of his
life were very serious.' That this was the case is evident
from a document found among his papers in his own handwriting, which is entitled 'Rules for my Future Conduct,'
and which was probably drawn up by him on entering the
University.[1] As these rules throw light upon his character
in his youth they are worth quoting :—

I. To fix it deep in my mind that I have but one business
upon my hands—to seek for eternal happiness by doing the will of
God.

II. To examine everything that relates to me in this view, as
it serves or obstructs this only end of life.

III. To think nothing great or desirable because the world
thinks it so ; but to form all my judgments of things from the
infallible Word of God, and direct my life according to it.

IV. To avoid all concerns with the world, or the ways of it,
but where religion requires.

V. To remember frequently, and impress it upon my mind
deeply, that no condition of this life is for enjoyment, but for trial ;
and that every power, ability, or advantage we have, are all so
many talents to be accounted for to the Judge of all the world.

VI. That the greatness of human nature consists in nothing else
but in imitating the divine nature. That therefore all the greatness of this world, which is not in good actions, is perfectly beside
the point.

VII. To remember, often and seriously, how much of time is
inevitably thrown away, from which I can expect nothing but the
charge of guilt ; and how little there may be to come, on which an
eternity depends.

VIII. To avoid all excess in eating and drinking.

IX. To spend as little time as I possibly can among such
persons as can receive no benefit from me nor I from them.

[1] See *Notes, &c., for a Biography of William Law*, printed for private
circulation.

X. To be always fearful of letting my time slip away without some fruit.

XI. To avoid all idleness.

XII. To call to mind the presence of God whenever I find myself under any temptation to sin, and to have immediate recourse to prayer.

XIII. To think humbly of myself, and with great charity of all others.

XIV. To forbear from all evil speaking.

XV. To think often of the life of Christ, and propose it as a pattern to myself.

XVI. To pray privately thrice a day, besides my morning and evening prayers.

XVII. To keep from —— as much as I can without offence.

XVIII. To spend some time in giving an account of the day, previous to evening prayer : How have I spent the day? What sin have I committed? What temptations have I withstood? Have I performed all my duty?

With these excellent rules for his conduct, Law entered as a Sizar at Emmanuel College, Cambridge, in 1705. He took his B.A. degree in 1708, was elected Fellow of his College and received holy orders in 1711, and took his M.A. in 1712.[1] With his strong sense of duty, it is scarcely necessary to say that Law was a diligent student in his University days. He told his friend Dr. Byrom that ' he was very diligent in reading Horace &c. at Cambridge ; '[2] and when Dr. Trap upbraided him for his want of taste for ' his *Virgil's*, *Horace's*, and *Terence's*,' he replied, ' I own when I was about eighteen, I was as fond of these books as the Doctor can well be now, and should then have been glad to have translated the *Sublime Milton*, if I had found myself able. But,' he adds, ' this *ardour* soon went off.'[3]

[1] The following is the register (not an original one) of Mr. Law's entry at Emmanuel, kindly supplied to me by the present librarian, Dr. Pearson : ' June 7, 1705, Lawe, Wm. S. (sizar). N. ton. Soc.; A.B. 1708, A.M. 1712; a celebrated enthusiast.'

[2] Byrom's *Journal,* ii. 366.

[3] *Appeal to all that Doubt &c.,* Law's ' Works,' vol. vi. p. 318.

The only other allusion, so far as I am aware, which Law
ever made to his early days in his printed works, occurs in
the same treatise, where, referring to the bigotry of party
spirit, he says : ' When I was a young scholar at the University I heard a great religionist say in my father's house,
that if he could believe the late King of France to be in
heaven, he could not tell how to wish to go there himself.
This was exceeding shocking to all that heard it.'[1]

Besides the classics, Law appears to have studied philosophy and also the so-called mystic writers, of whom in
later days he became so ardent an admirer.[2]   Law also
possessed some knowledge of Hebrew, which he learnt at
the University ' from his Hebrew master, old Eagle,'[3] and
his MSS. notes in the library at King's Cliffe show that
he had some knowledge of mathematics ; his acquaintance
with the modern languages was probably made at a later
date, with the exception of French, which he certainly
learned in his youth.   There is a tradition that he acted as
curate of Fotheringhay for a short time, but there is no
direct evidence of the fact ; while there *is* evidence that
after his election to the Fellowship he resided at Cambridge
and took pupils.[4]

Law's tenure of his Fellowship, however, was not destined to be of long duration.   It is well known that the
last four years of Queen Anne's reign (1710–1714) were
marked by a vigorous revival of those doctrines which had
led many conscientious men twenty years earlier to demur
to the Revolution Settlement.   The old watchwords of

---

[1] *Appeal to all that Doubt &c.*, Law's ' Works,' vol. vi. p. 278.
[2] See Byrom's *Journal*, vol. i. part i. p. 23, which shows Law's early
acquaintance with the mystic philosopher Malebranche.
[3] *Ibid.* for January 31, 1730.
[4] *Ibid.*   Letter from John Byrom to Mrs. Byrom, vol. i. part ii. p. 512.
' I was to-day,' writes Byrom, ' to call on Dr. Richardson, the clergyman ; . . .
he was pupil to Mr. Law at Cambridge.'

' divine, hereditary', indefeasible right,' ' passive obedience,'
and ' non-resistance,' began again to be heard. The logical
result of such doctrines was, of course, antagonistic to the
Protestant succession ; but all those who held them were
not prepared to follow out their principles to the logical
result. There were undoubtedly many, who, without going
the whole length of the Vicar of Bray, were inclined to
adopt the policy of a contemporary ballad :—

> We moderate men do our judgment suspend
> For God only knows where these matters will end.
> For Sal'sbury, Burnett, and Kennet White show
> That as the times vary so principles go :
> And twenty years hence, for aught you or I know,
> 'Twill be Hoadly the high and Sacheverell the low.[1]

William Law, however, was not one of these ' moderate
men, whose principles went as the times varied,' and, as he
was the last man in the world to conceal his principles,
they brought him into trouble. In the first mention which
Byrom, in his amusing ' Journal,' makes of his future mentor,
he tells us, ' there is one Law, a M.A. and Fellow of Emmanuel, has this last week been degraded to a Soph., for a
speech that he spoke on a public occasion, reflecting, as is
reported, on the Government. All I could learn of the
matter is of some queries that he asked the lads in the
middle of his speech, to such effect as these, viz. : Whether
good and evil be obnoxious to revolution ? Whether, when
the earth interposes between the sun and the moon, the
moon may be said to advocate herself ? Whether, when
the children of Israel had made the golden calf the object
of their worship, they ought to keep to their God *de facto*,
or return to their God *de jure* ? and such like. He is much
blamed by some and defended by others ; has the character
of a vain, conceited fellow.'[2] Byrom wrote this, April 27,

---

[1] Quoted in Mr. Wordsworth's interesting work on *University Life in the
Eighteenth Century*, p. 34.

[2] Byrom's *Journal*, vol. i. part ii. p. 20, 21.

1713, to his 'honoured mother, dear brother, and sisters,'
and three days later, repeating to another correspondent
the story of Law, he added, ' On account of a speech that
he made at the Trypos, a public meeting of the University.'
The account of Byrom (who is generally pretty accurate) is
confirmed by the following entry in the annals of the Tripos
speeches: ' April 17, 1713, Mr. Will. Law was suspended
for "his speech in the public schooles at the latter act." ' [1]
This same event is evidently alluded to by Hearne, though
the news appears to have been somewhat late in reaching
him, for it is dated July 30, 1713 : ' One Mr. Lawes, A.M.,
of Cambridge, was lately degraded by the means of
Dr. Adams, head of King's College, who complained to the
present lord-treasurer (who was zealous for his degradation)
upon account of some queries in his speech called tripos
speech, such as, Whether the sun shines when it is in an
eclipse ?   Whether a controverted son be not better than a
controverted successor ?   Whether a dubious successor be
not in danger of being set aside ? With other things of the
same nature.' [2]

Soon after his 'degradation' Law preached the one and
only sermon of his which is still extant. As the single
specimen we possess of his pulpit powers, it is worthy of
attention, but for this reason only. The sermon itself is
in no way remarkable. Many a pulpit rang with the same
sentiments on the same day. It is simply an energetic and
vehement defence of the Peace of Utrecht which the Tory
Government had lately concluded, and is about as unspiritual
a composition as one can well conceive ; in fact, there is
not one word of what we should call religion in it from
beginning to end. It is entitled, ' A Sermon preach'd at
Hazelingfield in the county of Cambridge, on Tuesday,

---

[1] See Wordsworth's *University Life in the Eighteenth Century*, p. 231.
[2] Hearne's *Diary*, i. 282.

July 7, 1713, being the day appointed by Her Majesty's Royal
Proclamation for Public Thanksgiving for Her Majesty's
General Peace, by W. Law, M.A., Fellow of Emmanuel
College, Cambridge.' The text is Titus iii. 1, and prefixed
to the printed sermon is this very suggestive motto : ' A
modest man would never meddle with another's business ;
a prudent man would never interpose in things above his
reach ; but least of all would any loyal subject entrench
upon Cæsar's rights' (Mr. Chiswell's Sermon at Hertford
Assizes). The sermon is mainly directed against those
audacious Whigs who ventured to find fault with 'a Peace
which nothing but the most consummate wisdom and la-
borious care, blessed with Providence, could have procured
us,' instead of 'giving God thanks and praise for as glorious
an affair as ever befel these nations.' ' Man,' says the
preacher, ' is equally averse to the government of God and
his vicegerents. Our duty to government in most cases must
be active, but in all passive.' He divides his subject into
four heads : ' (1) That every good Christian and loyal subject
must have a care of examining too nicely the affairs of his
Prince. (2) That if a wise man was pretty sure that some
parts of the Public Administration would admit of better
management, yet should he be very careful how he expressed
such sentiments ; and in such cases never suffer the wisdom
or care of government to be common topicks of Reflexion.
(3) The Reason why this Duty is now so much transgressed
by us. (4) The application to the Happy Occasion.' The
sermon reminds one of the strain in which Queen Elizabeth
used to address her Parliaments. We are to ' have a care
of examining too nicely the affairs of our Prince, (1) because
of the danger of becoming too wise in our own conceits to
be thankful, (2) because of our ignorance, (3) because of
our passions, (4) because of our party spirit.' Then follows
some violent abuse of those who railed at the ministry :

'Men are resty and unruly, bold and disloyal in their expressions.' They 'condemn an authority that has no superior but that of Heaven.' It is 'hard to say whether this
practice be more common or more abominable.' The
'meanest Mechanick pretends to be wiser than his Governor
and censure the Proceeding of Crown'd Heads.' Then
comes what in this day we should consider fulsome praise
of the Queen for her fostering care as a nursing mother of
the Church. 'Whilst the State thrives and triumphs under
her Protection how does our Church rejoyce in her true Defender, whilst she sees her faithful sons encouraged to be
good, whilst to defend her rights is to secure Anna's favour;
whilst she sees the Princely heart eager in the cause of
God, firm to the Faith as the undaunted martyr's, zealous
in devotion, and both in Principle and Practice unchange-
ably good.' Then the preacher apostrophises her : 'Thou
great, dear offspring of great Charles, how do his Royal
Virtues shine in thee! Glorious in every excellence that
can grace a Christian, adorn Government, and bless a nation ! Shame that we should murmur! Let us cast out
this evil spirit of discontent, and be thankful to the best of
Queens for this happy and honourable Peace!' After some
further diatribes against 'our rude, disloyal behaviour to
Government,' the preacher concludes by urging his hearers
to 'profess with boldness those good old principles of our
Religion, concerning the Divinity of our Sovereign's authority and the absolute passive obedience we owe to her.'

This sort of language was common enough at the time
when it was uttered, but within a few months of the preaching of the sermon 'the best of Queens' was no more. And
then how were such extravagant assertions of the divine
right and so forth to be reconciled with the recognition of
a Sovereign who had obviously no other than a Parliamentary title to the vacant throne ? Law hesitated not one

moment in answering the question. The two positions were absolutely irreconcileable. His intellect was far too clear-sighted to be satisfied with the flimsy arguments which many of the late assertors of the old High Church doctrines adopted to justify their adherence to the new dynasty; and his moral sense was far too acute to allow him to adopt a course in which his conscience would be sacrificed to his interest. He at once determined to refuse the oaths of allegiance to the new Government and abjuration of the so-called Pretender.[1] The letter which he wrote to his elder brother George announcing his determination is very characteristic, and therefore worth quoting: ' Dear Brother, —If your affairs will permit you to peruse the intent of this letter, you will oblige the affectionate writer. I have sent my mother such news as I am afraid she will be too much concerned at, which is the only trouble for what I have done. I beg of you, therefore, to relieve her from such thoughts, and contribute what you can to satisfy her about my affairs. It is a business that I know you love, and therefore don't doubt but you will engage in it. My prospect, indeed, is melancholy enough, but had I done what was required of me to avoid it, I should have thought my condition much worse. The benefits of my education seem partly at an end, but that same education had been more miserably lost if I had not learnt to fear something more than misfortunes. As to the multitude of swearers, that

---

[1] There is, of course, a marked distinction between the oath of allegiance and the oath of abjuration. Many persons could have conscientiously taken the former who could not with any consistency take the latter ; that is, they could tolerate the king *de facto* without altering their opinion as to who was the king *de jure*. I doubt, however, whether Law would have been among the number ; his sensitiveness of conscience was almost morbid, and even if the very unnecessary and injudicious oath of abjuration of the Pretender had not been imposed, the mere fact that he tacitly abjured his right by recognising King George as his sovereign would probably have been sufficient to deter Law from doing so ; at the same time an expression in his letter to his brother indicates that the abjuration oath was his great *crux*.

has no influence upon me ; their reasons are only to be
considered, and everyone knows no good ones can be given
for people swearing the direct contrary to what they believe.
Would my conscience have permitted me to have done
this, I should stick at nothing where my interest was concerned, for what can be more heinously wicked than heartily
to wish the success of a person upon the account of his
right, and at the same time in the most solemn manner, in
the presence of God, and as you hope for mercy, swear that
he has no right at all ? If any hardships of our own, or
the example of almost all people can persuade us to such
practice, we have only the happiness to be in the broad
way. I expected to have had a greater share of worldly advantages than what I am now likely to enjoy; but am fully
persuaded, that if I am not happier for this trial it will be
my own fault. Had I brought myself into troubles by my
own folly, they would have been very trying, but I thank
God I can think of these without dejection. Your kindness
for me, may perhaps incline you to wish I had done otherwise ; but as I think I have consulted my best interest by
what I have done, I hope, upon second thoughts, you will
think so too. I have hitherto enjoyed a large share of
happiness ; and if the time to come be not so pleasant, the
memory of what is past shall make me thankful. Our lot
is fallen in an age that will not be without more trials than
this. God's judgments seem now to be upon us, and I pray
God they may have their proper effect. I am heartily glad
your education does not expose you to the same hardships
that mine does, that you may provide for your family without expense of conscience, or at least what you think so ;
for whether you are of the same opinion with me or not, I
know not. I shall conclude as I began, with desiring you
to say as many comfortable things as you can to my
mother, and persuade her to think with satisfaction upon

that condition, which upon my account gives me no un-
easiness, which will much oblige your affectionate brother,
W. LAW.'

It is curious to contrast this letter with one on the same
subject from Law's future friend and disciple, John Byrom.
Byrom, too, was a strong Tory and High Churchman, and
'would sooner have had a drawn battle or a lost one in
Flanders, than have heard of the preferment of a man of
Mr. Hoadley's principles.' He, too, had strong Jacobite
tendencies. But, then, there was a Trinity Fellowship in
prospect to weigh down the balance on the other side.
'Thursday,' he writes, 'we buried Dr. Smith, one of our
Seniors, so now we have three Fellowships. But this oath·
I am not satisfied so well as to take it, nor am I verily persuaded of its being unlawful. It has always been the custom of nations to set aside those whom it was not found
for the good of the public to reign. Is it not the opinion
of present nations ? Why do they make kings of Sicily
&c., and order people to change their masters &c. ? And
may I not rely on the judgment of thousands, thousands of
good, pious, learned men for its being a lawful oath ? It
is very hard—everything so orderly settled in regard to
posterity, and all must be undone for the sake of a man who
has a disputed title to his birth and right too. I saw a book
in our library the other day where the Pretender's birth is
made very suspicious, and all your affidavits, allegations,
&c., made nothing of. I suppose you have seen the book,
what say you to it ? The Commons, I see, have taken the
abjuration oath &c. ; how is it likely this young fellow
should ever come among us ? The Queen and Parliament
have settled the succession in a Protestant family, and made
what provision they can for our religion and liberties, and
why must we not be content ? though, for what I hear, few
are otherwise. Our Dr. Bentley has been at London, and

he says everybody is for the succession.'[1] A year later, the
good man's mind is not yet quite made up, but it is evidently becoming so. 'The abjuration oath,' he writes to
the same correspondent,[2] 'hath not been put to us yet, nor
do I know when it will be ; nobody of our year scruples it,
and, indeed, in the sense they say they shall take it, I could.
One says he can do it and like the Pretender never the
worse ; another, that it only means that he won't plot to
bring him in, he doesn't trouble his head about him &c.
You know my opinion, that I am not clearly convinced that
it is lawful, nor that it is unlawful ; sometimes I think one
thing, and sometimes another ;' but what he thought finally
it is not very difficult to anticipate. It was well for Byrom's
prospects that his friendship with Law did not commence
till many years later. One can fancy what havoc the latter
would have made of the scraps of argument which Byrom
adduces with transparent simplicity for the course he meant
to adopt.

But to return to Law. How his letter was received in
Northamptonshire is not known. His mother, for whom
he showed so touching and tender a concern, had not long
lost her husband, whose epitaph is still to be read on a
monument in the chancel of King's Cliffe church : ' Here
lye the dear Remains of Thomas Law, lately Grocer in
this Parish : a kind, careful, industrious Father of a large
Family ; a tender and affectionate Husband ; a true and
faithful Friend ; and a peaceable honest Neighbour ; who
deceased on the tenth day of October, Anno Dei 1714.
" And now, Lord, what is my hope ? Truly my hope is
even in Thee." ' There is no reason for thinking that the
widowed mother had cause for anxiety about any of her
children ; but she would naturally look upon William as
the pride and hope of the family. A brilliant career

---

[1] Byrom's *Journal*, vol. i. part i. p. 25.   [2] *Ibid.* p. 31.

seemed to be open to the able young fellow of Emmanuel, and it must have been a disappointment to her to feel that all hopes of that seemed at an end.

Law's prospects as a nonjuror were dreary enough. He had not even the poor satisfaction of being able to join heart and soul with the active opponents of the new *régime*; for he had no mind to meddle with politics. It was a matter of indifference to him, personally, whether King James or King George were sitting on the throne;[1] he simply obeyed his conscience, and was prepared to take the consequences, whatever they might be.

[1] Not but that Law's sympathies were to the end of his life with the exiled Stuarts. Among other interesting memorials of her great relative in the possession of Miss Sarah Law, is a pincushion with this inscription on one side, 'Down with the Rump'; and on the other, 'God save K. J. P. C. D. H.', that is, King James, Prince Charles, Duke Henry.' See also Byrom's *Journal* for July 27, 1739, vol. ii. (part i.) 259.

CHAPTER III.

LAW AND THE BANGORIAN CONTROVERSY.

THERE is a tradition that, after the resignation of his fellowship, Law was a curate in London under the famous preacher Dr. Heylin, Rector of S. Mary-le-Strand, Vicar of Sunbury, and Prebendary of S. Paul's. Law himself, a few months before his death, alluded incidentally, in the course of conversation, to a time when he was ' curate in London.' [1] Byrom twice [2] mentions the report ; once on the authority of a Mr. Rivington, who, however, threw discredit upon the whole story by adding the very improbable piece of gossip that Law was then 'a gay parson, and that Dr. Heylin said his book ('The Serious Call') would have been better if he had travelled that way himself.' A Mrs. Collier also told Byrom that ' Mr. Law was a great beau, would have fine linen, was very sweet upon the ladies, and had made one believe that he would marry her ; that he made his great change in the year 1720 ; that he wore a wig again.' [3] All this, however, is mere gossip, unworthy of a moment's serious consideration. It is quite possible that Law's serious impressions may have been deepened about the year 1720 ; but that he was ever other than a grave, con-scientious, God-fearing man is highly improbable.

It is also reported that he was offered several pieces of valuable preferment by, or through the instrumentality of,

---

[1] See the *Memoirs of the Life, Death, Burial, and Wonderful Writings of Jacob Behmen, now first done at large into English &c.*, by Francis Okely. Northampton, 1780.

[2] *Journal*, Dec. 29, 1734, and Sept. 1739.

[3] *Ibid.* Jan. 3, 1731.

his friend Dr. Sherlock ; but how this could be, it is not easy to see. Of course, if Law persisted in refusing the oaths, he could not have held any preferment ; and Dr. Sherlock, then Dean of Chichester, if he knew Law's character at all, must have been aware that he might as well try to persuade his cathedral to walk into the sea, as try to persuade Law to change his convictions or to sacrifice them to his interests. The only evidence of Law's having officiated in church at all after he became a nonjuror is a notice in the ' Preacher's Assistant' that he published a single sermon in 1718 on the text 1 Cor. xii. 3 ; [1] but this sermon does not appear to be extant.

Law, however, was certainly not idle. In 1717 he wrote his ' Three Letters to the Bishop of Bangor,' which raised him at once to the very highest rank of writers in controversial divinity. The appearance of so powerful an ally was warmly and quickly welcomed by the High Church party. Mr. Pyle tells us he wrote against Law because ' his was thought to be the strongest and most impartial piece that has appeared against his Lordship.' [2] Law's friend, Dean Sherlock, himself one of the most clear-headed and powerful writers of the time, declared that ' Mr. Law was a writer so considerable that he knew but one good reason why his Lordship did not answer him.' [3] Some years later, Mr.

---

[1] See *Preacher's Assistant*, vol. ii. 1737.

[2] See a *Vindication of the Bishop of Bangor in answer to W. Law*, by T. Pyle, Lecturer of Lynn Regis, 1718. ' Mr. Law's performance,' writes Mr. Pyle, ' has been so much approved of by the rest, and particularly by Dr. Snape '—Dr. Snape being himself, it need hardly be said, one of the foremost opponents of Bishop Hoadly.

[3] Quoted in *A Full Examination of Several Important Points relating to Church Authority, &c.*, by Gilbert Burnet, 1718. See also Hoadly's *Works*, ii. 694-5, where the bishop gives his reasons to Dr. Sherlock for not answering Law ; but promises that, if the dean will ' publicly own any one of Mr. Law's main principles,' he will reply to him. This was a severe home-thrust ; for Hoadly knew that Sherlock was not prepared to identify himself with Law, whose uncompromising character was not of the stuff of which bishops were

Jones of Nayland, himself an able advocate of High
Church principles in their older and nobler sense, characterised Law's 'Three Letters' as 'incomparable for truth
of argument, brightness of wit, and purity of English.'[1]
Later still, Dean Hook singled out these alone among all
the voluminous literature on the subject, as 'perhaps the
most important of the works produced by the Bangorian
controversy;' and added, 'Law's "Letters" have never
been answered, and may indeed be regarded as unanswerable.'[2] Bishop Ewing thinks that the 'Letters to Hoadly
may fairly be put on a level with the "Lettres Provinciales"
of Blaise Pascal, both displaying equal power, wit, and
learning.'[3] Mr. F. D. Maurice is of opinion that 'the
"Letters" show that Law had the powers and temptations
of a singularly able controversialist.'[4]

One of the chief among the many merits of these fine
pieces of composition is that they always keep close to the
true point at issue.[5] As a rule, the writers on both sides
in the tedious but very important Bangorian controversy
show a constant tendency to fly off at a tangent to all
sorts of irrelevant questions. This Law never does.
Whether Bishop Hoadly was justified or not in having
a converted Jesuit as tutor in his family ; whether he did or
did not interpolate some modifying epithets in his printed
sermon which were not in the original MS. ; whether Sherlock had or had not once preached the same doctrines as

made in the eighteenth century. Though I do not agree with Bishop Hoadly's
principles, I admit that he was a very able controversialist, and not afraid of
any antagonist.

[1] See *The Scholar Armed.*

[2] *Church Dictionary.* Art. 'Bangorian Controversy.'

[3] *Present-Day Papers on Prominent Questions in Theology.*

[4] F. D. Maurice's *Introduction* to 'Remarks on the Fable of the Bees,'
p. xi. 1844.

[5] This is noticed by Mr. Leslie Stephen in his interesting account of Law.
See *English Thought in the Eighteenth Century*, ii. p. 161.

Hoadly ; whether occasional conformity ought or ought
not to be allowed ; whether the Test and Corporation Acts
ought or ought not to be repealed ;—these, and other more
or less irrelevant points were discussed in many an angry
pamphlet and letter.

But Law, in his attack upon the bishop, always keeps
to the main point, often hitting a hard, but never a foul,
blow ; never losing sight of his character as a Christian
and a gentleman. The one question which really required
an answer was whether Bishop Hoadly's assertions did or
did not tend to impair the nature of the Church in which he
held high office, considered as a spiritual society. Law
contends that they did, and drives his arguments home
with crushing force.

He begins by pointing out that the freethinkers, who
made no secret of their desire to dissolve the Church, did,
as a matter of fact, regard the bishop as their ally, simply
because they thought he agreed with them on this point.
And had they not good grounds for so thinking ? 'Your
Lordship is ours,' says Law, 'as you fill a bishopric ; but
we are at a loss to discover what other interest we have in
your Lordship.' Did not the Bishop plainly intimate that
if a man were only not a hypocrite, it was no matter what
religion he was of ? Did he not ridicule the 'vain words
of regular and uninterrupted succession' as 'niceties, trifles,
and dreams'? And what was this but saying in effect that
no kind of ordination was of any moment ? for, if ordination was not regular, or derived from those who had authority from Christ to ordain, what was the use of it ? 'Your
Lordship's servant might ordain and baptize to as much
purpose as your Lordship. You have left us neither priests,
nor sacraments, nor Church ; and what has your Lordship
given us in the room of all these advantages ? Why, only
sincerity. This is the great universal atonement for all ;

this is that which, according to your Lordship, will help us
to the communion of saints hereafter, though we are in
communion with anybody or nobody here.' If a private
person were to pretend to choose a Lord Chancellor, would
it not be an absurdity ? But was it more absurd to commission a person to act, sign, and seal in the king's name
than in the name of Christ ? If there were no uninterrupted succession, then there were no authorised ministers
from Christ ; if no such ministers, then no Christian sacraments ; if no Christian sacraments, then no Christian covenant, of which the sacraments were the visible seals.

The bishop affirmed that when he said Christ had left
no authority behind him he meant no absolute authority.
But Law shows that his reasons are equally against *any*
degree of authority. 'Absolute authority the bishop denies, and at the same time makes that which is not
absolute nothing at all.' But it was quite possible that
an authority might be real without being absolute : the
sacraments were *real* means of grace, though conditional ;
a limited monarchy was real, though not absolute. The
first letter ends with a stricture on the bishop's definition
of prayer as 'a calm and undisturbed address to God.' [1]

In his second letter, Law strives to prove that the
bishop's notions of benediction, absolution, and Church communion were destructive of every institution of the Christian

---

[1] There is a very amusing squib directed against this definition, entitled
'The Tower of Babel : an Anti-Heroic Poem, Humbly Dedicated to the
B——p of B ·-—r,' 1718. It commences :

> ' I must with decent Pride confess
> I've christen'd Prayer a calm address,
> And likewise added undisturb'd,
> For why should gentle steeds be curb'd ?
> A mind that keeps the Balance even,
> And hangs well-pois'd 'twixt Earth and Heaven—·
> What should molest its ease and quiet,
> Or set its passions in a riot ?'

religion. If, as the bishop said, 'to expect the grace of God
from any hands but His own was to affront Him,' how
could the bishop confirm ?   When he did so, he ought to
warn the candidates that he was only acting according to
a custom which had long prevailed against common sense,
but that they must not imagine that there was anything in
the action more than an useless, empty ceremony.   How
could he ordain ?   How could he consecrate the elements
in the Lord's Supper ?   After quoting several texts which
speak of grace conferred through the Apostles' hands, Law
asks with fine irony, 'Do we not plainly want new Scriptures ?   Must we not give up the apostles as furious High
Church prelates, who aspired to presumptuous claims, and
talked of conferring the graces of God by their own hands ?'
What a superstitious custom it must be to send for a
clergyman before death, if there is no difference between
sacerdotal prayers and those of a nurse !   Eliphaz should
have argued that it was a weak and senseless thing, and an
affront to God, to think that he could not be blessed without the prayer of Job !   Abimelech should have rejected
the prayer of Abraham as a mere essay of prophet-craft !
It was as absurd for the human hands of Moses or Aaron,
or the priests of the sons of Levi, to bless, as for those of
the Christian clergy !

After having shown that the clergy were as truly
Christ's successors as the apostles were, and that none can
despise them but those who despise Him that sent them,
Law contends with great energy against the notion that
this doctrine ought to terrify the consciences of the laity, or
to bring 'the profane scandal of priestcraft upon the clergy.'

'The clergy,' it was said, 'were only men.'   Yes, and
the prophets were only men, but they insisted upon the
authority of their mission.   Was it more strange that God
should use the weakness of men than that He should use

common bread and wine, and common water, as instruments for conveying His grace? Can God consecrate
inanimate things to spiritual purposes, and make them
the means of eternal happiness? And is man the only
creature that He cannot make subservient to His designs? If it is reasonable to despise the ministry and
benedictions of men, because they are men like ourselves,
it is surely as reasonable to despise the sprinkling of
water, a creature below us, a senseless and inanimate
creature. Naaman the Syrian was, on that principle, a
wise man when he took the water of Jordan to be only
water, as the bishop justly observed that a clergyman was
only a man.

Law then shows that the order of the clergy stood on
exactly the same footing as the Sacraments and the Scriptures, and that the uncertainty about the succession of the
clergy was not greater than about the genuineness of the
Scriptures. Both rested upon the same historical evidence.
It was said that there is no mention of the apostolical succession in Scripture. But the doctrine upon which it is
founded plainly made it unnecessary to mention it. Was
it needful for the Scriptures to tell us, that if we take our
Bible from any false copy it is not the Word of God?
Why, then, need they tell us that if we are ordained by
usurping false pretenders to ordination, nor deriving their
authority to that end from the apostles, we are no priests?

As a true priest cannot benefit us by administering a
false sacrament, so a true sacrament is nothing when it is
administered by a false, uncommissioned minister. So, the
apostolical benediction pronounced by a priest is not a bare
act of charity—one Christian praying for another; but it
is the work of a person commissioned by God to bless in
His name.

Law then shows that it is no injury to the laity to assert

these claims, 'for,' he says, 'if we are right, they will receive the benefit ; if wrong, we shall bear the punishment.'
But into what perplexity did the bishop's notions lead the
laity ! If a layman should pretend to ordain clergymen in the
diocese of Bangor, what could its bishop say ?   He could be
answered in his own words ; and this was the confusion which
the bishop was charged with introducing into the Church.

The bishop's objection that an authoritative absolution
must be infallible, might, says Law, be applied with equal
force against the administration of the Sacraments, and
indeed against the whole Christian religion.   As for the
clergy claiming such absolving power as to set themselves
above God, the bishop might as well have argued against
worshipping the sun, for who ever taught that any set of
men could absolutely bless or withhold a blessing independent of God ?   But is the prerogative of God impaired
because His own institutions are obeyed ?   In a word, the
clergy are only entrusted with a *conditional* power, and
every means of grace is conditional.

Law then touches upon the crucial text on the Power
of the Keys.   The bishop had suggested that it might
possibly refer only to the power of inflicting and curing
diseases.   On this principle, replies Law, the text must be
explained thus : ' Thou art Peter, and upon this rock I will
build my church '—that is, a peculiar society of healthful
persons—'and the gates of hell shall not prevail against it '
—that is, they shall always be in a state of health. 'Whatsoever thou shall bind on earth shall be bound in heaven'
—that is, on whomsoever thou shall inflict leprosy, for instance, on earth, shall be a leper in heaven ; and so forth.

Then follow some strictures upon a passage in which
the bishop ran perilously near to denying the Divinity
of Christ, and justifying the charge of Socinianism so frequently brought against him. 'Your lordship,' says Law,

'has rejected all Church authority, and despised the pretended power of the clergy, for this reason : because Christ
is the sole King, sole Lawgiver, and Judge in His Kingdom.   But, it seems your lordship, notwithstanding, thinks
it now time to depose Him.'

Law next makes merry over an objection of Hoadly's
against the necessity of Church communion, because it
puts the conscientious objector into a dilemma.   'Does it
prove,' he says, 'that Christianity is not necessary because
the conscientious Jew may think it is not so ?   It may as
well prove that the moon is no larger than a man's head,
because an honest, ignorant countryman may think it no
larger.   This is a new-invented engine for the destruction
of the Church, that if we have but an erroneous conscience
the whole Christian dispensation is cancelled.'

The letter ends with a refutation of the old charges of
Popery and priestcraft—charges which never failed to tell
in those excited times when the Protestant succession was
hardly yet secured.   But Law was not a man to be
frightened by bugbears.   'If,' he says boldly, 'this doctrine
is Popish simply because the Papists hold it as well as us,
we own the charge, and are not for being such true Protestants as to give up the Apostles' Creed, or lay aside the
sacraments because they are received by the Church of
Rome.'   And 'if it be a breach upon the layman's liberty, it
is only upon such as think the Commandments a burden.'
It is difficult to realise now the courage it would require
then to utter such matter-of-course sentiments.

To this letter Law added a postscript, answering some
objections which the bishop had raised against his first
letter, and unfolding at greater length some of the arguments which have already been referred to.   The first of
these was that the doctrine of an uninterrupted succession
is not mentioned in Scripture ; neither, replies Law, is it

expressly stated there that the Scriptures contain all things necessary to salvation, nor that the Sacraments are to be continued in every age of the Church, nor that we are to observe the Lord's Day. But the succession is *founded* on Scripture, and asserted by the voice of tradition in all ages of the Church. The same Scriptures which made it necessary that Timothy should be sent to Ephesus to ordain priests, because the priests who were there could not ordain, made it equally necessary that Timothy's successors should be the only ordainers. Nor is the Divine Right of Episcopacy founded merely on an apostolical practice which may or may not be binding. It is the nature of the Christian priesthood that it can only be continued in that method which God has appointed for its continuance ; and that method is episcopacy. To the objection which has always been the strongest that has been or can be urged against the doctrine, viz., that the uninterrupted succession is so uncertain, that, if it be necessary, no man can say if he be in the Church or not, Law's reply is very powerful. It is, he says, a matter of fact, founded on historical evidence, just like Christianity itself, just like the truths of Scripture. And this very doctrine that none but episcopal succession is valid in every age has been a constant guard upon the succession. It was morally impossible to forge orders or steal a bishopric in any one given age. This is the one reason, and an absolutely sufficient reason, why we believe the Scriptures cannot have been corrupted.

Law's third letter, which is by far the longest of the three, is a reply to the bishop's answer to the representation of the Committee of Convocation. The bishop explained that his description of the Church which had given so much offence applied ' not to *a* church but to *the invisible* Church of Christ.' This explanation called forth some of the most brilliant specimens of Law's irony. He does not, of course, deny that there *is* an invisible church, or 'a number of beings in covenant with God, who are not to be seen by human eyes;' but, he says, you might as well call all the number of people who believe in Christ and observe His institutions the invisible church as call them the order of angels or the church of seraphims. The *acts* which prove people Christians are visible. Our Lord, when He compared the Kingdom of Heaven to a net, which gathered fish of every kind, to the marriage of the king's son where the guests were good and bad, spoke of the Church as visible; and He never gave a hint that He founded two universal churches on earth—one visible, the other invisible.

How could the bishop think it possible that the committee could imagine him capable of hurting an invisible church ? They might as well think him capable of arresting a party of spirits. But they *did* think his description of a church 'which was the only true account of Christ's Church in the mouth of a Christian' was directly opposed to the description of the Church given by Our Saviour, and was in disparagement of the 19th Article of the Church of England. The bishop says not, because he is only speaking of the invisible church. Supposing, then, anyone should affirm that there is a sincere, invisible Bishop of Bangor, who is the only true Bishop of Bangor in the mouth of a Christian, would Dr. Hoadly think this no contradiction to his right as bishop ?

Again: Bishop Hoadly plainly set up his invisible church against outward and visible ordinances. But outward ordinances were as necessary to make men true Christians as outward acts of love were to make them charitable. In short, the world is divided upon the subject whether it be as safe to be in one external visible communion as in another, and the bishop comes in to end the controversy. How? By skipping over the whole question, and laying down a description of the universal Church ! He had been as well employed in painting spirits or weighing thoughts. The bishop thinks the main question is, whether this description is true and just. Supposing he had been describing an invisible king to the people of Great Britain, would the main question amongst the Lords and Commons be, whether he had hit off the description well ? No ; it would be, to what ends and purposes he had set up such a king, and whether the subjects of Great Britain might leave their visible, and pay only an internal allegiance to his invisible king. It was the same with the Church. He might erect as many churches as he pleased, if he only did it for speculative amusement, and to try his abilities in drawing ; but if it was to destroy the distinction between the Church and the Conventicle, they could no more admire the beauty and justness of his fine description than *he* would admire a just description of an invisible diocese. Here was a visible bishop at a visible court solemnly preaching in defence of a church which can neither be defended nor injured. Though it was as invisible as the centre of the earth, and as much out of reach as the stars, he was pathetically preaching and publishing volumes, lest this invisible church, which no one knew where to find, should be run away with ! With the same Christian zeal, he might at some other solemn occasion appear in the cause of the winds, desiring that they might rise and blow where they listed. If the Committee had so far forgotten the visible church of which they were members as to have engaged with him about his invisible church, the dispute would have been to as much purpose as a tryal in Westminster Hall about the philosopher's stone. It was very hard that when the bishop had an invisible church ready for them, they should have gone off to an article of the

Church of England which describes only an old-fashioned
visible church, as churches went in the apostles' days !
But, in point of fact, the Church of Christ was as truly a
visible, external society as any civil or secular society in
the world, and was no more distinguished from such societies
by the invisibility than by the youth or age of its members.

The bishop founded his arguments on the saying of
Our Lord : ' My kingdom is not of this world ; ' which does
not describe what His kingdom *is*, but what it is *not*. It
was simply an answer to the question whether Christ was
the temporal King of the Jews. Does it follow that because
He was not, therefore His kingdom was invisible ? Christ
told His disciples that they were not of this world ; is that
an argument that they immediately became invisible ? In
a word, all the doctrines which the bishop founded on this
little negative text had no more relation to it than if he had
deduced them from the first verse of the first chapter of
Genesis.

In the next chapter Law shows that the bishop's objection to Church authority would be equally applicable to all
authority in the world—to that of a prince over his subjects,
a father over his children, or a master over his servants ;
and, what is very rare in his writings, hints at his own
position as a nonjuror, turning against the bishop his
' Defence of Resistance.'

It is not necessary to follow Law in his defence of
excommunication, or of the advantages of external communion, or on the true value of sincerity, and the true
extent of private judgment, or on the reconcilement of his
doctrines with the principles of the Reformation.

The specimens already given will, it is hoped, be sufficient to show that these three brilliant and well-argued
letters were fully deserving of all the praise that they
received.

CHAPTER IV.

THE FABLE OF THE BEES.

IN 1723 Law published another controversial piece which fully sustained the reputation he had won by his ' Three Letters.' The circumstances which called it forth were these. In 1714, Dr. Bernard Mandeville, a physician, published a short doggerel poem, entitled ' The Grumbling Hive, or Knaves turned Honest,' in which he described a hive of bees who grew wealthy and great by the prevalence of fraud and luxury ; but having by common consent agreed to turn honest, lost thereby all their greatness and wealth. The moral is—

> T' enjoy the world's conveniences,
> Be famed in war, yet live in ease,
> Without great vices is a vain
> Eutopia seated in the brain;
> Fraud, luxury, and pride must live,
> While we the benefit receive.

The theory is a sufficiently startling one as it stands ; but, by way of improving matters, the author, nine years later, republished the poem with long explanatory notes, giving the full interpretation of the parable, under the title of the ' Fable of the Bees ; or, Private Vices, Public Benefits.' Mandeville's work was a sort of caricature, or *reductio ad absurdum*, of the doctrines of those ethical philosophers who taught the morality of consequences, as opposed to the morality of principles. It was the extreme reaction against the doctrine of Lord Shaftesbury, who took the nobler view of ethics, but stated it in a rhapsodical, overstrained fashion, which had the appearance of unreality.

Taken by itself, Mandeville's so-called poem might have passed for a rather flippant and eccentric brochure, hardly worthy of serious notice. But Law, who never made an attack without very strong cause, perceived that it harmonised too well with the prevalent looseness both of sentiment and practice to be innocuous ; and therefore, in the very year of its appearance (1723), he published his ' Remarks on the Fable of the Bees '—the most caustic of all his writings. It is hardly more than a pamphlet, but it is a perfect gem in its way, exhibiting in miniature all the characteristic excellences of the writer—a thorough perception of the true point at issue, and a close adherence to it, a train of reasoning in which it would be hard to find a single flaw, a brilliant wit, and a pure and nervous style. Whether the bees, thriving by their fraud, and ruined by turning honest, do or do not give a correct representation of human society—in other words, whether honesty is or is not the best policy—this is a question which Law does not care to discuss. Good Bishop Berkeley might think it worth while to enter into elaborate details to show, for example, that more malt was brought into the market to satisfy the demands of the sober than of the drunken.[1]   But Law saw there was a deeper fallacy underlying Mandeville's paradoxes.   If man was what Mandeville represented him to be—if virtue was, in its origin, what Mandeville said it was—it really made very little matter how masses of men throve best in society.   That man was only an animal, and that morality was only an imposture—these were the principal doctrines which Mandeville, ' with more than fanatic zeal,' recommended to his readers ; and on these points

---

[1] See Berkeley's *Minute Philosopher*, Dialogues I. and II. ; also 'Introduction' to *Remarks on the Fable of the Bees*, by F. D. Maurice, p. x.

Law is ready to join issue with him. ' I believe man,' said Mandeville, ' besides skin, flesh, bones, &c., that are obvious to the eye, to be a compound of various passions ; that all of them, as they are provoked and come uppermost, govern him by turns, whether he will or no.' ' The definition,' replied Law, with crushing force, ' is too general, because it seems to suit a Wolf or a Bear as exactly as yourself or a Grecian philosopher.' But, according to his definition, how could Mandeville say that he believed anything, unless believing could be said to be a passion, or some faculty of the skin or bones ? ' If,' proceeds Law, with a severity which, under the circumstances, was not undeserved, ' you would prove yourself to be no more than a brute or an animal, how much of your life you need alter I cannot tell ; but at least you must forbear writing against virtue, for no mere animal ever hated it.' ' The province,' he says, ' which you have chosen for yourself is to deliver man from the encroachments of virtue and to replace him in the rights and privileges of Brutality ; to recall him from the giddy heights of rational dignity and angelic likeness to go to grass or wallow in the mire.' As a contrast to this grovelling view of human nature, Law quotes with fine effect, ' And God said, Let us make man in our image, after our likeness,' and dwells in an elevated strain, which no one knew better than he how to sustain, on the ' declaration of the dignity of man's nature, made long before any of your sagacious moralists had a meeting.' [1]

---

[1] This allusion to the ' sagacious moralists ' refers to a passage in the *Fable of the Bees* in which the author says, ' Sagacious moralists draw men like angels in hopes that the pride, at least of some, will put them upon copying after the beautiful originals, which they are represented to be ; ' upon which Law remarks, ' I am loth to charge you with sagacity, because I would not accuse you falsely ; but if this remark is well made, I can help you to another full as just : viz. ' That sagacious advocates for immorality draw men like brutes in hopes that the depravity at least of some will put them upon copying after the base originals, which they are represented to be.'

Mandeville had given a sort of apologetic explanation, saying that in his inquiry into the origin of moral virtue, he was not speaking of Jews or Christians, but of man in a state of nature. But this is a distinction which Law will not for a moment allow. He maintains—and with perfect truth—that the origin of morality was the same to Jew, Christian, or heathen, that man in a state of nature was not savage and brutal, and that making the training of such supposed savage creatures a true account of the origin of morality was like making the history of curing people in Bedlam a true account of the origin of reason. Besides, Mandeville's own conduct was utterly inconsistent with his explanation. All the observations which he made upon human nature, on which his origin of moral virtue was founded, were only so many observations upon the manners of all orders of Christians. And yet he, good man, is not talking about Christians! He applies his definition of man as a vile animal to 'himself and his courteous reader.' Are he and his courteous readers, then, all savages in a state of nature ?

After having shown with admirable irony that Mandeville's account of the origin of virtue might be applied with equal force to the origin of the erect posture of man, Law proceeds to unfold in grave and dignified language the true origin of virtue. 'In one sense it had no origin—that is, there never was a time when it began to be—but it was as much without beginning as truth and goodness, which are in their natures as eternal as God. But moral virtue, if considered as the object of man's knowledge, began with the first man, and was as natural to him as it was natural to man to think and perceive or feel the difference between pleasure and pain. The reasonableness and fitness of actions themselves is a law to rational beings ; nay, it is a law to which even the Divine Nature is subject, for God is necessarily good and just, from the excellence of justice and goodness ; and it is the will of God that makes moral virtue our law, and obliges us to act reasonably. Here, Sir, is the noble and divine origin of moral virtue ; it is founded in the immutable relations of things, in the perfections and attributes of God, not in the pride of man or the craft of cunning politicians. Away, then, with your idle and prophane fancies about the origin of moral virtue ! For once, turn your eyes towards Heaven, and dare but own a just and good God, and then you have owned the true origin of religion and moral virtue.'

The transition from the sarcasms with which the section commences to the grave and elevated tone in which it closes is very striking. One can quite understand the enthusiasm with which John Sterling speaks of ' the first section of Law's remarks as one of the most remarkable philosophical essays he had ever seen in English.' Now this section,' he adds, ' has all the highest beauty of his (Law's) polemical compositions, and a weight of pithy right reason, such as fills one's heart with joy. I have never seen, in our language, the elementary grounds of a rational ideal philosophy, as opposed to empiricism, stated with nearly the same clearness, simplicity, and force.'

In the second section Law answers with convincing force the objection to the reality of virtue on the ground that what has the appearance of virtue proceeds from some blind impulse ; in the third he returns to his satirical tone and cuts up in his most slashing style Mandeville's assertion that there was no greater certainty in morals than in matters of taste. The next two sections deal with the immortality of the soul and the nature of hope ; the sixth and last comments on a defence which Mandeville had put forth and in

[1] Letter from John Sterling to F. D. Maurice, quoted in Maurice's ' Introduction ' to the *Remarks on the Fable of the Bees.*

which he had the audacity to affirm that the 'Fable of the Bees' was 'designed for the entertainment of people of probity and virtue, and was a book of severe and exalted morality!' 'I should,' exclaims Law, with pardonable indignation, 'have thought him in as sober a way if he had said that the author was a seraphim, and that he was never any nearer the earth than the fixed stars! He now talks of diverting persons of probity and virtue, having in his book declared that he had never been able to find such a person in existence; he now talks of morality, having then declared the moral virtues were all a cheat; he now talks of recommending goodness, having then made the difference between good and evil as fanciful as the difference between a tulip and an auricula!'

Attached to the 'Remarks' is a postscript attacking Mr. Bayle's assertion that religious opinions and beliefs had no influence at all upon men's actions.

CHAPTER V.

'THE UNLAWFULNESS OF STAGE ENTERTAINMENTS,'
AND 'CHRISTIAN PERFECTION.'

LAW wrote two more works before he emerged from his obscurity. The first is a tract entitled ' The Absolute Unlawfulness of Stage Entertainments fully Demonstrated.' It is decidedly the weakest of all his writings, and most of his admirers will regret that he ever published it. Regarded merely as a composition, it is very inferior to his usual standard. Unlike himself, he gives way to passion and seems quite to lose all self-control ; unlike himself, he indulges in the most violent abuse ; and unlike himself he lays himself open to the most crushing retorts. He makes no distinction whatever between the use and abuse of such entertainments. ' The stage is not here condemned, as some other diversions, because they are dangerous, and likely to be occasions of sin, but it is condemned as drunkenness, and lewdness, as lying and profaneness are to be condemned, not as things that may only be the occasion of sin, but such as are in their own nature grossly sinful. You go to hear a *play*: I tell you that you go to hear *ribaldry* and *profaneness* ; that you entertain your mind with extravagant *thoughts*, wild *rants, blasphemous speeches, wanton amours, profane jests*, and *impure passions.*' [1]

It has been said that Law was never worsted in argument, and, as a rule, the statement is true ; but every rule

[1] P. 5

has its exceptions. Law measured his strength with some
of the very ablest men of his day, with men like Hoadly
and Warburton and Tindal and Wesley ; and it may safely
be said that he never came forth from the contest defeated.
But, absurd as it may sound, it is perfectly true that what
neither Hoadly nor Warburton nor Tindal nor Wesley
could do, that was done by—John Dennis ! In the controversy between Law and Dennis, the latter assuredly has
the advantage. ' Plays,' wrote Law, ' are contrary to Scripture, as the devil is to God, as the worship of images is to
the second commandment.' To this Dennis gave the obvious and unanswerable retort that ' when S. Paul was at
Athens, the very source of dramatick poetry, he said a great
deal publickly against the idolatry of the Athenians, but
not one word against their stage. At Corinth he said as
little against theirs. He quoted on one occasion an Athenian dramatick poet, and on others Aratus and Epimenides.
He was educated in all the learning of the Grecians, and
could not but have read their dramatic poems ; and yet
so far from speaking a word against them, he makes use of
them for the instruction and conversion of mankind.' [1]

Dennis again convicts Law of something very like dis-
ingenuousness in quoting Archbishop Tillotson's strictures
against plays *as they were then ordered*, but omitting to add
the Archbishop's qualification that ' plays might be so
framed and governed by such rules as not only to be innocent and diverting, but instructive and useful.' It was the
whole purport of Law's treatise to show that this was impossible. It is really painful to quote the unmeasured
abuse which he pours not only upon the entertainment
itself but upon all who took part in it ; but it is the duty

[1] *The Stage defended from Scripture, reason, experience, and the common
sense of mankind for* 2000 *years, ... occasioned by Mr. Law's Pamphlet.*
By Mr. Dennis, 1726.

of a faithful biographer not to shrink from admitting the weaknesses of his subject. 'Perhaps,' writes Law, ' you had rather see your son chained to a *galley*, or your daughter driving a *plough* than getting their bread on the *stage*, by administering in so scandalous a manner to the vices and corrupt pleasures of the world ! The business of the player is not a more christian employment than that of robbers ! There is as much justice and tenderness in telling every player that his employment is abominably sinful as in telling the same to a thief!' ' The playhouse, not only when some very profane play is on the stage, but in its daily common entertainments, is as certainly the house of the devil as the church is the house of God.' 'Can pious persons tell you of any one play for this forty or fifty years that has been free from wild rant, immodest passions, and profane language ?' ' To suppose an innocent play is like supposing innocent lust, sober rant, or harmless profaneness.' 'The stage never has one innocent play ; not one can be produced that ever you saw acted in either house, but what abounds with thoughts, passions, and language, contrary to religion ! This is true of the stage in its best state, when some admired tragedy is upon it.'

When it is remembered that such a play, for example, as Addison's ' Cato ' had, within Law's lifetime been acted with immense success, and that Shakespeare's tragedies, though not so popular as they deserved to be, must have been perfectly well known to him, one can scarcely conceive how he could stigmatise all plays in such a sweeping tone of condemnation.[1] His scurrilous abuse of players, too,

---

[1] It is interesting to contrast the views of the master with those of one of his most distinguished disciples on this point. John Wesley, after condemning, as well he might, the barbarous amusements of bear-baiting, cock-fighting, &c., adds, ' It seems a great deal more may be said in defence of seeing a serious tragedy. I could not do it with a clear conscience ; at least not in an English theatre, the sink of all profaneness and debauchery, but possibly

was surely as uncharitable as it was unauthorised, and fully
justifies Dennis's remark that the pamphlet was written in
'downright anti-Christian language.'

It was a sad pity that Dennis, having so strong a case,
should have spoiled it by having recourse to the *ad captan-
dum* argument that Law wrote in the interests of Jacobitism. Law had no such object in view ; he wrote in perfect sincerity and honesty, and if he had followed the
example of the Archbishop whom he quoted, he might
have written with telling effect. For the state of the stage
was deplorably bad. If the efforts of Collier and others
had done a little to purify it from the utter degradation
into which it had fallen after the Restoration, it still was so
corrupt that even a worldly man like John, Lord Hervey,
was fain to confess that the law (passed ten years after
Law's pamphlet was written) requiring plays to be licensed
by the Lord Chamberlain was needed.[1] But Law spoiled
the effect which no one better than he could have produced
by his unreasonable violence ; and it is to be feared that
there is some truth in Dennis's remark that the ' wild enthusiasm of Law's pamphlet would afford matter of scorn and
laughter to infidels and freethinkers, and render our most
sacred religion still more contemptible among them !'
Those who had read none of Law's writings except this

others can.' Law, in point of fact, was far more of a Puritan, High Churchman though he was, than any of the Methodists or Evangelicals were; in some
points, indeed, as, for instance, that of clerical celibacy, he recommended and
practised an asceticism which the Puritans never did ; and, singularly unlike
them, he almost absolutely condemned all wars and all oaths. On the point of
plays he was thoroughly at one with the ' Histriomastix ' of the preceding
century.

[1] Lord Hervey's *Memoirs*, ii. 341. David Hume, also, who will hardly
be accused of Puritanism, writing a few years later, speaks of the English
stage being put to shame by a neighbour which has never been considered a
model of purity. ' The English are become sensible of the scandalous licentiousness of their stage from the example of the French decency and morals.'
—Essay on the ' Rise of the Arts and Sciences,' *Essays*, iii. 135.

pamphlet, might really say of him as one of his antagonists on this question did : ' I never read a more unfair
reasoner. He begs the question. He is a madman who
rails at theatres till he foams again.' [1] But we shall do Law
more justice if we remember that in this pamphlet he was
really unworthy of himself ; and we may close this painful
account of what one cannot but call his escapade, with the
judicious remark of Gibbon : ' His discourse on the absolute unlawfulness of stage entertainments is sometimes
quoted for a ridiculous intemperance of sentiment and
language ; . . . . but these sallies must not extinguish the
praise which is due to Mr. William Law as a wit and a
scholar ; ' [2] and we may add what the historian does not
add, ' as a most powerful advocate of the Christian cause
and a noble example of the Christian life.'

Law himself thought his remarks upon the stage so
important that he transferred them almost word for word
to the pages of his ' Christian Perfection,' the first of his
great practical treatises, which was published in the same
year as the Tract on the Stage (1726).

The merits of this treatise have been somewhat thrown
into the shade by the still greater reputation of its immediate successor, ' The Serious Call.' But the ' Serious Call '
is, perhaps, the only work of the kind published in the
eighteenth century to which the ' Christian Perfection ' is
inferior.

By ' Christian perfection ' Law did not exactly mean
what became soon afterwards the source of such fierce
dispute between the Wesley and Whitefield sections of the

[1] *Law Outlawed ; or, a Short Reply to Mr. Law's Long Declamation against
the Stage, wherein the wild rant, blind passion, and false reasoning of that
piping-hot Pharisee are made apparent to the meanest capacity.* By Mrs. S. O.,
1726.

[2] Autobiography. *Misc. Works,* i. 15.

Methodists. Intending the work to be exclusively what he
termed it, 'a practical treatise,' he carefully avoided all
nice points of doctrine, and defined 'Christian perfection,'
at the outset, in a way to which no one who accepted
Christianity at all could take exception :[1] viz. as 'the right
performance of our necessary duties;' it is 'such as men
in cloysters and religious retirements cannot add more,
and, at the same time, such as Christians in all states of
the world must not be content with less.'

In his 'Christian Perfection' Law takes a very gloomy
view of life—far gloomier than he took in his later works.
The body we are in is 'a mere sepulchre of the soul ;' the
world ' but the remains of a drowned world—a mere wilderness, a vale of misery, where vice and madness, dreams
and shadows, variously please, agitate, and torment the
short, miserable lives of men.' 'The sole end of Christianity is to separate us from the world, to deliver us from
the slavery of our own natures and unite us to God.' This
life is 'a state of darkness, because it clouds and covers all
the true appearances of things; and what are called worldly
advantages no more constitute the state of human life than
rich coffins or beautiful monuments constitute the state of
the dead.' ' The vigour of our blood, the gaiety of our
spirits, and the enjoyment of sensible pleasures, though the
allowed signs of living men, are often undeniable proofs of
dead Christians.' ' Christianity buries our bodies, burns
the present world, triumphs over death by a general resurrection, and opens all into an eternal state.' ' There is
nothing that deserves a serious thought but how to get out
of the world and make it a right passage to our eternal
state.' ' It is the same vanity to project for happiness on
earth as to propose a happiness in the moon. Christianity,

---

[1] So far as it went, that is. The Evangelicals would, of course, complain of
it, as being very inadequate, as savouring more of the law than the gospel.

or the Kingdom of Heaven, has no other interests in this
world than as it takes its members out of it ; and when the
number of the elect is complete, this world will be con-
sumed with fire, as having no other reason for its existence
than the furnishing members for that blessed society which
is to last for ever.' 'Every condition in the world is
equally trifling and fit to be neglected for the sake of the
one thing needful.'

Such being Law's theory of life, it naturally follows
that he should recommend a course of severe austerity.
Our cares and our pleasures are to be strictly limited to
the necessities of nature. 'Self-denial and self-persecution
are even more necessary now than they were in the first
days of Christianity, when there was persecution from
without.' 'There is no other lawful way of employing our
wealth (beyond our bare necessities) than in the assistance
of the poor.' 'Suffering is to be *sought*, to pay some of the
debt due to sin.' 'The word of Christ, " deny *himself*," points
to a suffering and self-denial which the Christian is to inflict upon himself. He must, in his degree, recommend
himself to the favour of God on the same account and for
the same reasons that the sufferings of Christ procured
peace and reconciliation. Repentance is a hearty sorrow
for sin ; and sorrow is a pain or punishment which we are
obliged to raise to as high a degree as we can, that we may
be fitter objects of God's pardon.' [1]

Law reminds us that he wrote in the eighteenth century by going on to prove the reasonableness of his views ;
for ' reasonableness ' was the very keynote of the theology
of the period, and the writer who did not pay his homage
to it would have had little chance of being listened to. He
shows that while self-abasement is strictly according to

[1] It is hardly necessary to remark how very inadequate and erroneous many
of these sentiments would seem to the later evangelical school.

reason, 'pride is the most unreasonable thing in the world —as unreasonable as the madman who fancies himself to be a king, and the straw to which he is chained to be a throne of state. Self-denial is no more unreasonable than if a person who was to walk upon a rope across some great river was bid to deny himself the pleasure of walking in silver shoes, or the advantage of fishing by the way. In both cases the self-denial is reasonable, as commanding him to love things that will do him good, or to avoid things that are hurtful.'

Law then descends into details ; and, first of all, insists strongly upon the duty of fasting, devoting no less than twenty-five pages to the subject. Almost every ill temper, every hindrance to virtue, every clog in our way of piety, and the strength of every temptation, chiefly arises from the state of our bodies. If S. Paul thought his own salvation in danger without this subjection of his own body, how shall we, who are born in the dregs of time, think it safe to feed and indulge in ease and plenty ?

Then idleness, ambition, and worldly occupations are dealt with in the same spirit, in connection with self-denial. In this part of his work Law begins the plan, which he elaborated more carefully and in greater fulness in the 'Serious Call,' of illustrating his meaning by imaginary characters. *Philo*, who thinks all time to be lost that is not spent in the search of shells, urns, inscriptions, and broken pieces of pavement ; *Patronus*, who never goes to the sacrament, but will go forty miles to see a fine altar-piece ; who goes to church when there is a new tune to be heard, but never had any more serious thoughts about salvation than about flying ; *Eusebius*, who would be wholly taken up in the cure of souls, but that he is busy in studying the old grammarians, and would fain reconcile some differences amongst them before he dies ; *Lucia*, who must be the same sparkling creature in the church as she is in the playhouse ; *Publius*, who died with little or no religion through a constant fear of popery ; *Siccus*, who might have been a religious man, but that he thought building was the chief happiness of a rational creature ; who is all the week among dirt and mortar, and stays at home on Sundays to view his contrivances, and who will die more contentedly if his death does not happen while some wall is in building ;—are all admirable touches, combining the sparkling wit of Addison and a little of the cynicism of Swift with an intense earnestness of Christian conviction which is all Law's own.

Law next dwells largely upon the baneful effects of idle and unprofitable conversation— a favourite topic with him, for of all things he disliked ' a talkative spirit ;' and he then condemns sweepingly the reading of ' all corrupt, impertinent, and unedifying books,' and especially books of plays. But he does not sufficiently distinguish between books which are, to say the least, harmless, if not instructive, and those which are positively noxious. It is true that the majority of works of imagination, which, in Law's day, mostly took the dramatic form, were utterly abominable, and unfit reading for any Christian ; but it is unlike Law's usual acumen to argue from what was obviously only the abuse of a thing against the use of it. And the worst of such wholesale, indiscriminate censure is, that it tends to aggravate the very evil which it deplores. When all writers who appeal to the imagination are thus put under one general ban, they naturally become reckless, and thus one important element of the human mind has poison, not food, administered to it.

The next chapter, on the constant state of devotion to which Christians are called, is full of beautiful thoughts, beautifully expressed. We are here reminded that we are

still under the guidance of the High Churchman, for we
are told that ' we are most of all to desire those prayers
which are offered up at the altar where the Body and
Blood of Christ are joined with them.' [1]   The connection
between self-denial and prayer is well worked out.   His
arguments also against short prayers are ingenious and
unanswerable ; but, as this subject is more fully dealt with
in ' The Serious Call,' it is not necessary to say more of it
here.   Nor need we dwell on the arguments adduced to
show that Christians are required absolutely and in the
minutest particulars to imitate the life and example of
Christ.   The subject is a well-worn one, but, like almost
every subject which Law touches upon, it is presented to
us by him in a forcible and original manner.   In the last
chapter he gives a summary of the whole treatise ; and
concludes with a persuasive exhortation to all to aim at
nothing short of this Christian perfection.

As, above all things, it is desired to be perfectly fair,
it is necessary to notice some of the defects of the ' Christian
perfection.'

1. In this work Law begins that crusade against all
kinds of human learning which henceforth almost amounted
to a life-long craze with him.   The most illiterate of
Methodist preachers did not express a more sublime contempt of mental culture than this refined and cultured
scholar.   Every employment which is not of a directly
religious tendency is contemptible in his eyes.   ' If a man,'
he says, ' asks why he should labour to be the first mathe-
matician, orator, or statesman, the answer is easily given,
because of the fame and honour of such a distinction.'
The answer may be easily given, but it is by no means a
conclusive or satisfactory answer.   Law altogether ignores
the higher and less selfish motives which surely may

<hr>

[1] *Christian Perfection, Works,* vol. iii. c. xii. p. 367.

stimulate the nobler kind of men to follow such pursuits. What! had Newton, when he was engrossed with his mathematics and astronomy, no higher object than fame? Is not truth of all kinds a worthy object of pursuit? Was it no advantage to mankind to know the true nature of the glorious work of the Creator? When Demosthenes was stirring the hearts of his countrymen in behalf of their native country, was he actuated by no higher motive than a love of fame? Is there no such thing as a pure, disinterested patriotism? Had such statesmen as the two Pitts and Burke no higher object than the gratification of their own personal vanity? [1]

This tendency in Law is noticeable on account of the widespread and by no means wholly beneficial effects which it produced. It was obviously a convenient doctrine for those who could never have distinguished themselves to hold that all such distinction is contemptible. The alienation of Christianity from mental culture is a most disastrous thing. Law himself, indeed, by a happy inconsistency, was saved from the extravagances which the strict application of his own principles is apt to engender. Though he abused scholarship, he always wrote as a well-read scholar.

2. The 'Christian Perfection' is a somewhat melancholy book: the brighter side of Christianity is certainly not brought out into full relief; Law's own character was, particularly at this period, of the stern, austere type, and his book reflects his character. These defects, however, will be more fully considered in connection with ' The Serious Call.'

3. Once more. Law himself was the most unselfish

---

[1] It is only fair, however, to add that the politicians of Law's day were, as a rule, very different from the Pitts and the Burkes. Disinterested patriotism was quite at a discount in the age of the Walpoles and Pelhams.

of men, and yet there is some ground for the charge that this book advocated too much a selfish religion. You are to aim at Christian perfection because it is your only chance of happiness here and hereafter. It is true that the means by which this end is to be attained are the very reverse of selfish. Self-denial and mortification are of the essence of his scheme ; but it is mortification and denial of the lower self for the advantage of the higher. Beyond the actual requirements of nature, the rich are to spend nothing upon themselves, but give all to the poor. Is this selfishness ? In one sense, no ; but in another, possibly, yes. If the poor are regarded simply as a sort of 'spiritual plate-powder for polishing up our own souls' (to use a rather flippant but very forcible expression of a writer of our own day), there may lurk selfishness even in this apparently most unselfish rule. It must be added that nothing was further from Law's thoughts than selfishness ; but that is not to the point.

In spite, however, of these blemishes, the 'Christian Perfection' is a great work—a noble protest against the prevalent irreligion ; and the practical good which it effected far overbalanced the possible harm which a misuse of some of its sentiments may to a slight extent have caused.

Weighty testimony to the beneficial effects which it produced might be multiplied to an almost indefinite extent. A few of the most striking evidences must here suffice. The saintly Bishop Wilson says of it : 'Law's "Christian Perfection" fell into my hands by providence ; and after reading it over and over, I recommended it so heartily to a friend of mine near London, that he procured eighteen copies for each of our parochial libraries ; I have recommended it to my clergy after the most affecting manner, as the likeliest way to bring them to a most serious temper.[1]   The elder Venn (his biographer tells us) tried to realise Law's 'Christian Perfection.' John Wesley, who was himself deeply impressed by the work, informs us that all the Methodists were greatly profited by it.[2]   Bishop Horne (says Bishop Ewing) either copied, or was sufficiently conversant with the 'Christian Perfection' to quote from memory whole passages from it in his sermon 'On the Duty of Self-denial.'[3]   And, not to weary the reader, it may suffice to quote one more very practical illustration of the influence which the 'Christian Perfection' exercised. Shortly after its publication, it is reported that as Law was standing in his publisher's shop, in London, a stranger, after inquiring whether his name was the Rev. Mr. Law, placed in his hands a letter, which, on being opened, was found to contain a banknote for 1,000*l.*, sent, it is presumed, by some anonymous writer who was impressed with his practical treatise.   It is rumoured that with this money Law founded part of the school which still exists in his native village.

[1] *Letter from Bishop Wilson to Lady Elizabeth Hastings,* dated Warrington, September 13, 1729.
[2] Wesley's 'Sermons,' vol. iii. p. 228; *Sermon CVII.* on 'God's Vineyard.'
[3] *Present-Day Papers on Prominent Questions in Theology,* p. 13.

CHAPTER VI.

LAW AT PUTNEY.

AFTER a period of about ten years' occultation, which Law probably spent in London, and, as we may gather from an incidental notice, in somewhat straitened circumstances,[1] he emerges from his obscurity and appears before us in very distinct individuality henceforth to the end of his life—thirty-four years later. It is said to have been about the year 1727 when he became an inmate of the family of Mr. Gibbon, grandfather of the historian, at Putney, acting in the capacity of tutor to his only son, Edward. The story of the life at Putney is immortalised in perhaps the most finished piece of literary biography in the English language—Gibbon's 'Memoirs of My Life and Writings.' Mr. Gibbon, the master of the house, had been

---

[1] The incidental notice is in a pamphlet entitled, ‘An Account of all the Considerable Pamphlets that have been published on either side in the present controversy between the Bishop of Bangor and others to the end of the year 1718, with occasional observations on them by Philagnostes Criticus, 1719.’ The writer has a very strong bias in favour of Bishop Hoadly, and against Law. After vehemently condemning Law's letters, he writes, ‘ There has been for some time advertised a “ Reply to the Bishop of Bangor's Answer to the Representation ” by Law, to be published by subscription, and the following right zealous and orthodox divines of the Church of England, Dr. Pelling, Dr. Fiddes, Dr. Astry, and Mr. Thorold, have charitably taken the trouble of solliciting (*sic*) and receiving subscriptions for this great nonjuring defender of the rights of the clergy.’ I think that slight as this notice is, we may certainly gather from it that Law was at the time in straitened circumstances; otherwise, with his independent character, he would never have allowed such an arrangement.

one of the directors of the disastrous South Sea Company ; and, when the bubble burst, he lost, not only his fortune, but also, like the rest of the directors, to a great extent his reputation. He appears, however, to have been an excellent man of business, and to have succeeded in a comparatively short time both in repairing his shattered fortune and in re-establishing his good name ; so that at the time when Law became a member of his household he was again a reputable and wealthy man. ' He had realised a very considerable property in Sussex, Hampshire, Buckinghamshire, and the New River Company ; and had acquired a spacious house with gardens and lands at Putney, in Surry, where he resided in decent hospitality.'[1] In this ' spacious house ' we find Law comfortably located, certainly not later than 1727, and possibly much earlier. In fact, I am by no means sure that a considerable portion of the time during which we seem to have lost sight of Law may not have been passed in Mr. Gibbon's family. Gibbon the historian is provokingly vague on the subject, but his account will at least admit of such an explanation. ' A parent,' he writes, ' is most attentive to supply in his children the deficiencies of which he is conscious in himself ; my grandfather's knowledge was derived from a strong understanding, and the experience of the ways of men ; but my father enjoyed the benefits of a liberal education as a scholar and a gentleman. At Westminster School, and afterwards at Emanuel College, in Cambridge, he passed through a regular course of academical discipline, and the care of his learning and morals was entrusted to his private tutor, the same Mr. William Law,'[2] Now, as Mr. Edward Gibbon (Law's pupil) was born in 1707, he would be twenty years old at the time when Law is reported to have entered the family ;

---

[1] Gibbon's ' Miscellaneous Works,' vol. i. p. 13. *Memoirs of my Life and Writings.*   [2] *Ibid.* i. 15.

and as it was evidently intended that he should be tutor
at Putney as well as at Cambridge, it seems highly probable that he commenced his labours before his pupil
had reached so ripe an age. The reasons which induced
Mr. Gibbon to select Law as a tutor for his son are obvious. Though not actually a Jacobite, Mr. Gibbon, like
many other country gentlemen, had probably in his heart
of hearts a strong sympathy with the cause of the exiled
Stuarts. He was a staunch Tory, and had been one
of the Commissioners of Customs under the famous Tory
Ministry during the last four years of Queen Anne. He
had acquitted himself so well in this post that, as his
grandson proudly informs us, ' Lord Bolingbroke had been
heard to declare that he had never conversed with a
man who more clearly understood the commerce and
finances of England.' He had, as we have seen, suffered
severely under the Whig Ministry which succeeded with
the accession of George I., and was always an implacable
opponent of Sir Robert Walpole. The *protégé* of Bolingbroke and the foe of Walpole could hardly be without
Jacobite proclivities ; and thus the fact that William Law
was a nonjuror would be a strong recommendation rather
than a hindrance to the favour of Mr. Gibbon. Like many
other shrewd but self-educated men, he probably valued
the benefits of education all the more because he had felt
the want of it in his own person. A man of the attainments and abilities of Mr. Law was not to be met with
every day ; and his sturdy, independent, masculine character, his intense piety without a scrap of cant about it,
and his evident firmness, which Mr. Gibbon no doubt felt
that his son required in a tutor, would all commend him to
his employer.

The office of half-tutor, half-chaplain and companion,
in a gentleman's family was a very common resource
for the nonjurors. Lord Macaulay's description of the

degeneracy into which many of them fell is well known. Whether it be in the main true or not need not here be discussed ; but it is quite clear that it would not apply to William Law. *He*, at any rate, was in no danger of ' sinking into a servile, sensual, drowsy parasite.' *He* never set himself ' to discover the weak side of every character, to flatter every passion and prejudice, to sow discord and jealousy where love and confidence ought to exist, to watch the moment of indiscreet openness for the purpose of extracting secrets important to the prosperity and honour of families,' &c.[1] From his general character we might assume with perfect certainty that he belonged to neither of these classes ; but, apart from this, we have the express testimony of his pupil's son, who certainly would not be prejudiced in favour of a man holding the views that Law did. ' In our family,' writes the historian, ' he (Law) had left the reputation of a worthy and pious man, who believed all that he professed, and practised all that he enjoined.'[2]

In 1727 Law accompanied his pupil to Emmanuel College, Cambridge,[3] and thus once again, under very different circumstances, entered within the walls from which he had been excluded eleven years before for conscience' sake. It would be interesting to know Law's feelings and behaviour on his return to a society of which he had once been a distinguished member. Most men look back to their old college days with affectionate regard. But we have no record whatever of Law's sentiments on this point. The 'Serious Call' was probably written, in part at least, at Cambridge, but no allusion of any kind to the University is found in that great work ; and beyond a few scattered

[1] Macaulay's *History of England*, vol. ii. chap. xiv. p. 110.
[2] Gibbon's *Miscellaneous Works*, vol. i. p. 14.
[3] The register of Mr. Gibbon's entry at Emmanuel is as follows: 'July 10, 1727, Gibbon, Edw., F.C. [Fellow Commoner], Alderman of London.'

hints, to be noticed presently, Law's second stay at Emmanuel is a perfect blank to us.

Of Law's pupil little need be said. It would seem as if in the family of Gibbon force of character, like the gout in some families, passed over a generation. It is seen in a very remarkable degree in the grandfather and the grand-son. The stout old gentleman who repaired a shattered for-tune and an almost shattered reputation, and who earned the complimentary remark of Lord Bolingbroke, was certainly not deficient in moral and intellectual vigour; still less was the great historian. But the second Gibbon, boy and man, was a vague, purposeless, uninteresting character. His son, indeed, always spoke of him and treated him with affection and respect, and when he died paid a pious tribute to his 'graceful person, polite address, gentle manners, and unaf-fected cheerfulness, which recommended him to the favour of every company.' But he is obliged to acknowledge his father's weakness and inconstancy. To fritter away his time when he was a youth, and his money when he grew to be a man, seems to have been his habit. Such a character was not likely to commend itself to a man like the elder Gibbon. On one occasion Law had to interpose his good offices to prevent the old gentleman from turning his son out of doors; and at his death Mr. Gibbon enriched his two daughters at the expense of his son, because, the his-torian tells us, he did not altogether approve of the latter's marriage, but probably in part also because, as a man of business, he knew that money would be thrown away upon so feeble a character. It may be that Law was not exactly the man to draw out the latent faculties of a youth like Gibbon; at any rate he did not succeed in doing so.

One can hardly help speculating what might have been the result if Law's pupil had been the grandson instead of the son. There certainly were some very noble elements in the character of the historian ; but, so far as Christianity was concerned, he never had a fair chance. His experiences at Magdalen College, Oxford, were not likely to give him a very exalted opinion of the established religion. M. Pavilliard, the worthy Swiss pastor who was employed to win him back from Romanism, though a man of respectable abilities and attainments, was not a strong enough man to deal with such a mind as Gibbon's. And, so far as is known, Gibbon never *was* brought into contact with sufficiently powerful Christian influences until he had drifted away from the Christian faith. What the influence of a Christian of real genius, as well as of intense earnestness and blameless life, like Law, might have done for him, can of course only be a matter of conjecture. On the one hand, Gibbon had little of what the Germans call 'religiosität' in his composition, and it is therefore quite possible that the austere and uncompromising character of Law's religion might only have precipitated the catastrophe which subsequently befel his faith. But then, on the other hand, if Gibbon had not a very strong sense of piety, he had a very keen relish for intellectual questions connected with Christianity ; from his earliest youth he had always a hankering after religious controversy ; and his enthusiastic exclamation in describing his conversion to Romanism through the instrumentality of Bossuet, 'Surely I fell by a noble hand,' &c., shows what a hold a powerful controversialist could gain upon his mind. No man living was more competent to gain this hold than Law ; one can fancy into what ribbons he could have torn the arguments which Gibbon's boyish mind loved to frame. Gibbon's own account of the curious sort of arithmetical process by which he was reconverted from Romanism, while it shows the interest he took in such questions, shows also how crude and unformed his views were. As one reads the sad story of what a Christian cannot help calling the wreck of a noble character, one is tempted to cry 'exoriare aliquis' to lead this great but erring spirit from darkness into light. And the 'aliquis' was at hand in the honoured friend and spiritual director of the family, William Law.

Nor would the advantages of such a connexion as we have imagined between these two great men have been all on one side. It was distinctly a misfortune to Law that he never came into close personal relationship, except upon paper, with a man of real genius. John Wesley was the nearest approach to such a man who knew Law intimately; but Wesley's genius was, as we shall see presently, not at all of the kind which Law was likely to appreciate. As a rule, Law was a very Saul among his Christian brethren, intellectually taller by the head and shoulders than any of them. At no period of his life, so far as we know, did he make any friends who could converse with him on at all equal terms. He was invariably the oracle of his company, and oracles are not wont to be contradicted. This manifest superiority to his surroundings rather tended to encourage a certain peremptoriness of tone and abruptness of manner which were natural to him. Had he been brought into that intimate relationship which subsists between a conscientious tutor and an intelligent pupil, with a young man of the calibre of Gibbon, and continued the intimacy when the relationship ceased, the result might have been beneficial to him. Such, however, was not his good fortune; his lot was cast with the feeble father, not with the strong son.

Law's pupil quitted the University without taking a degree, and commenced his travels, leaving his tutor behind him in the 'spacious house' at Putney. The historian cannot resist a sneer at this arrangement. 'The mind of a saint is above or below the present world, and while the

pupil proceeded on his travels, the tutor remained at Putney;' but he does Law the justice to add, 'the much
honoured friend and spiritual director of the whole family;'
and at a later period he acknowledges his obligations to
the tutor for 'some valuable editions of the classics and
the fathers, the choice, as it should seem, of Mr. Law.'
These he found in his father's study at Buriton, which was
also 'stuffed with much trash of the last age, with much
High Church divinity and politics, which have long since
gone to their proper place ';—possibly this ' High Church
divinity and politics,' which he is pleased to call trash, may
also have been the choice of Mr. Law. Not a trace, however, of the influence of Mr. Law can be found in his
pupil's character and after career. It is difficult to conceive a greater difference than between the life of Mr.
Gibbon and the ideal life sketched by Law in the ' Serious
Call ' at the very time when Gibbon was under his charge.
Law did not succeed in making his pupil even tolerant of
Jacobitism ; for Gibbon the historian tells us of a certain
unhappy Mr. John Kirkby, 'who exercised about eighteen
months the office of my domestic tutor ;' and adds, ' His
learning and virtue introduced him to my father, and at
Putney he might have found at least a temporary shelter,
had not an act of indiscretion again driven him into the
world. One day, reading prayers in the parish church, he
most unluckily forgot the name of King George ; his
patron, a loyal subject, dismissed him with some reluctance,
and a decent reward.' Well might the pupil of Mr. Law
show 'some reluctance' in punishing a man for doing
inadvertently what his tutor had no doubt always done
deliberately !

Law's life at Putney, which lasted at least twelve years,
was by no means an inactive or useless one. Besides
being busy with his pen during this period, he acted as a

sort of spiritual director, not only to the family of the house, but also to a coterie of earnest men who, in that time of spiritual torpor, both inside and outside the national church, might well require some more religious guidance than either church or conventicle could supply them with. The widespread and profound impression which Law's two practical treatises had produced, caused him to be greatly sought after as a kind of *ductor dubitantium*. In many respects he was admirably adapted for the office. In the first place, he was always accessible. He appears to have had what in this day we should call the ‘ run of the house ’ at Putney, with full liberty to receive his friends there, as well as to correspond with them, as often as he chose. Nothing can better illustrate the force of Law's character than this curious arrangement. When we remember that too many domestic chaplains, especially nonjurors, held a very subordinate, not to say degrading, position at this period, when we bear in mind that the master of the house was evidently a strong-willed old gentleman, and one more-over whose pursuits and habits were not of the kind which lead a man to do homage to a scholar and a divine simply as such ; when we further take into account that, from a worldly point of view, the obligations were entirely on one side, we shall see what a strong man Law must have been, to have become, as he obviously did, complete master of the situation. But the power he obtained he never abused ; he employed it, as was his invariable way, for no selfish purposes, but for the spiritual good of all who came within its sphere.

Again, oracle as Law was, he never expressed himself oracularly. You might disagree with him, but you could not mistake what he meant. Neither could you doubt the thorough genuineness of the man. He varied his opinions not unfrequently, and his disciples must have found some difficulty in keeping pace with his various changes ; but from first to last he was manifestly desirous only to discover the truth and to glorify the God of truth.

Perhaps, too, he was all the more calculated to fascinate, because there was always a certain amount of fear mingled with the love which his disciples bore him. His natural temper was cheerful and very kindly ; but there was an asperity of manner, a curtness of expression, an impatience of everything that appeared to him absurd and unreasonable,—and he had a wonderfully keen perception of what *was* absurd and unreasonable,—which made most men with whom he came into contact rather afraid of him. Indeed, if this natural asperity had not been softened by Divine grace, he would have been, in spite of his greatness and goodness, a somewhat repelling man. Even as it was, he was rather a Gamaliel to be looked up to by a select few than a friend to be loved by a large number.

If we compare him with two of his contemporaries, who in many respects greatly resembled him—John Wesley and Dr. Johnson—we shall at once see the difference. All three were good Christians, of a very different type indeed, and by no means reaching the same spiritual standard, but all genuine in their way. All three exercised a vast influence for good in their generation. They were, each of them, the centre of a circle of admiring disciples. There were many personal characteristics common to the three. A certain massiveness and strength of character, a rather grim sense of humour, a real benevolence of nature concealed under an external roughness which made them feared at least as much as loved—these belong to all. But Johnson and Wesley are still household words in the mouth of every educated Englishman ; Law is almost forgotten. And yet in their many excellences Law was fully equal to the other two ; while in point of purely intellectual power

he was, I venture to think, superior to both. Johnson and
Wesley could no more have written such powerful works
as Law wrote than they could have won Marlborough's
victories. This seems a bold assertion, but let any one
compare the still extant works of the three, and he can
hardly fail to admit its truth. In what single work of
either Johnson's or Wesley's is there the same originality
of thought, elegance of diction, or force of argument, which
are to be found in almost every one of Law's works ? Of
course, it may be said that neither Wesley's nor Johnson's
reputation rests on his literary merit ; the former having
immortalised himself as a practical worker, the latter as a
conversationalist. Still, the literary work of both has
survived ; while, in one sense, Law was as truly a practical worker as Wesley ; and, from the scattered hints
which yet remain to us, we may gather that, like Johnson,
he had very remarkable conversational powers. The secret
of their success and of his comparative failure probably
lies in the fact that they both possessed bonds of sympathy
with their fellow men which Law never possessed. Both
Wesley and Johnson were thorough eighteenth century
men ; Law was a sort of *lusus naturæ* in his day. Of course,
the oblivion into which he has fallen is partly owing to the
fact of his having in his later years adopted a set of very
unpopular opinions. But with his force of intellect, Law
might surely to a great extent have overcome this unpopularity, if he had possessed that sympathy with his age
which both the others did. Johnson, in spite of his rug-
gedness, was full of *bonhomie* ; he took a broader view of
life than Law did ; he thought the world was to be leavened,
not renounced, by the Christian ; and thus he was able to
extend his influence over a far wider area during his lifetime, and to leave works behind him which would be read
by a far wider class of readers after his death than Law

did. Wesley, again, in spite of much that has been said to
the contrary, was in reality a thoroughly genial man. He,
too, took a broader view of life than Law did ; and, moreover, he possessed a wonderful faculty of organising and
governing masses of men, of which Law was quite destitute.
Hence it happened that he who was really the ablest of
these three good Christians is much the least known of the
three.

But all this time we are leaving Law at Putney, the
centre of a very small circle of admirers, who looked up to
him as their 'guide, philosopher, and friend.' A brief description of some of the more prominent members of this
circle will enable us better to understand the great central
figure round which they were grouped.

First in order of intimacy, if not of merit, comes John
Byrom. In common gratitude we are bound to place him
first on the list, because it is to him that we are indebted
more than to any man, except Law himself, for the 'materials which enable us to estimate Law's character. It seems
to have been the fashion for the gods of the eighteenth
century to have had each his flamen. As Addison had his
Steele, Warburton his Hurd, Johnson his Boswell, so Law
had his Byrom.

John Byrom had considerable merits, both as a man
and an author ; but there is a certain absurdity about him
in both capacities which rather mars them. Like Law, he
was, though the son of a tradesman, the scion of an old and
honourable family ; and, like Law, he had the benefit of a
liberal education. He was a Fellow of Trinity, Cambridge,
at the same time that Law was Fellow of Emmanuel ; but
they do not seem to have become personally acquainted at
the University ; and, as we have already seen, the reports
which Byrom then heard of his future mentor did not at
all impress him in his favour. At the early age of twenty-

three, Byrom wrote a pastoral entitled ' Colin and Phœbe,'
or, as he generally terms it, from its first line : ' My time,
O ye Muses, &c.,' which had the honour of being inserted
in the eighth volume of the ' Spectator,' with the complimentary remark of the editor, ' It is so original, that I do
not much doubt it will divert my readers.'[1]   It *is* a diverting little piece, prettily conceived and smoothly written,
equal, in fact, to the best pastorals of Shenstone or Philips,
and nearly equal to those of Gay ; but what would Law
have said if his pupil had been guilty of perpetrating this
amatory trifle in later years ?   The history of this pastoral
gives us so curious a glimpse into the way in which matters
were managed at the Universities in the eighteenth century,
that it is worth noticing.   The ' Phœbe ' of the poem was
Joanna, daughter of the famous Dr. Bentley, then Master of
Trinity ; and young Byrom immortalised her, not because
he wished to win her affections, but because he desired to
secure her father's interest for the fellowship for which he
was a candidate.   It is satisfactory to be able to add that
the ingenious plan was successful ; for through Dr. Bentley's influence he was elected.   However, this kind of
trifling was soon ended.   Phœbe married a bishop,[2] and
Colin, under the tuition of his ' Master Law,'[3] sang afterwards in a very different strain ; but to the last he seems to

---

[1] *Spectator,* vol. viii. No. 603.   Byrom also wrote Nos. 586, 587, 597,
the former under the pseudonym of ' John Shadow.'
[2] Dr. Dennison Cumberland, afterwards Bishop of Clonfert in Killaloe.
[3] Byrom always called Law ' his master,' and explained what he meant by
so doing, *more suo,* in rhyme.

> O how much better he from whom I draw,
> Though deep yet clear, his system—' Master Law.'
> *Master* I call him ; not that I incline
> To pin my faith on any one divine.
> But man or woman, whosoe'er he be
> That speaks true doctrine, is a pope to me.
>
> *Epistle to a Gentleman of the Temple.*

have been proud of ' My time, O ye Muses, &c.,' and to have considered it as his *chef-d'œuvre.*

We have already seen that Byrom, like Law, was attached to the exiled Stuarts ; but he had not, like Law, the courage of his opinions. Still, their political sympathies were, no doubt, a bond of union between them. But there were other bonds stronger than this. Byrom resided for a time in France, and there met with Malebranche's ' Search after Truth,' and some of the works of Madame Antonia Bourignon. Both these authors fascinated him extremely, and of course prepared the way for those mystic views which, under the direction of Law, he afterwards ardently embraced.

It is from Byrom's private journal that we derive our best information about Law at Putney. His accounts of his continual meetings with Law, and the reports of the conversations between them are most interesting and amusing, perhaps none the less so for being mixed up in a rather bewildering way with the minutest details about the writer's own habits and tastes. In fact, they are so good that it is provoking that they were not made still better by being worked up into a regular life of his friend, instead of appearing as mere disjointed fragments. Byrom might perhaps have done for Law what Boswell did for Johnson. There is a very curious resemblance between the relations of the two men to their respective heroes. Both not only received with perfect complacency the snubs which their patrons were continually administering to them, but also chronicled those snubs with the utmost simplicity. Both were rewarded by the great men with compliments and expressions of love and esteem. Both fought their principals' battles with more than their principals' ardour. But, as Law was a more strictly religious man than Johnson,[1] so

---

[1] Dr. Johnson's attitude towards Christianity is very happily hit off by Mr. Leslie Stephen. ' Johnson, as we know him, was a man of the world, though

Byrom was a more reputable man than Boswell. We hear of no such escapades on the part of Byrom as those which Boswell naively reports about himself. Still, Byrom was as much more lax than Law as Boswell was than Johnson. His journal indicates a curious conflict between the Church and the world on the part of the writer. One finds such odd medleys as these : ' April 4, 1735. Captain Mainwaring, from Chester, called, and we drank a bottle of old hock, 30 years old, and talked about religion and Mr. Law. ' Jan. 31st, 1730. Supper at Mitre with Chilton, Hough, &c. ; talked about Hebrew points, happiness, Mr. Law, stage plays ; we paid 2s. ; I had two bottles—too much for a defender of Law to drink.' ' Rose at 10 o'clock, rose at 9.30, rose at 11,' are entries of constant occurrence, in utter defiance of Law's rule that early rising was almost essential to the Christian character.

This, however, is anticipating. The first entry in the journal which indicates any intimacy between Byrom and his mentor is dated March 1729. On February 15 of the same year he records ' Bought Law's " Serious Call " of Rivington.' Three days later he writes to Phœbe Byrom, ' I have bought Mr. Law's book since I came to town, but have had no time to read him yet. I find the young folks of my acquaintance think Mr. Law an impracticable, strange, whimsical writer, but I am not convinced by their reasons. Yesterday, Mr. Mildmay bought it because I said so much of it ; he is a very pretty young gentleman. But, for Mr. Law and Christian religion, and such things, they are mightily out of fashion at present.' About a fortnight afterwards we find that Byrom had made time not only to read Mr. Law's book, but also, after his wont, to turn a

a religious man of the world. He represents the secular rather than the ecclesiastical type.'—*Johnson* (' English Men of Letters '), p. 10. Law most decidedly represents the ecclesiastical.

passage of it into rhyme. On March 4, 1729, is the first
recorded interview between Law and his future disciple,
which is well worth quoting in full. Byrom writes : ' We,'
(i.e. himself and the ' pretty young gentleman ' mentioned
in the last entry) ' went to the Bull Inn, Putney, and sent
to Mr. Law that we should wait on him in the afternoon ; it
was then near two o'clock ; while we were eating a mutton
chop Mr. Law came to us, and we went with him to Mr.
Gibbon's, where we walked in the gardens and upstairs
into some rooms, the library, and then we sat in a parlour
below with Mr. Law and young G., who left us after a
little while over a bottle of French wine. We talked about
F. Malebranche much ; Mr. Law said he owed it to him that
he kept his act at Cambridge upon "Omnia videmus in
Deo ;" that meeting with the book without any recommendation of it, he found all other books were trifling to
this ! Nay, so far does he admire the author, that if he knew
anybody who had conversed with him much he would go to
Paris on purpose to talk with him. I told him I would go
with him. We talked about his book, and I made some of
the common objections. . . . . I repeated the verses about
the *Pond* to him[1] and Mildmay, and they laughed, and
Mr. Law said he must have a copy of them, and desired I
would not put the whole book into verse, for then it would
not sell in prose—so the good man can joke !' After a few
more observations not worth repeating, Byrom concludes,
' He lent me the Eloge upon Father Malebranche, and said
he would find me out at London ; we left directions where
we both lived. He brought us to the water-side, &c.'

---

[1] The verses about the ' Pond ' were a poetical version of the capital story
in the ' Serious Call ' of the man who spent his life in getting from all sources
water to fill his pond, and, when it was filled, drowned himself in it. Wrenched
from its context, as it appears in Byrom's poem, the story seems absurdly
extravagant ; introduced as it is by Law in the ' Serious Call,' it is an admirable one ; to say nothing of the superiority of Law's prose over Byrom's verse.

This interview between Law and Byrom evidently ended
to the satisfaction of both, and from that time sprang up an
odd intimacy between these two good men who were in
most respects singularly unlike one another.   We next find
them both at Cambridge—Law in his capacity of tutor or
governor to young Mr. Gibbon, Byrom apparently on an
expedition after pupils for a new system of shorthand which
he had invented, and by teaching which he at this time
mainly supported himself and his family.   He was particularly anxious to secure Gibbon on account of his connexion with Law, but found him a difficult pupil to catch,
and not a very satisfactory one when caught.   Thus, we find
him writing to Mrs. Byrom : ' Jan. 30, 1730.   Going to
Emmanuel. . . . . I had a mind not to miss a gentleman
or two whom I like, and especially had a desire to enter
Mr. Law's pupil, but question now whether I shall, because
he is always saying he will learn, but not to me, or else I
would fain have him for his tutor's sake.'   The shy bird,
however, was caught, for within a few days we have the
entry: ' Mr. Gibbon had appointed to come and begin
shorthand, which he did.   Mr. Gibbon, of Emmanuel (Mr.
Law's pupil), began Candlemas Day, 1730.'   The pupil was
not an apt one, but Byrom was more than repaid by the
approbation of his tutor.   At the second lesson, he finds
that ' Gibbon, who had been " playing," he said, at quad-
rille [what did Mr. Law say to that ?] had writ a little, but
very ill, for he makes his letters wretchedly, but reads
pretty well.   Mr. Law came in while we were at it, and sat
with us, and I ran over the theory of it with him, and he
took it immediately and seemed much pleased with it ; said
he had never so good a notion of it before, that it was of
great use and well contrived, that he was much tempted to
learn it ; I exhorted him to try ; he said the theory of it he
saw plainly, and I could say nothing of it, but he would

allow all the fine things that could be said ; I was much
pleased that it pleased a man for whom I have a great
veneration ; he said I should have more pains with Mr. G.,
because he wrote a very bad hand ; he asked me if I
smoked, but I said " No, not alone ;" we had a bottle of
wine ; he drank none, I think, I two or three glasses ; . . .
appointed to call to-morrow. . . . . Mr. Law made Mr.
Gibbon go to the porter's with me to let me out.'   On the
morrow, Byrom found 'Mr. Gibbon had done nothing.'
' What a pity,' he adds, ' he should be so slow, for Law's sake.'
There was a reward, however, in store for him.   The next
day, 'going to Emmanuel, I met Mr. Gibbon and Bridgman, so appointed to-morrow.   N.B.—Bridgman said that
he had been with Law, who had commended our shorthand much, was glad that Gibbon had learned it, and said
that it was THE SHORTHAND.'   Gibbon, however, would
not learn it ; it was impossible to fix the volatile pupil.
One day, Byrom ' went to Gibbon, but Law said he was gone
to the Westminster Club ;' on another, ' went to Gibbon's,
but he was gone to Huntingdon, Law said ;' on another,
' went to Emmanuel, Gibbon was in the Combination, Law
sent for him,' and so forth.   Trifling as these details are in
themselves, they are well worth noting as illustrative not
only of the character of Law's pupil, but also to a certain
extent of Law's own capacity for the office of tutor.   He
and Gibbon were evidently in no way congenial spirits, and
Law appears to have had little or no influence over his
pupil.   One can well understand, therefore, why, when the
Cambridge career was over, the pupil should have gone
forth on his travels alone, and the tutor have been left behind at Putney, where there were others who appreciated
him better, and where he found more congenial and useful
occupation than managing a dull, vacillating young man.
The only other allusion in Byrom's journal to Law's unsatis-

factory pupil occurs thirteen years later, when Byrom, who
was rather given to asking awkward questions, asked Law
'about the story of his setting young Gibbon and his father
at odds about his smoking;' to which Law replied 'that he
had never spoken to him in his life about it; that he had
reconciled them when he was turned out of doors.'

In March 1731 we have an entry in Byrom's journal
which is provoking on account of its brevity. 'Met Dr.
Bentley in the park, and Mr. Abbot, and we had talk about
Mr. Law, charity, and religion.' Mr. Abbot was an Emmanuel man and doubtless knew Law well; but as he was
in no way remarkable, there would have been no particular
interest in hearing what he had to say about Law. But
one *would* have liked to know what the greatest scholar
and critic of his age thought of the only man who had
shown himself capable of writing a piece of slashing controversial divinity equal to his own immortal 'Remarks
on a Discourse of Freethinking;' for I have no hesita-
tion in saying that Law in his 'Remarks on the Fable of
the Bees' as completely annihilated Mandeville as 'Phile-
leutherus Lipsiensis' annihilated Collins.

In May of the same year, Byrom gives his wife a pretty
picture of a somewhat unwonted scene for Law to figure in.
'I told Phœbe,' he writes, 'how Mr. Houghton, Lloyd,
Chaddock, and I and Mr. Law came in a boat from Putney to London, and what kind of conversation we had;
when I asked him first what he thought of Mrs. Bourignon,
he said he wished he could think like her, by which thou
mayst guess that he and I should not much disagree about
matters. Our young brethren were mightily pleased with
him, as anybody must have been, and have seen by the
instance of a happy poor man that true happiness is not
of this world's growth. I wish thou hadst been there and
Josiah, &c. I think you would all have liked him, for all he

is such an unfashionable fellow—perhaps for that reason among others.

Passing over such unimportant notices as—'I met Mr. Law in the street to-day and had a great deal of talk with him. I wish thou [Mrs. Byrom] hadst been with us ;' ' Put on a shirt to go to Mr. Law ;'—which are of constant occur-rence, we come to a long entry which is singularly interest-ing as illustrative of Mr. Law's opinions at this period on a variety of subjects expressed with all the frankness which a man uses when he pours out his soul to a confidential friend. It will be remembered that Byrom before his acquaintance with Law had been much fascinated with the writings of Madame Bourignon ; to wean him from his excessive attachment to this interesting, pious, but wildly extravagant writer was evidently one of the objects of Law's remarks. The sort of half-fear, half-love with which Byrom was beginning to regard Law ; the touching *naïveté* with which he records the severe rebukes which he submis-sively received from his mentor ; the austere views which mysticism had not yet toned down in the author of the 'Serious Call ;' and, finally, the utter want in Law of that power of influencing the lower classes which his fellow-reformer John Wesley possessed in so remarkable a degree ; —all this is very vividly illustrated in the following entry : ' June 7, 1735. I went to Putney afoot, and walked past the house and into a field '—evidently because he could not yet summon up courage to meet the great man [1]—'and about three inquired for Mr. Law, and Miss Gibbon came to me and went with me into the garden, and brought me to him,

---

[1] This is clear from what goes before. 'Having,' he tells us, ' put on my boots and coat and trunk-hose, and gone up to shave and powder, . . . I went to Putney, where I light at the King's Arms in Fulham, and stayed there till two o'clock, it being near one when I came.' Having fortified his courage with 'four Brentford rolls and half a pint of cider,' he went 'to Putney afoot,' as recorded above.

walking by the green grass by a canal ; he asked if I had
dined ? I said Yes ; and after salutation and a turn or two :
" Well, what do you say ? " to which I answered that I had
a great many things to say, but I dare not. It was not
long before Mrs. Bourignon became the subject of his
discourse, and he said much about her and against her ;
seemed to think she had great assistance from the Spirit of
God, but questioned much if she did not mix her own as
Luther did ; said that he had locked her up that Miss
Gibbon might not find her among his books, that he had
not met with anybody fit to read her, and mentioned her
saying that there were no Christians but herself ; and,
above all, her rendering the necessity of Christ's death
needless, which was the very foundation of all Christianity ;
and that she would puzzle any man what to do, and that she
thought the world would be at an end. He mentioned
Mr. John Walker some time in the afternoon, that he had
left his father because he could not comply, and yet he
heard since that he went to assemblies, which was impossible for a true Christian to be persuaded to do ; mentioned
one that came to ask about some indifferent matter his
advice, and he heard that since he was going to join holy
orders and matrimony together ; I suppose he meant
Houghton. He said that Taulerus had all that was good
in Mrs. Bourignon, but yet the humblest man alive. Upon
my asking if Rusbrochius [1] was the first of those writers,
he said, " You ask an absurd question. Excuse me," says
he, " for being so free ; " that there never was an age since
Christianity but there had been of those writers. Mentioned H. Suso's three rules for possessing money : first, to
take necessaries only ; second, to impart to any Christian
that wanted ; thirdly, if lost, not to be at all concerned ; and

---

[1] For an account of Rusbrochius, Taulerus, Suso, and Madame Bourignon,
see *infra.*

this Suso did not know where to hide himself for humility. He said that the bottom of all was that this world was a prison into which we were fallen, that we had nothing to do but to get out of it, that we had no misery but what was in it, that to be freed from it was all that we wanted, that this was the true foundation of all ; that if he was to preach, he would tell the people that he had nothing to tell them but this, that once knowing this they knew enough and had a light that would set everything in a true view ; that the philosophers Epictetus, Socrates, had, by the grace of God and their own search, observed that this world could not be what God made it. He said that there was a necessity for everyone to feel the torment of sin ; that it was necessary for them to die in this manner and to descend into hell with Christ, and so to rise again with Him ; that every one must pass through this fiery trial in this world or another. He said I must tell the people to whom I had recommended Mrs. Bourignon that I meant only to recommend what she had said about renouncing the world, and not any speculations ; that it was wrong to have too many spiritual books, that the first time a man was touched by the reading of any book that was the time to fall in with grace, that it passed into mere reading instead of practice else ; that if we received benefit from reading a book, the last person we ought to say so to should be the author, who might receive harm from it, and be tempted to take a satisfaction in it which he ought not ; that a man suffering ought to abandon himself to God and rejoice " Gloria Patri," that some justice was done to God by his suffering ; there was such music in " Our Father which art in heaven, hallowed be Thy name ; Thy kingdom come ; Thy will be done." He said what little difference there was between a king upon a throne and a king in a play, between calling a man a lord in earnest and in jest. That he had reason to remember Dr. Richardson, his pupil, whom he called Richards, but was not sure that his father was minister of Putney, I think ; that the preachers durst not speak upon the subject of the cross ; that we do not know what our Lord suffered, that the sacrifice of His human body was the least thing in it. There were two men drawing the rolling-stone, and he said how fine it would be if they would learn piety, but they would not be taught ; that Mr. Gibbon's other daughter was married ; that it was such an absurdity to come to the communion with patches or paint, which no Christian would have bore formerly.'

No one who is acquainted with Mr. Law's writings can doubt for one moment that we have in this queer, dis-jointed, fragmentary report a very faithful reproduction of his conversation. Not only are the sentiments his exactly, but, making allowance for its dilution in its pas-sage through Byrom's mind, we have also Law's style—its curtness, its raciness, its keenness, and its vigour. It gives one the impression that Law was a good talker, as well as a good writer ; and, as Byrom gives us the only materials we possess for judging of Law's powers in this department, as well as of Law's mode of life at Putney, there is hardly need to apologise for transcrib-ing the accounts of other interviews between the two friends.

On Wednesday, April 13, 1737, Byrom writes : ' I went to Mr. Gibbon's, where the dinner was just going up. Mr. Law was in the dining-parlour by himself. I went in and came out again ; and, upon Miss Gibbon telling me that it was he, I went in again ; and he said, " Are you but just come in ?" and I sat down by the fire, and they came in to dinner ; and, being asked, I excused myself, and said that I had dined, and Mr. Gibbon saying " Where ?" I said, ' On the other side of the bridge." He asked, among

other questions, how shorthand went on, and I said that
more persons were desirous to learn. After dinner I sat to
the table, and drank a few glasses of champagne. Mr. Law
eat of the soup, beef, &c., and drank two glasses of red
wine—one, Church and King ; the other, All Friends. Mr.
Gibbon fell asleep. . . . . He (Mr. Law) read over Slater's
catalogue, and not one book could he find that he wanted.
His grace before meat the same as ours ; and that after
not much different, ending with God bless the Church
and King. He asked me if I cared to walk out in the
afternoon, and we did ; and when we were out he said,
Well, have you made any more Quakers? And we
went up to the high walk, when we soon fell a-talking
about Mr. Walker, and how it was all owing to Mrs.
Bourignon,[1] who was all delusion, which he argued much
about, as if it was the chief topic that he intended upon at
that time, and mentioned a manuscript of Freyer's wherein
it was said that he had sent her forty-five contradictions
extracted from her works. He said that she was peevish,
fretful, and plainly against the sacrifice of Christ, which
Mr. Poiret vindicated, and mentioned the Lamb slain from
the foundation of the world (this was as we were going in
again), and seemed to say that she was a Quaker, though
she wrote against them ; that she made nothing of it ; that
she could not tell what to do with the people that came to
her, nor they with her ; that she kept her money ; that she
was against priests; and then, when to write against the
Quakers, she pretended to honour them ; that if he had
been of her admirers he would have burnt that book, that
it should not have been known that she had writ such a
book ; and, upon my interjecting some little excuses for
her, he seemed to be very warm. When I mentioned that
the greatest things that could be said had been, in short,
by the apostles, as, " Be ye followers of me as I am of

Christ;" "The life which I live, not I, but Christ that liveth in me,"—he said, "Why, you are worse than he, I think," meaning Mr. Walker; and when I was for not condemning her, but taking the good only wherein she agreed with others, he said that it was not enough to do so; but, if she was a deluded person, to talk of her as such, or to that effect. I find much repugnancy in me to condemn her.'

'On Friday, 15th, Mr. Law said of Madam Guion[1] that, though she was much more prudent than Mrs. Bourignon, yet, carried away, that she played at cards with Ramsay; and I said that it was as easy to suppose that Ramsay might tell a lie, being such a gay one as he said, as that she might play at cards with him, and he seemed to say so, that it might. He said, when I mentioned her commentaries upon the New Testament, that they would not do in English, nor Mrs. B.'s; but that they were flat and not bearable (that is, Mrs. Bourignon's).'

The suggestion of Byrom, in which Law also seems to have acquiesced, that, because a man played at cards and was ' a gay one,' he might probably be a liar—illogical and uncharitable as it may sound to us—was thoroughly characteristic of that tone of thought which made hardly any distinction between what it called 'worldly' and what was positively immoral. Soon after this interview, Byrom met the Mr. Walker referred to in it, and ' mentioned his going to see Mr. Law, whom he said he should be glad to meet, but not to go in the rain to Putney. I said that he that had gone beyond sea [he had just returned from a visit to Holland] to see three gentlemen, not to go such a little way to see one that had been friendly to him, and was a proper person!—till he broke out at last, that I knew not his reasons for acting, and— and so he went away, and I

---

[1] For an account of Madame Guyon, see infra pp. 158-168.

desired him to stay ; but he went, and just came up again
to say, " Pray, when you see Mr. Law, my service to him ; "
and I said, " Stay, come up ! hark ye ! " but he went away.'
And really, knowing as we do the warm reception which
this disciple of Madame Bourignon would have met with
from Law, we can hardly help feeling a sense of relief to
hear that he did not beard the lion in his den.   It looks at
first sight as if Byrom wished to let him into a trap ; but it
was not so.   Byrom was the kindliest and humblest of men
living ; he was only anxious for his friend's good, and he
knew no more ' proper person ' to effect this than Mr. Law ;
nor was he in the least ironical when he spoke of Law as
'friendly.'   He knew, no doubt, that Law had a rod in
pickle for Mr. Walker ; but it was only ' to smite him
friendly,' and he never dreamt of the possibility of anyone
objecting to be scolded by the Putney sage any more than
he did himself.

Other friends, however, were quite willing to accompany Byrom in his visits to Putney.   It is hoped that the
reader will not be wearied with the account of one more
such visit.   In April 1737, Byrom tells us, ' W. Chaddock
asked if I was for going to Putney ; and we went thither ;
and I told him to go himself, and if Mr. Law was there,
and gave opportunity, I would come to them, and he would
let me know ; and I walked in the lane thereby.   So he
went, and soon after they both came out, and I came to
them, and Mr. Law said nobody but one that was vapoured
with drinking tea would have not come in ; and he talked
about Madame Guyon and her forty books, though she
talked of the power of quiet and silence, which he believed
was a good thing—that, indeed, it was all, if one had it ;
but that a person that was to reform the world could not
be a great writer ; that the persons who were to reform the
world had not appeared yet ; that it would be reformed to

be sure ; that the writers against Quakerism were not
proper persons, for they writ against the Spirit, in effect,
and gave the Quakers an advantage ; that the Quakers
were a subtle, worldly-minded people ; that they began
with the contempt of learning, riches, &c., but now were a
politic, worldly society, and strange people, which word he
used for them after I had shown him Thos. Smith's letter
to S. Haynes, and F. H.'s to Mary Sutton, to which last,
Well, and what is there in all this ? And when I said,
a little while after, that they would be glad to know in
what manner to answer Smith's letter, or whether to take
any notice of it, he said there was nothing in it worth
notice, or required answering, if they had no mind. I told
him of Smith's leaving a copy of verses with her, and then
it was that he said they were strange people. He commended Taulerus, Rusbrochius, T. à Kempis, and the old
Roman Catholic writers, and disliked, or seemed to condemn, Mrs. Bourignon, Guion, for their volumes, and
describing of states which ought not to be described.
When I mentioned J. Behmen as a writer of many books,
he said that it was by force that he had writ ; that he desired that all his books had been in one ; that, besides, he
did not undertake to reform the world as these persons
had done ; that, if Mrs. Bou. had lived, why she would
have writ twenty more books, and Poiret had published
them ! I mentioned the old people, Hermas, Dionysius,
Macarius, whom he commended—especially, I think,
Macarius. I just asked him which particular books were
the best and safest, and, at our coming away, W. Chad.
asked that question particularly ; but he said, Another
time, and gave no answer to it then, having asked us
before if we lay in town all night, and me, if I was not
afraid of being robbed ; to which I said, No, no ; and
thought after that it was better to be robbed of money

than instruction. We came away late, it being just near ten when we got to Richard's coffee-house, where we drank a dish of tea.'

Byrom little knew the deep interest which would attach to the following entry in his journal, which, though only indirectly connected with my subject, I cannot forbear quoting : ' Putney, Sund. May 15, 1737. They have had great doings here at the christening of Mr. Gibbon's son. . . . Our landlady says that his lady had no fortune, but was a young lady of good family and reputation, and that old Mr. Gibbon led her to church and back again.' It need scarcely be said that the child was afterwards England's greatest historian.

A few months later, ' old Mr. Gibbon ' was himself ' led to church,' never to come ' back again ; ' and his death broke up the establishment at Putney—not, however, immediately. Mr. Law appears still to have remained, off and on, at Putney for two or three years, but evidently in an unsettled state. Byrom never visited him there again ; but the two friends continually met in Somerset Gardens, at the back of the Strand. Law, at this time, seems to have had lodgings in London ; for we constantly find such entries as these in Byrom's journal : ' Went to Somerset Gardens ; found Mr. Law there. Went home with him to his room.' One entry is quite plaintive : ' I have been walking in Somerset Gardens a long while, in expectation of meeting Mr. Law there, who is in town, and I am welly tired.' The entries at this period seem to me to indicate that Law was a good deal worried, as he might well be, since the comfortable home in which he had lived for at least ten years was broken up, and the good man knew not what he was to do next. This may account for the increased asperity of his conversation, which Byrom faithfully records, though it often bears hardly upon himself. For instance, we read :

'Aug. 1, 1739. To Somerset Gardens. Mr. Law there ;
asked me if I had scholars ; I said Yes ; he said he thought
it was to be published after I had said that I was desired,
&c. [*sic*], and I took out my book and showed him the
proposal ; but he just looked at it, and gave it me again,
and seemed to say that, if he knew it, it would be no use
to him ; that he could write faster than he could think ;
that, for them, indeed, that wanted to write down what
others said, it might do. I said, *valeat quantum valere
potest.* He said that they talked of the Pretender's coming
—was not I afraid of it ? I said, No, not at all ; and he
talked in his favour. [Then follows a sentence in cipher.]
And, as we came away, gave him (the father) a most excellent character for experience, wisdom, piety. I said
that I saw him once. He said, Where ? I said, At A.
He said, Did you kiss hands ? I said, Yes ; and
parted. He said that Mr. Morden and Clutton had been
with him ; that there should not be so much talk about
such matters ; that the time was not now ; that he loved a
man of taciturnity.' This, with the exception of one other
incidental hint, is the only allusion, so far as I am aware,
which Law ever made—either in conversation or writing—
to Jacobitism.

It would be wearisome to relate all these meetings in
Somerset Gardens : all of them give one the idea of Law
being in a troubled, weary, and, to tell the truth, rather a
petulant frame. Now we find him telling Byrom that 'he
has been to the city, and is tired ;' now that 'he has a
tooth-ache, and he said, " Well, what say you ?" as he does
often ; and I said, Say ! I say nothing, but how do you
do ? I am glad to see you—what would you have me to
say ?' Now we find him complaining that 'Charles
Wesley had brought to him Mr. Cossart, who said nothing,
but sighed deeply.' Now he rebukes poor Byrom 'for his

incontinency ;'[1] now he tells him that 'learning had done more mischief than all other things put together,' and that it was useful only 'like a carpenter's business, or any other.' Now, on Byrom's showing him a book he had 'writ to him about the gift of tongues,' he tells him, 'Well, go on and finish it ; I am busy while I am here.' Now 'he mentioned the philosopher's stone as what he believed to be true, but not to be found by philosophers.' On Byrom's complaining, after he had rebuked his incontinency, 'I will be continent, but I have none to converse with, and it is a desolate condition, he said that when our king came over I should go into orders. I said, Probably you think too well and ill of me ; for that is so far too well that—— He said [evidently cutting his disciple short rather impatiently], He had conversed with clergymen, and thought he knew.' After these accounts, the reader will not be surprised at the following entry : 'Mrs. Hutton came and said, she, having asked a young man—one Ackers, of Barbadoes—how Mr. Law did, he said that he was strangely altered—grown sour.' The fact is, that Law was an excellent Christian ; but, like other excellent Christians, he had his human infirmities, and circumstances, at this time, tended to aggravate the irascibility and impatience of temper to which he was naturally prone. As a fitting conclusion to this sketch of the relationship between Law and Byrom at this period of the life of the former, I may quote one more entry which illustrates very fairly the difference between the two men. ' I went home with Mr. Law, and in his room he told me that his thought and mine had great sympathy ; but that I was more easily wrought upon, and that his strings were more hard. I said that I was like an instrument that was pinned too soft, and wanted to be better quilled.' Here, for the present, we may dismiss this quaint, gentle, lovable

---

[1] I.e. in talk.

man. We shall meet him again when Law's life at King's Cliffe comes before our notice.

Two far more illustrious disciples of Mr. Law, at Putney, were the brothers John and Charles Wesley. These two great and good men were deeply impressed with Law's practical treatises, and for some time they were both respectful admirers of the author. The relation between Law and John Wesley, in especial, is a very interesting study. 'I was at one time,' wrote Law, 'a kind of oracle with Mr. Wesley;' and the oracle was frequently consulted, both in person and by writing. On one occasion we find Wesley demurring to Law's view of Christian duty as too elevated to be attainable; whereupon Law silenced and satisfied him by saying, 'We shall do well to aim at the highest degree of perfection, if we may thereby, at least, attain to mediocrity.' On another, Wesley complained to Law that he felt greatly dejected because he saw so little fruit of his labours, and received from his mentor this very sensible advice : 'My dear friend, you reverse matters from their proper order. You are to follow the Divine Light, wherever it leads you, in all your conduct. It is God alone gives the blessing. I pray you calmly mind your own work, and go on with cheerfulness, and God, you may depend upon it, will take care of His. Besides, sir, I see you would fain convert the whole world ; but you must wait God's own time. Nay, if after all He is pleased to use you only as a hewer of wood and drawer of water, you should submit ; yea, be thankful to Him that He has honoured you so far.' On another occasion Law gave Wesley some counsel which evidently made a very deep impression upon him, and which, as we shall see, he retorted upon Law many years later. 'You would have,' said Law to him, 'a philosophical religion ; but there can be no such thing. Religion is the most plain, simple thing in the world.; it is only, "We love Him because He first loved us."' / On another occasion we find Wesley writing to Law for advice as to how he should treat a young man who 'had left off the Holy Eucharist.' After detailing the symptoms of the case, he concludes : ' I therefore beseech you, sir, that you would not be slack, according to the ability God shall give you, to advise and pray for him.' When Law became fascinated with mysticism, which happened while he was still at Putney, Wesley for a time followed the example of his friend, and succumbed to the same charm, though always somewhat doubtfully, and never entering fully into the spirit of the system ; and, finally, when Wesley was in doubt as to whether it was his mission to go to Georgia, he at once consulted the Putney oracle, and was, to a great extent, determined by Law's advice. Wesley's visits to Putney were all made on foot, that he might save the money for the poor.[1]

It is easy to see the reasons why Law gained this ascendency over John Wesley. From his childhood Wesley had been brought up with persons of earnest piety, without a tincture of cant about it ; of principles of a very marked High Church type ; of plain, straightforward good sense, sometimes rather bluntly and curtly expressed. These were more or less the characteristics of his father, mother, brothers, and sisters ; above all of his mother, whose influence over her son John was deservedly almost unbounded. All these characteristics he found in an eminent degree in William Law. The thorough reality of the man, his ardent piety, his clear and logical intellect, his raciness, his strong and vigorous common sense, his outspokenness, the very bluntness and abruptness of his manner, his uncompromising High Churchmanship,—all these features in his character would commend him to the founder of Methodism.

[1] Wesley's first visit to Putney was in 1732.

G

The rupture between these two great and good men is a painful subject, but it cannot be wholly passed over in a life of Law. It occurred during the latter part of Law's residence at Putney, soon after Wesley's return from Georgia. It appears to be now the popular opinion that Wesley's conduct in the matter is wholly to be blamed.[1] This is an opinion with which I must venture utterly to disagree. Let us examine the circumstances of the case. In the spring of 1738 Wesley gained, through the instrumentality of Peter Böhler, an abiding peace and joy in believing which he had not found under the guidance of Mr. Law. This is plain matter of fact. Whether the fault lay with the master or the disciple is not now the question. The letter which Wesley wrote to Law upon his conversion may have been ill-judged—Wesley's judgment was often at fault; it may have laid him open to the crushing retort which he received ; but that it was written in a real spirit of Christian charity, that the writer had no other motive than anxiety for the spiritual welfare of Law himself (whom he still loved and respected more than almost any living man) and of those over whom Law was exercising a vast influence, that there was no conscious presumption or rudeness in it,—no one, I think, who examines dispassionately the circumstances, can deny. In fact, believing what he did, Wesley, as a Christian, could hardly, in common charity, have helped writing as he did. If Law was taken by many as their spiritual director, and was directing them wrongly or inadequately, was it not the duty of the discoverer of the wrong to deliver his own soul, and for the sake both of the guide and the guided to tell the former of his error ? Bearing these circumstances in mind, let us now turn to the famous letter, and its still

---

[1] This seems to be the view even of Mr. Tyerman. See his *Life of Mr. Wesley*, vol. i. p. 188.

more famous answer. Wesley's letter runs : ' It is in obedience to what I think the call of God that I, who have the
sentence of death in my own soul, take upon me to write
to you, of whom I have often desired to have the first
elements of the gospel of Christ. If you are born of God,
you will approve of the design ; if not, I shall grieve for
you, not for myself. For as I seek not the praise of men,
so neither regard I the contempt of you or any other. . . .
For two years I have been preaching after the model of
your two practical treatises, and all who heard allowed that
the law was great, wonderful, and holy ; but when they
attempted to fulfil it, they found that it was too high for
man, and that by doing the works of the law should no
flesh be justified. I then exhorted them to pray earnestly
for grace, and use all those other means of obtaining which
God hath appointed. Still I and my hearers were more
and more convinced that by this law man cannot live ; and
under this heavy yoke I might have groaned till death, had
not a holy man to whom God has lately directed me answered my complaint at once by saying, " Believe, and thou
shalt be saved." Now, Sir, suffer me to ask, how will you
justify it to our common Lord that you never gave me
this advice ? Why did I scarcely ever hear you name the
name of Christ ?—never so as to ground anything upon
faith in His blood ? If you say you advised other things
as preparatory to this, what is this but laying a foundation
below the foundation ? Is not Christ the First as well as
the Last ? If you say you advised this because you knew
that I had faith already, you discerned not my spirit at all.
Consider deeply and impartially whether the true cause of
your never pressing this upon me was this, that you had
it not yourself.' Wesley concluded by warning him, on the
authority of Peter Böhler, whom he called a man of God,
that his state was a very dangerous one ; and asked him

whether his extreme roughness, and morose and sour behaviour, could possibly be the fruit of a living faith in
Christ.

To this letter Law sent the following reply: ' May 19,
1738. Rev. Sir,—Yours I received yesterday. As you
have written that letter in obedience to a Divine call, and
in conjunction with another extraordinary good young
man, whom you know to have the Spirit of God, so I assure
you that, considering your letter in that view, I neither
desire nor dare to make the smallest defence of myself. . . .
But now, upon supposition that you had here only acted
by that ordinary light which is common to good and sober
minds, I should remark upon your letter as follows: How
you may have been two years preaching the doctrine of
the two practical discourses, or how you may have tired
yourself and your hearers to no purpose, is what I cannot
say much to. A holy man, you say, taught you this:
" Believe and thou shalt be saved, &c." I am to suppose
that till you met with this holy man you had not been
taught this doctrine. Did you not above two years ago give
a new translation of Thomas à Kempis ?[1] Will you call
Thomas to account and to answer it to God, as you do me,
for not teaching you that doctrine ? Or will you say that
you took upon you to restore the true sense of that divine
writer, and instruct others how they might profit by reading him, before you had so much as a literal knowledge of

---

[1] It is interesting to find in Law's library at Cliffe three copies of this
edition of à Kempis by Wesley, one of them evidently much read. Law had
also several other editions of his favourite author ; one so curious that it is
worth noting. T. à Kempis has doubtless afforded comfort to many troubled
spirits, but one may doubt whether the following edition would quite answer
the purpose for which it was published : *7. à Kempis—4 Books of the Imitation
of Christ ; together with his Three Tabernacles of Poverty, Humility, and
Patience,* by W. Willymott, Vice-Provost of King's, Cambridge. *Dedicated
to the Unhappy Sufferers by the great National Calamity of the South Sea !*
(1722).

the most plain, open, and repeated doctrine in his book?
You cannot but remember what value I always expressed
of à Kempis, and how much I recommended it to your
meditations. You have had a great many conversations
with me, and I dare say you never was with me half an
hour without my being large upon that very doctrine which
you make me totally silent and ignorant of. How far I
may have discovered your spirit and the spirit of others
that may have conversed with me may perhaps be more a
secret to you than you imagine. But granting you to be
right in your account of your own faith, how am I charge-
able with it? I am to suppose that you had been meditating upon an author that of all others leads us the most
directly to a real, living faith in Jesus Christ ; after you
had judged yourself such a master of his sentiments and
doctrines as to be able to publish them to the world with
directions and instructions on such experimental divinity,
that after you had done this you had only the faith of a
Judas or devil, an empty notion only in your head ; and
that you were thus through ignorance that there was anything better to be sought after ; and that you were thus
ignorant because I never directed or called you to this
faith. But, sir, à Kempis and I have both of us had your
acquaintance and conversation, so pray let the fault be
divided betwixt us, and I shall be content to have it said
that I left you in as much ignorance of this faith as he did,
or that you learnt no more of it by conversing with me
than with him. If you had only this faith till some
weeks ago, let me advise you not to be hasty in believing
that because you change your language and expressions,
you have changed your faith. The head can as easily
amuse itself with a living and justifying faith in the blood
of Jesus as with any other notion ; and the heart, which
you suppose to be a place of security, as being the seat of

self-love, is more deceitful than the head. Your last paragraph, concerning my sour, rough behaviour, I leave in its
full force ; whatever you can say of me of that kind without hurting yourself will be always well received by me.'

Mr. Southey calls this a 'temperate answer,' and so it
is, but it is difficult to conceive a more cutting one ; and
its edge is all the keener on account of its temperateness.
Any abuse would not only have been unchristian, but it
would have spoilt the force of the answer. It would have
been worse than a crime, it would have been a blunder.
And none knew this better than William Law. The letter,
in fact, shows on a small scale what almost all Law's controversial pieces show—the handiwork of a consummate
master of the art of controversy. Law had a marvellous
knack, without overstepping the boundaries of Christian
courtesy, of making his opponents look particularly foolish.
In this case it was a singularly unequal match. For Law
had age and experience, as well as incomparably superior
argumentative powers, on his side. Wesley was, in more
senses than one,

Infelix puer atque impar congressus Achilli,

and no one was more conscious of this than Wesley himself ; only, perhaps, instead of comparing himself to Troilus,
and Law to Achilles, he would rather have compared himself to David and Law to Goliath. He knew that he had
an intellectual giant to deal with, and that he in comparison
was but an intellectual stripling ; but he knew also that
' the battle is not always to the strong ;' he believed that
his cause was God's cause, and that by God's help he
might with his little sling and stone pierce through the
strong man's armour. After he had written his letter, and
received his answer, it would, perhaps, have been wiser in
Wesley to have let the matter rest. He had delivered his

own soul by uttering his protest, and he might have seen that there was nothing to be gained by continuing a controversy with Law. But Wesley was a thorough Englishman, and Englishmen proverbially never know when they are beaten. The very day after receiving Law's reply he wrote him another letter, and received from him an answer which, if possible, was more crushing than the first.

But it is neither a pleasing nor a profitable task to descant upon the disputes between two good Christians. It is far pleasanter to record that Wesley's after-conduct was thoroughly characteristic of the noble and generous nature of the man. Though the divergence between him and his late mentor increased rather than diminished with years, yet he constantly referred to Law in his sermons, and always in terms of the warmest admiration and respect. ' In how beautiful a manner,' he exclaims in his sermon on ' Redeeming the Time,' ' does that great man, Mr. Law, treat this important subject !' [1] ' The ground of this,' he says, in his sermon on ' Christian Education,' is ' admirably well laid down by Mr. Law !' [2] In another sermon Law is described as ' that strong and elegant writer, Mr. Law.' [3] Even when speaking of Law's mysticism, which at the time was the object of his special abhorrence, he asks almost indignantly, ' Will any one dare to affirm that all mystics, such as Mr. Law in particular, ... are void of all Christian experience?' [4] Speaking of the origin of the Methodists, he admits that ' there was some truth ' in Dr. Trapp's assertion that ' Mr. Law was their parent.' For ' all the Methodists carefully read his books [i.e. the ' Christian

[1] *Sermon XCIII.* vol. iii. p. 79.
[2] *Sermon XCV.* vol. iii. p. 97.
[3] *Sermon CXVIII.* vol. iii. p. 333.
[4] *Sermon XX.*, on the ' Lord our Righteousness,' preached Nov. 24, 1765, vol. i. p. 269.

Perfection' and ' Serious Call '], and were greatly profited thereby.'[1]

What Wesley intimates in this last passage about the value which the early Methodists set upon Mr. Law is perfectly true. It is only of later years that it has become the fashion to depreciate him. The contemporaries of Wesley and their immediate successors, widely as they differed from Law, always recognised in the warmest way his intense earnestness and piety, his splendid intellectual powers, and the inestimable services he had rendered to the cause of true religion in England. Whitefield, for example, always speaks of him as ' the great Mr. Law ; ' and even when expressing his strong disagreement with many things in the ' Spirit of Prayer,' is careful to add, ' But the sun hath its spots, and so have the best of men.'[2]   Not to weary the reader with evidence which it would be easy to multiply, it will be sufficient here to quote a very remarkable testimony from John Wesley's earliest biographers.   Dr. Coke and Mr. Moore, writing, be it remembered, the very year after Wesley's death (1792), in a very marked manner, name Mr. Law, and Mr. Law alone, as a sort of Abdiel among the clergy.   After asserting that in 1738 ' true religion was little known in England,' that ' the great leading truths of the Gospel were not credited, or at least not enforced by the clergy of the Establishment in general,' and that ' the Dissenters in general were in no better situation,' they add : ' The great Mr. Law was an exception indeed ; ' and then, after speaking of the services rendered by ' his excellent pen,' they own distinctly that ' he was the great forerunner

---

[1] *Sermon CVII.* on ' God's Vineyard,' vol. iii. p. 228.
[It is scarcely necessary to add that all these sermons were preached long after Wesley's breach with Law.]

[2] He also says that in the ' Spirit of Prayer' there are ' many things truly noble, and which I pray God to write upon the tables of my heart.' See Whitefield's *Letters*, vol. ii. p. 359 and *passim.*

of the revival which followed, and did more to promote it than any other individual whatever ; yea, more, perhaps, than the rest of the nation collectively taken.'[1]   Such language stands forth in striking contrast to the language which has been used about Law in later days.

We are forcibly reminded of this when we turn from John Wesley to the modern account of his brother Charles's intimacy with Law and its termination.   'He had,' writes his biographer, ' the highest opinion of William Law, upon whose writings he might be said to meditate day and night. This eloquent but erring man was then resident at Putney ; and, for the purpose of being benefited by his counsel, Charles visited him there on August 31, and September 9, 1737.   Their interviews led to no beneficial result.   ' Nothing I can either speak or write,' said he, ' will do you any good.' While he avoided all reference to the atonement of Christ, the true nature of which he appears never to have understood, his advices concerning spiritual religion only tended to lacerate the conscience, and discourage the anxious inquirer.   He set his pupils upon the hopeless task of attaining to holiness without showing them by what means they might obtain the pardon of their past sins and the blessing of a clean heart.   Happily for Mr. Charles Wesley, by the merciful providence of God he was brought into intercourse with other men who were better qualified to instruct him in divine things.'[2]

It is almost needless to say that I disagree *in toto* with this passage ; but it is fair to add that the prejudice which the later Methodists conceived against William Law was not altogether unnatural.   There is a sort of poetical justice in it ; for Law never did full justice to the Methodists. John Wesley in especial appreciated William Law better

[1] See Coke and Moore's *Life of Wesley*, Introduction.
[2] *Memoirs of the Rev. Charles Wesley*, by Thomas Jackson, c. ii. p. 52.

than William Law appreciated John Wesley. Law greatly underrated the extent and permanency of the work for God which the Wesleys were doing. Time has shown that he was wrong when he said, ' These gentlemen have no bottom but zeal to stand upon.' When he could only bestow upon the founder of Methodism the grudging praise, ' I never knew any harm in him,' and even spoilt that by adding, ' but I always judged him to be too much under his own spirit,' he *mis*-judged him, though he only said what was very commonly said by many of Wesley's contemporaries in far more unchristian language.

But to return to Charles Wesley. He himself gives us an interesting account of an interview he had with William Law, after his change of views. ' To-day ' (Friday, August 10, 1738), he writes, ' I carried T. Bray [a brazier in Little Britain, near Smithfield, who had become a convert to Methodism] to Mr. Law, who resolved all his feelings into fits, or natural affections, and advised him to take no notice of his comforts, which he had better be without than with. He blamed Mr. Whitefield's journals and way of proceeding ; said he had great hopes that the Methodists would have been dispersed by little and little in livings, and have leavened the whole lump. I told him my experience. " Then am I," said he, " far below you (if you are right), not worthy to bear your shoes." He agreed to our notion of faith, but would have it that all men held it ; was fully against the laymen's expounding, as the very worst thing both for themselves and others. I told him he was my school-master, to bring me to Christ ; but the reason why I did not come sooner to Him was my seeking to be sanctified before I was justified. I disclaimed all expectation of becoming some great one. Among other things he said, " Was I talked of as Mr. Whitefield is, I should run away and hide myself entirely." " You might," I answered,

"but God would bring you back like Jonah." Joy in the
Holy Ghost, he told us, was the most dangerous thing
God could give. I replied, "But cannot God guard His
own gifts?" He often disclaimed advising, seeing we had
the Spirit of God, but mended upon our hands, and at last
came almost quite over.'

Let us now see how the matter is described from a
very different point of view, that of our old friend Dr.
Byrom. The following entry in his journal is important
as showing that the divergence between Law and the two
brothers had begun some time before the memorable letter
of 1738 was written. It is dated July 1737 (two months,
be it observed, before the interview described by Dr. Jackson), and begins : 'Mr. C. Westley called as I was shaving.'
It then goes on to mention several objections which
Charles raised against Law's teaching, especially against
his mysticism, ' which,' says Byrom, ' as it seems to me, he
very little understood. He defined the mystics as those
who neglected the use of reason and the means of grace.'
Byrom goes on in his odd, fragmentary way, ' There was the
expression of " If any like reading the Heathen Poets let
them have their full swing of them," or to this effect, at which
I wondering, he said that it was the advice of Mr. Law, and
talked very oddly I thought upon these matters.' Then
Charles noticed ' a palpable mistake in Mr. Law's " Serious
Call," that there is no command for public worship in
Scripture.' ' I believe,' concludes Byrom, ' he has met with
somebody that does not like Mr. Law. I believe that Mr.
Law had given his brother or him or both very good and
strong advice which they had strained to a meaning very
different from his.'¹ Whatever the circumstances may
have been, the fact is certain that both the brothers Wesley
discarded their former mentor in 1738. Unhappily,

¹ Byrom's *Journal*, vol. ii. part i. pp. 181-2.

another collision between the elder of them and Mr. Law
will have to be noticed at a later period.

Another disciple of Mr. Law at Putney was Dr. George
Cheyne, a physician of great eminence [1] and a voluminous
writer. Dr. Cheyne incidentally influenced Law more
than any living man, having been, as Law himself told
Byrom, 'the providential occasion of his meeting or knowing of Jacob Behmen, by a book which the Doctor mentioned to him in a letter, which book mentioned Behmen.' [2]
According to the same authority, Law had so very high an
opinion of Dr. Cheyne that he made the amazing assertion
that 'the reputation of Dr. Cheyne served to balance that
of Bishop Bramhall.' One can scarcely, however, imagine
that, in his calmer moments, Law would have compared
the Doctor to the great ' Athanasius Hibernicus.' The fact
seems to have been that when Law made this very absurd
comparison, he was somewhat nettled with Bramhall for
having spoken slightingly of one of his most favourite
authors ; for on the same occasion he told Byrom that
' Bishop Bramhall, in answer to an argument used for the
Romish Church from their saints such as Taulerus, had said
something like, You may take your foolish Taulerus to
yourselves.' No man who did not admire Tauler was
likely to find favour in the eyes of Law. Byrom himself
furnishes us with reasons for thinking that this or some such
explanation must be supposed of Law's wild statement ;
for he inserts a letter from Dr. Cheyne on the subject of
M. Marsay, a French enthusiast, who combined mysticism
proper with many visionary notions which have no necessary
connection with mysticism. The letter gives us a curious

[1] He was, in fact, the fashionable doctor of the day. Thackeray, with
that admirable knowledge of details which he invariably shows in his semi-
historical works, represents Lord Castlewood in ' Esmond ' going to consult
the famous Dr. Cheyne.

[2] Byrom's *Journal*, vol. ii. part ii. p. 364.

illustration of the extent and variety of the subjects on which Mr. Law was consulted and is therefore worth quoting in part. I had written,' says the Doctor, ' in much the same strain with mine to you, to one I think the most solid judge in these sublime and abstracted matters known to me, whose first answer I found grounded on a mistake of the character and writings of Mr. Marsay, author of the " Témoignage d'Enfant," &c. ; I therefore sent him all the history of the person, adventures, and methods of proficiency I had learned of this wonderful author, with the number of his books, which I suspected by his first answer he had not thoroughly known.   But Mr. Law, being a man who never judges, nor gives characters rashly without entering deeply into the spirit of his author, in more than two months has never given me an answer to this my second letter, and I hope by his delay he is reading and pondering Mr. Marsay's " Témoignage," which, consisting of eight or ten octavo volumes, must require time under his hands.   I have waited hitherto for this answer, whereon to form a small judgment of the author and his works.   It would be the greatest mortification to me to give up a line or thought, or even a whim (if any such there be), of his. . . . . But, if a person whom I admire so much as I do Mr. Law rejects his accessories . . . . I will so far give them up as not to propagate them with that blind zeal I might do otherwise.' [1]   If Mr. Law was often expected to read ' eight or ten octavo volumes ' on such profound subjects as ' new scriptural manifestations and discoveries about the states and glory of the invisible world, and the future purification of lapsed intelligences, human and angelical ' (these being the ' accessories ' to which Dr. Cheyne refers), and to read them so carefully that on his opinion their publication or non-publication was to depend, he certainly had his work cut out for him.   But

[1] Byrom's *Journal*, vol. ii. part iii. p. 331.

alas ! Dr. Cheyne's assumption that the delay was caused by
Mr. Law's 'reading and pondering' the formidable volumes
does not appear to have been correct ; for some little time
after, Law 'mentioned' to Byrom, ' Dr. Cheyne and his not
writing to him upon some matters, because his letters would
fall into the hands of his executors ; that the Doctor was
always talking in coffee-houses about naked faith, pure
love, &c.'

This rather contemptuous opinion of Dr. Cheyne's
incontinency seems hardly consistent with the flattering
comparison of him with Bramhall noticed above.

Perhaps this is as fitting an occasion as may be found
for suggesting a caution as to the value which should be
attached to the conversational remarks of Law and other
great men. As illustrations of character they are, if faithfully reported, invaluable ; but surely it is unfair to the
speakers, no less than to the subjects, to take random utterances, made in all the freedom from responsibility and
'abandon' of a convivial meeting of friends, as necessarily
expressing final and deliberate convictions. We have a
very notable instance of the erroneousness of such a plan
in connection with Law himself. Everybody knows
Dr. Johnson's famous remark, reported by Boswell, that
'William Law was no reasoner.' That the Doctor made
the remark I have no manner of doubt ; but I have also
no manner of doubt that it was not the expression of his
deliberate conviction, but simply a chance utterance, made,
partly in the spirit of pure contradiction, and partly in
maintenance of his dignity. He had just made the
sweeping assertion that 'no nonjuror could reason,' and
being reminded of Charles Leslie, he yielded so far as to
allow very properly that he was an exception. But it
would have compromised his dignity to yield farther ; and
therefore he preferred doggedly to maintain that though

William Law had written 'the finest piece of paraenetic divinity in the language' he was no reasoner. But what was this piece of paraenetic divinity but reasoning from beginning to end ? and when the Doctor owned on another occasion that 'William Law was quite an over-match for him,' in what was he an overmatch except in reasoning ?

But to return to Dr. Cheyne. Regarded from one point of view, he would have seemed to be about the last man in the world one would have expected to be a *primum mobile* of English mysticism. For he was a kind of eighteenth century Banting. Being afflicted with corpulency, he adopted and recommended in print a milk diet ; and, to his great annoyance, was made a butt for the wits of the day in consequence. He also wrote a treatise on the gout, and another on the spleen and the vapours, which he termed 'the English malady.' But though one side of his mind was engrossed with these very material topics, there was another side of it which was filled with the most trans-cendental speculations. He was, in fact, not only the recommender of German mysticism to William Law, but himself a mystic of a very marked type. This tendency is traceable in almost all his works, but most of all in his 'Philosophical Principles of Religion Natural and Revealed.' This work, which is oddly enough based upon mathematics, touches upon most of the points on which mystics love to dwell. It shows us how 'there is a perpetual analogy (physical, not mathematical) running on in a chain through the whole system of creatures up to their Creator,' how 'the visible are the images of the invisible, the ectypical of the archetypical, the creatures of the Creator, at an abso-lutely infinite distance,' how 'if gravitation be the principle of the activity of bodies, that of reunion with their origin must by analogical necessity be the principle of action in

spirits,' how 'material substances are the same with spiritual substances of the higher order at an infinite distance,'
how 'the pure and disinterested love of God and of all His
images in a proper subordination is the consummate perfection of Christianity.' The fall of man is described, the
philosophy of Locke argued against, and, in fact, most of the
topics dwelt upon which are discussed, only with infinitely
greater power, in Law's later works.

It will appear in the sequel that this combination of
mysticism with the more mundane subjects on which Dr.
Cheyne wrote was not so unusual as one might have expected. Dr. Cheyne is perhaps best known at the present
day as a correspondent of David Hume. It is difficult
to conceive a more complete contrast than between the
Doctor's two friends, William Law and David Hume—that
is, so far as religious questions were concerned. Intellectually, however, there were some points of resemblance
between them. The same clearness of thought, the same
luminous and pure style, the same strong logical power is
seen in both ; but to what widely different conclusions did
they lead the two men !

Upon the rest of Law's friends and disciples at Putney
it is not necessary to dwell at length. Among them may
be noticed the daughter of the house, Miss Hester Gibbon,
who was a far more docile pupil of Mr. Law's, at least in
spiritual matters, than her brother or her more worldly
sister Katherine, and of whom Byrom 'heard it said that
she was a very good lady, though some people said she was
mad ;'[1] Miss Dodwell (daughter of the famous nonjuror),
to whom (probably) Law wrote three long and interesting
letters which will be noticed among his writings during this
period ; Mr. Archibald Hutcheson, M.P. for Hastings, who
had so high an opinion of Mr. Law that on his death-bed

---

[1] Byrom's *Journal*, vol. ii. part i. p. 124.

he recommended him to his wife as her spiritual director ; and Mr. Archibald Campbell, a relation of the above ; Dr. Stonehouse, who, however, on the rupture between Law and Wesley wavered between the two mentors, and finally seems to have sided with the latter ; and others whom it is needless to specify.

CHAPTER VII.

THE 'SERIOUS CALL.'

IN the early part of his residence at Putney, or to speak more accurately, when he was alternating between Putney and Cambridge, Law wrote that work which probably constitutes to nine-tenths of those who have heard his name at all his one title to fame. If one desires to let people know whom one means by William Law, the best—perhaps, in most cases, the only—way of doing so, is by saying that he was the author of the 'Serious Call.' It is his only work which can, as a matter of fact, be called an English classic, though it certainly is not his only work which deserves that somewhat vague title of honour ; some may think that it is by no means the work which deserves it best. Still, the popular verdict in such cases is generally correct ; or, at any rate, so far correct that there is always some substantial reason for it. In this case the verdict is stamped by the approval of the great name of Gibbon, who calls the 'Serious Call' Law's master work. From Gibbon's point of view, one can well understand his selection. He could hardly be expected to appreciate controversial writings, in which he would certainly have taken the other side of the controversy. And still less was he likely to sympathise with Law's mysticism, a subject which was utterly repulsive to his frame of mind.[1] But, Sybarite as he was in his own life,

---

[1] 'Gibbon,' wrote Mr. Kingsley, 'however excellent an authority for facts, knew nothing about philosophy, and cared less' (*Alexandria and her Schools*, p. 81). This is true, at least so far as anything approaching to idealism or mysticism is concerned.

Gibbon could thoroughly appreciate self-denial and piety in others, and a more persuasive and forcible recommendation of these graces was surely never written than is to be found in the 'Serious Call.' And men of much less mark than Gibbon were quite capable of appreciating the book. It is, in fact, of all Law's works the one most calculated to impress the multitude, and on this ground it may fairly be called his 'master work;' though as mere specimens of intellectual power his controversial works are more remarkable, and in originality of thought and beauty of expression, in tenderness and maturity both of style and sentiment, he rises to far greater heights in his later mystic works. But there is no need to compare Law with himself. Taken by itself the 'Serious Call' is unquestionably a great work, more than worthy of the high reputation which it won. We may now proceed to examine it in detail.

Its full title is 'A Serious Call to a Devout and Holy Life. Adapted to the State and Condition of all Orders of Christians.' It travels over very much the same ground as the 'Christian Perfection,' but it is a more powerful work than its predecessor, and deserved in every way the greater popularity which it enjoyed. Its style is more matured, its arguments more forcible, the range of subjects which it embraces more exhaustive, its wit more sparkling, and its tone more tender, affectionate, and persuasive.

In the first chapter the author shows that devotion means not merely prayer, public or private, but a *life* devoted to God. By some well-drawn instances he exposes the inconsistency of those whose lives are a contradiction to their prayers, and declares that the majority of church-goers only add Christian devotion to a heathen life—pray as Christians, but live as heathens.

In the second chapter he contends that the real cause of the inconsistency is simply this : that men have not so

much piety as to *intend* to please God in all the actions of
their lives, as the happiest and best thing in the world.
This is the real distinction between the modern and primitive Christians.   Law then illustrates what would be the
necessary result of having such an intention, first, in the
case of a clergyman, then in that of a tradesman, then in
that of a private gentleman.

The author then passes on to show the danger and folly
of not having such an intention, and introduces a very
striking picture of a dying tradesman, who had lived well,
as the world calls well, but, by his own confession, had
never had this intention.

He next insists that every employment, lay as well as
clerical, must be conducted with the single view to God's
glory, ' for all want the same holiness to make them fit for
the same happiness.'   A man may do the business of life,
and yet live wholly to God by doing earthly employments
with a heavenly mind.   The same rule which Christ has
given for our devotion and alms is to be brought to all our
actions if we would live in the spirit of piety.

He then specially addresses himself to those who are
under no necessity of working for their livelihood.   In
fact, though the whole treatise is of universal application, it
is more particularly addressed to this class of persons.[1]
' You are no labourer or tradesman, you are neither mer-
chant nor sailor,' he writes in a very beautiful sentence ;
' consider yourself, therefore, as placed in a state in some
degree like that of the good angels, who are sent into this
world as ministering spirits, for the general good of mankind, to assist, protect, and minister for them who shall be
heirs of salvation.'

He dwells at great length upon the right use of wealth,

[1] Law expressly asserted this, many years later, both of the ' Serious Call'
and the ' Christian Perfection.'   See *Works*, vol. vi. p. 91.

by no means falling in with the notion that it is useless. 'If we waste it, we do not waste a trifle that signifies little, but we waste that which might be made as eyes to the blind, as a husband to the widow, as a father to the orphan.' Money may be made either a great blessing or a great curse to its possessor. 'If you do not spend your money in doing good to others, you must spend it to the hurt of yourself. You will act like a man that should refuse to give that as a cordial to a sick friend, though he could not drink it himself without inflaming his blood.' The use and abuse of riches is then illustrated by two of the most elaborate portraits which Law ever drew—those of the two maiden sisters, Flavia and Miranda. Flavia 'is very orthodox, she talks warmly against heretics and schismatics, is generally at church, and often at the sacrament. If any one asks Flavia to do something in charity, if she likes the person who makes the proposal, or happens to be in a right temper, she will toss him half-a-crown or a crown, and tell him if he knew what a long milliner's bill she had just received, he would think it a great deal for her to give. She is very positive that all poor people are cheats and liars, and will say anything to get relief, and therefore it must be a sin to encourage them in their evil ways. You would think Flavia had the tenderest conscience in the world if you was to see how scrupulous and apprehensive she is of giving amiss. She would be a miracle of piety if she was but half so careful of her soul as she is of her body. The rising of a pimple in her face, the sting of a gnat, will make her keep her room two or three days, and she thinks they are very rash people that do not take care of things in time. If you visit Flavia on the Sunday, you will always meet good company, you will know what is doing in the world, you will hear the last lampoon, be told who wrote it, and who is meant by every name that is in it. You will

hear what plays were acted that week, which is the finest
song in the opera, who was intolerable at the last assembly,
and what games are most in fashion, &c., &c.   But still she
has so great a regard for the holiness of the Sunday, that
she has turned a poor old widow out of her house, as a
prophane wretch, for having been found once mending her
cloaths on the Sunday night.'   After some more admirable
hits, Law concludes : 'I shall not take upon me to say that
it is impossible for Flavia to be saved, but her whole life is
in direct opposition to all those tempers and practices which
the Gospel has made necessary to salvation.   She may as
well say that she lived with our Saviour when He was upon
earth as that she has lived in imitation of Him.   She has
as much reason to think that she has been a sentinel in an
army as that she has lived in watching and self-denial. . . .
And this poor, vain turn of mind, the irreligion, the folly
and vanity of this whole life of Flavia is all owing to the
manner of using her estate.'

From this sad portrait Law turns with evident relief to
a still more elaborate description of the other sister, Miranda.
The mentor of the founder of Methodism very characteristically introduces this model of Christian perfection by a
strong recommendation of living by rule or method. Miranda
is 'a sober, reasonable Christian.   She is not so weak as to
pretend to add what is called the fine lady to the true
Christian.   She has renounced the world to follow Christ
in the exercise of humility, charity, devotion, abstinence,
and heavenly affections, and that is Miranda's " fine breed-
ing." '   As to her fortune, ' she is only one of a certain number of poor people who are relieved out of it, and she only
differs from them in the blessedness of giving.'   As to her
dress, she has but ' one rule, to be always clean, and in the
cheapest things.   If you was to see her, you would wonder
what poor body it was that was so surprisingly neat and

clean.' As to her devotions, they are so regularly marked
out that 'she does not know what it is to have a dull half-
day. She seems to be as a guardian angel to those that
dwell about her, with her watchings and prayers blessing
the place where she dwells, and making intercession with
God for those that are asleep.' As to her food, ' she eats
and drinks only for the sake of living, and with so regular
an abstinence, that every meal is an exercise of self-denial,
and she humbles her body every time that she is forced to
feed it.' As to her reading, ' the Holy Scriptures, especially
of the New Testament, are her daily study. When she has
the New Testament in her hand, she supposes herself at
the feet of our Saviour and His apostles, and makes everything that she learns of them so many laws of her life.
She receives their sacred words with as much attention and
reverence as if she saw their persons, and knew that they
were just come from heaven on purpose to teach her the
way that leads to it.' ' She is sometimes afraid that she
lays out too much money in books, because she cannot
forbear buying all practical books of any note, especially
such as enter into the heart of religion, and describe the
inward holiness of the Christian life. But of all human
writings, the lives of pious persons and eminent saints are
her greatest delight. In these she searches as for hidden
treasure, hoping to find some secret of holy living, some
uncommon degree of piety which she may make her
own.' As to her charity, ' to relate it would be to relate
the history of every day for twenty years,' and then follows an account of some of the benevolent acts she has
done.

Tempting as the subject is, we must not linger on this
inimitable portrait. It concludes : ' When she dies, she
must shine amongst apostles, saints, and martyrs ; she
must stand amongst the first servants of God, and be

glorious amongst those that have fought the good fight, and finished their course with joy.'

In the next chapter Law goes on to show that every-one may imitate Miranda, in the spirit if not in the letter. He dwells particularly on her dress, enforcing his argu-ment by one of those happy illustrations at which one can hardly help smiling though one feels how grave the subject is. 'Let us suppose,' he says, 'that some eminent saint, as, for instance, that the holy Virgin Mary was sent into the world to be again in a state of trial for a few years, and that you was going to her to be edified by her great piety. Would you expect to find her dressed out, and adorned in fine and expensive clothes? No! You would know in your own mind that it was as impossible as to find her learning to dance. A saint genteelly dressed is as great nonsense as an apostle in an embroidered suit.' He then vindicates Miranda's choice of voluntary poverty, virginity, and retirement, quoting (a thing which he very rarely does) an author outside the canon of Scripture,[1] to show that such a state was considered the highest state in the early and purest state of Christianity.

Before quitting the subject of these two exquisitely drawn portraits, a few words seem requisite on their sup-posed originals. 'Under the names,' writes Gibbon, 'of Flavia and Miranda he has admirably described my two aunts—the heathen and the Christian sister.'[2] If Gibbon means by this that the two ladies in question unconsciously sat for their portraits, the presumption is very strong against it. At the time when the 'Serious Call' was pub-lished, Miss Hester Gibbon was only twenty-four years of age, and could have passed through scarcely any of the experience which belonged to Miranda. And, apart from this, it was singularly unlike Law to hold up as a model of

---

[1] Eusebius.   [2] *Memoirs of my Life and Writings*, p. 15.

perfection one who would of course read what he wrote, and recognise herself in the character. It was the very way to foster that pride and self-love which Law held to be the root of all sin. On the other hand, Law had far too much Christian feeling to gibbet the daughter of his friend and benefactor under the character of Flavia. Another tradition makes the Baroness de Chantal the original of Miranda. But probably Law had no one model in his eye when he drew either of the sisters. Miranda was simply the ideal Christian, as Flavia was the ideal worldling. It was Miranda who was to be the model for Miss Gibbon, as for all her sex, not Miss Gibbon who was the model of Miranda.

Law dwells with great beauty and force in the 'Serious Call' on a subject which he had put rather too much in the background in his 'Christian Perfection,' viz. the nature of the peace and happiness enjoyed by those who make their whole lives one continued course of devotion; and this gives him the opportunity of drawing some neat sketches of those who sought happiness in other ways. The ingenious have discovered in the restless Flatus, who seeks for happiness now from tailors and peruke-makers, now from gaming, now from drinking, now from hunting, a portrait of Law's own pupil, Edward Gibbon. But the Gibbon family are probably as free from the discredit of furnishing models for Flatus and Flavia as from the credit of furnishing one for Miranda. Passing over Feliciana, the lady of fashion, and Succus, the glutton, we come to a painfully lifelike portrait of a character happily more rare now than when Law wrote, Cognatus, the clerical pluralist and farmer, and then to Negotius, the diligent, honourable, and liberal man of business, but mainly intent upon dying a rich man: 'As wise an aim,' says Law, 'as if the object of his life was to die possessed of more than a hundred thousand pairs of boots and spurs and as many greatcoats.'

The remainder of the treatise—that is, the longer half of it—is taken up with the subject of devotion, in the popular sense of the word, as confined to acts of prayer, praise, and thanksgiving. It would be impossible to analyse this part of the work without spoiling the effect. It will suffice to remark on one or two points in it which seem specially worthy of attention.

1. We are reminded that we are still under the guidance of the writer of the three famous letters to Bishop Hoadly —that is, of a pronounced Churchman. Law's stated hours of devotion are not evolved out of his own inner conscious-ness; they are simply the canonical hours of the Church.

2. We are also reminded that we are under the guidance of the early mentor of Wesley. Law insists as strongly as Wesley himself and the early Methodists did on the advantages, indeed the necessity, of early rising—a rule which he himself consistently followed, as he did all the rules which he laid down. He also devotes no less than twenty-six pages to the subject of psalm-singing, as a part not only of public, but also of private devotion—a fit prelude to that wonderful outburst of sacred song which was one of the most marked features of the Methodist movement. Law was himself passionately fond of music, and he held the somewhat untenable opinion that every one can sing.

3. Law, like every right-minded man, respected women and loved children. He has therefore much to say on the subject of education. He protests against what he conceives to be the radical error of modern educa-tion, viz. its encouraging in children a spirit of emulation, which, he says, is only another name for envy; and this leads him into one of the most touching passages of the

book, the advice of Paternus to his son. Its tenderness,
its simplicity, its affectionate tone, evidently come from
the heart of one who loved the little ones whom his
Divine Master loved. The education of girls seemed to
Law to be particularly faulty. Recognising the vast influence which a mother has in forming the character of a
child ('as,' he says, 'we call our first language our mother-
tongue, so we may as justly call our first tempers our
mother-tempers'), he saw the importance of training these
possible mothers aright. He had a very high opinion both
of the intellectual and spiritual capacities of women. He
has 'much suspicion that if they were suffered to dispute
with us the proud prizes of arts and sciences, of learning
and eloquence, they would often prove our superiors ;' he
believes 'that, for the most part, there is a finer sense, a
clearer mind, a readier apprehension, and gentler disposi-
tions in that sex than in the other ;' and, 'if many women
are vain, light, gew-gaw creatures, they are only such as
their education has made them.' Law illustrates his meaning by two of those graphic portraits which he alone could
draw : Matilda, who represents the mother as she is ;
Eusebia, the mother as she ought to be.

4. On these portraits we must not linger ; but there
is yet another which, for our present purpose, is the most
important in the book, because it gives us the ideal which
Law set before himself personally, which he earnestly strove
to realise, and *did* realise, so far as his circumstances permitted : this is Ouranius, the good country parson. The
subject has been a favourite one with poets : Chaucer, George
Herbert, Oliver Goldsmith, William Cowper, and Alfred
Tennyson have all tried their hands at it, and have all succeeded ; but not one of them has surpassed William Law.

Ouranius, 'when he first entered into Holy Orders, had
a great contempt for all foolish and unreasonable people ;

but he has prayed this spirit away. When he first came to his little village, it was as disagreeable to him as a prison ; his parish was full of poor and mean people that were none of them fit for the conversation of a gentleman, and he thought it hard to be called to pray by any poor body when he was just in the midst of one of Homer's battles. *Now* he is so far from desiring to be considered as a gentleman that he desires to be used as the servant of all. He has sold a small estate that he had, and has erected a charitable retreat for ancient poor people ; he is exceeding studious of Christian perfection, because he finds in Scripture that the intercessions of holy men have an extraordinary power with God ; he loves every soul in his village as he loves himself, because he prays for them all as he prays for himself; he visits everybody in his village, among other reasons, that he may intercede with God for them according to their particular necessities ; '— and so forth. Of course, Law's position as a nonjuror prevented him from having, like Ouranius, the cure of souls ; but in other respects who can fail to see the resemblance ? That natural impatience of what was foolish and unreasonable ; that natural inclination to enjoy Homer's battles— that is, the beauties of heathen literature ; that determination, when circumstances forced him to retire into a remote and uncongenial seclusion, to do all the good he could in it, to found hospitals, and give almost all his goods to feed the poor ;—it is partly the story, partly the prophecy, of what Law's own experience had been or was to be. Those who know the character and career of Ouranius know, *mutatis mutandis*, the character and career of William Law himself.[1]

5. It is only fair to Law to draw special attention to

---

[1] It was so recognised by his contemporaries. Law's neighbour, Mr. Harvey, had Law in his eye when he drew 'Ouranius,' in 'Theron and Aspasio.'

the concluding caution of the treatise, because he evidently
lays very great stress upon it, rightly feeling that his purport was liable to be misunderstood.   He recommends a
life of strict devotion ; it was the one object of his work to
do so.   But he does *not* recommend, as absolutely necessary, any particularity of life ; for, as he says, ‘ Christian
perfection is tied to no particular form of life.’   Virginity,
voluntary poverty, devout retirement, and such other re-
straints of lawful things, are, in his opinion, highly beneficial to those who would make the way to perfection the
most easy and certain ; and so far he recommends them,
but only so far.   They are only helps and means to an
end which may be attained without them.   A devout spirit
is the one thing needful.   He who attains to this has heard
and obeyed the ‘ Serious Call.’

Before quitting the subject of this the most famous, if
not the greatest, of all Law’s works, it seems desirable to
refer to some of the evidences of the influence which it exercised, and the admiration which it excited in the last century, and also to notice some of its excellences and defects.

The mere fact that, next to the Bible, it contributed
more than any other book to the rise and spread of the
great Evangelical revival of the eighteenth century, is of
itself sufficient to show the importance of the work.

But the testimony of some of the most famous individuals who were influenced by it may enable the reader
to realise this the more vividly.   First and foremost stands
the great name of John Wesley.   We have already seen
Wesley confessing to Law, in the famous letter of 1738, that
‘ for two years he had been preaching after the model of Mr.
Law’s practical treatises,’ which had made so deep an impression upon himself.   But it was not only in his ‘ unconverted ’ days that Wesley expressed his admiration of the
‘ Serious Call.’   Only eighteen months before his death he

spoke of it publicly as 'a treatise which will hardly be excelled, if it be equalled, in the English tongue, either for
beauty of expression or for justness and depth of thought ;'[1]
and he gave a practical proof of his appreciation of its value
by making it a text-book for the highest class in his school
at Kingswood.   Charles Wesley was as much impressed by
the book as his brother John.[2] So was George Whitefield.
'Before I went to the University,' he writes, 'I met with
Mr. Law's " Serious Call," but had not money to purchase
it.   Soon after my coming up to the University, seeing a
small edition of it in a friend's hand, I soon purchased it.
God worked powerfully upon my soul, as He has since upon
many others, by that and his other excellent treatise upon
" Christian Perfection."'[3]   So was Henry Venn. 'Law's
" Serious Call," says his biographer, 'he read repeatedly,
and tried to frame his life according to that model.'[4]   So
was Thomas Scott. 'Carelessly taking up,' he tells us,
' Mr. Law's " Serious Call," a book I had hitherto treated
with contempt, I had no sooner opened it than I was
struck with the originality of the work, and the spirit and
force of argument with which it is written. . . . By the
perusal of it I was convinced that I was guilty of great
remissness and negligence ; that the duties of secret devotion called for far more of my time and attention than
had been hitherto allotted to them ; and that, if I hoped to
save my own soul and the souls of those that heard me, I
must in this respect greatly alter my conduct, and increase
my diligence in seeking and serving the Lord.   From that
time I began,' &c.[5]   So, probably, was John Newton.[6]

---

[1] *Sermon CXVIII.* on a 'Single Eye,' vol. iii. p. 333.
[2] See Jackson's *Memoirs of Rev. Charles Wesley*, p. 52.
[3] *Life and Times of the Rev. George Whitefield*, by Robert Philip, p. 16.
[4] *Memoir of Henry Venn* prefixed to the 'Complete Duty of Man,' published by the Religious Tract Society.
[5] *Force of Truth*, part iii.   Scott's 'Theological Works,' p. 18.
[6] See Newton's *Works* (Cecil's edition), vol. vi. p. 247.

So, certainly, was Thomas Adam, an eminent Evangelical of his day, and himself the author of a devotional work of no small merit and of great popularity. So, too, was Adam's pious and accomplished biographer, James Stillingfleet, of Hotham, who, at a time when Law had fallen into discredit with the Evangelical school (1785), wrote : ' I must beg leave to differ from those who would utterly discard Mr. Law's writings, and to assert that we have not perhaps in the language a more masterly performance in its way, or a book better calculated to promote a concern about religion, than Mr. Law's " Serious Call to a Devout and Holy Life." ' [1]

Nor was it only the Methodists and Evangelicals of the last century who were deeply touched by the ' Serious Call.' Dr. Johnson's opinion of it is well known. ' I became,' he says, ' a sort of lax *talker* against religion, for I did not much *think* against it ; and this lasted till I went to Oxford, when I took up Law's " Serious Call to a Holy Life," expecting to find it a dull book (as such books generally are). But I found Law quite an over-match for me ; and this was the first occasion of my thinking in earnest.' [2] On another occasion he called it ' the finest piece of hortatory theology in any language,' and on another, ' the best piece of paraenetic divinity.' Gibbon, the historian, says of it : ' Mr. Law's master work, the " Serious Call," is still read as a popular and powerful book of devotion. His precepts are rigid ; but they are founded on the Gospel. His satire is sharp ; but it is drawn from the knowledge

---

[1] See *Life of the Author* prefixed to Adam's ' Private Thoughts on Religion,' p. xxvi. Speaking generally of Mr. Law's writings, the same writer says, ' They are admirably adapted to awaken the conscience, and beget in the mind of the reader a conviction of the futility of nominal profession and mere decency of conduct ; and have in them such a strength of easy reasoning, level to every capacity, as almost irresistibly wins the reader's assent to the necessity of vital religion.

[2] Boswell's *Life of Johnson*, in 10 vols., i. 67.

of human life, and many of his portraits are not unworthy of the pen of La Bruyere. If he finds a spark of piety in his reader's mind, he will soon kindle it to a flame ; and a philosopher must allow that he exposes, with equal severity and truth, the strange contradiction between the faith and practice of the Christian world.'[1] The first Lord Lyttelton, the poet and historian, is said to have taken up the ' Serious Call ' about bed-time, at a friend's house, and to have been so fascinated with it that he read it quite through before he could go to rest. He expressed himself as 'not a little astonished to find that one of the finest books that ever were written had been penned by a crack-brained enthusiast.'[2] Bishop Horne was so impressed with it that 'he conformed himself in many respects to the strictness of Law's rules of devotion.'[3] A clergyman, writing under the title of 'Ouranius,' to 'Lloyd's Evening Post,' in a letter dated ' Scarborough, December 21, 1771,' gives this remarkable testimony to the value of the ' Serious Call,' which is worth quoting in full: ' Though I live (when at home) in a small country village, I have had sufficient work upon my hands to bring my parishioners to any tolerable degree of piety and goodness. I preached and laboured among them incessantly ; and yet, after all, was convinced that my work had been as fruitless as casting pearls before swine : the drunkard continued his nocturnal practices, and the voice of the swearer was still heard in our streets. I purchased many religious books, and distributed them among them ; but, alas ! I could perceive no visible effects. In short, I had the grief to find that all my labour had proved in vain. . . . About this time I happened

---

[1] *Memoirs of my Life and Writings*, p. 15.

[2] Byrom's *Journal*, vol. ii. part ii. p. 634.

[3] Jones of Nayland's *Life of Bishop Horne*, prefixed to his edition of Horne's ' Works,' vol. i. p. 67.

to peruse a treatise of Mr. Law's, entitled " A Serious Call to a Devout and Holy Life," with which I was so charmed, and greatly edified, that I resolved my flock should partake of the same spiritual food. I therefore gave to each person in my parish one of those useful books, and charged them upon my blessing (for I consider them as my children) to carefully peruse the same. My perseverance was now rewarded with success, and I had the satisfaction of beholding my people reclaimed from a life of folly and impiety to a life of holiness and devotion.' The writer then speaks of 'the strong and nervous style,' and the ' sublime thought' of the ' Serious Call,' and concludes : 'I will venture to add, that whoever sits down, without prejudice, and attentively reads it through, will rise up the wiser man and better Christian.' It would be wearisome and needless to quote further evidence to prove the admiration which this work excited and the effects which it produced ; it will suffice to add that the ' Serious Call ' was, if possible, more popular in America than in England, and it is certainly better known and more admired there than here in the present day.

Its popularity in England has certainly not been advanced by the well-meant, but strangely misdirected, efforts of those who— sometimes under the sanction of high authority [1]—have endeavoured to popularise it by abridging it. Abridgments are rarely successes ; but few have been such dismal failures as those of the ' Serious Call.' All they have succeeded in doing is in giving their readers a totally erroneous impression of the book. By a

---

[1] I was never more struck with the contrast between the interesting little works with which the Society for the Promotion of Christian Knowledge now supply us and the very uninteresting ones which they used to issue forty years ago, than I was on turning from one of the ' Fathers for English Readers ' to ' Tract, No. 163, A Serious Call,' abridged from the abridgment of the original work.

I

provokingly perverted ingenuity they have transmuted one of the raciest and most forcible books that ever was written into a dreary little tract, whose prim propriety does not at all compensate for its intolerable dulness. In fact, Tate and Brady give one about as good a notion of the poetry of David as the various abridgments of the ' Serious Call ' give one of the powers of Law.

It was hardly possible that such a book as the ' Serious Call,' dealing as it did with all the popular shortcomings of the day in the most trenchant and uncompromising fashion, should fail to give offence in many quarters. Of course the Flatuses and Cognatuses, the Flavias and Matildas of real life would strongly object to see themselves held up to the scorn of the world. Byrom was ' a little surprised ' to hear two ladies ' mention Mr. Law's book of the " Serious Call " as a silly, ridiculous book, because of Eusebia, dress, &c.,' and he naively adds, ' Probably the gay, pleasant, diverting life may render even innocent people blind.' [1] For ' probably,' Law would no doubt have said ' certainly,' and would have added that it was the very object of his book to displease such people, or rather to make them displeased with themselves. He himself was inundated with criticisms of such a conflicting kind that, as he told Byrom, ' there was hardly any passage in the book but what had been both admired and condemned.' This class of objection, however, need not be dwelt upon. Neither is it necessary to comment upon the cavil that ' the apportioning of hours for devotion is too monkish and unearthly for a Christian ;' because Law himself expressly guards against the notion that this ' method of devotion was to be pressed upon any sort of people as absolutely necessary ;' [2] and, moreover, it is quite sufficient apology to say that as a good Churchman

[1] *Journal*, vol. i. part ii. p. 541.   [2] *Serious Call*, ch. xx. *ad init.*

he was simply following out the rules of the Church.[1] Nor for the same reason, need we comment upon the alleged drawback that there is 'nothing said of the benefits from the association of Christians for prayer and religious conference ;' for Law would, of course, have replied that such associations were already provided for by the Church system, if properly carried out. Charles Wesley hit upon a more serious blot when he said to Byrom, 'Do not you think that a palpable mistake in Mr. Law's " Serious Call," that there is no command for public worship in Scripture ?'[2] Byrom calls this a 'trifling objection ;' but, with all due deference to the good doctor, I cannot but think that Law expresses himself far too strongly when he says, 'It is very observable that there is not one command in all the Gospel for publick worship, and perhaps it is a duty that is least insisted upon in Scripture of any other. The frequent attendance at it is never so much as mentioned in all the New Testament.'[3] The fact is, Law was so struck with the inconsistency of people who were very particular about attending public worship and not at all particular about leading a corresponding life, that, unlike himself, he was carried away, and maintained an untenable position. This was, however, only a casual slip. The general tone of the 'Serious Call' is certainly in favour of public worship.

The commonest, and perhaps the strongest, objection alleged against the 'Serious Call' is that there is too little of the Gospel in it. No doubt, this term 'the Gospel' became, in the next generation, as John Wesley said, 'a mere cant term, with no determinate meaning.'[4] But surely it has in itself a very real meaning ; and this is not put

---

[1] This answer, however, would not have satisfied one of the editors of the 'Serious Call' who makes the objection—the Rev. David Young, of Perth, a Presbyterian minister.

[2] *Journal*, vol. ii. part i. p. 182.   [3] *Serious Call*, c. i. p. 8.

[4] See Tyerman's *Life of Wesley*, iii. 278.

sufficiently forward in the 'Serious Call.' Not that the distinctive doctrines of Christianity are ignored, or that the arguments which Law urges are not based on distinctively Christian motives. But there is, to say the least of it, too little of the Gospel in the literal sense of the term; that is, too little of the glad tidings, the bright, joyous side of Christianity. Though this defect is not so marked as in the 'Christian Perfection,' there is still a certain austerity about the 'Serious Call' (as perhaps there was about the writer at this period of his life) which has a tendency to 'break the bruised reed.' The mortifications and renouncements which Christianity requires are put forward not, indeed, too prominently, for Law has chapter and verse for all that he asserts, but too exclusively. The work, in fact, is more calculated to alarm than to attract. The comforts of the Gospel are not ignored, but they are described too vaguely, and with not sufficient particularity.

But this is not altogether what the Evangelicals meant when they complained of the absence of Gospel teaching in the 'Serious Call.' They used the term 'Gospel' in a wider and also a more technical sense than its literal meaning. Nor was it only to Law's omissions that they would take exception. Many of his positive assertions would be specially offensive to them; such, for instance, as the following: 'True religion is nothing but simple Nature governed by right reason;'[1] 'you are to honour, improve, and perfect the spirit that is within you, you are to prepare it for the Kingdom of Heaven;'[2] 'with what tears and contrition ought you to purge yourself from the guilt of sin;'[3] and many more which might be quoted. Whitefield, on one of his voyages home from America, commenced the task of 'Gospelising' the 'Serious Call.' It

[1] *Serious Call*, c. xviii. p. 343.   [2] *Ibid.* c. xix. p. 363.
[3] *Ibid.* c. xxiii. p. 473.

required a stronger pen than Whitefield's to supplement Law, and there is no need to regret that the project was abortive ; but one can hardly wonder that it was attempted. Neither can one wonder that Thomas Scott, in the very passage in which he expresses his deep admiration of the 'Serious Call,' and thankfully acknowledges his obligations to its author, should add, ' There are many things in it that I am very far from approving, and it certainly contains as little *Gospel* as any religious work I am acquainted with.'[1]   There is, in fact, much force in a remark of one of the editors of the 'Call :' ' It tells the reader what he ought to be, but not how he is to attain it.'[2]   It is difficult to conceive any one permanently resting content with the system of the 'Serious Call.'   And, as a matter of fact, those who expressed most strongly their obligations to it did not.   Law himself certainly did not.   Within a very few years of its publication he found a lifelong fascination in a system which is not, indeed, antagonistic to that of the 'Serious Call,' but hardly one vestige of which can be found in that famous treatise.   The Methodists and Evangelicals, who were roused from their spiritual lethargy by it, went on to a very different system.   And the old-fashioned, high and dry Churchmen who admitted it to an honoured place in their theological libraries, certainly did not as a rule carry out its precepts in all their literal strictness.

Perhaps, however, the objections to the 'Serious Call' have partly arisen from a misconception of its nature and scope.   It is not, properly speaking, a devotional book ; still less is it a complete body of divinity.   It is simply, as its name indicates, a 'Call.'   Regarded in this, its proper

---

[1] *Force of Truth*, part ii.   Scott's 'Theological Works,' p. 17.

[2] *Introductory Essay* prefixed to an edition of the 'Serious Call,' by the Rev. David Young, of Perth.

light, it must be admitted that it has been wonderfully
effective. The 'Call' reached the ears of thousands, and
appealed to them not in vain.

As a composition, it is difficult to speak too highly of
it. The epithets which Wesley applied to its writer, ' strong '
and ' elegant,' express exactly two out of its many excellences. As one reads it, one feels under the guidance of
a singularly strong man. There is no weak, mawkish
sentimentality, no feeble declamation, no illogical argument. It is like a strong man driving a weighty hammer
with well-directed blows. Every stroke tells, and you
cannot evade its force. And both in style and matter it
is a singularly elegant composition. There are no offences
against good taste, no slipshod sentences, no attempts
at fine writing in it. Its illustrations (though, perhaps a
little too frequent) are always apposite, and often very
beautiful.

But besides being ' strong ' and ' elegant,' it has also
another characteristic, which Wesley would have thought
wrong to mention in a sermon, and which Law would
probably have disclaimed. The ' Serious Call ' is full of
humour, and sparkles with wit in every page. It never
forfeits its title to be a *serious* call, but wit and humour, so
far from being inconsistent with seriousness, often shine the
brighter from their contrast with their surroundings. If
one could conceive—as one cannot—Law taking part in
such light productions, what admirable papers he could
have contributed to the ' Spectator ' ! Steele and Addison
at their very best do not rise higher as humourists than
Law did.

But, after all, it is not the beauties' of composition—
many and great as these undoubtedly are—which attract
us most in the ' Serious Call.' It is the intense earnestness, the obvious reality and thoroughness of the man, the

knowledge that his ' Call ' to others was only to do what he meant to do and *did* himself. The book is (to use the language of an able writer of our own day, who cordially admires and appreciates Law, though he differs very widely from his views) ' a book which throughout palpitates with the deepest emotions of its author. Law, whose sensitiveness to logic is as marked as his sensitiveness to conscience, is incapable of compromise. He not only believes what he professes, but he believes it in the most downright sense, and he is not content until it is thoroughly worked into his whole system of thought,'[1] and, it may be added, ' of action.'

In short, if Law had written nothing whatever except the ' Serious Call,' he would have written quite enough to deserve a prominent and honoured place in English literature ; and, what is better still, he would have written quite enough to earn the gratitude of all who value true piety.

[1] Mr. Leslie Stephen's *English Thought in the Eighteenth Century*, vol. ii. pp. 395, 396.

CHAPTER VIII.

THE 'CASE OF REASON,' ETC., AGAINST TINDAL.

'WHETHER,' writes a correspondent to the 'Gentleman's
Magazine' in October 1800, 'the "Serious Call" be Mr.
Law's masterpiece, I have some doubt; I should give the
palm to his "Case of Reason," stated in answer to "Christianity as old as the Creation."' It is difficult to compare
works of so different a scope and character; each is good
of its kind, but it may safely be asserted that Law did not
diminish the reputation he had justly won by his 'Serious
Call' by his next work, published probably about three
years later, in 1732.

Law always selected foemen worthy of his steel to do
battle with. As he had formerly pitted himself against the
ablest champion of the Low, or, as we should now call it,
the Broad, Church party, so now he pitted himself against
the ablest champion of Deism; and the unprejudiced
reader will admit that he at least holds his own as success-
fully in the one case as he does in the other. Tindal was
an old enemy, or perhaps we should rather say friend, of
Law's; for Law had found his book, written thirty years
earlier, the 'Rights of a Christian Church,' a useful ally
in his controversy with Hoadly, as tending to show what
was the real conclusion of the bishop's argument— a conclusion to which the bishop would naturally have objected,
since it gave him no *locus standi* as a bishop at all. It will

be remembered that Law was constantly twitting Hoadly for not recognising the author of the ' Rights of a Christian Church ' as his ally. Tindal's ' Christianity as old as the Creation ' was a more able and important work than its predecessor. No book on the Deist's side created so great a sensation ; and justly so, for it marks the climax of Deism. Oddly enough, the title of the book contained a truth which Law, especially in his mystic days, not only held, but actually made the cardinal point of his whole system. As we shall see presently, Law insisted as strongly as Tindal did that Christianity was as old as the Creation, in one sense ; only that sense was certainly not Tindal's sense. It is worth remarking, however, that in the work now before us Law never finds fault with the title of Tindal's book ; but the contents of the book were not necessarily indicated by the title. The way that Tindal proved that Christianity was as old as the Creation was by magnifying Reason at the expense of Revelation, and on this point Law joined issue with him. He will by no means admit what Tindal had laid down as an almost self-evident axiom, viz. that man is obliged to abide by the sole light of his own reason. He contends *à priori* that this may be a mere groundless pretension. If humility be a duty, then this lofty claim for reason may be nothing better than spiritual pride. This being in Law's view the true point of the controversy, he discusses it at some length, and it need scarcely be said with what result.

The earlier part of the ' Case of Reason ' is concerned with a question which belongs to the province of Ethics as much or more than to that of Theology. Whether morality depended upon the will of God, or upon the eternal and immutable fitness of things, had long been a bone of contention between moral philosophers. Tindal took the latter view, but turned it to a purpose which its

Christian advocates (among whom Law himself may to a certain extent [1] be reckoned) never intended. The way in which Law deals with his adversary on this point affords a good specimen of that adroitness which he always showed as a controversialist. 'You argue,' he says in effect, 'that the relation of things and persons, and the fitness resulting from thence, is the sole rule of God's actions. I grant it most readily; but I contend that instead of proving what you suppose, it proves the exact opposite. I appeal to this one common and confessed principle as a sufficient proof that man cannot walk by the sole light of his own reason without contradicting the nature and reason of things and denying this to be the sole rule of God's actions. For, God's nature being divinely perfect, the fitness of things implies that He must necessarily act by a rule *above* all human comprehension.' This idea is powerfully worked out by a reference to Creation, Providence, the miseries of life, the nature and origin of the soul, the origin of evil— in fact, to all the topics of natural religion. 'What,' he asks, 'can we know of such matters by such means as our own poor reason can grope out of the nature and fitness of things?' 'We have the utmost certainty that we are vastly-incompetent judges of the fitness or unfitness of any methods that God uses in the government of so small a part of the universe as mankind are.'

Law shows how the line of argument which Tindal was using must end in 'horrid Atheism.' 'For,' he says, 'it is just as wise and reasonable to allow of no mysteries in revelation as to allow of no mysteries or secrets in Creation and Providence. And, whenever this writer or any other shall think it a proper time to attack natural religion with as

[1] I say 'to a certain extent,' because Law rather held that the 'eternal and immutable fitness of things' and the 'will of God' were only different modes of expressing one and the same thing.

much freedom as he has now fallen upon revealed, he need not enter upon any new hypothesis or different way of reasoning. For the same turn of thought, the same manner of cavilling, may soon find materials in the natural state of man for as large a bill of complaints against natural religion, and the mysteries of Providence, as is here brought against revealed doctrines.' It is interesting to remark, as illustrative of the clearness with which Law always saw the exact drift of an argument, how he here anticipates and, in fact, obviates an objection which was made in the last century, and has been repeated more than once in our own, against Butler's famous argument in the 'Analogy.' To prove that there are the same difficulties in natural religion as there are in revealed is, it is said, 'a dangerous process, because it may lead to Atheism.'¹ 'It not only *may,*' says Law in effect, ' but it *must* lead either to Atheism or to the complete dislodgment of the Deist from his position.' Now, when it is remembered that the Deist (as his very name implies) based his whole position on the assumption that God's existence, wisdom, power, love, &c., were all knowable without revelation, the force of this argument, as against Tindal, will be apparent. In fact, Law, by anticipation, carried Butler's train of reasoning to its logical conclusion, and in so doing hit exactly upon the true weakness of the Deist's position. That position was, in fact, quite untenable, because his weapons might be turned against himself. This was the chief reason of the sudden and utter collapse of Deism. And no one saw this more clearly than William Law. Others, no doubt—Bishop Butler among the number—pursued more or less decidedly the same course of argument ; but no one, in my opinion, realised its full force as the true key of the position so thoroughly as Law. He

¹ See *inter alia,* Miss Hennel's essay ' On the Sceptical Tendency of Butler's Analogy,' and Mr. Martineau's ' MS. Studies of Christianity.' The objection is as old as the days of the first Pitt.

recurs to the same argument when he deals with the special objections which Tindal raised against the Christian revelation. Instead of answering them in detail, he felt— and felt quite rightly—that, as against a Deist, it was sufficient to take the line marked out in the following fine passage: ' There is nothing half so mysterious in the Christian revelation, considered in itself, as there is in that *invisible* Providence, which all must hold that believe a God. And though there is enough plain in Providence to excite the adoration of humble and pious minds, yet it has often been a rock of *Atheism* to those who make their own reason the measure of wisdom.' Again: ' Though the *creation* plainly declares the glory, and wisdom, and goodness of God, yet it has more mysteries in it, more things whose fitness, expedience, and reasonableness human reason cannot comprehend. Thus does this argument [of Tindal] tend wholly to Atheism, and concludes with the same force against Creation and Providence as it does against revelation.' He then applies the same kind of reasoning to the miracles and the prophecies.

Remembering, again, that Law was addressing a *Deist*, that is, a man who professed to have the highest reverence and appreciation of the perfection of the Deity, we shall see that there is something very telling and apposite in his dignified exposure of Tindal's somewhat grovelling and anthropomorphic conception of God. Writing, for instance, on what he calls the ' relative characters of God '—that is, God's relations to us as our Father, Governor, and Preserver, Law says: ' That which is plain and certain in these relative characters of God plainly shows our obligations to every instance of duty, homage, adoration, love, and gratitude. And that which is mysterious and inconceivable in them is a just and solid foundation of that profound humility, awful reverence, internal piety, and tremendous

sense of the Divine Majesty, with which devout and pious
persons think of God, and assist at the offices and institutions of religion. . . . And if some people, by a long and
strict attention to reason, clear ideas, the fitness and unfitness
of things, have at last arrived at a demonstrative certainty,
that all these sentiments of piety and devotion are mere
bigotry, superstition, and enthusiasm ; I shall only now observe, that youthful extravagance, passion, and debauchery,
by their own natural tendency, without the assistance of
any other guide, seldom fail of making the same discovery.'

Tindal, again, objected to the popular conception of God
as 'an arbitrary Being, acting out of humour and caprice.'
How finely Law meets this objection ! ' Though will and
power, when considered as blind or imperfect faculties in
men, may pass for humour and caprice, yet as attributes of
God they have the perfection of God. His own will is
wisdom, and His wisdom is His will. His goodness is
arbitrary, and His arbitrariness is goodness.' In the same
vein Law answers Tindal's question, ' Was it not as easy for
God to have communicated His revelation to all nations as
to any one nation or person, or in all languages as in any
one ?' ' This argument,' he replies, ' is built upon the truth
and reasonableness of this supposition, that God does
things because they are easy, or forbears things because
they are difficult to be performed ;' and then, summing up
generally the argument on this point, ' We will not,' he
says, ' allow a Providence to be right, unless we can comprehend and explain the reasonableness of all its steps ;
and yet it could not *possibly* be right, unless its proceedings
were as much *above* our comprehension as our wisdom is
below that which is infinite.'

In the latter part of his treatise, Law turns, as it were,
to the reverse side of the medal. Having vindicated the
greatness of God, he now asserts the littleness of man.

Perhaps on this topic he is in some danger of being run away
with by his favourite hobby ; certainly he was in some
danger of offending the popular feeling of the day, which
on both sides, Christian and Deist alike, ran strongly in
favour of reason, and of proving religion to be of all things
reasonable.   But whether we can quite endorse all his assertions or not, we can hardly help admiring the ingenuity
and adroitness with which he cuts away the whole ground
from under his antagonist.   He shows that this grand discovery of the Deists that man has the right to judge and act
according to reason, is really nothing else than the discovery
of a mare's nest.   It was no more than if they said, a man
has a right to see only with his own eyes, or hear only with
his own ears.   It was not a matter of duty, but of necessity.
The real question between Christians and unbelievers was
not whether reason is to be followed, but when it is *best*
followed.   But, after all, what do we mean by ' our own
reason ' ?   We have by nature only a bare capacity of
receiving good or bad impressions ; our light is really little
more than the opinions and customs of those among whom
we live.   Talk of the perfection and sufficiency of our own
reason !   Why we are nothing better than a kind of foolish
helpless animals till education and experience have *revealed*
to us the wisdom and knowledge of our fellow-creatures.
Tindal himself calls education a second nature.   There are,
then, according to him, two natures.   This pleader for the
sufficiency of the light of nature should have told us to
which of the two natures we are to resign ourselves, the
first or the second.   They may be as different as good and
evil ; yet, as they are both natures, both internal lights,
which are we to follow ?   Which of the two is ' the perpetual,
standing rule for men of the meanest as well as the highest
capacities, which carries its own evidence with it, those
internal and inseparable marks of truth ?' [1]

[1] *Christianity as old as the Creation.* p. 243.

Law, who appears to have perceived almost instinctively the weakest points of his adversaries' position, dwells with great force upon another flaw in Tindal's argument, a flaw which belonged to him in common with most Deists, and which was probably one of the chief causes of the utter collapse of Deism. It is this : The Deists boldly asserted the perfection of human reason, but they offered no proof, nor even a pretence of proof, from fact or experience, of their assertion. ' The history,' says Law very truly, ' of all ages for near six thousand years past demonstrates quite the contrary. And yet the matter rests *wholly* upon fact and experience ; all speculative reasonings upon it are as idle and visionary as a sick man's dreams about health.' So far, most thoughtful people will agree with Law ; but they will not perhaps be disposed to follow him so readily when, pursuing his raid against his pet aversion, he goes on to declare that ' all the disorders of human nature are the disorders of human reason,' and that ' all the perfection or imperfection of our passions is nothing else but the perfection or imperfection of our reason. Medea, when she killed her children, and Cato, when he killed himself, acted as truly according to the judgment of their reason at that time as the confessor who chooses rather to suffer than deny his faith ; the difference is purely the different state of their reason. For the passions may be said to govern our actions only as they denote the disordered state of our reason.' Law finally sums up the whole ' case of reason,' which in this part might more fairly be called a case against reason, in the following vigorous manner : ' In a word, when self-love is a proper arbitrator betwixt a man and his adversary ; when revenge is a just judge of meekness ; when pride is a true lover of humility ; when falsehood is a teacher of truth ; when lust is a fast friend of chastity ; when the flesh leads to the spirit ; when sensuality delights in self-denial ; when partiality is a promoter of equity ; when the palate can taste the difference between sin and holiness; when the hand can feel the truth of a proposition ;—then may human reason be a proper arbitrator between God and man, the sole, final, just judge of all that ought or ought not to be matter of a holy, divine, and heavenly religion.'

When it is remembered that the title of Locke's famous treatise—the 'Reasonableness of Chiistianity'—gave the keynote to the dominant theology of Law's day, one can hardly be surprised that this vigorous crusade against reason should have been received by the friends of the Christian cause with indifference, if not with actual hostility. At any rate, such appears to have been the fact. Although the 'Case of Reason' was published when the 'Serious Call' was just in the first flush of popularity, and although the writer had long been recognised as one of the most powerful and successful contributors to the Bangorian controversy, his new controversial piece was certainly not appreciated. Leland barely mentions Law as one of the answerers to Tindal, without one word of commendation, although he can find room for a word of praise for 'the ingenious Mr. Anthony Atkey' (whoever he may have been), and has a panegyrical epithet for almost all the rest of the many replies to 'Christianity as old as the Creation' which he notices.[1] Dr. Waterland gives all the weight of his great name against Law's performance,[2] and the majority of contemporary or nearly contemporary writers simply ignore the work. But Law has been better appreciated in later years, and few who read the 'Case of Reason' in the present day will deny that it is a powerful work, fully worthy of the great writer who penned it. It was reprinted at the request of a friend in 1755.[3]

[1] See Leland's *View of the Deistical Writers*,' Letter IX., pp. 79–85.
[2] See Waterland's 'Works' (Van Mildert's edition), vol. vi. p. 454.
[3] This is worth noting, because one might perhaps have expected that it would not have accorded with Law's later views. See 'Works,' vii. (2) 10, 11, 15, 16, 17, 29.

CHAPTER IX.

LAW ON THE ROMAN QUESTION.

DURING the years 1731–32, Law wrote three letters which
are worthy of a short separate chapter, among other reasons because they furnish us with almost the only materials
which we possess for judging of his attitude towards the
Church of Rome. Like other nonjurors, he was constantly
charged with a tendency to Romanism. His three letters
on the Bangorian controversy, in especial, were accused of
leading men in this direction. ' The Papists,' wrote Gilbert Burnet, ' should rejoice in your doctrines, which would
do you little service but be of great advantage to them.' [1]
Mr. Pyle, another antagonist, spoke of Law as ' triumphing
over his lordship [Bishop Hoadly], under no banner but that
of the Pope ;' [2] and, in another work, declared that ' Law's
principles can possibly serve nobody but a Romanist.' [3] The
same accusation was hinted at, if not actually made, by
Mr. Jackson, of Rossington, and others.[4] The charge was

[1] *An Answer to Mr. Law's Letter to the Bishop of Bangor in a letter to
Mr. Law.* By Gilbert Burnet (second son of the Bishop of Salisbury). Published 1717.

[2] *Vindication of the Bishop of Bangor in Answer to Law.* By T. Pyle,
Lecturer of Lynn Regis 1718.

[3] *Second Vindication.* By the same. 1718.

[4] See *An Answer to Mr. Law's Letter to the Bishop of Bangor concerning
his late Sermon and Preservative.* By John Jackson, rector of Rossington. 1718;
and the literature on the Bangorian controversy, *passim.* Mr. Jackson was
subsequently vicar of Doncaster, and became well known in connection with the
controversy between Drs. Waterland and Clarke on the subject of the Trinity.

K

utterly unfounded. Law, like the rest of the nonjurors, had no sympathy whatever with the Roman system. His position in the Church of his baptism was perfectly clear and logical. At the same time, his attitude towards Romanism was very different from that of the majority of his contemporaries. He was no Romanist, but he was also no violent anti-Romanist. Though he had no inclination to meddle with politics, he was always a staunch Jacobite at heart ; and the religion of him whom he considered the rightful claimant to the throne was, in his opinion, no sufficient bar to his right. But circumstances did not require Law to give his opinion on the Roman controversy, and hence, with the exception of these letters, we have little direct intimation of his views on the subject.

The letters were written to a lady, probably, but not certainly, Miss Dodwell, daughter of the learned but eccentric nonjuror Henry Dodwell. The circumstances of the Dodwell family agree with what is said or hinted in these letters about the personal characters of those referred to in them. But then, so also, to a certain extent, do the circumstances of the Lee family—a name which will come before us again in connection with Law's mystic period.[1] However, it is not a matter of importance to identify the individual to whom the letters were addressed. It is sufficient to note that, whoever she was, her frame of mind was very similar to that of many, who in the present, and indeed in every, age, have been attracted to Romanism as the shortest way of getting rid of their difficulties. Law's advice is not only pious, sensible, and admirable in every respect, but it is quite applicable, *mutatis mutandis*, to all

---

[1] Mr. Edward Fisher wrote to Miss Gibbon in 1789, respecting these letters, 'They were published in 1779 and intituled " Letters to a Lady, &c." This lady, it seems, was of the name of Dodwell, not a member of any sect, but of the Church of England, and daughter to the pious and learned Mr. Henry Dodwell, &c. ;' but he does not give any reason why ' it seems ' so.

who feel the same attraction in the present day. For their
practical utility, therefore, the letters are well worth noticing. They are also noticeable in a life of Law as being
thoroughly illustrative of the character of the writer. That
curious mixture of severity and extreme tenderness which
is conspicuous in Law's intercourse with Byrom meets us
again in these letters. They are full of heart; but while
they could hardly have failed to make the recipient love
the writer, they were also calculated to make her fear him.
While she must have felt that Law had a most affectionate
regard for her welfare, she must also have felt the sternness of his rebukes. The fault which some perhaps will
find with the letters will not be that they are too High
Church, but rather that they are too Broad. But the letters,
or rather extracts from them, for they are too long to be
quoted in full, shall speak for themselves. They are
entitled : ' Letters to a Lady inclined to enter into the Communion of the Church of Rome, by W. Law, M.A.' They
were not intended for publication ; and were, in fact, not
published until some years after the writer's death, being,
as is stated in the title-page, ' now [1779] first printed for
H. Payne,' a devoted admirer of Law, and himself the
author and editor of several works.

The first letter is dated ' May 24, 1731,' and is a reply
to a most curious medley of reasons which the lady appears
to have given for desiring to join the Church of Rome.
Among these were the licentiousness of the press—which
Law not unnaturally terms ' an unreasonable complaint ; '
the old difficulties about the doctrines of predestination and
absolute decrees ; and the objection that God's grace would
attend more sensibly the use of His ordinances if He
approved of the Church of England. On this latter difficulty Law dwells more at length than on the rest. He
contends—(1) that before the Reformation the same objec-

tion might have been made, and therefore the Reformation
was not to blame ; (2) that there was the same reason to
put the question in the Church of Rome ; (3) that the
fact of the Jews falling into idolatry was no objection to
their ordinances ; and (4) he administers to his correspondent a grave rebuke on the presumption implied in
the objection. 'How,' he asks, 'can you tell who are receiving benefit from ordinances ? The prophet had need
to be reminded that there were seven thousand who
were not bowing the knee to Baal. And, nowadays, people,
who have never been out of the town in which they
were born, are apt to think they know the state of the
religious world.' But, even supposing the corruption of
Christianity to be as great as his correspondent supposed,
'it should only move us to profound humility, zeal, tenderness, charity, and intercession for those who neglect
it.' To ask 'how, supposing a sufficiency of Divine grace,
men should be in such a state,' is blamable curiosity.
'What is there in the Bible to make us think ourselves
qualified to ask or answer such questions, or that any part
of our duty depends upon our knowledge of them ? It
is the end of revelation to silence such inquiries. It tells
us of the blindness and disorder of our nature and the
depths of Infinite Providence.' He then touches upon the
fall of angels, to which his correspondent had probably
referred, and finely adds : 'It is no subject for inquiry ;
there is no place in the meek and lowly spirit of the followers of Christ Jesus for such questions ; they are all to
be buried in a profound resignation to the adorable providence of God ; we should resist them, if, through our weakness, they intrude on us, like other thoughts contrary to
piety.'

On some points Law agreed with his correspondent's
premisses, but demurred to the conclusions she drew from

them. For instance : ' I agree with you,' he says, ' about the method of the Reformation ; the bare history of it is satire enough. But the history of Popes, written by persons of their own communion, is as large and undeniable a history of scandal ; there is little room for private judgment on the excellency of one Church above another on that account. You wonder God's judgments did not overtake the reformers ; others, that papal tyranny has so long escaped them. Hence we may gather, how much we are out of the way when we are guessing at the fitness of God's judgments ; and perhaps they may then be executing in the severest manner when we are wondering why they do not fall. The means of salvation are fully preserved both in the English and Roman communion for all who are disposed to make a right use of them. The sins both of reformers and papists are personal ;' and so forth. These last sentences were strangely out of accord with the strong anti-papal feeling then almost universally prevalent, and Law probably felt that they were.[1] For he goes on to speak of the bitterness of controversy, and quaintly adds : ' He who says, " Sirs, ye are brethren," is like to have Moses' reward for his pains.' Then, again pressing the lesson which he appears to have considered specially needful for his correspondent, he proceeds : ' Every part of the Church is in division ; let us live in these divided, schismatical, uncharitable parts of Christendom, free from schismatical principles and passions, and intent on love to God and our neighbour. God's goodness overrules this vast disorder and differences in churches. Better say, I am a private member of a Church which has full means of salvation in it ; I have no ability, no call or commission to judge

---

[1] ' How different is this from our modern Protestant Divinity !' is the reflection in Mr. Law's handwriting on the text— in a Bible, evidently much read and annotated by him, now in the possession of Miss S. Law.

in these matters ; they belong to those who, by the providence of God, have the care of this Church.'

. On another point, Law quite agreed with the premisses
of his correspondent, though he denied her conclusion.
' You say,' he writes, '" I inclined to the Church of Rome
because of the excellent books written by persons of that
communion ; and they must have been very acceptable to
God, and had large assistance from Him." Right in both
respects ! I think the same of many of their writers, and
bless God for the knowledge I have had of them. And as
I consider their Church and all its members my brethren
in Christ, and as nearly related to me as any Protestants,
so it is the same benefit to me to receive benefit from their
Church as from that of England. In my own heart I drop
and forget all divisions and distinctions which the enemy
hath set up among us ;' with much more to the same
effect.

The second letter opens in the same strain. Law bids
the lady ' love the Churches of Rome and Greece with the
same affection and sense of Christian fellowship as she
loved the Church of England, and consider herself, not as
an external member of one in order to renounce communion
with the others, but as necessarily forced into one externally
divided part because there is no part free from external
division.' Strange sentiments from the pen of a clergyman
in the middle of the eighteenth century ! The rest of the
letter does not bear very directly upon the subject of this
chapter, but it contains one or two personal references
which, if for no other reason, deserve notice for their rarity,
Law, as a rule, carefully abstaining from writing anything
about himself. We learn, for instance, that he was not un-
conscious of his own powers. After one of his usual tirades
against human learning, he adds : ' Was the world to see
this remark upon learning, they would impute it to my want

of learning ; and though they would be very right in judging my pretensions to learning not to be great, yet it would
be unjust to think me an entire stranger to the nature of it.
But I profess to you that whatever parts or learning I am
possessed of, I think it as necessary to live under as continual apprehension of their being a snare and temptation
to me as of any worldly distinctions, &c.' Then, after
touching upon a subject about which he was very chary of
speaking, but upon which he unquestionably held strong
opinions—the restoration of all things—he adds a rebuke
of the curiosity of his correspondent about such deep questions, which gives us some insight into her family history. ' I hope I shall not offend you by observing of your
great and good father, whose memory I esteem and reverence, that his chief foible seems to have lain in a temper
to speculation, and perhaps you may have some reason to
resist and guard against it as a temper to which you have
a natural inclination.' The ' foible ' was common both to
Dodwell and Lee, but it would certainly be brought more
under Law's notice in connection with the latter than with
the former. On the other hand, the fact that the lady to
whom Law was writing had a dearly loved brother, whose
falling away from Christianity was one of the chief sources
of her perplexities, exactly tallies with the known lapse of
the younger Dodwell, but not with what is known of the
Lee family.

The third letter, which is dated ' May 29, 1732,' is an
answer to an evidently heartrending account of the sister's
sad state on the falling away of her brother. She had vindicated herself for loving her brother too well, declared that
she would not be able to keep her senses if he were taken
before her, and repeated her desire to ' be of the Church of
Rome, to be free from the danger and anxiety of thinking
for herself on religion.' ' Why not,' replied Law, ' resign

yourself to God instead of the Church of Rome ? A restless, inquisitive, self-seeking temper is the rock on which
you split. Resignation is the best cure. You seem to be
affected with the "Serious Call"; I pray God you may
have benefit by it, and desire you will think the chapter
upon resignation to the will of God deserves most of your
attention. Your desire to go to the Church of Rome proceeds from this restless temper.' The rest of the letter
deals with her excessive love for her fallen brother, and
therefore does not throw much light upon the subject of
this chapter ; but it may be noted in passing, that if Law's
correspondent was really Miss Dodwell, the brother would
be the author of ' Christianity not founded on Argument,'
one of the most remarkable works which the Deistic controversy produced, and about which Law, among many others,
doubted whether it was written on the Christian or the
Deist side.

It has been stated that, with the exception of these
three letters, there is little to show what were Law's views
with regard to the Church of Rome. There is, however,
one remarkable passage written several years later, which
shows that the mystic views which he had then embraced
increased rather than diminished his admiration of some of
the Romish writers, though he was still, as ever, without the
slightest sympathy with Romanism, as a system. His
sentiments, however, were not certainly those of the typical
protestant of the eighteenth century. How many, for instance, would have been found to echo such a sentiment as
this : ' If each Church [Roman and Anglican] could produce but one man a-piece that had the piety of an apostle,
and the impartial love of the first Christians in the first
Church at Jerusalem, a protestant and a papist of this
stamp would not want half a sheet of paper to hold their
Articles of Union, nor be half an hour before they were of

one religion'? Taken by itself, this might seem to show that Law thought there was but little difference between the Church of England and that of Rome. But this was not his meaning ; he was not insensible of the importance of an orthodox faith, but he *did* think (and who will blame him for thinking ?) that, after all, a Christian spirit was at least as important as orthodoxy. This is evident from the following passage which is worth quoting, both for its own intrinsic beauty of thought and expression, and also as a corrective to the false impression which the sentence quoted above might be liable to produce. 'The more,' he writes, ' we believe or know of the corruptions and hindrances of true piety in the Church of Rome, the more we should rejoice to hear, that in every age so many eminent spirits, great saints, have appeared in it, whom we should thankfully behold as so many great Lights hung out by God to show the true way to Heaven ; as so many joyful proofs that Christ is still present in that Church, as well as in other Churches, and that the gates of Hell have not prevailed, or quite overcome it. Who that has the least spark of Heaven in his soul, can help thinking and rejoicing in this manner at the appearance of a St. Bernard, a Teresa, a Francis de Sales,' &c. in that Church ? Who can help praising God that her invented devotions, superstitious use of images, invocation of saints, &c., have not so suppressed any of the graces and virtues of an evangelical perfection of life, but that among Cardinals, Jesuits, Priests, Friars, Monks and Nuns, numbers have been found who seem to live for no other end but to give glory to God and edification to men, and whose writings have everything in them that can guide the soul out of the corruption of this life into the highest union with God ? And he who, through a partial

---

[1] Among Mr. Law's books is a copy of the ' Introduction à la vie dévote du bien-heureux François de Sales,' evidently never read.

orthodoxy, is diverted from feeding in these green pastures
of life, whose just abhorrence of Jesuitical craft and worldly
policy keeps him from knowing and reading the works of
an Alvares du Pas, a Rodigius, a Du Pont, a Guillorée, a
Père Surin, and such like Jesuits, has a greater loss than he
can easily imagine. And if any clergyman can read the Life
of Bartholomeus a Martyribus, a Spanish archbishop, who
sat with great influence at the very Council of Trent, without being edified by it, and desiring to read it again and
again, I know not why he should like the Lives of the best
of the Apostolical Fathers ; and if any Protestant Bishop
should read the "Stimulus Pastorum," wrote by this Popish
Prelate, he must be forced to confess it to be a book that
would have done honour to the best archbishop that the
Reformation has to boast of. O my God, how shall I
unlock this mystery of things ? in the land of darkness,
overrun with superstition, where Divine Worship seems to
be all show and ceremony, there both among priests and
people Thou hast those who are fired with the pure love
of Thee, who renounce everything for Thee, who are
devoted wholly and solely to Thee, who think of nothing,
write of nothing, desire nothing but the Honour, and Praise,
and Adoration that is due to Thee, and who call all the
world to the maxims of the Gospel, the Holiness and
Perfection of the Life of Christ. But in the regions where
Light is sprung up, whence Superstition is fled, where all
that is outward in Religion seems to be pruned, dressed
and put in its true order, there a cleansed shell, a whited
sepulchre, seems too generally to cover a dead Christianity.'[1]

No one can read this splendid passage without seeing
that Law's admiration of many Romanists was in spite of,
not in consequence of their Romanism. The errors of
Rome he thoroughly abjured, her persecuting spirit he

---

[1] *An Appeal to all that Doubt, &c.,* 'Works,' vol. vi. p. 282.

thoroughly abhorred. 'The error of all errors,' he writes, 'and that which makes the blackest charge against the Romish Church, is *Persecution*, a religious sword drawn against the liberty and freedom of serving God according to our best light, that is against our "worshipping the Father in spirit and in truth": This is the great Whore, the Beast, the Dragon, the Antichrist.' But he adds: 'Though this is the frightful monster of that Church, yet even here, who, except it be the Church of England, can throw the first stone at her? Where must we look for a Church that has so renounced this persecuting Beast, as they who have renounced the use of Incense, the sprinklings of Holy Water, or the Extreme Unction of dying persons? What part of the Reformation abroad has not practised and defended persecution? What sect of Dissenters at home has not, in their day of power dreadfully condemned Toleration?'[1] Certain practices of the Church of Rome—e.g. the celibacy of her clergy, her recommendation of the state of virginity, her comparative freedom from State control —Law also approved of, but, in spite of all this, he was no Romanist.

[1] *An Appeal to all that Doubt, &c.*, 'Works,' vol. vi. p. 284.

CHAPTER X.

ON MYSTICISM AND MYSTICS.

A VAST interval in point of thought separates those writings of Law which we have been hitherto considering from those which subsequently came from his pen. The 'Case of Reason,' and 'Letters to a Lady inclined to enter the Church of Rome,' were written between 1731 and 1733; his next work was not published until 1737. Almost immediately after the former date he became acquainted with the writings of Jacob Behmen ; and before the latter date he had virtually embraced, though not yet, perhaps, in all their fulness, those views which made him known as emphatically ' *The* English mystic.' The occasion, causes, and results of this transformation in Law's mind will be noticed presently. Before doing so, it seems necessary to say a few words on the subject of mysticism generally.

And, first of all, let us not be frightened by the name. The term ' mysticism ' implies something vague, obscure, impalpable, something, in short, which English people, of all people, from their natural love of clearness, specially abhor. Whether its original reference be to the initiation of the privileged into that which is veiled from common eyes, or whether it refer, as the literal derivation of the word seems to imply, to the closing of the avenues of the senses, that the mind may be susceptible of supra-sensuous impressions, or whether we adopt any other of the numerous definitions of the word,[1] the name 'mysticism' certainly has to many an evil sound. But we must not be misled by a name. We must remember at the outset that the appellation of 'mystic' was not chosen by the mystics themselves. They called themselves the 'spiritual,' or the 'illuminated,' if they called themselves by any special name at all, which they rarely did. But they seldom, as a rule, called themselves mystics. *That* is simply a term of reproach applied to them by their enemies, and applied most loosely and indeterminately to men who held the utmost variety of opinions. In order, therefore, to do common justice to the heterogeneous mass of writers who are lumped together under the opprobrious appellation of 'mystics,' we must divest ourselves of all sinister associations connected with the name, and strive to look at them as they really were.

Again, we must beware of taking exaggerated forms of mysticism as its normal type. No form of thought that ever existed in the world could bear to be judged by such a test ; and as mysticism is specially liable to exaggeration, it would be specially unfair to mystics to judge them by such a standard.

---

[1] It has been defined or described in the following ways :

'Theologica mystica est sapientia experimentalis, Dei affectione divinitùs infusa, quæ mentem ab omni inordinatione puram, per actus supernaturales fidei, spei, et charitatis cum Deo intime conjungit.' . . . 'Mystica theologia, si vim nominis attendas, designat quamdam sacram et arcanam de Deo divinisque rebus notitiam.' [He then explains the well-known classical usage of the term μυστήριον.]—Isagoge Balthasaris Corderii Soc. Jesu Theologi ad Mysticam Theologiam S. Dionysii Areopagitæ.

'La mystique est la science de l'état surnaturel de l'âme humaine manifesté dans le corps et dans l'ordre des choses visibles par des effets également surnaturels.' Dictionnaire de Mystique Chrétienne, par l'Abbé Migne.

'Le mysticisme consiste à substituer l'illumination directe à la révélation indirecte, l'exstase à la raison, l'éblouissement à la philosophie.'—Victor Cousin, 'Religion, Mysticism, Stoicism.'

'Mystische Theologie entstand, als die Menschen von Gott abgefallen waren, und sich Wiedervereinigung mit ihm sehnten.'—J. L. Ewald, 'Briefe über die alte Mystik und den neuen Mysticismus,' p. 20.

And, once more, we must beware of confounding the accidents with the essence of mysticism. For not only is mysticism peculiarly liable to be pushed to extremes, it is also apt to gather around it a number of accretions which are really no part of itself. We must in this connexion beware of the old 'post hoc ergo propter hoc' fallacy. Many mystics have advanced from mysticism pure and simple to build up wild theories for which mysticism has no right to bear the blame.

Bearing these cautions in mind, let us now examine what this much-abused system really is.

'The Divine Word (Logos) is instilled into all men. In all something Godlike has been breathed. You bear the image of God.' This is the *starting-point*, one might almost say the postulate, of all mysticism.

The complete union of the soul with God—this is the *goal* of all mysticism ; and the Christian mystic would add, through a mediator, Jesus Christ.

The means by which this union is to be effected are faith and love, which to the mystic are hardly distinguishable, even in thought, and are quite inseparable, in fact, for love implies faith, and faith can only work by love.

As, according to this view, the soul is in itself a part of the Divine Nature, the mystic must seek this union by looking, not without, but within. God is within him, and he is only separated from God when he turns away from his own inner Divine nature. Not that the true mystic— at any rate the true mystic of later days - despised the world without ; that, too, spoke to him of God ; but the true sanctuary of the Deity was within his own soul ; his gaze therefore must be introverted if he would find true union with God.

In seeking this union with God, all thoughts of self must be entirely abandoned ; he must be content, yea, happy, to sink into his own nothingness and see and know nothing but God ; this is true humility, the cardinal virtue of Christian mysticism.   Hence it follows that the love by which this union with God is to be brought about must be totally free from any thoughts of his own happiness ; it must be pure and disinterested, without regard either to reward or punishment ; in a word, it must be simply love.

The more this union with God is effected, the more the mystic learns to see God in all things, and all things in God. Hence this outer world and all that is in it, from the noblest work of creation down to the smallest insect or the commonest weed that grows in the field, is to the mystic a copy of the Deity ; everything visible is a type of the invisible, all outer matter a symbol of the inner ; and that not by any fanciful analogy, but in actual reality.

But to enter into all this there is need of a religious sense—not reason, not conscience, but something higher than either.   This religious sense must be felt to be understood.   To attempt to explain what it is to one who is destitute of it, would be like trying to point out the sunrise on the sea to a blind man, or to teach one who is born deaf and dumb to enjoy sweet music.

How is this religious sense to be acquired ? A man must enter into the holy place of his own heart, and he will find it there.   Then he will gain a new birth, not in any figurative, but in the most literal sense of the term.

It must not, however, be supposed that, because he lays so much stress upon the Inner Light and the Inner Life, the true mystic depreciates the outward Written Word. On the contrary, the ' spiritual writers ' (as Law generally calls them) brought out a depth of meaning from that Word which has never been so well brought out by others. In fact, to many well-read men, the very word ' mysticism ' chiefly conveys the notion of a mode of interpreting Holy

Scripture which is rightly called 'the mystical interpretation': that is, the development of a latent, figurative sense
over and above the literal sense, which shows, as S. Augustine says, that 'in the Old Testament the New was fore-
shadowed, and the New was nothing else than the revealing
of the Old.' It was in this sense chiefly that the early
Fathers of the Church were mystics, though many of them
were also mystics in the other sense as well. Indeed, the
two phases of mysticism are very closely connected together,
for the same tone of mind which would attract a Christian
to the one, would also, as a rule (Law was an exception on
this point), attract him to the other. He who loved to
trace a latent spiritual meaning throughout the Book of
Nature would also love to trace a latent spiritual meaning
in the Written Book of Revelation.[1]

At the same time, the true mystic would be the very
last man in the world to allow the mystical meaning of
Holy Scripture to take the place of the literal or historical
sense. On the contrary, the very stronghold of mysticism
is the extreme literalness of its interpretations of Scripture.
The mystic contends that he has chapter and verse for
every one of his fundamental tenets, and that it is not he
but his opponents who have to explain away the plain
letter of Scripture. He would ask, for example, how could
language express more unmistakably that 'the Divine
Word is instilled into all men,' than the text : ' That is the
True Light which lighteth every man that cometh into the
world ' (John i. 9) ; or, that the union of·the soul with
God is to be the Christian aim, than the prayer of our
Lord, in John xvii. ; or, that this union is to be effected

---

[1] For modern specimens of this form of mysticism, see the *Mystical Sermons* of that good man, the late Rev. W. R. Wroth, of S. Philip's, Clerken-
well, edited by the Rev. J. E. Vaux ; also Dr. Littledale's *Commentary on
the Song of Songs*; Dr. Neale *On the Psalms*, etc.

through love, than 'He that dwelleth in love dwelleth in God, and God in him' (1 John iv. 16); or, that this love must be disinterested, than 'Love seeketh not her own' (1 Cor. xiii. 5); or, that the Christian must look within if he would find God, than 'The kingdom of God is within you' (Luke xvii. 21); or, that the outer world is in all its parts a type of the unseen world, than 'The invisible things of Him from the creation of the world are clearly seen, being understood by the things that are made' (Rom. i. 20), and, in fact, almost every parable of Christ?

Having thus seen what mysticism is, a brief sketch of a few of the principal mystic writers may help us the better to understand Law's position. We shall be travelling over ground which he travelled over before us, for 'of these mystical divines,' he writes, 'I thank God I have been a diligent reader through all ages of the Church; from the apostolical Dionysius the Areopagite down to the great Fénélon, Archbishop of Cambray, the illuminated Guion, and M. Bertot.'[1] Of course such a sketch must necessarily be very imperfect and superficial, and strictly limited to what bears upon the subject of this biography, otherwise it would quickly swell into a bulky volume instead of a single chapter.

In one sense, mysticism is as old as mankind. There is a mystic element in every man's nature. For who has not sometimes felt a tendency to turn from the world that is without him and is no part of him, to the world which is within and which is the very centre of his life? Who has not sometimes thought that there is something in this outer world more than meets the eye, something that is but a type of the invisible? So far as a man follows these tendencies, so far he is a mystic. The Christian mystic

---

[1] *Some Animadversions upon Doctor Trap's 'Reply.'* Law's 'Works,' vol. vi. p. 319.

would certainly assert that he owed his mysticism to no human teacher, but that he was taught by none other than by God Himself; by God speaking both internally to his soul, and externally through the Holy Scriptures.

The points of resemblance between Christian mysticism and Platonism, and even older philosophies, need not here be discussed ; for, whether they were as striking as they have been affirmed to be or not, they are never referred to by William Law, and do not, therefore, come within our purview. For the same reason, it is unnecessary to dwell upon the mysticism of the later Platonists at Alexandria. In fact, the first mystics who attract our attention in connexion with William Law are those whom he terms the ‘ Fathers of the Desert.' Among these the most famous were the two hermits Macarius, who, in the enthusiastic language of the editor of one of them, ‘ shone like two lights of Heaven in those deserted places.' Macarius Ægyptius was read and admired greatly by William Law. The fragments of his letters which have come down to us are full of the most pronounced mysticism.[1]

In speaking of the Fathers of the Desert as the earliest mystic Christians who attracted William Law, it is assumed that the Epistles of the so-called Dionysius the Areopagite are spurious. If, as many of the mystic writers, William Law among the number, believed, these writings were really the product of S. Paul's convert at Athens, he must of course be regarded as the founder of Christian mysticism. It is, however, now pretty generally agreed that the works belong to a later date. Still the writer, whoever he may have been, cannot have lived later than the sixth century.

---

[1] See ‘ Macarii Ægyptii Epistolæ,' ed. Floss. (1850) *passim.* In one of the epistles (p. 234) occurs this fine sentence, 'Ο θρόνος τῆς θειότητος ὁ νοῦς ἐστιν ἡμῶν. Among Law's books are *Les Vies des Saints Pères des Déserts* and the *Spiritual Homilies of S. Macarius Ægyptius.*

His writings were deeply valued both in early and mediæval times; and, if they are now less thought of, it cannot be denied that, through them, a nobler and more spiritual element was introduced into the arid region of Aristotelian scholasticism.[1] They contain all the crucial points of mysticism, and one can well understand that they would be deeply appreciated by Law, and his ' wish might be father to the thought' that their author derived his instruction directly from the mouth of an apostle.

In the eleventh and twelfth centuries mysticism flourished greatly, especially in France. The two great abbots of S. Victor, Hugo and his pupil and successor, Richard, and the still greater abbot of Clairvaux, Bernard, ' the last of the Fathers,' were the most remarkable among a host of mystics belonging to this period, and their names alone were sufficient to shed a lustre upon any cause. It is somewhat remarkable that Law makes few if any allusions to mystics of this date. One would have thought that S. Bernard in especial would have been a mystic after his own heart. No doubt this great and good man was a mystic of a very moderate and sober type. Many of the characteristic features of mysticism are not found in his writings; but on many points—such, for instance, as the mystic ecstasy, the abstraction from earthly things, the application of terms of human love to the relation between

---

[1] ' La traduction des ouvrages de St. Denis l'Aréopagite par Scot Érigène marque la date précise de l'introduction du mysticisme dans la philosophie scolastique.'—*De la Controverse de Bossuet et de Fénelon sur le Quiétisme*, L. A. Bonnel, Introd. See also Enfield (ii. 314), who was thoroughly in accord with the spirit of the eighteenth century in strongly condemning Dionysius. ' It was the translation of this book [of Dionysius] which revived the knowledge of Alexandrian Platonism in the West, and laid the foundation of the mystical system of theology which afterwards so generally prevailed. Thus philosophical enthusiasm, born in the East, nourished by Plato, educated in Alexandria, matured in Asia, and adopted into the Greek Church, found its way, under the pretext and authority of an apostolic name, into the Western Church, and there produced innumerable mischiefs.'

Christ and the Christian—he expresses himself as strongly as the most advanced mystics ; and, more perhaps than any of his predecessors, he brought into prominence that very side of mysticism which was most fascinating to William Law—the discovery of a mystical meaning in all outward nature as the shadow and emblem of the things invisible.[1]

Passing over the mystics of the thirteenth century, of whom Bonaventura was the most remarkable,[2] we next come to a group of mystic writers who attracted and influenced Law more than any others, with the single exception of Jacob Behmen. These were the mystics, mostly German, of the fourteenth century.

The chief representatives of this form of mysticism were Eckart, commonly called ' Master Eckart,' of Cologne, John Tauler, a Dominican friar of Strasbourg, Henry Suso, also of Strasbourg, Ruysbroch, an Augustinian friar and prior of Grünthal in Brabant, and a little later, Henry Harphius. They were all mystics of a singularly robust and manly type, and this characteristic, among others, probably tended to attract Law to their writings. The tenderness which constitutes one of the chief charms of mysticism is apt to degenerate into effeminacy and sickly sentimentality. Law's natural infirmities lay all the other way : he described himself rightly when he said that his ' strings were hard,' though they were considerably softened by his mysticism. But, whatever William Law was, he was always a thorough man ; and anything approaching to mawkishness was particularly distasteful to him. Now there was nothing of this kind about these fourteenth century

---

[1] See *inter alia*, Morison's *Life of S. Bernard*, p. 22.

[2] It does not appear that this phase of mysticism had any special connexion with William Law, though *Bonaventuræ Speculum Disciplinæ* is one of the books in his library.

mystics. Whatever they wrote was hardy and masculine. It would have been well if they had been equally free from wildness and extravagance. But in this respect they were certainly offenders, especially Eckart their chief, who appears at times to lose all self-control, and utters sentiments about the inward freedom of the spirit, and the virtual abolition of the distinction between the creature and the Creator, which were not only liable to grievous perversion by those who sought an occasion for sin, but which actually were so perverted by the Beghards, or Brethren of the Free Spirit, who found, or professed to find, in them a justification of the grossest and most barefaced Antinomianism. Law does not often allude to Eckart, and he certainly would have strongly disapproved of his extravagances, which touched on the very verge of Pantheism. But I think there is very little doubt that he was well acquainted with his writings. This is shown, among other ways, by one of Byrom's mystic poems, which were nothing else than Law in verse. One of the prettiest of these odd compositions is entitled ' The Soul's Tendency towards its True Centre,' and commences :

> Stones towards the earth descend ;
> Rivers to the ocean roll ;
> Every motion has some end ;
> What is thine, beloved soul ?
> Mine is where my Saviour is :
> There with him I hope to dwell ;
> Jesu is the central bliss ;
> Love the force that doth impel.

And so forth. Now, nearly four hundred years earlier, Eckart had written : ' Consciously or unconsciously all creatures seek their proper state. The stone cannot cease moving till it touch the earth, the fire rises up to heaven : thus a loving soul can never rest but in God ; and so we say that God has given to all things their proper place :

to the fish the water, to the bird the air, to the beast the earth, to the soul the Godhead.'[1]   If Byrom versified Law, had not Law read Eckart?

In the above quotation from Eckart there is nothing extravagant or liable to abuse. 'O si sic omnia!' But what will be said of the following?—'When the will is so united that it becometh a one in oneness, then doth the Heavenly Father produce his only begotten Son in Himself and in me. Wherefore in Himself and me? I am one with Him. He cannot exclude me. In the selfsame operation doth the Holy Ghost receive His existence and proceed from me as from God. Wherefore? I am in God, and if the Holy Ghost deriveth not His being from me, He deriveth it not from God. I am in no wise excluded.'[2] Ruysbroch—the 'divine Rusbrochius,' as Law termed him —sometimes expressed himself hardly less wildly. 'Our created,' he writes, 'is absorbed in our uncreated life, and we are, as it were, transformed into God. Lost in the abyss of an eternal blessedness, we perceive no distinction between ourselves and God.' One can hardly call this by a milder name than blasphemy; and my apology for venturing even to quote it is, that I desire to be perfectly fair; and if this chapter is intended to bring out the good points of mysticism, it seems due to those who strongly objected to the system generally, and to Law's exposition of it in particular, to admit that the objectors had some

---

[1] Cf. S. Augustine's famous remark at the very beginning of his Confessions :' 'Thou madest us for Thyself, and our heart is restless until it repose in Thee.'

[2] It is only fair to Eckart, however, to add, that in other passages he expressly denies that the union with God makes us part of God. He writes: 'Wir haben zwar alle, über unser erschaffenes Wesen auch ein ewiges Leben in Gott, als in unserer lebhaften Ursache, der uns aus dem Nichts geschaffen hat. *Aber doch sind wir nicht Gott selbst.*' He is very highly praised by Chevalier Bunsen, who calls 'Meister Eckart, the Dominican, the Socrates of the Rhenish School.' See *Letter from Chevalier Bunsen*, prefixed to the translation of 'Theologia Germanica,' by S. Winkworth.

grounds for their objections, so far as the more extreme exponents of mysticism were concerned. It seemed also necessary, in illustration of our subject, to show into what perilous quicksands Law was in danger of running when he embarked on his mystic voyage.

It was not, however, Eckart or Ruysbroch whom Law studied and valued most among these fourteenth century mystics.[1] It was a man of a far more sober type—John Tauler—who in fact did his very best to check, and prevent the ill effects of, the extravagances both of his master Eckart and his friend Ruysbroch. Tauler, indeed, sometimes soars to heights where it is somewhat difficult for an ordinary mortal to follow him ; but on such occasions he generally adds a caution which shows that he felt the danger of such speculations to some minds. Take, as an example, the following passage from his sermon on ' Whose is this image and superscription ? '—' He that would be truly united to God must dedicate the penny of his soul, with all its faculties, to God alone, and join it unto Him. For if the highest and most glorious unity, which is God Himself, is to be united to the soul, it must be through oneness. Now when the soul hath utterly forsaken itself, and all creatures, and made itself free from all manifoldness, then the sole Unity, which is God, answers truly to the Oneness of the soul, for there is nothing in the soul besides God.' But thinking, probably, that if he went on much further in this strain there was danger lest some of his hearers should become what has been rather flippantly termed ' God-intoxicated,' he adds : ' But there are some who will fly before they have wings, and pluck the apples before they are ripe, and at the very outset of the Divine life be so

---

[1] Among Law's books, however, are *Rusbrochii Opera Omnia*, underlined and evidently much read. Tauler appears in Law's library both in a Latin and a German dress.

puffed up that it contents them not to enter in at the door and contemplate Christ's humanity, but they will apprehend His highness and incomprehensible Deity only. . . . Beware of such perilous presumption. Your safe course is, to perfect yourselves first in following the lowly life of Christ, and in earnest study of the shameful cross.' As Tauler unquestionably exercised a very deep and lasting influence upon William Law, it may be well to quote one or two more specimens, which will show us what sort of a man he was. In the following passage we have another instance of this double tendency, noted above, of rapture checked by practical good sense. ' The ground,' writes Tauler, ' or centre of the soul, is so high and glorious a thing that it cannot properly be named, even as no adequate name can be found for the Infinite and Almighty God. In this ground lies the image of the Holy Trinity. . . . God pours Himself out into our spirit as the sun rays forth its natural light into the air and fills it with sunshine, so that no eye can tell the difference between the sunshine and the air ; how far less this Divine union of the created and the uncreated spirit. Our spirit is received and utterly swallowed up in the abyss which is its source. Then the spirit transcends itself and all its powers, and mounts higher and higher towards the Divine Dark. Yet let no man in his littleness and nothingness think of himself to approach that surpassing darkness ; rather let him draw nigh to the darkness of his ignorance of God, let him simply yield himself to God, ask nothing, desire nothing, love and mean only God, yea, and such an unknown God ! . . . . Moreover, if a man, while busy in this lofty, inward work, were called by some duty in the providence of God to cease therefrom and cook a broth for some sick person, or any other such service, he should do so willingly and with great joy.' In the same practical spirit Tauler set himself against the extravagances of asceticism. 'There are some who thoughtlessly maim and torture their miserable flesh, and yet leave untouched the inclinations which are the root of evil in their hearts. Ah, my friend, what hath thy poor body done to thee that thou shouldst so torment it? Oh, folly! mortify and slay thy sins, not thine own flesh and blood.' When we remember that the sermons from which the above extracts are quoted were written chiefly in the first half of the fourteenth century, we shall appreciate what remarkable productions they were for so early a date. Hallam calls Tauler 'the first German writer in prose.'[1] Heinsius says that 'Tauler, in his German sermons, mingled many expressions invented by himself, which were the first attempt at a philosophical language, and displayed surprising eloquence for the age in which he lived. It may be justly said of him that he first gave to prose that direction in which Luther afterwards advanced so far.'[2] Luther himself deeply valued Tauler, and said 'he was a teacher such as had been none since the time of the apostles.'[3]

But it was the character of Tauler, even more than his writings, which helped to recommend the doctrines he taught. At a time of deep depression, when his countrymen were ready to sink into despair, Tauler stood forth as their undaunted champion against the formidable combination of temporal and spiritual weapons wielded by the King of France and the Pope.[4] When Strasbourg was visited by a deadly pestilence, it was Tauler who sustained

---

[1] *Literature of Europe*, i. 48. In another passage of the same work (ii. 378) the writer says: 'Tauler's sermons in the native language (German) are supposed to have been translated from Latin.'
[2] Heinsius, iv. 76, quoted by Hallam.   [3] See Ewald, p. 35.
[4] For an interesting account of the state of Germany in Tauler's time, see Miss Winkworth's *Introduction* to the translation of 'Theologia Germanica,' p. xxxiii. All the 'Friends of God' (Gottes Freunde) were more or less mystics.

the spirits of the survivors, and taught them to find in religion the support they sorely needed.[1] On the whole, Tauler was perhaps as exemplary a specimen of the Christian mystic as one can find in any age, and thoroughly deserved the high esteem in which he was held by William Law.

His reputation is all the more remarkable when we remember that the account of him has come down to us mainly through sources which were greatly prejudiced against him. Not only did he at Cologne oppose the pantheistic notion of the Beghards, not only did he fearlessly attack the vices and follies of his fellow-monks, but he set himself, so far as politics were concerned, against the whole hierarchy of Rome. He never separated, or wished to separate, himself from the Roman obedience ; but he was always a patriot first, a Romanist afterwards. And, in point of fact, though perhaps unintentionally, he was, in his doctrine, as well as in his conduct, a precursor of Luther. Indeed, all these mystics of the fourteenth century, and Tauler more than all, tended to pave the way for the Reformation. And therefore Romish writers speak of them with grave suspicion, and while admitting their merits, warn their readers against the tendency of their teaching.[2]

Belonging to this same group, though somewhat later in date, is a little anonymous work entitled '_Theologia Germanica._' It contains a sort of summary of mystical

---

[1] See *inter alia*, Winkworth, p. xlv., and Vaughan's *Hours with the Mystics.*

[2] 'Maître Eckart fut en rapport avec les Beghards, Taulère fut un des plus ardents propaga eurs de l'association des *Amis de Dieu*, dont quelques-uns se séparèrent plus tard ouvertement de l'église, sous le nom de *Vaudois.* Ces mystiques exaltés et hardis de la Germanie du xive siècle justifièrent, par l'influence diverse qu'eurent leurs écrits, et l'indulgence avec laquelle on les traita, et la défiance qu'ils avaient excitée.' (Bonnel : *De la Controverse de Bossuet et de Fénelon sur le Quiétisme.* Introd. xiii.) See also Ullmann's *Reformatoren vor der Reformation.*

theology, expressed in pointed and pithy language, and deeply affected many minds of various casts. William Law valued it very highly, and recommended it to the more advanced among his disciples, as appears from his second letter to John Wesley in 1738. Referring to some depreciation of the 'Theologia Germanica' which Wesley made in his reply to Law's first answer to him, Law writes : ' If you remember the " Theologia Germanica " so imperfectly as only to remember something of Christ our Pattern, but nothing express of Christ our Atonement, it is no wonder that you can remember so little of my conversations with you. I put that author into your hands not because he is fit for the first learners of the rudiments of Christianity, who are to be prepared for baptism, but because you were a *clergyman*, that had made profession of divinity, had read, as you said, with much approbation and benefit the two practical discourses ['Christian Perfection' and the 'Serious Call'], and many other good books ; and because you seemed to me to be of a very inquisitive nature, and much inclined to meditation : in this view, nothing could be more reasonable for you than that book, which most deeply, excellently, and fully contains the whole system of Christian faith and practice, and is an excellent guide against all mistakes, both in faith and works. What that book has not taught you, I am content that you should not have learnt from me.'

Other minds of a very different tone from Law's were equally fascinated with the work. Luther published an edition of it,[1] and wrote in his Preface, 'This precious little book, poor and unadorned as it is in words of human wisdom, is so much the more costly and rich in Divine wisdom. As to myself, next to the Bible and S. Augustine,

[1] Indeed, according to its English translator, 'he *discovered* the work and first brought it into notice in his edition of 1512.'

not one book has been published from which I have learned more of what God, Christ, man, and all things are. I thank God that I can thus seek and find my God in the German tongue, as I have hitherto not been able to find him, either in the Greek, Latin, or Hebrew tongues. God grant that this little book may become better known ; so shall we find that the " German Theology " is without doubt the best theology.[1] Arndt, a sort of reviver of Luther's work in the succeeding century, published a new edition and spoke most highly of it.[2] Spener, a reviver of Arndt's work in the later part of the century, and the founder of the school of Halle pietists, says of it : ' It must be profitable, that this simple little book, the " German Theology," as well as the writings of Tauler, from both of which equally, next to the Scriptures, our dear Luther became what he was, should be more placed into the hands of students, and its use recommended to them.'[3] Henry More, the famous Cambridge Platonist, speaks of it as ' that golden little book which first so pierced and affected me.' In later times Charles Kingsley admired it greatly, and wrote a preface to a new edition of it ;[4] and Ewald devotes more than twenty pages to this little work in his small volume on Mysticism.[5] The Chevalier Bunsen placed it next to the Bible.

A somewhat kindred treatise to the ' Theologica Germanica,' but far better known, is the famous ' De Imitatione

---

[1] Luther cannot be called a mystic, yet in many respects he agreed with the mystics. He was a professed enemy of the conventional Aristotle and the dogmas of the scholastic philosophy ; he had some leaning towards Platonism, and was a deep admirer of Augustine ; his regard for Tauler and the ' Theologia Germanica ' appears from the text.

[2] See *A Short Defence of the Mystical Writers*, &c., appended to ' Paradise Restored,' &c., by T. Hartley, Rector of Winwick.

[3] See Ewald, p. 201.

[4] See *Life of Kingsley*, i. 426 ; and Miss Winkworth's translation of *Theologia Germanica*. Seventeen editions of the work appeared during Luther's lifetime. [5] Ewald, pp. 200–222.

Christi.' But the two works have not altogether the same scope. The 'German Theology' is a mystic treatise, and nothing else ; the author of the ' Imitation of Christ ' was an ascetic at least as much as a mystic.[1] None but those who have a tendency to mysticism would care about reading the former ; but the latter has found readers and admirers among all classes, mystic and non-mystic, Romanist and Protestant. The former certainly helped to prepare the way for the Reformation. The latter, though it dwells largely upon the interior life, still devotes a fair share of its pages to the advocacy of doctrines and practices which were decidedly opposed to those of the Reformers. The ' Imitatio Christi,' however, may be regarded as a mystic treatise, inasmuch as most of the essential features of mysticism are found in it. The duty and blessedness of turning from the outer to the inner life,[2] the entire abnegation of self,[3] the doctrine of the cross expressed after the mystic fashion,[4] the Christian's pure and disinterested love to God,[5] rest in God as the highest blessing,[6] the union of the soul with God,[7] the blessedness of silent

[1] It is needless to enter into the vexed question of the authorship of the *De Imitatione.* Law evidently assumed it to be the work of à Kempis. Those who desire to see the claims of à Kempis fully stated may be referred to Mr. Kettlewell's interesting work on *The Authorship of ' De Imitatione Christi.'*

[2] ' Learn to despise exterior things, and give thyself to the interior, and thou shalt see the kingdom of God will come into thee.' (Book II. c. i.) ' Happy ears, indeed, which hearken to truth itself teaching within, and not to the voice which soundeth without. Happy eyes which are shut to outward things and attentive to the interior.' (Book III. c. i.)

[3] ' One thing is chiefly necessary for him, and what is that ? That having left all things else, he leave also himself and wholly go out of himself,' &c. (Book II. c. xi.)

[4] See the whole chapter ' Of the King's Highway of the Holy Cross.' (Book II. c. xii.)

[5] See Book III. chap. vi. (the whole): ' Of the Proof a True Lover.'

[6] See Book III. chap. xxi : ' That we are to rest in God above all goods and gifts.'

[7] ' Join me to Thyself by an inseparable bond of love,' &c. (Book III. c. xxiii. § 10). ' Ah ! Lord God, when shall I be wholly united to Thee, and absorpt in Thee,' &c. (Book IV. c. xiii.)

waiting,[1] the mystic ecstasy,[2]—on all these crucial points
the treatise is express ; and thus, while the work was valued
by Law before his mystic days, it would be certainly all
the more valued by him after he became a mystic.'[3]

It would transcend the limits of this work to dwell upon
the distinctively Romish mystics. The monastic system
was favourable to the development of mysticism ; hence it
flourished, especially in the fifteenth and sixteenth centuries,
in those countries which were most devoted to the Roman
See—in Italy, in Spain, and in France. It was encouraged
in the fifteenth century by the revival of Platonism by
Ficinus, Picus, and others under the patronage of the
Medici. Some mystics, like S. Theresa, were visionaries as
well ; as such, they would find no favour with William
Law, but as mystics he read and admired them heartily,
as we have already seen. The Church of Rome utilised
these mystics to her own purpose. It may seem at first
sight as if she was not so wise in her generation in the
seventeenth century as she had shown herself at an earlier
date ; her treatment of Fénélon, Molinos, Madame Guyon,
Père Lacombe, Falconi, and Malaval, was apparently based
on a very different principle from that on which she treated
S. Theresa, S. Francis de Sales, and S. John of the Cross.
But the contrast is only an apparent, not a real, one. In
point of fact, she showed the same keen perception of her

---

[1] 'If thou walkest *interiorly*, thou wilt make small account of flying words.
It is no small prudence to be silent in the evil time, and to turn within,' &c.
(Book III. c. xxviii.)

[2] 'Cleanse, cherish, enlighten, and enliven my spirit, that it may be
absorbed in Thee with ecstacies of joy' (Book III. c. xxxiv.)

[3] Dean Milman regards the author of the 'Imitation' as a mystic of the
mystics. 'In one remarkable book was gathered and concentrated all that
was elevating, passionate, profoundly pious in all the older mystics. Ger-
son, Ruysbroch, Tauler, all who addressed the heart in later times, were
summed up and brought into one circle of light and heat in the single small
volume, the "Imitation of Christ."'—*Hist. of Latin Christianity*, vol. ix.
p. 161, &c.

own interests when she suffered Molinos to die in the prisons of the Inquisition, when she condemned Fénelon's ' Maxims of the Saints' to the Index, and forced him to retract his sentiments ; when she drove Madame Guyon from pillar to post ; when she imprisoned Père Lacombe, as she did when she canonised the earlier mystics. For, while it was easy for her to turn to account the visions of a Theresa, the raptures of a Francis, and the almost morbid craving for suffering of a John of the Cross, it was not easy for a Church which lays great stress on externals, and whose whole system is objective, to utilise the intensely subjective speculations of the Quietists. The prayer or silence, the passive state, the almost exclusive recommendation of the introverted gaze,— these doctrines were very liable to prove antagonistic to the whole Romish system. Besides, there was a most suspicious resemblance between the French and Italian mystics of the seventeenth century and the German mystics of the fourteenth,[1] who had contributed so largely to the undermining of the power of Rome, and to preparing the way for the Reformation. One need not therefore be surprised to find the Church of Rome setting her face against this new phase of mysticism ; but it certainly is strange that she should have selected so apparently harmless a doctrine as that of ' pure and disinterested love' for the chief point of her attack. ' Harmless,' indeed, is too negative an epithet to apply to the doctrine. For surely, in point of fact, purity and disinterestedness are of the very essence of love. A love which is not disinterested is not love. A mother who loved her child only for the pleasure or advantage she derived from it, would not love it with a mother's love. A

---

[1] ' Ces mystiques exaltés et hardis de la Germanie du xiv⁵ siècle . . . . sont les ancêtres directes de nos Quiétistes du xviiᵉ siècle.'—*De la Contro-verse de Bossuet et de Fénelon sur le Quiétisme.* L. A. Bonnel, Introduction, xiii.

novel which represented its hero as loving his mistress only for the sake of her fortune would be universally condemned for holding up to admiration so mercenary a lover. And ought the love which the Christian bears to his God to be of a baser and more selfish character than that poor, faint shadow of love between creature and creature?

William Law would, of course, have answered this question in the negative. In the famous controversy between Bossuet and Fénelon he was decidedly on the side of Fénelon—'the great Fénelon,' as he terms him. He does not, so far as I am aware, refer to the subject anywhere in his writings, but we learn his opinion upon it from our old informant, Dr. Byrom. In the last interview between the two friends in Somerset Gardens in 1739, 'I asked,' writes the Doctor, 'why Mr. Poiret was so angry at Father Malebranche; he said that Father had writ against the pure love; I said that the doctrine appeared to me to be true, for must it be impure? He seemed to be quite for it, that interest and love were different things.'[1] When we remember that Law said this at a time when he was generally disposed to snub rather than to agree with his friend, and that he said it in opposition to one who was so prime a favourite with him as Father Malebranche, we may consider it as conclusive on the matter of his sentiments; but, if further evidence be needed, I may quote a little poem of Dr. Byrom, who, on such a subject, of all subjects, would certainly not have dared to write what his mentor would not have approved of. It is 'On the Disinterested Love of God,' and commences —

> The love of God with genuine ray
> Inflam'd the breast of good Cambray;
> And banish'd from the prelate's mind
> All thoughts of interested kind ;

He saw, and writers of his class
(Of too neglected worth, alas!),
Disinterested love to be
The Gospel's very A B C,' [1]

&c. &c. Law himself, however, very rarely mentions any of this group of mystics. There is, indeed, frequent allusion to Madame Guyon in the earlier interviews between Law and Byrom ; but the subject was obviously introduced by Byrom, who was attracted to her by her resemblance to his favourite, Madame Bourignon. Law's remarks on both ladies are by no means complimentary. To that most lovable of men and fascinating of writers, Archbishop Fénelon, Law hardly ever refers.[2]

And yet one would have thought that both Fénelon's and Madame Guyon's writings would have been full of attraction to anyone who sympathised with mysticism. They both expressed in very touching and beautiful language just those sentiments which Law echoed in all his later works. Are not, for example, such passages as the following, from Fénelon's 'Maxims of the Saints,' the very counterpart of what may be found over and over again in Law ?—' Those who love God only out of regard to happiness, love Him just as a miser loves his gold, a voluptuous man his pleasures. Such love, if it be called love, is un-worthy of God. Pure love is not inconsistent with mixed love, but is mixed love carried to its true result. When this result is attained, the motive of God's glory so expands itself and fills the mind, that the other motive, our own happiness, becomes so small, and so recedes from our in-ward notice as to be practically annihilated. It is then

---

[1] See Byrom's *Poems*, in ' Chalmers' Edition of the English Poets from Chaucer to Cowper, in 21 vols.' Vol. XV.

[2] But in Law's library there are three copies of the Life of Fénelon, with many passages marked, and also many of Fénelon's works.

that God becomes what He ever ought to be, the Centre of
the soul, to which all its affections tend ; the great moral
Sun of the soul, from which all its light and warmth proceed. We lay ourselves at His feet. Self is known no
more, not because it is wrong to regard and desire our
own good, but because the object of desire is withdrawn
from our notice. When the sun shines, the stars disappear.
When God is in the soul, who can think of himself? So
that we love God and God alone, and all other things in
and for God.' And what could be more in accordance with
Law's later teaching than Madame Guyon's account of her
own conversion to the spiritual, interior life ? After having
striven in vain to find comfort, amid uncongenial surroundings, in religious exercises, she consulted ' a holy Franciscan,'
and was told by him : ' Your efforts have been unsuccessful,
madam, because you have sought without what you can
only find within. Accustom yourself to seek God in your
heart and you will not fail to find Him.' ' These words,'
she says, ' were to me like the stroke of a dart which
pierced my heart asunder. Oh my Lord ! Thou wast in
my heart, and demanded only the turning of my mind inward, to make me feel Thy presence. Oh, Infinite Goodness ! Thou wast so near, and I ran hither and thither seeking Thee, and yet found Thee not ! My life was a burden
to me, and my happiness was within myself. I was poor
in the midst of riches, and ready to perish with hunger near
a table plentifully spread with a continual feast.'[1] Her
husband allowed her a stated time for prayer; but ' I often,'
she writes, ' exceeded my half-hour, and then he was angry,
and I was sad. . . . In time I understood. When months
and years had passed away, God erected His temple fully

---

[1] See *Life, Religious Opinions, and Experience of Madame de la Mothe
Guyon*, &c., by T. C. Upham, p. 36.

in my heart. He entered there, and I entered with Him. I learned to pray in that Divine retreat ; and from that time I went no more out.' [1]

Now, surely here was a mystic after Law's own heart ; a perfect illustration of the truth of his favourite text, ' Neither shall they say, Lo here ! or, lo there ! for, behold the kingdom of God is within you' (S. Luke xvii. 21). Moreover, Madame Guyon had a strong sympathy with that particular phase of mysticism which most of all fascinated William Law, the seeing in the visible a symbol of the invisible. How beautifully, for instance, she works out that favourite illustration from natural things of the soul's finding its true rest in God ! ' All fountains and rivers have a tendency to ocean. They often flow with great violence ; overcoming obstacles, dashing against rocks, foaming and rushing around them with great noise ; but when they meet and mingle with the mighty ocean, all is peaceful, because they have reached the place of their rest. So,' &c. How ingeniously she traces the analogy between pure water and a holy soul! ' Nothing is more simple than water, nothing more pure. It is a fitting emblem of the holy soul. Water has the property of yielding to all impressions. As it yields to the slightest human touch, so the holy soul yields without resistance to the slightest touch of God, the slightest intimation of the Divine will. Water is without colour, but susceptible of all colours. So the holy soul, colourless in itself, reflects the hues, whatever they may be, which emanate from the Divine countenance. Water has no form, but takes the form of any vessel in which it is contained. So the holy soul takes no position or form of itself, but only that which God gives it.' [2]

Numberless other quotations might be given to show

[1] Upham, p. 88.　　　　[2] *Ibid.* pp. 388-9.

how both these writers harmonised with William Law.
He expressly mentions both 'the great Fénelon and the
illuminated Guion' as mystic writers whom he had read,
and yet we may gather, from his distinct words in one case
and from his silence in the other, that neither of them was
a real favourite of his. With the knowledge we have of
Law's character it is not difficult to conjecture why they
were not. In the first place, it is highly probable that the
very name 'Quietist' may have had an ominous sound to
him. For Law, though he constantly depreciated human
learning and never paraded his own, was nevertheless a
thoroughly well-read man. He was, no doubt, well aware
that under this name of Quietist, or its Greek equivalent,
the wildest enthusiasts had, some centuries earlier, propa-
gated notions which were calculated to bring mysticism
into derision. Little has hitherto been said of the Greek
or Oriental phases of mysticism, because it seemed necessary rigorously to confine this sketch to those mystics who
influenced Law ; and, with the exception of course of the
earliest mystics of this school who have been already mentioned, this form of mysticism does not appear to have
attracted him. But the name 'Quietists' suggests that of
' Hesychasts,' a set of fanatics in the monasteries of Mount
Athos, whose fanaticism may be judged of from the following instructions which they were required to carry out.
' Being alone in thy cell, close the door, and seat thyself in
the corner. Raise thy spirit above all vain and transient
things ; repose thy beard on thy breast, and turn thine eyes
with thy whole power of meditation upon thy navel. Re-
tain thy breath, and search in thine entrails for the place of
thy heart, wherein all the powers of the soul reside. At
first thou wilt encounter thick darkness ; but by persevering
night and day thou wilt find a marvellous and uninterrupted
joy ; for as soon as thy spirit shall have discovered the

place of thy heart, it will perceive itself *luminous* and full of discernment.'[1]

The Quietists of the seventeenth century showed none of the extravagances of their namesakes of the fourteenth, but we can readily see that there was much in Fénelon and still more in Madame Guyon which would not find favour in the eyes of William Law. In the first place, both of them wrote too much and were too diffusive in their style to please him. They were, neither of them, robust enough for Law's taste. In fact, although on the main points at issue, Law agreed with Fénelon and not with Bossuet, yet in their personal characters, the 'Eagle of Meaux' would in some respects be more in harmony with the thoroughly masculine and somewhat stern nature of Law, than his gentler and more lovable opponent. For instance, though he never said one word upon the subject, I should much doubt whether Law would have sympathised with Fénelon's submission to the See of Rome, and virtual retractation of his most cherished sentiments. Law himself never yielded one inch when he believed himself to be in the right. He preferred sacrificing all his prospects in life to abating one jot even of his political principles. Of course his position in the English Church was somewhat different from that of Fénelon in the Roman Church, where there is no alternative between submission and exclusion. Still, one can scarcely conceive even all the thunders of the Vatican making the slightest impression upon William Law ; and though he would be slow to condemn a Romanist who submitted to recant his private opinions at the bidding of his Church, yet one can quite understand that the man who had consented to make such a submission would not be the kind of man to commend himself greatly to Law.

---

[1] Quoted in Dean Waddington's *History of the Church*, p. 609.

Again, Law was not the kind of character to sympathise
with a man who at one period of his career seems to have
put himself under the guidance of a woman. Some of the
letters which passed between Fénelon and Madame Guyon
are really written as if *she* were the spiritual director, and
he the humble disciple.[1] And, moreover, that woman was
one of whom he could write to another woman : 'I have
never felt any natural inclination to her or her writings. I
think nothing of her pretended prophecies or revelations.'[2]
In fact, though Fénelon was not exactly effeminate, there
was a certain softness about him which, indeed, constitutes
one of the many charms of his exquisitely charming
character ; but it was not at all the sort of charm to fascinate William Law. The hardier, more rugged type of
mystic, like Tauler and Ruysbroch, would be more in his
vein.

As to Madame Guyon, the very fact that she held many
of Law's sentiments would naturally make him all the more

---

[1] Thus Madame Guyon wrote to Fénelon in November 1688: 'Your soul
is not yet brought into full harmony with God, and therefore I suffer. My
prayer is not yet heard. God's designs *will* be accomplished in you. You
may delay the result by resistance ; but you cannot hinder it. Pardon Christian plainness.' And again: 'God appears to be making me a medium of
communicating good to yourself, and to be imparting to my soul graces which
are ultimately destined to reach and bless yours. My mind does not form its
conclusions by extraordinary methods of dreams, inward voices, and spiritual
lights, but *intuitively*. The instrumentality cannot fail to be beneficial, *provided there is a proper correspondence on your part.* Do not regard this instrumentality as a useless thing. Be so humble and childlike as to submit to the
dishonour, if such it may be called, of receiving blessings from God through
one so poor and unworthy as myself. Our souls shall become like two rivers
mingling in one channel and flowing on together to the ocean.' On his
appointment as preceptor to the Duke of Burgundy, she wrote to him: 'Act
always without regard to self. The less you have of self, the more you will
have of God. You are called in God's providence to aid and superintend in
the education of a prince, whom with all his faults God loves, and whom, as
it seems to me, He designs to restore spiritually to Himself.' See Upham,
pp. 337–9.

[2] Fénelon to Madame de Maintenon. See *Œuvres de Fénelon*, vol. xviii.
p. 367.

intolerant of her other views which were likely to bring those sentiments into disrepute. For instance, Law would unquestionably have regarded with extreme repugnance such expressions as the following, which are reported to have been uttered in a conversation between her and her implacable foe, Bossuet :—

B. : Do you really deny that you can ask anything of God ?

Mad. de G. : I do.

B. : You cannot offer the petition, Forgive us our trespasses ?

Mad. de G. : I can say the words by heart, but as to conveying any meaning to my heart, the state of *oraison pure* and gratuitous love to which I am raised does not admit of it.[1]

The spectacle of a poor, weak woman badgered and baited by the greatest theologian of the age is a cruel one, and it is hardly fair to judge of her by what she said, or rather what was drawn out of her, under such an ordeal. But apart from these extorted confessions, there were many things both in her life and writings which would be extremely distasteful to William Law. He would have regarded with considerable suspicion her prophecies and revelations ; he would have disapproved of her comparing herself in any way with the woman in the Apocalypse ;[2] he would hardly have relished her illustrations borrowed

---

[1] *Œuvres de Bossuet,* vol. xxviii. p. 563.

[2] It is, however, only fair to Madame Guyon to see her own account of this comparison:—

B. : I was surprised to see you speak of yourself as the Woman in the Apocalypse.

Mad. de G. : As I read the passage in the Apocalypse, which speaks of the woman who fled into the wilderness, I thought of myself as driven from place to place for announcing the doctrines of the Lord, and it seemed to me the expression might be applied not as prophetic of me, but as illustrative of my condition.

from sexual love, for in the most high-flown of his own mystic writings he always scrupulously avoided any expressions or sentiments of what may be called an amatory character; her spiritual adaptation of the Song of Solomon, therefore, would not have been at all to his taste; still less her extraordinary 'Act of Consecration,' which is worth quoting in full as illustrative of that element of romantic enthusiasm in her character, which would assuredly find no echo in the breast of William Law. 'I henceforth take Jesus Christ to be mine. I promise to receive Him as a husband to me. And I give myself, unworthy though I am, to be His spouse. I ask of Him in this marriage of spirit with spirit that I may be of the same mind with Him, meek, pure, nothing in myself, and united in God's will. And, pledged as I am to be His, I accept as a part of my marriage portion the temptations and sorrows and crosses and contempt which fell to Him.' This extraordinary document was signed with her name and sealed with her ring.

Again, mysticism would come to William Law in a very questionable shape, when it appeared in the form of a very beautiful and fascinating woman, appealing to every sentiment of chivalry by the persecutions she suffered from overbearing prelates and not over-scrupulous monks. There is not one jot of trustworthy evidence to show that her life was aught but that of a pure and honourable lady; but there is no question that she owed much of her influence to more mundane attractions than Law would at all have approved. The spectacle of young dandies fluttering round her in the *salons* of Paris like moths fluttering round a candle, and talking about the mystic ecstasy and pure love, would be an utter abomination in the eyes of Law. Thus, when we come to look into the matter, it need cause us no surprise that one whose writings have been truly called 'the very abstract and model of the true, pure mysticism "¹ should still have been regarded with doubtful favour by William Law.

As for that other mystic lady, Madame Bourignon, a very few words will suffice to explain the reasons of that strong antipathy to her which, as we have seen, Law constantly expressed in his conversations with Byrom. Law had the deepest reverence for the Divine Person of the Blessed Jesus, whom he believed to be 'God of God, Light of Light, Very God of Very God,' Who was not made manifest in the flesh, until, in the fulness of time, He was 'born of the Virgin Mary.' With what abhorrence, then, must he have regarded Madame Bourignon's wild, not to say impious theory, that Jesus was born of Adam in his state of innocence! Law had a profound distrust in 'visions and revelations.' Was it likely that he would agree with a writer who spoke of 'the high, secret mysteries which God had revealed to her'? Law, though he deplored the state of the Church in his own day, and by no means approved of the sentiments and practice of many of the clergy, always held the highest views of the ministerial office, and carefully abstained from all personal abuse of his clerical brethren. Could he possibly approve of a writer—and that writer a woman—who ventured to contrast the preaching of the clergy of her day with that of the apostles, in the following unseemly language?—' Their sermons are nothing else but apish mummeries. If an ape saw an excellent painter drawing a curious picture, and if in his absence it should take the pencil and colours and so scratch upon the same table, it would entirely daub, all though [*sic*] it made use of the same pencil and colours, because it wanted the painter's spirit. This is the true emblem of most of the preachers and writers

¹ Ewald (*Briefe über die alte Mystik und den neuen Mysticismus*, p. 176) says of Madame Guyon's works, 'Sie sind der Inbegriff und Grundriss der echten, reinen Mystik '

nowadays in religion.' But it is needless to dwell on the many points of disagreement between Law and Madame Bourignon ; as in other cases, these would be all the more annoying to him because they tended to bring into discredit the other points—and they were many and striking—in which he agreed with her.[1]

The last of the mystic writers whom Law mentions is M. Bertot. He is generally known as ' Le Directeur Mystique,' and among his spiritual children was Madame Guyon herself. He was a native of the diocese of Coutances in Normandy, in which diocese he officiated as a parish priest until his removal to the famous Abbey of Montmartre, near Paris, where he remained until his death, his special employment being the spiritual direction of the religious Benedictines. Ewald, who, oddly enough, declares his inability to discover anything about Bertot's life, though there is no difficulty in ascertaining the details of it, gives some interesting extracts from his writings, which he had learned from a friend. There is no need to quote them, as they differ in no wise from the ordinary views of mystics ; and Bertot does not appear to have exercised any special influence over Law.[2]

But there is one mystic of the seventeenth century whose influence over Law was second only to that of Jacob Behmen himself. That man is Father Malebranche. Malebranche is in himself a singularly interesting character, and

[1] See Bourignon's *Nouv. Ciel* (pp. 166–170), *Renouv. de l'Espr. Ev.*, Preface, p. 110-2, &c. Also Preface to Leslie's *Snake in the Grass*, and *Bourignonism Detected*, and, on the other side, *An Apology for Mad. Antonia Bourignon*. The anonymous author of the last work asks plaintively, ' Does she deserve to be treated either as a heretick or mad, whimsical woman ? ' (p. 56). I am afraid the answer of most people will be that she does.

[2] For the same reason it is unnecessary to notice in detail the writings of Molinos (the most notorious, if not the greatest, of this group of mystics, with the exception of Fénelon and Madame Guyon), or of Malaval, or of Père Lacombe, or of Falconi.

doubly interesting to us on account of his connection with William Law. He was a mystic of the seventeenth century in point of date, but only in point of date. In his type of character, no less than in his opinions, he differed widely from the other mystics of that period. In the first place, the Roman Church certainly could not complain of him, as she did of the Quietists,[1] that he was a Protestant in disguise. She might condemn his ' Traité de la Nature et de la Grâce ' to the Index, but she could not deny that he was himself her faithful son. When Dom Lamy quoted some passages out of Malebranche's ' Récherche de la Vérité,' in support of Fénelon's doctrine of pure love, Malebranche at once wrote a pamphlet indignantly repudiating any sympathy with the Quietists, and satisfied even Bossuet himself that he was sound on these points. Malebranche was, however, in one sense, unquestionably a mystic of the mystics. His mysticism was much fostered by his connection with the Oratory in the Rue St. Honoré, in which he passed the greater part of his life. The attitude of the Oratory in regard to mysticism could not be better described than in the language of the Abbé Blampignon, which I shall therefore make no apology for venturing to translate.[2] ' From its commencement the Oratory declared against the ancient school and its Aristotle of convention, by showing

[1] ' C'est, sans doute, cet esprit mal déguisé d'indépendance et de révolte qui valut aux Quiétistes l'appui du Protestantisme. Nous voyons, dans la correspondance de Bossuet et de Fénelon sur le Quiétisme, que les Protestants ne cessaient de publier, en faveur de Quiétistes, des lardons dans les journaux, *pamphlets,* &c. Mme de Guyon ne trouva d'éditeurs, que parmi Protestants, d'abord le ministre Poiret, et ensuite Dutoit Mambrini, ministre à Lausanne.' Bonnel, Introd. xxviii.

[2] *Etude sur Malebranche,* par l'Abbé E. A. Blampignon, pp. 100-1. ' De ses commencements . . . . la main de Dieu.' I have thought it better to translate the passage quite literally at the expense of the English idioms. Those who have not leisure to read the voluminous writings of Malebranche (though for the mere style alone, independently of the matter, they would amply repay careful study) will find an admirable picture of him, painted as a Frenchman alone could do, in this work.

itself generally attached to S. Augustine and to Descartes.
The Cardinal de Berulle had supported by his authoritative
language the reform which Descartes projected.   From
S. Augustine came naturally to the society a lively attachment to the ideas of Plato ;[1] this affection for Plato, this
devotion to Descartes, developing itself gradually among
the Oratorians, inspired them to write many excellent works.
The mysticism of S. Theresa necessarily exercised a great
influence upon the society.   Berulle, aided by Madame
Acarie, had brought from Spain into France the spiritual
daughters of Theresa, and he directed them during his
whole life ; the genius of S. Theresa entered into the heart
of the pious Cardinal ; there is the same silence imposed
on the senses, the same feeling of the Divine Presence, the
same endeavour to seek in everything the hand of God.'
Breathing such an atmosphere, and entering thoroughly
into the spirit of the place, Malebranche could hardly fail
to be a mystic.

It would far transcend the limits of this work to enter
into the philosophy of Malebranche ; all we have to do
with is that one point, which, indeed, is the culminating
point of the whole, viz. that we see all things in God.   This
magnificent conception Malebranche held not merely in
vague, conventional terms, but worked out thoroughly and
made the grand climax of his whole system.   This it was
which thoroughly fascinated William Law.   It is therefore
necessary to investigate it more in detail.   ' We must,' says
Malebranche in effect, ' distinguish between the mysteries of

---

[1] S. Augustine cannot be called a mystic, but he was more or less a Platonist.   See especially his *De Civitate Dei*, Book VIII.   In fact, the way
was prepared for his conversion by the perusal of the writings of some of the
later Platonists.   As a specimen of his idealism and (so far) Platonism, take the
following passage: ' Sat est enim ad id quod volo, Platonem sensisse duos esse
mundos, unum Intelligibilem in quo ipsa veritas habitaret, istum autem Sensibi-
lem quem manifestum est nos visu tactuque sentire.   Itaque illum verum hunc
verisimilem et ad illius imaginem factum.'—*Contra Academ.* Lib. iii. chap. xvii.

faith and the things of nature. To be a Believer, one must believe blindly, but to be a philosopher, one must see evidently ;[1] for the Divine authority is infallible, but all men are subject to error. Let us try to deliver ourselves by degrees from the illusions of our senses ; of our sight, of our imagination, of the impressions which the imagination of other men have made upon our spirits. Let us reject all the confused ideas which we have through the dependence in which we are upon our bodies, and only admit the clear and evident ideas which the spirit receives by the union which it necessarily has with the Word or Wisdom or Eternal Truth. It is only God that we see with a sight immediate and direct. In this life it is only by the union which we have with Him that we are capable of knowing what we do know. We must let God speak ; turn back into ourselves and seek in ourselves for that which never quits us, and which always enlightens us. He speaks low, but His voice is distinct ; He enlightens but a little, but His light is pure. Nay, rather, His voice is as strong as it is distinct, His light is as bright as it is pure. The knowledge of the truth and the love of virtue can be nothing else than the union of the spirit with God, and a kind of possession by God. When the spirit sees the truth, not only is it united with God, it possesses God, it sees God in a manner, it sees also in one sense the truth as God sees it. We discover by the clear light of the spirit that we are united to God after a manner far more close and far more essential than to our own bodies. Men are more certain of the existence of God than of that of their bodies ; and when they turn back into themselves they

---

[1] What Malebranche said in all sober seriousness, the author of *Christianity not founded upon Argument* (Dodwell the younger) said, probably, in irony. It is no wonder that Law supposed, though, I think, erroneously, that this latter author was in earnest, for Law certainly agreed in the main with his argument.

discover more clearly certain wills of God, according to which He produces and preserves all beings, than those of their best friends, of those whom they have studied all their lives. For the union of their spirit with God and that of their will with His, I might say, with the Eternal Law or with the Immutable Order, is an immutable union, is an immediate, direct, and necessary union.'[1]

An intelligent man like Law reading with delight such sentiments as these, set off as they were with all the graces which a most pure, forcible, and luminous style can lend, could hardly fail to become favourably impressed with the ground-doctrine of mysticism which they contain. Thus, in Law's early undergraduate days, the seed was sown by Malebranche which was many years later to grow and bear fruit in full-blown mysticism.

Apart from this dominant idea, the other details of Malebranche's philosophy were by no means in accordance with Law's later views. It is a curious fact that, deeply as he was indebted to Malebranche's writings for his mystic bias, the only mention he makes of the Oratorian by name in his later works is to express his strong disagreement with him. Mystic as Malebranche was, so far as the great aim of all mysticism, the union of the soul with God, is concerned, his system was quite incompatible with that other phase of mysticism, so dear to William Law, which

---

[1] These expressions are taken mainly from the *Recherche de la Vérité*, and especially from chap. vi. book 3: 'Que nous voyons toutes choses en Dieu'— the thesis, it will be remembered, which Law elected to maintain, avowedly on the authority of Malebranche, at his Act at Cambridge. But the same sentiments permeate all Malebranche's writings. For example, in the *Méditations Chrétiennes* (ii. 15), addressing 'the Divine reason' he exclaims: 'C'est donc vous-même dans le plus secret de mon esprit, et c'est votre voix que j'entends. O mon unique maître ! que les hommes sachent que vous les penetrez de telle manière que lorsqu'ils croient se répondre à eux-mêmes, et s'entretenir avec eux-mêmes, c'est vous qui leur parlez et qui les entretenez.' See also *Traité de Morale*, t. ii. p. 46, i. 242 ; also *Entretiens sur Métaphysiques*, i.; and, in a word, Malebranche's works *passim*.

traces the essential connection between the visible and the invisible world. In Law's view, 'body and spirit are not two separate, independent things, but are necessary to each other, and are only the inward and outward conditions of one and the same being.'[1] This Law rightly conceives to be totally opposed to the doctrine of Malebranche ; he represents both the schools of philosophy—that of Locke on the one side, and that of Descartes and Malebranche on the other—though they agreed in little else, as agreeing in this, that they supposed spirit and body not only without any natural relation, but essentially contrary to one another, and only held together in a forced conjunction by the arbitrary will of God.' ' Nay,' he adds indignantly, ' if you was to say, that God first creates a soul out of nothing, and when that is done, then takes an understanding faculty, and puts it into it, after that a will, and then a memory, all as independently made as when a taylor first makes the body of a coat, and then adds sleeves or pockets to it ; was you to say this, the schools of Descartes, Malebranche, or Locke could have nothing to say against it.'[2] The reason why Malebranche has to be gibbeted in such evil company as that of Locke, the arch-enemy of mysticism, is, that he has unhappily never sat at the feet of Jacob Behmen ! But this is anticipating.

In more respects than one there was a curious resemblance between Malebranche and Law, both in their tones of mind and, *mutatis mutandis,* in their circumstances of life. In the first place, there was in both that same strange intellectual inconsistency which made them depreciate the very points in which one secret of their strength lay. The study of languages was in the eyes of Malebranche worse than waste of time. It might be necessary to learn just

---

[1] *Spirit of Love,* ' Works,' vol. viii. p. 33.   [2] Ibid, p. 31.

enough Latin to read Augustine, but 'as for Greek!—so many languages weary the brain and impede the reason. How is it possible to justify the passion of those who turn their heads into a library of dictionaries?' He would have made a clean sweep of all literature and sciences, with the exception of algebra and a little natural science; history, geography, &c., are all pedantry and puerility. 'Adam was perfect, and he knew neither history nor chronology.' He anathematised style as the product of sin, yet his own style was singularly polished and attractive;[1] his own writings show in every page of them the mind of the well-read scholar as well as the profound thinker, and, strangest of all, they are constantly interlarded with most apposite quotations from those very classical authors whom he abjured. The same curious inconsistency has already been noticed in Law. It may be added that neither in Law nor in Malebranche is there the slightest trace of affectation or unreality in their inconsistency.

Again, in France during the latter half of the seventeenth century, and in England during the first half of the eighteenth, 'there were giants in the land.' Bossuet, Fénelon, Pascal, in France; Butler, Waterland, Bentley, Sherlock, in England,—were great names. Both Malebranche and Law fully reached the stature of the tallest of their contemporaries,[2] but they were content, and they were allowed

---

[1] Even Enfield, who had no sympathy with Malebranche's system, and could only see in his theory of 'seeing all things in God' a singular and paradoxical dogma, still owns 'the work (*Recherche de la Vérité*) was written with such elegance and splendour of diction, and its tenets were supported by such ingenious reasonings, that it obtained general applause, and procured the author a distinguished name among philosophers and a numerous train of followers.' (ii. 534.)

Norris of Bemerton says of Malebranche: 'He is indeed the great Galileo of the intellectual world. He has given us the point of view, and whatever farther detections are made, it must be through his Telescope. He has search'd after Truth in the proper and genuine Seat and Region of it, has open'd a great many noble Scenes of the World we are now contemplating [the

to live and work and die unnoticed and unrewarded. Both Malebranche and Law were born for the recluse life, and both of them found it; for Malebranche was as much a recluse amid the hubbub of Paris as Law was amid the green fields of Northamptonshire. For simplicity and purity of life, for intense piety and self-denial, there was nothing to choose between these two saintly mystics. But in one point they differed widely. Malebranche was always the philosopher as well as the theologian. Law, though he was constantly accused of blending philosophy with religion, had in reality no taste for philosophy, for Behmenism can hardly be dignified, or, as Law would say, degraded, by that name. The study of mathematics, too, which was regarded by Malebranche as a sort of handmaid to mysticism, was not thus looked upon by William Law. But it is needless to pursue the contrast and comparison further.

With the great name of Malebranche this brief sketch of the mystics who influenced William Law may fitly close. There were many others, both sects and individuals, of a mystic tendency, with whom Law was brought into connection. But to treat of them under the head of mystics would be to encourage the very error against which a protest was entered at the beginning of this chapter. It would be to confound the mystics proper with those who, together with a large admixture of mysticism, blended much which, whether better or worse, was really a different element. Platonists, Philadelphians, Swedenborgians, Moravians, Quakers, will all have to come before us in connection with Law. All were tinged with mysticism ; but all were some-

---

ideal world] ; and would perhaps have been the fittest Person of the age to have given a just and complete Theory of its Systems. But even this great Apelles has drawn this Celestial Beauty but half way, and I am afraid the excellent piece will suffer, whatever other hand has the finishing of it.'— *Theory of the Ideal World*, vol. i. p. 4.

thing more, and also something less, than mystics. Even Jacob Behmen was not, exclusively at least, a mystic ; he has not therefore been mentioned in his chronological order among the mystics, partly for this reason, and partly also because his influence over Law was so great that he ought not to be confounded with the minor factors which contributed to form the totality of Law's mind, but deserves such prominence as a separate chapter devoted entirely to him can give.

CHAPTER XI.

ON JACOB BEHMEN.

THE exact date at which Law first became acquainted with the writings of Jacob Behmen cannot be ascertained ; but it was certainly between the years 1733 and 1737, probably immediately after the former date. The circumstances and results of his first meeting with the Teutonic theosopher are happily known to us from his own words, reported by Mr. Okely. 'In a particular interview,' writes this gentleman, 'I had with Mr. Law a few months before his decease, in answer to the question, *when* and *how* he first met with Jacob Behmen's works, he said that he had often reflected upon it with surprise that, although when a curate in London, he had perhaps rummaged every bookseller's shop and book-stall in that metropolis, yet he never met with a single book, or so much as the title of any book, of Jacob Behmen's. The very first notice he had of him was from a treatise called " Ratio et Fides." [1] Soon after which he

---

[1] I imagine that this is the treatise described by Law himself in a letter to his friend Langcake, in 1759, in the following words : ' The name of the author of *Faith and Reason* is Mittenach, a German count. All his later works are in a book called *Fides et Ratio* ; they are chiefly translations from Madam Guion.' But there is also a work by Peter Poiret bearing the same title. It is entitled in full, *Fides et Ratio collatæ ac suo utraque loco redditæ adversus principia Johannis Lockii*, published in 1707. It has already been seen that Poiret was not altogether a favourite of Law's, but they would be thoroughly at one in their disagreement with Locke's philosophy. Whether the work referred to in the text be Mittenach's or Poiret's I do not know ; probably the former.

lighted upon the very best and most complete edition of his works. ' When I first began to read him,' says he, ' he put me into a perfect sweat. But as I discovered sound truths and the glimmerings of a deep ground and sense, even in the passages not then clearly intelligible to me, and found myself, as it were, strongly prompted in my heart to dig in these writings, I followed this impulse with continual aspirations and prayer to God for his help and divine illumination, if *I was called* to understand them. By reading in this manner again and again, and from time to time, I perceived,' said he, ' that my heart felt well, and my understanding opened gradually ; till at length I found what a treasure was hid in this field.'[1] A slightly different but not inconsistent account of the same event is given by Dr. Byrom in his ' Journal.' ' Mr. Law,' he writes, ' said that Dr. Cheyne was the providential occasion of his meeting or knowing of J. Behmen, by a book which the Dr. mentioned to him in a letter, which book mentioned Behmen.'[2] The book was, no doubt, the ' Ratio et Fides ' mentioned by Mr. Okely.

It would scarcely be an exaggeration to say that this meeting with Jacob Behmen was the most important era in William Law's life. Other mystics only touched the surface of his nature ; Behmen penetrated to its very depths.

---

[1] *Memoirs of the Life, Death, Burial, and Wonderful Writings of Jacob Behmen, now first done at large into English, &c.*, by Francis Okely. Northampton, 1780. Page 105, note. Mr. Walton, in his ' Notes, &c., for an adequate biography of William Law,' printed for private circulation, relates this incident with a few verbal differences and one that is more than verbal. Instead of ' the most complete edition,' he describes Law as having met with ' one of the best of all his [J. B.'s] works,' and adds in a bracket that it was ' the *Signatura Rerum*.' I do not know whence Mr. Walton (who is generally most accurate) derived his information ; but as I derived mine from Mr. Okely's own book, a copy of which is in the British Museum, I have thought it better to let the passage stand as it does in the text.

[2] Byrom's *Journal*, part ii. vol. ii. p. 363.

If he had never met with Behmen, his sympathy with mystics, even such as Malebranche and Tauler, who affected him most of all, would have attracted little attention. He would have been known only as one of the very ablest among the many able writers against Deism and Erastianism, and as one of the few really successful authors of works of practical divinity. But the Teutonic theosopher took possession of his whole soul, and gave to all his later writings a bias which makes them far more attractive to a small minority, and far more repulsive to a vast majority, of divinity students than any of his earlier works are. Having found this treasure, Law characteristically at once threw himself heart and soul into the examination of it. ' I taught myself,' he tells us, ' the High Dutch language, on purpose to know the original words of the blessed Jacob.' He made diligent search after other theosophical writers, and studied especially the writings of Andreas Freher, a commentator and illustrator of Behmen, who had died only a few years previously (1728). He not only made himself master of Freher's writings, but took the trouble to copy out many portions of them ; he also obtained possession of some wonderful symbolical illustrations of Behmenism drawn by Freher, which are still extant. He procured and studied the MSS. of the learned Dr. Francis Lee, and other Philadelphians, who were tinged with Behmenism. He purposed publishing a new edition and translation of the whole of Behmen's works, which purpose, however, he did not live to carry out ; but there is not one single work of his own written after this period which does not show obvious traces of the influence which Behmen exercised over him.

Before inquiring what was the secret of this influence, it seems necessary to describe briefly the life and the general characteristics of the writings of this extraordinary man.[1]

Jacob Behmen, or Böhme—for that was his proper name, though I have preferred to call him by the name under which he was known by Law and the majority of English readers—was born in 1575 at Old Seidenburg, a village one mile and a half from the town of Gorlitz in Upper Lusatia. His father was a herdsman, and in his early years Jacob helped him to tend the cattle ; and it is highly probable that in this employment he acquired that love of nature which he afterwards manifested so remarkably. When he grew older, he was placed at a school, where he learned to read and write, but apparently little else. He was then apprenticed to a shoemaker at Gorlitz, married the daughter of a butcher, and in due time became a master shoemaker.

Such was his outer life, and it is scarcely possible to conceive one less favourable to the development of mysticism. But, under these unpromising outward circumstances, he was cultivating an inner life of which his friends little dreamed. In the intervals of shoemaking he found time to read controversial divinity, and was so shocked at the bitterness displayed by the theologians of the day that he began to be troubled with doubts about the truth of Christianity altogether. But he was of a pious nature, and he prayed to God earnestly and continually to send him light. And he found what he sought. ' He began to ob-

---

[1] The principal authorities I have used in sketching Behmen's life are the *Works of Jacob Behmen, the Teutonic Theosopher, and Life of the Author*, in four volumes published in 1764, and falsely attributed to William Law ; Ewald's *Briefe über die alte Mystik, &c.; Memoirs of the Life, Death, Burial, and Wonderful Writings of Jacob Behmen, now first done at large into English*, by Francis Okely, 1780 ; Enfield's *History of Philosophy*, book ix. chap. iii. ' Of the Theosophists' ; Hallam's *Literature of Europe*, the article on ' Böhme' in the *Penny Cyclopædia ;* Dorner's *History of Protestant Theology*, vol. i.; Blunt's *Dictionary of Sects, &c.*

serve a wonderful connection between all things, a unity in
their variety, a harmony in the thousand voices of creation.'
A light poured in upon his soul, but he kept his thoughts
within himself till he could do so no longer. In 1610 he
began to write them down, and at last they took the form
in which they appear in his first work, 'Aurora, or the
Morning Redness.' Still he had no intention of publishing;
he only felt that he *must* pour forth what was in him. But
a nobleman of the neighbourhood, who was visiting him,[1]
found the manuscript on the table, begged permission to
read it, and was so impressed with its contents that he had
several copies taken in writing. These were passed from
hand to hand, and one of them fell into the hands of
Gregory Richter, superintendent of Gorlitz, who denounced
Behmen by name from the pulpit, and persuaded the
Senate of Gorlitz to convene him, to seize the book, and to
admonish the author to write no more, but 'stick to his
last.' Behmen, who throughout the whole business appears
to have acted in a truly humble, Christian spirit, obeyed as
a dutiful citizen the admonition, and for seven years abstained from writing anything. 'Then,' he tells us, 'the
gate was opened to me, and in a quarter of an hour I saw
and knew more than if I had been many years together at
a university.' From this time until his death in 1624
(only seven years) compositions flowed forth from his pen
with marvellous rapidity. The very titles of his books are
of portentous length, and would fill many pages. It will
suffice here to state that his best known works are, 'Aurora,
or Dawning of Day in the East, or Morning Redness, &c.
&c.,' the 'De Signatura Rerum, &c.,' the 'Three Principles
of the Divine Essence, &c.,' the 'Threefold Life of Man,' &c.,

---

[1] Behmen was constantly visited by the higher classes, who took a very intelligible interest in the 'inspired cobbler.'

the ' Humanity of Christ,' and the ' Mysterium Magnum,'
which is an explanation of the Book of Genesis.'[1]

If we were to judge of Behmen simply by the language
which was used about him in England during the eighteenth
century, after Law had made him better known to the
English world, we should conclude that he was either a
madman or a conscious impostor, or, in plain words, a
messenger of Satan.   Bishop Warburton writes in the true
Warburtonian language: ' When we find a pretender to inspiration such as Jacob Behmen delivering to us, under this
character, a heap of unmeaning, or, what comes to the same
thing, unintelligible, words, we reasonably conclude, that if
indeed this wisdom did come from above, it hath so de-
generated in its way down as to be ever unfit to return ;
but must be content, with the other lapsed entities of celestial original, to seek employment amongst fools and knaves
here below ; ' and, after several other choice expressions,
he concludes as a climax: ' Behmen's works would disgrace
even Bedlam at full moon.'[2]   John Wesley over and over
again calls Behmen's writings ' unintelligible jargon,' and
asks : ' May we not pronounce with the utmost certainty of
one who thus distorts, mangles, and murders the Word of
God, that the light which is in him is darkness ; that he is
illuminated from beneath rather than from above ; and
that he ought to be styled a demonosopher rather than a

---

[1] Here is a specimen of the full title of one of these works : *The Three
Principles of the Divine Essence ; of the Eternal Dark, Light, and Temporary
Worlds showing what the Soul, the Image, and the Spirit of them are ; as also
what Angels, Heaven, and Paradise are ; how Adam was before the Fall, in
the Fall, and after the Fall ; and what the wrath of God, Sin, Death, the
Devils, and Hell are ; How all things have been, now are, and shall be at the
last.*   Ex uno disce omnes.

[2] *Doctrine of Grace*, book i. pp. 625-6, in vol. 4 of Warburton's ' Works '
in seven volumes.   The expression ' a pretender to inspiration ' is very misleading, as it would convey to most readers the impression that Behmen placed
himself, in some measure, on a level with the inspired writers of the Holy
Scriptures, which most assuredly he did not.

theosopher ?'[1] Forty years earlier he had read the ' Mysterium Magnum.' 'And what,' he asks, 'can I say concerning
the part I read ? I can and must say this much (and that
with as full evidence as I can say that two and two make
four), it is most sublime nonsense, inimitable bombast, fus-
tian not to be paralleled.'[2] Good Bishop Horne sums up
Behmen's writings in the following neat dilemma : ' Either
Jacob Behmen's scheme is a new revelation, or an explanation of the old. If the latter, why is it wrapt up in mystic
jargon, never heard of in the Christian Church before ? If
the former, it is an imposture and delusion, for extraordinary inspirations are not to be credited, unless vouched by
miracles ; if they are pretended to come from Him, and
are not, it is a demonstration they come from the Devil.'
Mr. Jones of Nayland speaks of the ' stupendous reveries,'
'the wild dreams of Jacob Behmen,' 'the ignorance and
impudence of this impostor ;' and what poor Jacob calls
' the root and ground of the depth,' he calls ' the depths of
Satan.'[3] Dr. Johnson, when told that Law alleged Behmen to have been somewhat in the same state with S. Paul,
and to have seen unutterable things, replied in his own
racy manner: ' Were it even so, Jacob would have resembled
S. Paul more by not attempting to utter them !'[4] Gibbon
speaks of ' the incomprehensible visions of Jacob Behmen.'[5]
And in later times the Teutonic theosopher does not appear to have fared much better with our countrymen. Mr.

---

[1] See *A Specimen of the Divinity and Philosophy of the Highly-Illuminated
Jacob Behmen*, by John Wesley ; also *Extract of a Letter to Rev. W. Law*
and *Thoughts upon Jacob Behmen*, passim in vol ix. of Wesley's ' Works' ;
also his *Journal* passim.

[2] *Journal* for Friday, June 4, 1742. The passages quoted before this were
written in 1780 and 1784.

[3] See *Jones' Life of Bishop Horne*, pp. 67 and 69; and *Letters to a Lady
on Jacob Behmen's Writings*, in the same volume, p. 210.

[4] Boswell's *Life of Johnson* (edition of 1822 in four volumes), ii. 112.

[5] *Memoirs of My Life and Writings*, by E. Gibbon, p. 14.

Southey refers to his writings as 'the nonsense of the German shoemaker;'[1] and the calmest and most evenly-balanced historian of our own day terms Behmen's speculations 'the incoherencies of madness.'[2]

This is one side of the picture. In common fairness to Behmen himself and to William Law, his admirer, we must now turn to the other side. Little favour as Behmen has found with the majority of Englishmen, he is very differently spoken of by many illustrious writers of his own land. It is true that Mosheim, whose mind was of a cast the very opposite of that which is likely to be attracted by mysticism of any kind, is of opinion that Behmen's philosophy was 'more obscure than that of Heraclitus' [surnamed σκοτεινός, the obscure], and that Behmen himself was mad.[3]   But, on the other hand, Schlegel while admitting that 'Böhme is much ridiculed by the general race of literary men,' adds : 'These are themselves sensible that they understand neither the good nor the bad that is in his writings ; but they are ignorant that they know absolutely nothing either respecting the man himself, or the relation in which he stood to his contemporaries.' He then proceeds to give his own estimate of Behmen, which, considering the vast influence which the theosopher exercised over Law's mind, it will not, I trust, be out of place to quote. 'Jacob Böhme,' he writes, 'is commonly called a dreamer ; and it is very true that in his writings there may be more marks of an ardent imagination than of a sound judgment. But we cannot at least deny this strange man the praise of

---

[1] Southey's *Life of Wesley*, chap. ii.

[2] Hallam's *Literature of Europe*, ii. 380.

[3] Jac. Böhmius, Sutor Görliensis : 'Hic, cum naturâ ipsâ proclivis esset ad res abditas pervestigandas et Rob. Fluddii et Rosæcrucianorum scita cognovisset, Theologiam, igne duce, imaginatione comite, invenit, ipsis Pythagoricis numeris et Heracliti notis obscuriorem ; ita enim Chymicis imaginationibus et tantâ verborum confusione et caligine omnia miscet ut ipse sibi obstrepere videatur.'-- Quoted by Warburton, *Doctrine of Grace*, p. 625.

a very poetical fancy. If we should consider him merely as a poet and compare him with those other Christian poets who have handled subjects connected with the supernatural world—with Klopstock, with Milton, or even with Dante—we shall find that he rivals the best of them in fulness of fancy and depth of feeling, and that he falls little below them even in regard to individual beauties and poetical expression. Whatever defects may be found in the philosophy of Jacob Böhme, the historian of German literature can never pass over his name in silence. In few works of any period have the strength and richness of our language been better displayed than in his. His language possesses, indeed, a charm of nature, simplicity, and unsought vigour, which we should look for in vain in the tongue which we now speak, enriched as it is by the immense importation of foreign terms, and the invented phraseologies of our late philosophers.'[1]

It may be said, indeed, that this does not touch the point in question, for it was not from a literary, but from a theological, point of view that Law regarded Behmen, and Schlegel's view at most vindicates Law's taste, not his judgment. The same, however, cannot be said of other judgments respecting Behmen. Spener says of Behmen's writing: ' Should much of it be unintelligible to any person, as I do not deny it to be the very case with my own self, yet let him not condemn it ; but rather reflect that the fault of it may be in his own self ; he being not as yet advanced under the experience of the Holy Ghost's operation, or heart's work, so far as to be in a capacity of comprehending it all.'[2] Semler, of whose piety and splendid intellectual powers there can be but one opinion, whatever may be thought of

---

[1] Schlegel's *History of Literature*, Lecture xv., p. 395.
[2] Dr. P. J. Spener on *Jacob Behmen's Works*, prefixed to the German edition of Thaulerus, Frankfort, 1692.

his views, found both pleasure and profit in reading Behmen's writings ; it was, indeed, with especial reference to
Behmen that he wrote: 'We may in general know and
praise the mild and pure spirit of the mystics, and the
earnest and holy sentiment of such Christians, without going so far as to approve and imitate all their steps and all
their opinions.'[1] Hochmann, whose zeal and piety stimulated him to attempt in Germany the same work of reformation which Wesley did in England,[2] but with very
different success, was an ardent admirer of Behmen. Schel-
ling, who, so far as I can understand him, seems to desire
to make an alliance between the Kantian philosophy and
Christianity, but who, whatever his opinions might be,
was not a man whose judgment can be passed lightly over,
derived great advantage from Behmen. Fouqué, a true
poet, and an earnest seeker after truth, found in Behmen's
works 'a Christian satisfaction which he had in vain sought
elsewhere.' Hagenbach calls Behmen ' the father of Protestant mysticism.'[3] Hegel was a reader of Behmen ; J. L.
Ewald appreciated him so highly as to assert that ' if he
had had a learned education and been able to express his
meaning clearly, he might perhaps have been a German
Plato.'[4] Dorner speaks of 'the wondrous beauty and
plasticity of his language' and of 'many a noble germ in
the fermenting chaos of his notions.'[5]

---

[1] *Lebensbeschreibung*, p. 269.

[2] When one reads of Hochmann travelling about Germany, attacking the
lukewarmness of the clergy, occupying the pulpit where he could, and conducting devotional services in houses, one cannot help being reminded of the
early Methodists; but the resemblance ceases when we consider the doctrines
taught. On a vast variety of points Hochmann differed from the orthodox
standards, the Wesleys in none.   [3] *History of the Church*, ii. 290.

[4] 'In seiner Aurora hatte er seine eigenthümlichsten Ideen oder Anschauungen niedergelegt. Sie enthält viel Tiefes und Wahres. Hätte er gelehrte Bildung
gehabt, und seine Anschauungen zum klaren Bewusstseyn bringen können, so
hätte er vielleicht ein deutscher Plato werden können.'—Ewald's *Briefe über
die alte Mystik, &c.*, p. 230.   [5] *History of Protestant Theology*, i. 184.

The above authorities arc not quoted as being all orthodox, but simply to show that, in the opinion of many able
men, Behmen was not at any rate the madman or impostor
that he was thought to be in England during parts of the
eighteenth and nineteenth centuries.[1] But even in England, at an earlier date, he was not without his admirers
among men of eminence. Not to mention here Dr. Pordage, Mrs. Lead, and other enthusiasts whom we shall
meet again, it may be noted that more than one member
of the noble family of Hotham,—men of mark in their day,
though now forgotten,—that Dr. Francis Lee, whom we
shall meet again, and that Sir Isaac Newton were readers
of Behmen. I do not presume to offer an opinion upon
Law's assertion that Newton was indebted for his famous
discoveries to the Teutonic theosopher ; but Law's statement of the fact that copies of extracts from Behmen's
works in Newton's own handwriting were found among
that great man's papers after his death, has not, so far as I
am aware, ever been impugned.[2]

---

[1] It should be added, however, that thorough justice is done to Behmen
in the *Encyclopædia Britannica.* 'Behmen,' it is owned in the article on
'Mysticism,' 'was a genial, manly mystic, free from everything effeminate
and sentimental. His whole life resembled one great dream ; but he strove
with as much zeal as ever man displayed to benefit his fellow-mortals and
exalt the name of God.'

[2] Law wrote to Dr. Cheyne : 'When Sir Isaac Newton died, there were
found amongst his papers large abstracts out of Jacob Behmen's works written
with his own hand. This I have from undoubted authority. No wonder that
attraction, with its two inseparable properties, which make in Jacob Behmen
the first three principles of eternal nature, should come to be the grand foundation of the Newtonian philosophy.' See also Law's *Works,* vol. vi. (2) 314-5.
' Sir Isaac, ploughed with Behmen's heifer.' Law told Byrom ' that Sir I. Newton shut himself up for three months in order to search for the philosopher's
stone from J. Behmen, that his attraction and three first laws of motion were
from Behmen.' *Journal,* ii. (2) 364. Law's account is quoted by Sir David
Brewster, in his *Life of Newton,* vol. ii. pp. 371-2, without one word to show
that it was incorrect ; on the contrary, he adds ' that this statement ' (viz. that
' Sir Isaac was formerly so deep in Jacob Behmen that he, together with Dr.
Newton, his relation, set up furnaces and were for several months at work in

From these conflicting opinions as to the value of Behmen's works, one naturally turns to the works themselves. And one can quite understand that the first impulse of the reader, after having dipped into one or two pages, would be to toss them aside in disgust. ' Stupendous ' is the only epithet that adequately expresses their nature. They amaze, bewilder, take away one's breath. Let the reader judge from one single specimen which can hardly be called an unfair one, because it is taken from what the author terms, in his ' Preface to the Reader,' the A B C of all his writings ; and, moreover, the particular passage is introduced with the remark, ' It must be set down more plainly and intelligibly.'[1]   This, then, is the way in which our author renders particularly plain what he considers to be the most elementary part of his works : ' Mark what Mercurius is ; it is Harshness, Bitterness, Fire, and Brimstone Water, the most horrible essence ; yet you must understand thereby no materia, matter, or comprehensible thing ; but all no other than Spirit and the source of the original nature.   Harshness is the first essence, which attracts itself ; but it being a hard, cold Virtue or Power, the Spirit is altogether prickly and sharp.   Now, the sting and sharpness cannot endure attracting, but moves and resists and is a contrary will, an enemy to the Harshness, and from that Stirring comes the first mobility which is the third form.   Thus the Harshness continually attracts harder and harder, and so it becomes hard and tart so that the Virtue or Power is as hard as the hardest Stone, which the Bitterness cannot endure, and there then is a great anguish in it like the horrible brimstone Spirit and the sting of the Bitterness, which rubs itself so . hard that in the Anguish there comes to be a twinkling

quest of the tincture') is substantially true is proved by Dr. Newton's own letter.   Law was the very last man in the world to make a statement of this kind without the strongest grounds for doing so.

[1] See *The Three Principles of the Divine Essence.* Behmen's Works, vol. i.

Flash which flies up terribly and breaks the harshness, &c. &c.' And so he goes on for an interminable number of pages. Even the above extract is by no means the most amazing of Behmen's utterances. If one desired to take an extreme case, perhaps the verbal interpretation of Scripture would be that in which Behmen most of all out-Herods Herod. It really would seem at first sight as if he thought that Moses wrote, and Christ spoke, in German. He did not do so, for he speaks vaguely of a 'language of nature,' which he evidently distinguishes from any known tongue; [1] but it is difficult to attach any meaning to such an amazing passage as the following, except on the assumption that he did : 'Am Anfang erschuff Gott Himmel und Erden.' 'These words must be considered exactly what they are. For the word "Am" conceives itself in the Heart and goes forth to the lips ; but there is captivated and goes back again sounding, till it comes to the place from whence it came forth. And this signifies how that the Sound went forth from the Heart of God, and encompassed the whole Place or extent of this World ; but when it was found to be evil, then the Sound returned again into its own Place.' [2] All the rest of the verse is explained syllable by syllable in the same way. The whole of the Lord's Prayer is interpreted by a similar process ; [3]

---

[1] See *Memoirs of the Life, Death, Burial, and Wonderful Writings of Jacob Behmen, now first done at large into English*, by Francis Okely. 'He would,' writes Mr. Okely, 'from the outward signature and formation of flowers and herbs, immediately intimate their inward virtues, &c., together with the letters, syllables, and words of the name inspoken and ascribed to them. It was his custom first to desire to know their names in the Hebrew tongue, as being one that had the greatest affinity to that of nature ; and if its name were unknown in that language, he inquired what it was in Greek,' &c.

[2] *Aurora, &c.*, chap. xviii.

[3] See *The Threefold Life of Man*, chap. xvi., which is entitled 'A Summary Explanation of the Lord's Prayer ; how it is to be understood in the language of nature from syllable to syllable, as it is expressed in the words of the high Dutch tongue, which was the author's native language.' Behmen's 'Works,' in four volumes (1764), vol. ii. p. 175.

and the same principle is applied to other parts of Scripture.[1]   One can hardly wonder that such passages roused the ire of John Wesley, who of all things loved plainness, and one is certainly inclined to echo his indignant inquiry : 'Did any man in his senses from the beginning of the world ever think of explaining any treatise, human or divine, syllable by syllable ? If any Scripture could be thus explained, if any reason could be extracted from the several syllables, must it not be from the syllables of the original, not of a translation, whether English or German ?'[2]

After these portentous samples of Behmen's style, it is high time to relieve the reader's mind at once by stating that it will not be necessary for our present purpose to expound Behmenism from the works of Behmen.   There is no need to dwell further on the obscurities of Behmen, for as Byrom very truly, if not very poetically, remarks in one of his poems :—

> All the haranguing, therefore, on the theme
> Of deep obscurity in Jacob Behme
> Is but itself obscure ; for he might see
> Farther, 'tis possible, than you or me.[3]

Very possibly he might ; but still we may be thankful that our present task is concerned, not with Behmen, as he appears in his own writings, but with Behmen as he appears after passing through the crucible of Law's powerful mind ; with Behmen, not as he expressed himself in his own obscure and complicated style, but in the nervous and luminous style of his English exponent.

We may pass over, therefore, for the present the discussion of Behmen's theology, or rather theosophy, until it comes before us in Law's mystic writings.   But it is neces-

[1] See *inter alia*, Behmen's ' Works,' vol. ii. chaps. ii. and iii.

[2] *A Specimen of the Divinity and Philosophy of the Highly-Illuminated Jacob Behmen*, Wesley's ' Works,' vol. ix.

[3] *Socrates' Reply concerning Heraclitus' Writings.*   Byrom's Poems.

sary to add that Behmen has not done justice to himself if he desired the first extract which has been quoted to be a fair example of the way in which he could make himself intelligible. Some parts of his writings we may at any rate understand, whether we agree with him or not; and some parts contain passages of singular beauty, both of idea and expression. Take, for example, the following very beautiful vindication of the efficacy of infant baptism, which, with one or two omissions, might be used in a church pulpit at the present day : ' Say not, What does Baptism avail a child which understandeth it not ? The matter lies not in our understanding ; we are altogether ignorant of the kingdom of God. If thy child be a bud, grown in thy tree, and that thou standest in the covenant, why bringest thou not also thy bud into the covenant ? Thy faith is its faith, and thy confidence towards God in the covenant is its confidence. It is, indeed, thy essence, and generated in thy soul. And thou art to know, according to its exceeding worth, if thou art a true Christian, in the covenant of Jesus Christ, that thy child also (in the kindling of its life) passes into the covenant of Christ ; and though it should die in the mother's womb, it would be found in the covenant of Christ. For the Deity stands in the centre of the Light of Life ; and so now, if the tree stands in the covenant, then the branch may well do so.'[1] Or take again the following description of ' the Lord's Supper': ' Christ gave not to his disciples the earthly substance, which did but hang to Christ's body, in which he suffered death, which was despised, buffeted, slain, for then he had given them the mortal flesh ; but he gave them his holy body, his holy flesh, which hung also upon the cross in the mortal substance, and his holy blood which was shed together with the mortal,

[1] *The Three Principles of the Divine Essence,* Behmen's ' Works,' vol. i. chap. xxiii. p. 252.

as an immortal flesh and blood which the disciples received
into their body, which was put on to the soul, as a new
body out of Christ's body.'[1] Again, the following is a very
striking description of the future state, and, with the exception of one or two peculiar expressions, intelligible, at any
rate, to the meanest capacity : ' If we will speak of our
native country, out of which we are wandered with Adam,
and will tell of the Resting-place of the Soul, we need not
to cast our minds far off ; for far off or near is all one and
the same thing with God ; the Place of the Holy Trinity is all
over. . . . The Soul, when it departs from the Body, needs
not to go far, for at that Place where the body dies, there
is Heaven and Hell ; and the man Christ dwells everywhere. God and the Devil is there ; yet each in his own
kingdom. The Paradise is also there ; and the Soul needs
only to enter through the deep door in the Centre. Is the
Soul holy ? Then it stands in the Gate of Heaven, and
the earthly Body has but kept it out of Heaven ; and now
when the Body comes to be broken, then the Soul is already
in Heaven ; it needs no going out or in ; Christ has it in
his arms, &c.'[2] Many other passages might be quoted,
strangely wild and fanciful, but with a certain weird and
dreamy fascination about them, which none but a man of
genius with a true poet's eye could have written ; but as
they seem to me to be entirely without foundation in the
only Book which the Christian can recognise as an authority
on subjects so utterly beyond human ken, I refrain from
quoting them.[3]

---

[1] *The Threefold Life of Man*, Behmen's 'Works,' vol. ii. chap. xvi. p. 175.
[2] *The Three Principles of the Divine Essence*, Behmen's ' Works,' vol. i.
chap. xix. *ad fin* ; see also chap. ix. p. 61, on the same subject. ' There is
nothing nearer to you than Heaven, Paradise, and Hell . . . . then it becomes a paradisical child.'
[3] For examples, such passages as that in the Aurora, commencing : ' It is
most certain and true that there are all manner of Fruits in Heaven, and no
merely Types and Shadows.   Also the Angels pluck them with their Hands and
eat them, as we do that are men; but they have not any Teeth, &c.'(chap.viii.).

Not that Behmen ever professed to have received any revelation which was to supersede the Bible, or even to supplement it in any way ; but, as the inner light always existed in his own mind, and only required to be developed or ' opened ' (to use his own expression), so the truths which he proclaimed were all contained in the Bible, and only required to be ' opened.' Thus, with regard to the Creation and the Fall, which were the very hinges on which his whole system turned, he thought at first that his discoveries were not in the Bible. ' But,' he says, ' when I found the Pearl, then I looked Moses in the face, and found that Moses had wrote very right, and I had not rightly understood it.'[1] Neither is it correct to say that Behmen regarded himself as inspired ; there was simply an ' opening ' of God in him ; that is, the impulse came from within, not from without,—strictly in accordance with the fundamental principle of all mysticism, that Christ is *within* us.

Nor does he at all claim for himself the sole possession of the revelation which he had to make to the world ; others had potentially what he had actually. ' O thou bright Crown of Pearl,' he exclaims, ' art thou not brighter than the Sun ? There is nothing like thee ; thou art so very manifest, and yet so very secret, that among many thousand in this world, thou art scarcely rightly known of any one ; and yet thou art carried about in many that know thee not !'[2] Once more, Behmen, like most mystics, though in this respect unlike his admirer William Law, loved to find allegorical meanings in every part of Scripture ; but he did not, like the later mythical school, explain away the literal meaning of the historical facts. The sufferings of Christ, for example, were real, external facts, as well as being mystical. ' The outward man Christ underwent

[1] *The Three Principles of the Divine Essence,* chap. xvii. §§ 18, 19.
[2] *The Threefold Life of Man,* ' Works,' vol. ii. p. 69, chap. vi.

this Pain also outwardly when He was scourged ; for all
the inward Forms which the man Christ must bear inwardly
for our sakes, which caused him to sweat drops of Blood,
they stood also outwardly on his Body.'[1]

In fact, Behmen's position in regard to God's Revealed
Word could not be better described than in the following
words of William Law: ' He has no right to be placed
among the inspired Pen-men of the New Testament ; he
was no Messenger from God of anything new in Religion ;
but the mystery of all that was old and true both in
Religion and Nature was *opened* in him. This is the
particularity of his character, by which he stands fully
distinguished from all the Prophets, Apostles, and extraordinary Messengers of God. They were sent with occasional Messages, or to make such alterations in the
œconomy of Religion as pleased God ; but this man came
on no particular Errand, he had nothing to alter, or add,
either in the Form or Doctrine of Religion ; he had no new
Truths of Religion to propose to the World, but all that lay
in Religion and Nature, as a Mystery unsearchable, was in
its deepest Ground opened in this Instrument of God. And
all his Works are nothing else but a deep manifestation of
the Grounds and Reasons of that which is done, that which
is doing, and is to be done, both in the kingdom of Nature
and the kingdom of Grace, from the Beginning to the End
of Time. His Works, therefore, though immediately from
God, have not at all the Nature of the Holy Scriptures ;
they are not offered to the World, as necessary to be received, or as a Rule of Faith and Manners, and therefore
no one has any Right to complain, either of the Depths of
his Matter, or the Peculiarity of his Stile : They are just as
they should be, for those that are fit for them ; and he that

---

[1] *The Three Principles of the Divine Essence*, chap. xxv. ; ' Works,' vol.
i. p. 267.

likes them not, or finds himself unqualified for them, has no obligation to read them.'[1]

In spite of the marked and wide distinction which Law draws between the writers of Holy Writ and Behmen, it will be thought perhaps that he claims for his favourite a sufficiently exalted mission ; and though he admits that no man is obliged to read Jacob's writings as necessary to salvation, yet in another passage he expresses pretty clearly what his opinion is of those who do not appreciate them. ' I have given,' he says, ' notice of a Pearl ; if any one takes it to be otherwise, or has neither skill or value for Pearls, he is at Liberty to trample it under his feet.'[2] We all know what is the kind of animal which tramples Pearls underfoot.

It will be asked, What were the reasons for the fascination which Behmen exercised over a man of undoubted genius and piety like William Law?   These will appear more fully when we come to Law's mystic writings, but one reason may be noted here, viz., the contrast between the mean condition and want of education in Behmen, and the spirituality and beauty of his writings. For years, Law had been taking up his parable on the utter insufficiency of human learning to discern spiritual truths ; nay, on the positive hindrances which it gave to the discernment of them.   Here was a very case in point ! A pearl had been cast before these learned swine, cram-full of the husks of school-divinity, heathen mythology, profane poetry,—everything, in short, except the one thing needful,—and they trampled it under their feet, and turned again to rend him who had cast it before them ! Over and over again Law refers with inexpressible gusto to Behmen's want of human

---

[1] *Appeal to all that Doubt, &c.*; Law's ' Works,' vol. vi. p. 323-4.
[2] *Ibid.* p. 329.

learning. ' In his natural capacity and outward condition of
Life, he was as mean and illiterate as any one that our Lord
called to be an Apostle.'[1] ' The poor illiterate Behmen
was so merely an instrument of Divine Direction, as to have
no ability to think, speak, or write anything but what
sprung up in him or came upon him as independently of
himself, as a shower of rain falls here or there independently
of the place where it falls. His works, being an opening
of the Spirit of God working in him, are quite out of the
course of man's reasoning wisdom, and proceed no more
according to it than the living Plant breathes forth its
virtues according to such rules of skill as an Artist must
use to set up a painted dead Figure of it,'[2]—and to the same
effect in innumerable other passages.[3]

And Law was surely so far right, in thinking that the
learned men of his day utterly failed to appreciate the true
character and value of Behmen and his writings. We have
seen that many of them avowed point-blank, without any
circumlocution, that Behmen's inspiration came from the
_Devil,—the source, by the way, from which Wesley, White-
field, and the early Methodists were frequently said to
derive their impulse.[4]

Behmen was no ' Demonosopher' (to adopt Wesley's
happy phrase). His motives were perfectly pure and disinterested. His life was perfectly guileless and transparent ;

---

[1] *Appeal to all that Doubt, &c.,* p. 322.

[2] *Fragment of a Dialogue by W. Law,* prefixed to the translation of
Behmen's ' Works' of 1764 falsely attributed to Law. Though these volumes
can by no means be depended upon always, there is no doubt whatever that
this Dialogue was, as it purports to be, the work of Law. Law's style is un-
mistakable ; it was not to be imitated by any one, and least of all by the
translators of this work, of whom more anon.

[3] See especially the whole of the Second and Third Dialogues in *The Way
to Divine Knowledge,* Law's ' Works,' vol. vii. pp. 83-251.

[4] See Bishop Lavington's *Enthusiasm of Papists and Methodists compared,*
passim ; also Bishop Warburton's *Doctrine of Grace,* passim, &c.

and through his wild soul there flashed many noble and elevating thoughts, to which he struggled, and often in vain, to give an imperfect utterance. Those who follow him blindly as a guide will probably fall into intellectual quagmires, from which Law himself did not altogether escape ; but those who can see nothing in his writings but the disordered fancies of an unsound mind, have either imperfectly studied them, or else are unable to recognise genius when they meet with it.

CHAPTER XII.

'GENERAL REMARKS ON MYSTICISM.

LONG as this digression has already been, it seems necessary to add a few general remarks on Mysticism before
returning to the subject of Law's outer life.

It will have been gathered from the preceding pages
that I have a deep, but not indiscriminate, admiration for
the characters and writings of many of the mystics. And
surely their ardent piety, their intense realisation of the
Divine Presence, their spiritual-mindedness, their unsel-
fishness, their humility, their calm and serene faith, the
refinement, nay, the poetry of their style and matter, their
elevating view of the heavenly meaning of outward nature,
their cultivation of the inner life,—the ' life that is hid with
Christ in God,'—and many other points in their system,
are worthy of admiration.

But it may naturally be asked, How is it, if mysticism
really be what it has been described as being, that it has
not found more favour with a people so religious as the
English, on the whole, decidedly are ?

This question requires an answer. It will have been
observed that in the foregoing sketch the name of not one
single Englishman appears. The sketch, it will be remembered, was confined to those mystics exclusively who
influenced William Law ; and, though there were many
Englishmen of a mystical tendency who would come under
that category, and who will therefore be noticed presently,

there was assuredly not one who can fairly be called a
mystic proper. It would be too sweeping a statement to
assert that there were no English mystics, but they were
few and far between. Mysticism is a plant which seems
to thrive on English soil hardly better than an Alpen-rose
would on the top of Helvellyn. A fair and full account of
Christian mysticism is still a want in English literature.
Perhaps the most popular English book on the subject—
the book from which many who have not made mysticism
their special study derive their knowledge of it—is Mr.
Vaughan's ' Hours with the Mystics,' and its popularity
is not undeserved. The writer is full of information ; he
writes cleverly, and evidently desires to do justice to
his subject. But his very plan shows that he is hardly
in sympathy with it. His work is in the form of a
dialogue, or rather of a series of narratives, read by a
lawyer, on which the hearers—a country gentleman, his
sharp-witted wife, a lively young artist, and a rather flippant young lady—make their comments. The subject is
introduced as ' Three friends sat about their after-dinner
table, chatting over their wine and walnuts,'—not very
favourable circumstances under which to discuss the deep,
spiritual thoughts of devoted and self-denying Christians.
A good deal of smart badinage goes on over the narratives.
Now and then the subject seems likely to be slow, and the
ladies cut the performance. The writer loves to quote all
the extravagant expressions which mystics, carried away
by the heat of devotion, may have used. Those passages
in the history of mysticism are chiefly dwelt upon which
have a smack of romance about them ; such, for example,
as the account of Madame Guyon, who, being a fascinating
woman with a romantic history, occupies a space far beyond the proportion of her merits. The whole account of
Tauler's efforts as a patriot, though it has nothing directly

to do with mysticism, is given at full length ; and the
treatise ends very appropriately with the ringing of the
marriage bells for the wedding of the lively young artist
and the pert young lady.[1]

This sort of thing is all very well when the subject is
like those, for instance, discussed in the ' Noctes Ambrosi-

[1] Here are one or two specimens of the manner, that the reader may judge
for himself whether the description in the text is exaggerated or not.
Gower : Let me bring some prisoners to your bar. Silence in the court
there ! [Then follows an account of some mystics' views.] Guilty of mysticism, or not ?
Atherton : Can you call good evidence to character ?
Gower : First rate ! &c. (I. 27.)

.   .   .   .

Willoughby: Here's another definition for you : mysticism is the romance
of religion. What do you say?
Gower : True to the spirit ; not scientific, I fear.
Willoughby : Science be banished ! &c. (I. 29.)

.   .   .   .

Gower (flourishing a ruler, turning to the four points, and reading with
tremendous voice a formula of incantation from Hörst) : Lalla Bacheram !
Willoughby (springing upon Gower): Seize him! He's stark, staring mad !
Gower : Hands off ! were we not to discuss to-night the best possible order
for your mystics ?
Atherton : And a neat little plan I had set up—shaken all to pie at this
moment by your madcap antics !
Gower : Thanks, if you please, not reproaches. I was calling help for
you ; I was summoning the fay.
Willoughby : The fay?
Gower : The fay. Down with you in that arm-chair and sit quietly.
I now that I was this morning reading Anderson's Märchen—all about Luk-
Oie, his ways and works, the queer little elf, &c. (I. 39.)

.   .   .   .

Gower : Don't you think Atherton has a very manuscriptural air to-night ?
Kate : There is a certain aspect of repletion about him.
Mrs. Atherton : We must bleed him, or the consequences may be serious.
What's this? (Pulls a paper out of his pocket.)
Kate: And this ? (Pulls out another.)
Willoughby : He seems better.
The MS. is the long account of Tauler. The two impostors in Sir W.
Scott's novels, Sir A. Wardour's Dousterswivel and Leicester's Alasco, are
instanced as specimens of one kind of mystic (vol. ii. p. 34). Swedenborg is
' the Olympian Jove of mystics '—whatever that may mean (II. 279). And
yet the writer admits at the beginning of his work that ' the mystics were the
conservators of the poetry and heart of religion,' and that ' their very errors
were often such as were possible only to great souls.' (I. 15.)

ance,' or ' Friends in Council.' But questions which, to say the least of them, are of the profoundest spiritual moment, and works whose every page palpitates with the deepest emotions of their authors, surely deserve a little more serious treatment.

And there are a few English writers, and those men of high mark, who *have* treated the subject, though only slightly and incidentally, in a more serious and sympathetic tone. Foremost among these stands the honoured name of John Keble. He was attracted to the subject, partly by his reverence for patristic authority, and partly by his poetical instinct. The author of the ' Christian Year ' could hardly be insensible to the deep vein of devotional poetry which runs through the prose writings of the mystics, especially those parts of them which treat of the analogies between the visible and the invisible worlds. It would be difficult, indeed, to find a more thoughtful and appreciative estimate of Christian mysticism than in the beautiful fragment (alas! that it should be only a fragment) in Tract 89 of the ' Tracts for the Times.' The title of the tract is ' On the Mysticism attributed to the Early Fathers,' and the primary object of the writer is to vindicate the Fathers from the supposed stigma attaching to them on account of their mysticism. His remarks on the prejudices against mysticism were perhaps more applicable forty years ago than they are now ; but the prejudices still exist, if they are not so virulent, and therefore the weighty words of the departed saint are well worth quoting. ' It [the word mysticism],' he writes, ' touches the very string which most certainly moves contemptuous thought in those who have imbibed the peculiar spirit of our time. Mysticism implies a sort of confusion between physical and moral, visible and invisible agency, most abhorrent to the minds of those who pique themselves on having thoroughly clear ideas, and on their power of distinctly analysing effects into their proper causes, whether in matter or mind. Again, mysticism conveys the notion of something essentially and altogether remote from common sense and practical utility ; but common sense and practical utility are the very idols of the age. Further, that which is stigmatised as mysticism is almost always something which makes itself discerned by internal evidence. . . . . In the eyes of a world full of hurry and business, there is a temptation to acquiesce over lightly in any censure of that kind. . . . . How meanly even respectable persons allow themselves to think of the highest sort of poetry—that which invests all things, great and small, with the noblest of all associations—when once they have come to annex to it the notion of mysticism ! Perhaps its mischievous effects on theology are as great as any attributable to a single word.'

The frame of mind in which such a subject as mysticism should be studied is well described. 'A person who would go into this question with advantage should be imbued beforehand with a kind of natural piety, which will cause him to remember all along that perhaps, when he comes to the end of his inquiry, he will find that God was all the while really there. He will " put off his shoes from off his feet " if he do but think it possible that an angel may tell him by and by, " the place whereon thou standest is holy ground." So it must be in some measure with every right-minded person in the examination of every practice and opinion against which the charge of mysticism is brought. Whatever may appear in the case at first sight, likely to move scorn or ridicule, or tempt to mere lightness of thought, it will be an exercise of faith, a trial of a serious heart, to repress for the time any tendency of that kind ; the loss and error being infinitely greater, if we are found trifling with a really sacred subject, than if we

merely prove to have been a little more serious than was
necessary. In this sense—that is to say, in regard of the
reverent or irreverent *temper* in which such inquiries may
be approached—superstition is surely a great deal better
than irreligion. . . . . The noblest and most refined devotional tendencies have always had to bear the imputation
of mysticism, or some other equivalent word ; as if to cultivate them were a mere indulgence of a dreamy, soaring,
indistinct fancy. In this use of it, the word " mysticism "
has done probably as much harm in checking high, con-
templative devotion, as the kindred term " asceticism " in
encouraging Christian self-discipline.'
    The grounds on which mysticism was attributed to the
early Fathers were (1) their allegorical way of interpreting
Scripture ; (2) their tendency to spiritualise the works of
nature. With the first of these we are not concerned ; but
on the second Keble's remarks are very applicable to William Law. He calls it the symbolical or sacramental view
of nature. ' The works of God in creation and providence,
besides their immediate uses in this life, appeared to the
old writers as so many intended tokens from the Almighty
to assure us of some spiritual fact or other, which it concerns us to know :' and then, having referred to several passages of Scripture in which this analogy is obviously worked
out, he asks : ' What if the whole scheme of sensible things
be figurative ? What, if all αἰσθητὰ answer to νοητὰ in the
same kind of way as these which are expressly set down ?
What if these are but a slight specimen of one great use
which Almighty God would have us make of the external
world and of its relation to the world spiritual ? The form
of speaking would imply some such general rule ' (' That
was the *True* (ἀληθινόν) Light,' &c.), 'taking for granted that
there was somewhere in the nature of things a true counterpart of these ordinary objects, a substance of which they

were but unreal shadows; and only informing us, in each
case with authority, what that counterpart and substance
was.[1]   The Scriptures deal largely in symbolical language
taken from natural objects.   The chosen vehicle for the
most direct Divine communication has always been that
form of speech which most readily adopts and invites such
imagery, viz. the poetical.   Is there not something very
striking to a thoughtful, reverential mind in the simple fact
of symbolical language occurring in Scripture at all? that
is, when truths *supernatural* are represented in Scripture by
visible and sensible imagery.   Consider what this really
comes to.   The Author of Scripture is the Author of
Nature.   He made his creatures what they are, upholds
them in their being, modifies it at his will, knows all their
secret relations, associations, and properties.   We know
not how much there may be, far beyond metaphor and
similitude, in his using the name of any one of his creatures, in a translated sense, to shadow out some thing
invisible.   But thus far we may seem to understand, that
the object thus spoken of by Him is so far taken out of
the number of ordinary figures of speech and resources of
language, and partakes henceforth of the nature of a Type.'
Then, after having illustrated his position by a great variety
of passages in Scripture, he concludes: ' The text, " The
invisible things from the creation of the world are clearly
seen, being understood by the things that are made," lays
down a principle or canon of mystical interpretation for the
works of nature. . . . . It is the characteristic tendency of
poetical minds to make the world of sense from beginning to
end symbolical of the absent and unseen ; and poetry was
the ordained vehicle of revelation, till God was made mani-

---

[1] It will at once be seen how exactly all this agrees with the Platonic
idealism of S. Augustine, whom, indeed, Keble frequently quotes in this Tract.

fest in the Flesh.' The Tract from which these quotations have been made is little known, perhaps ; but every one knows the hymn, ' There is a book who runs may read.' That hymn is the poetical rendering of Keble's views on one phase of mysticism.

Few men differed more widely in their general tone of thought than John Keble and Charles Kingsley. But they might have found a common bond of sympathy in the attractions which mysticism presented to both. Moreover, it was, in part, the same aspect of mysticism which fascinated both. Kingsley, like Keble, was deeply impressed with the mystic harmony between the visible and invisible worlds. Nay, he went beyond Keble in the extent to which he would adopt the plan of spiritualising nature. ' The great mysticism,' he writes, ' is the belief, which is becoming every day stronger with me, that all symmetrical natural objects, aye, and perhaps all forms, colours, and scents which show organisation or arrangement, are types of some spiritual truth or existence, of a grade between the symbolical and the mystic type. Everything seems to be full of God's reflex, if we could but see it.' [1] ' The visible world is in some mysterious way a pattern or symbol of the invisible one ; its physical laws are the analogues of the spiritual laws of the eternal world.' [2] Like Keble, he observes with regret that ' our popular theology has so completely rid itself of any mystic elements,' and he attributes this avoidance of mysticism to the influence exercised by the philosophy of Locke.[3] There was, however, another phase of mysticism which attracted Kingsley, but would probably have repelled Keble ; that is, its breadth.

---

[1] *Life of C. Kingsley*, i. 77.
[2] *Miscellanies*, by C. Kingsley, Review of Vaughan's *Hours with the Mystics*, i. 329.
[3] *Ibid.* p. 325.

The Christ in every man, the 'light which lighteth every man that cometh into the world,' was a doctrine which, like the mystics, Kingsley understood in its most literal sense, and 'realised with extraordinary vividness.'[1] His mode of reconciling the wrath of God with the love of God exactly tallied with William Law's explanation. 'Because,' he writes, 'I believe in a God of absolute and unbounded love, therefore I believe in a loving anger of his, which will and must devour all, destroy all, which is decayed, monstrous, abortive in his universe.'[2] Like Law, he left it to be inferred as the necessary consequence of this theory, rather than actually stated his belief in the final restitution of all things. It seems strange that Kingsley should never have referred to Law in any of his frequent allusions to mysticism, particularly when we remember how deeply Law was appreciated by Kingsley's friend, F. D. Maurice. Possibly Law's reputation as a nonjuror and distinct high churchman may have repelled him ; possibly, also, Law's best known work, 'The Serious Call,' may have led him to avoid an author who in that stage of his career certainly took a widely different view of life from his own. But, assuredly, if any such prejudices as these prevented Kingsley from reading Law's later writings, he lost much which would have thoroughly harmonised with his own deepest convictions.[3]

There is another English writer, differing in tone of mind both from Keble and Kingsley as widely as Keble and Kingsley differed from each other, who shows some appreciation of the mystics, not because he had the least

---

[1] See *Life of C. Kingsley*, i. 160.

[2] *Ibid.* p. 396.

[3] Take, for example, the following sentence, in which he speaks in a tone of sadness of a want which the popular theology could not supply to him: 'I want to love and honour the absolute, abysmal God himself, and none other will satisfy me. This Lockism infects all our pulpits' (*Life*, i. 397). Would not the 'Spirit of Prayer' and the 'Spirit of Love' have helped him to supply this want?

sympathy with any phase of mysticism, but simply because he has made it his laudable aim to be fair all round. The late Dean Waddington certainly cannot be claimed by the mystics as their own ; indeed, he was so very much the reverse, that he seems almost ashamed of the approbation which his sense of justice forced him to bestow upon them, and half takes away with one hand what he has given with the other. His testimony, however, is all the more valuable on this very account, because it is, as it were, extorted from him in spite of himself. He preludes his account of some of the wilder sects which hung on the outskirts of mysticism with these very sensible and much-needed cautions : ' In a religious society, the purest characters are commonly those which shun celebrity ; it is rare that they throw their modest lustre on the historic page. On this account it is that, while the absurdities of mysticism are commonly known and derided, the good effect which it had in turning the mind to spiritual resolves and amending the hearts of multitudes imbued with it, is generally overlooked.'[1] Again : ' Under the respectable name of Mysticism much genuine devotion was concealed, and many ardent and humble aspirations poured forth before the Throne of Grace.'[2] And speaking of the prevalence of mysticism in every age of the Church, he writes : ' The aspirations of mysticism, sometimes degraded into absurdity, sometimes exalted into the purest piety, have unquestionably pervaded and warmed every portion of the ecclesiastical system, from the earliest era even to the present.'[3]

These three writers have been taken as typical instances of three very different classes of minds which have been more or less favourably impressed with the lives and writings of the mystics. Of course many more might have been

[1] Waddington's *History of the Church*, chap. xxvi. p. 608.
[2] *Ibid.* chap. xxviii. p. 700.   [3] *Ibid.* p. 708.

added ;[1] but they are certainly the exception, not the rule.
The general tendency of English divines has been to regard
mysticism with suspicion, and never more so than in the days
of Law, when the popularity of Lockism was at its zenith.

Nor is this suspicion altogether unnatural ; for the abuse
of mysticism leads to just those faults which are specially
odious to the English mind. Let us briefly consider what
these faults are.

(1.) Mysticism is charged with being unpractical and
leading men to neglect active duties and good works. The
lives of some false mystics, and some extravagant expressions in the teaching of true mystics, may lend countenance
to the charge ; but assuredly this is not, as it has been
repeatedly stated to be,[2] the legitimate tendency of the
system, nor has it been, as a matter of fact, its general
result. The lives of the most distinguished mystics rebut
the charge. When the wretched Strasburgers were stricken
to the ground by the double curse of the Black Death and
the Papal Interdict, it was the mystic Tauler who showed
his faith by his works of untiring benevolence, and, while

---

[1] E.g., S. T. Coleridge, through whose writings a vein of mysticism runs,
though he never, so far as I am aware, wrote directly on the subject. See
especially his *Lay Sermons*, pp. 74-9, 98-9, and *passim*. Bishop Berkeley's
'Siris' is essentially a mystic work. See also Ashwell's *Life of Bishop Wil-
berforce*, pp. 125 and 239.

[2] Thus M. Bonnel writes: 'Le mysticisme confiné dans les étroites limites
d'un certain monde intérieur, non-seulement n'inspire par lui-même l'exercice
d'aucune vertu, mais, poussé à ses dernières conséquences, il peut devenir un
principe d'inertie nuisible à la société ; il rapproche du ciel, mais c'est en
faisant perdre de vue la terre, c'est-à-dire en détournant les âmes de la grande
vocation de l'humanité.'—*De la Controverse de Bossuet et de Fénélon sur le
Quiétisme*, Introduction III.

Dr. Hey: 'It [mysticism] makes men useless when it runs to excess ; it
furnishes them with means of evading such duties as they cannot be ignorant
of, and it prevents them from learning many others ;' with much more to the
same effect. (*Lectures in Divinity*, vol. i. pp. 471-2, &c.) The same idea
runs through the whole of Alexander Knox's letter to D. Parken, Esq., ' On
the Character of Mysticism.' See *Knox's Remains*, vol. i. pp. 328, 329,
343, &c.

other religious teachers fled from the devoted city, manfully remained at his post, and, almost by his sole efforts, sustained the faith of his afflicted countrymen. When Fénélon retired to Cambray in semi-disgrace, he astonished the people of his diocese by taking the hardest duties upon himself, by visiting the poor in their cottages, sympathising with their griefs, and 'partaking of their black bread as though he had never shared the banquets of Versailles.' [1] The Mystic, S. Bernard, was the very incarnation of active Christianity. Madame Guyon was as energetic in attending to the patients at hospitals, as she was in recommending Quietism. Even the recluse Malebranche never forgot the claims of practical benevolence in the studies of philosophical mysticism. William Law, though he was always ready to show his faith by his good works, had not scope for the exercise of his charity until he had long been a Mystic ; while the sect in England, which has been most conspicuous for its mystic views, has also been most remarkable for its deeds of practical Christianity I mean, of course, the Quakers.

Nor can it be said that, in the case of those practical Christians who were attached to Mysticism, the men were better than their opinions. They give a perfectly consistent account of the principle on which a Mystic, while holding that the one aim of the Christian must be complete union with God, that he must have no will but God's will, that he must resign himself wholly to God and be passive in his hands, may yet, or rather, *therefore*, be active in all outward Christian duties. Thus Macarius is writing nothing out of harmony with his system when he says, ' If we would be born of the Heavenly Father we must do something better than the rest of men, that is, live in faith

---

[1] See Bishop de Bausset's *Life of Fénélon*, translated by Mudford, passim.

and fear, with all diligence, pains, zeal, love, and good works. The Lord quickens and awakens dead and corrupt souls through the good works and teaching of the Apostles.' Rusbrochius was in no way inconsistent when he declared, ' God requires obedience from us, according to his Gospel. Use thou only the grace that is in thee and take heed to thyself of that which can hinder thy culture. Therefore, not only plough and till, but also root out the thorns. Shouldst thou be lazy, thy field will become a wilderness.' Tauler's teaching to the same effect has already been quoted. Fénélon drew, in his own beautiful language, a perfectly logical distinction between quietism and idleness. ' Holy indifference is not inactivity. It is the furthest possible from it. It is indifference to anything and every-thing out of God's will ; but it is the highest life and activity to everything in that will. Self-renunciation is not the renunciation of faith or of love, or of anything except selfishness.' And again, ' The state of continuous faith and consequent repose in God is called the *passive* state ; but the more pliant and supple the soul is to divine impressions, the more real and efficacious is her own *action*, though with-out any excited or troubled movement. Nothing disturbs it ; and being thus peaceful, it reflects distinctly and clearly the image of Christ ; like the placid lake, which shows in its own clear and beautiful bosom the exact forms of the objects around and above it.'[1] In short, Madame Guyon's explanation of the mystic passivity, though somewhat clumsily expressed, is substantially correct. ' Better,' she says, ' call it *passively active*, because the sanctified soul, though it no longer has a will of its own, is never strictly inert. There is always an act of co-operation with God.'[2] Or, as a distinguished modern mystic expresses it, ' Perfect

[1] *Maximes des Saints.*
[2] Upham's *Life of Madame Guyon*, p. 378.

self-surrender differs wide as the Poles are asunder from inactivity. No true mystic withdraws himself wilfully from the business of life, no, not even from the smallest business.'[1] The worst that can be said is that the mystic teaching on this head has been sometimes misunderstood, and perverted to an abuse which no true mystic ever intended.

(2.) It is not so easy to vindicate mysticism from another charge which has been brought against it, viz., that it tends to make men think lightly of the outward ordinances of religion. It is true that the more moderate mystics expressly disclaim any such intention ; but even these lay so much more stress upon the duty of retiring into the inner temple of one's own heart that it can hardly be wondered at if their more extravagant disciples have concluded that worship in any other temple was a matter of minor consideration. Take, for example, the following passage from Tauler, the most reasonable and practical of mystics, on the Christian progress :—' They turn their thoughts inward, and remain resting on the inmost foundation of their souls, simply looking to see the hand of God with the eyes of their enlightened reason, and await from within their summons to go whither God would have them. And this they receive from God without any means, but what is given through means, such as other mortal men, is as it were tasteless ; moreover, it is seen as through a veil, and split up into fragments, and within it is a certain sting of bitterness. It always retains the savour of that which is of the creature, which it must needs lose and be purified from, if it is to become in truth food for the spirit, and to enter into the very substance of the soul.'[2] Behmen is never weary of dwelling upon the blessedness of this introversion

---

[1] Ewald's *Briefe über die alte Mystik und den neuen Mysticismus*, p. 280.
[2] Sermon for Advent Sunday.

of the soul. 'Turn away your heart and mind from all contention, and go in very simply and humbly at the door of Christ into Christ's sheepfold ; seek that in your heart ;'[1] and many more passages to the same effect. His admission of the possible use of outward ordinances is very faint and reluctant, and contrasts strangely with the fire and enthusiasm with which he speaks of the blessedness of retiring into the temple within. 'Where,' he says, 'the living knowledge of Christ is, there is the altar of God in all places where the hungry soul may offer the true, acceptable, holy offering in prayer, &c. Not that we would hereby wholly abolish and raze the stone churches, but we teach the temple of Christ which ought to be brought along into the stone church, or else the whole business of the stone church is only a Cain's offering, both of preacher and hearer. . . . Cain goes to church to offer, and comes out again a killer of his brother.'[2] Ewald gives from his own experience a curious instance of the results of this kind of teaching. 'I am preacher,' he writes, 'in a place where there are many Behmenists. They attended no church, took no part in the Lord's Supper. But, on closer acquaintance, I found among them some very candid, moral, and well-instructed men. I asked the cause why they attended no church ; they answered me that they edified themselves every Sunday and feast-day with Behmen's writings. I persuaded some of them to come to my church, and I gave myself much trouble to speak in their language, which was already popularised through the expression and imagery of the Bible.'[3] But it could hardly be expected that many clergy could adapt themselves so conveniently to the idiosyncrasies of the Behmenists.

[1] *The Threefold Life of Man*, Behmen's Works, vol. ii. chap. xi. p. 125.
[2] *Mysterium Magnum*, Behmen's Works, vol. iii. chap. xxvii. p. 132.
[3] *Briefe über die alte Mystik und den neuen Mysticismus*, p. 225-6.

Law himself personally never neglected the means of grace ; he and all who were under his influence attended every service, week-day and Sunday, at their own parish church, and he never intended one syllable of his teaching to direct his readers otherwise. But some of his sentiments might not unreasonably be construed as depreciating outward ordinances. Take, for example, that magnificent passage in the ' Spirit of Prayer,' which gave such deep offence to John Wesley : ' This pearl of eternity is the *Church*, or temple of God *within thee*, the consecrated place of divine worship, where alone thou canst worship God *in spirit and in truth. In spirit*, because thy spirit is that alone in thee, which can unite and cleave unto God, and receive the working of His Divine Spirit upon thee. *In truth*, because this *adoration* in spirit is that *truth* and *reality*, of which all outward *forms* and *rites*, though instituted by God, are only the *figure* for a time, but this worship is eternal. Accustom thyself to the holy service of this inward temple. In the midst of it is the fountain of living water, of which thou mayst drink and live for ever. There the mysteries of thy redemption are celebrated, or rather opened in life and power. There the Supper of the Lamb is kept ; *the bread that came down from Heaven, that giveth life to the world*, is thy true nourishment : all is done and known in real experience, in a living sensibility of the work of God on the soul. There the birth, the life, the sufferings, the death, the resurrection and ascension of Christ are not merely remembered, but inwardly found and enjoyed as the real state of thy soul, which has followed Christ in the regeneration. When once thou art well-grounded in this *inward worship*, thou wilt have learnt to live unto God *above time* and *place*. For every day will be *Sunday* to thee, and wherever thou goest thou wilt have a *priest*, a *church*, and an *altar* along with

thee.'[1]   John Wesley drew inferences from this passage
which Law never intended, but Wesley was a practical man
and saw whither, as a matter of fact, such doctrines tended
when imbibed by ordinary mortals.

(3.) 'Mysticism,' wrote Alexander Knox, ' is hostile to
Christianity, because it necessarily disqualifies the mind for
that distinct and intelligent contemplation of *Immanuel.*
The contemplation of the deity, to which the embodied
spirit is unequal, is contrary to the incarnation.'[2]   This is
far too strongly stated, but it points to a peril against which
all who have a tendency to mysticism should be on their
guard.   Law over and over again affirms, as Behmen
affirmed before him, that the doctrine of the Christ within
in no wise weakened his belief in the historical Christ who
was ' born of the Virgin Mary, suffered under Pontius Pilate ; '
and all the more moderate mystics affirm the same.   But
there is among the more extravagant mystics unquestionably a tendency to ignore the glorious truth that by the incarnation God, as it were, came down from the clouds in order
to prevent men from losing themselves in the clouds.   This
question, however, is in fact part of a greater : Does mysticism tend to sap the foundation of dogmatic theology ?
Here, again, we must answer, Not necessarily, but still there
is a danger of the system being so perverted.   To men who
are accustomed to soar to the lofty heights of mystic ecstasy, ' to lose themselves in the divine dark,' it is apt to
appear slavish, grovelling work to be tied down to articles
of faith.   Law himself was by no means free from this
danger.   He is never weary of crying down the learned
labours of divines, apparently forgetful of the fact that,
after all, Christianity is, in one sense, an historical religion,
which requires its proofs like any other history, that after
all it is a system of distinct articles of belief, which must

[1] *Spirit of Prayer*, Law's Works, vol. vii. p. 74 5.   [2] *Remains*, vol. ii. p. 333.

be defended and proved like those of any other system. Mysticism avowedly addresses itself to the feelings, not to the reason ; the eighteenth century was essentially an age of reason not of feeling ; each mode of viewing the matter has something to say for itself ; each has its peculiar snares ; and assuredly, if there be danger on the one hand of the heart of religion being frozen out by cold dogmas, there is, at least, equal danger on the other, of the *rationale* of religion evaporating in mere heat of feeling and in airy speculation.

(4.) The charge against mysticism of giving too little prominence to Christian dogmas is unquestionably a grave one, which the *Christian* mystic cannot afford to neglect ; but he need not be so careful to answer another similar objection raised against his system on the grounds of philosophy. It may be necessary, from the philosopher's point of view, to explain philosophically this phenomenon of the human mind ; but certainly, from the mystic's own point of view, any such explanation would seem strangely out of place. ' Sensationalism, idealism, scepticism, mysticism, eclecticism,'[1] would appear to him to be what the logicians call a cross division. He would ask himself ' What in the world am I doing in this galley ? ' He has been conscious of no such intellectual process as that by which the historian of philosophy supposes him to have arrived at his conclusions, if we are to call those conclusions which *he* would call simply intuitions or illuminations. He would say in effect to the philosopher, ' Settle these matters among yourselves. I know nothing about all these processes of the human mind ; one thing I know, whereas I was blind, now I see, and that is enough for me.'[2]

---

[1] This is Mr. Morell's division of the various systems of philosophy. See his *History of Philosophy*, passim.

[2] ' We cannot,' writes Dr. Dorner (*Hist. of Prot. Theology Eng. Tr.* i. 52), ' with some recent writers, regard it (mysticism) only as a kind of philosophy, or as the preliminary stage of a modern speculative mode of thought,

(5.) A very favourite expression of reproach against the mystics is that they are 'visionary ; ' if by visionary be meant apt to see and believe in visions, the epithet cannot be applied with truth to the genuine mystic.[1]   It is true that many mystics, such as S. Theresa, did see visions, but not *quâ* mystics.   The very essence of mysticism is that a man should retire into the temple of his own soul, and he will find God there.   He has no need of any vision or appearance from without,—no, not even from God ; his state of ecstasy or contemplation is not a manifestation of God from without, but an opening of God from within.   Law was in this respect a true mystic ; he held that visions were not to be sought ; and he looked with considerable suspicion and reserve on those who professed to have been favoured with them.

(6.) 'Mysticism encourages vanity or spiritual pride.'[2] Theoretically it might be enough to answer that humility is the very cardinal grace of the mystic ; but then there is a pride which apes humility, and it is quite possible that spiritual pride might lurk under the garb of mystic self-abasement.   But, as a matter of fact, the most pronounced mystics have without exception, so far as I know, been in very truth the humblest of men ; nor can I think of one instance in which true mysticism has led to self-conceit.

(7.) Mysticism is charged with using too familiar, not to say improper, expressions to describe the relation between Christ and the Christian.   It has been seen that, according

which fell with its time, a stage, however, which retires in obscure idealism into itself, to find in itself all truth and reality.   The whole essence of mysticism lies in a real religious fellowship of the subject with the personal God and of God with him.   The religious element must be regarded as the original principle, as the life-germ of mysticism.'

[1] ' Ceux qui traitent les mystiques de visionnaires seraient fort étonnés de voir quel peu de ces ils font des visions en elles-mêmes.'—*Dictionnaire de Mystique Chrétienne,* Introduction par l'Abbé Migne.

[2] Hey's *Lectures on Divinity,* i. 470.

to the mystic theory, perfect union of the soul with God is to be the aim of the Christian ; that this union is to be effected through love ; and that all earthly and visible things are types, or rather, more than types, actually lower forms of things spiritual and invisible.   It naturally follows that the best figure under which this spiritual union can be represented is the union of two human beings through earthly love.   That there *is* a beautiful analogy between the earthly and the heavenly in this respect no one of course will deny.   God has ' consecrated the state of matrimony to such an excellent mystery, that in it is signified and represented the spiritual marriage and unity betwixt Christ and his church.'   But in this ' mystical union ' of which our prayer-book speaks, the bride is the church collectively, not the individual Christian.   Some mystics not only married the individual soul to Christ, but closely followed out the analogy in the minutest particulars, and, it must be confessed, outraged sometimes one's notions not only of reverence but even of decency.   No one worked out this analogy more elaborately than Jacob Behmen ; in fact it would be quite impossible to transfer to these pages many passages from him on this subject.   Happily, on this point Law did not follow his master ; not only is there not one syllable in his writings which could shock the most fastidious ; he hardly ever alludes to the analogy at all.

To sum up, it appears to me that the prejudices against mysticism have been excessive, but not altogether without foundation ; and that William Law, though he has escaped many of the snares to which mysticism is exposed, has, to some little extent, laid himself open to the charges which were only too freely brought against his system. We may now, after this long discussion return to his outer life.

CHAPTER XIII.

IT will be remembered that we left William Law in London at the close of the year 1739, in a very unsettled condition. Owing to the death of Mr. Gibbon and the consequent breaking up of the establishment at Putney, his occupation was gone. I do not suppose that he either felt or anticipated the pressure of poverty. He had inherited a little property ; possibly, Mr. Gibbon had left him a small legacy. His books were popular, and were selling well ; and he might easily have made an arrangement with his publishers which would have secured him at least a moderate competency. But writing with the intense earnestness of purpose that Law did, with no other motive than to do good, he would have regarded it as a prostitution of his pen to write simply for bread and cheese. A ripe scholar of Law's reputation and experience might easily have gained his living by tuition ; but his failure with young Gibbon had probably disgusted him with that mode of life, for which he was really not adapted. Other men, again, in Law's circumstances, would have turned their thoughts to matrimony. It is true that Law was now past the prime of life, being fifty-three years of age ; but he was wonderfully young and vigorous for his years ; he was a personable, and, when he chose, a remarkably agreeable man, and would have had no difficulty in finding a wife. There was one lady, at any rate, with a fortune of her own, who would, we may be quite sure, have lent a favourable ear to his suit, Miss Hester Gibbon. But this resource was quite out of the question. Law never swerved one single inch from what he believed to be right. Given Law's opinions, and you might be absolutely certain what his conduct would be, for from the very beginning to the end of his career, it would be impossible to find a single instance of his acting on the principle—

> Video meliora proboque,
> Deteriora sequor.

Now, no hermit in his cell ever held stricter views on the subject of clerical celibacy than William Law did ; and at the very time of which we are speaking, he expressed those views in print with remarkable vigour. 'When,' he wrote in 1739, 'a clergyman excuses himself from any Heights of the Ministerial Service, by saying, "*he has married a wife, and therefore cannot come* up to them," it seems to be no better excuse than if he had said, "*he had hired a farm*," or "*bought five yoke of oxen*."' It was true that 'the Reformation had allowed Priests and Bishops, not only to look out for wives, but to have as many as they pleased, one after another, but from the beginning it was not so.' The sight of 'Reverend Doctors in Sacerdotal robes, making love to women,' was an abomination to him. He introduces one of those pictures at which one hardly knows whether to smile or be serious. 'John the Baptist came out of the wilderness burning and shining, to preach the Kingdom of Heaven at hand. Look at this great saint, all ye that desire to preach the Gospel. Now, if this holy Baptist, when he came to Jerusalem, and had preached a while upon Penitence, and the Kingdom of Heaven at hand, had made an offering of his Heart to some fine young *Lady of great accomplishments*, had not this put an end to all that was burning and shining in his character ?' And surely

'those clergy who date their mission from Jesus Christ
Himself, who claim being sent by Him as He was by His
Father, to stand as His representatives, &c. &c., should look
upon Love-addresses to the Sex, as unbecoming, as foreign,
as opposite to their character, as to the Baptist's. ✗Were
not Our Blessed Lord's own words ' (Matt. xix. 12) 'more
than a volume of human eloquence in praise of the Virgin
State.   And had not St. Paul done everything to hinder a
Minister of Jesus Christ from entering into marriage, except calling it a sinful state ?   Did not the apologists in
primitive times appeal to the members of both sexes consecrated to God in a Virgin Life, as one great Proof of the
Divinity of the Christian Religion.   But when such arguments as these were used to set forth the glory of the Gospel, need anyone to be told that it must have been *highly
shameful* in those Days for a Priest of such a Religion, to
be *looking out* for a wife ?'   And so he goes on for several
pages.   Holding such opinions as these, and always having
the courage of his opinions, Law certainly was 'not a
marrying man.'/

At the close, therefore, of 1740, he quietly retired to
King's Cliffe, his native village, where both his parents
were buried, where his eldest, and apparently most beloved,
brother George still resided, and where he himself owned a
house.   Here he lived alone for nearly three years, occasionally paying visits to London, for a letter from him to
Mr. Spanaugle is preserved by Dr. Byrom, dated April
1742, in which Law says that 'he is about to leave town,'
and in another entry in his 'Journal' (May 1743), Byrom
describes a visit which he paid to King's Cliffe, when Law
'received a letter [from London] while I was with him,
and said he should have gone that day but for me.'   As
this entry gives us the only glimpse which we can catch of
Law in his solitude, a short extract from it is worth insert-

ing. 'I went,' writes Byrom, 'to Wansford on Sunday
night, and on Monday morning to King's Cliff, where I
light at the Cross Keys, and understanding that Mr. Law
was at his house by the church, and his brother very ill of
the stone, I went to him. Mr. Law rid out with me over his
brother's grounds ; I dined and supped with him and lay at
the Cross Keys.' Then follows a full report of Mr. Law's
conversation which need not be recorded ; but we learn
from it that Law had all his books around him, for Byrom
mentions that Law pointed out to him a passage in Bertot,
and showed him a ' German book of distiches upon
Behmenish principles,' and that ' Rusbrochius lay upon his
table in folio.' We may gather, therefore, what was the
course of Law's studies at this period.

His solitude, however, was not destined to last long.
In 1740 Mr. Archibald Hutcheson died. In his last illness
he was visited by Mr. Law, to whom he expressed his desire that his widow should lead a retired and religious life ;
he expressed the same wish to the lady herself, and added
that he knew no one so well suited to help her to carry out
the pious plan as his friend Mr. Law, if she could take up
her residence within reach of his society. Mrs. Hutcheson at
once determined to accede to her dying husband's wishes,
and upon his death consulted Mr. Law on the subject. Mr.
Law, who was always very careful in his relations with the
other sex, appears to have shrunk from undertaking the
spiritual guidance of a rich widow, lest his motives should
be misinterpreted. But there was another lady who was
also left desolate, and who had for many years been taught
to look up to Mr. Law with the deepest reverence and admiration. This was Miss Hester Gibbon ; and it was probably on Mr. Law's suggestion that Mrs. Hutcheson proposed to her that they should live together, and partake
jointly of the benefits of Mr. Law's spiritual direction. The

proposal was accepted, and a house was taken for them by
Mr. Law at Thrapstone. There they took up their abode
in the summer of 1743. Their joint income amounted to
nearly 3,000*l.* a year, more than two-thirds of which belonged to Mrs. Hutcheson ; and their intention was to carry
out literally the counsel of the ' Serious Call,' and to devote
the whole of their fortune, after the supply of their own
necessary wants, to the relief of the poor. But Thrapstone
was not a suitable place for their purpose ; it was then, as
now, a very small place, and did not furnish sufficient scope
for their benevolence. Moreover, at Thrapstone, they must
have been at an inconvenient distance from their spiritual
director, King's Cliffe being ten miles away, a serious
matter in those days of bad roads. King's Cliffe contained
many more poor, and Mr. Law had on his hands there a
very suitable house for the ladies ; he therefore proposed
that they should remove thither, and, on their consent,
fitted up the house for their accommodation. Whether
this was ' Mr. Law's house by the Church ' at which Byrom
found his friend in May 1743, we need not stop to enquire ;
but as King's Cliffe was undoubtedly his residence during
the whole of the remainder of his life, it may be interesting
to the reader to know what sort of a place it was and
still is.

King's Cliffe is probably not very much changed since
the days of Law. The houses are for the most part old ;
and as the village lies off the main high road, and has not
until the present year been invaded by the railway, it has
been little affected by modern alterations. Nevertheless, it
is a place of some importance in its way, and was comparatively more so in Law's time. It is the capital of the East
Bailiwick of the Forest of Rockingham, which originally
included fifteen parishes. The pilgrim whose respect for
Law's memory may lead him to Cliffe will not be disap-

pointed. The ' Cross Keys,' where Byrom used to lie when he came to drink in wisdom at the fountain head is still the chief inn ; and though it has slightly modernised its exterior, it is still substantially the same old house which we connect with Law's quaint and gentle disciple. The parish church, at every service in which, week-day and Sunday, Law was a constant attendant, is the same externally as it was in his day, though internally it has succumbed to the modern spirit of restoration. There is a new rectory, a few new houses, and a handsome new school, very different from the humble and now venerable little schoolhouse, still standing but disused, which owed its existence to the munificence of the good people whose lives we are about to trace. But, happily, ' Mr. Law's house by the Church ' is still unaltered, and still occupied by one who bears the honoured name of Law. This, historically and æsthetically, as well as through its associations with ' the English Mystic,' is by far the most interesting object in King's Cliffe. It stands in an open space called the ' Hall Yard,' and is partly on the site of what was once a royal residence. Several monarchs lodged for a while at their ' Manor House at Clive ' when they came to hunt in the neighbouring Forest of Rockingham, or when they made their royal progresses through the country. King John probably rebuilt the house, for it went by the name of ' King John's palace.' ' I hope,' wrote Law to Byrom in 1751, ' you will make King John's house, not the Cross Keys, your inn.' The front part of the house has the date ' 1603 ' over the door, but the back part is much older. The garden and the little close of pasture stand just as they were in the days of Law, and there still remains the little wooden bridge over the brook (a tributary of the Nene) which Law crossed almost every day of his life when he went to visit his favourite schools and alms-houses. These, too, stand just as Law

left them, and, though plain and unpretentious, have a pic-
turesque and venerable appearance. In one corner of the
garden of the manor house, stands a fine oak grown from
an acorn planted by Mrs. Hutcheson immediately after her
settlement at Cliffe in 1744. In the main street of the
village there still stands the house which Law's father built
and where he earned an honourable living as a grocer and
chandler, but it is no longer used as a shop. You may still
meet in the streets of Cliffe boys and girls dressed in the
quaint but not unbecoming costume of the charity, through
which Law, 'being dead yet speaketh.'[1] In fact, King's Cliffe
is the only one of the places connected with any of the great
revivers of practical religion in the eighteenth century which
still retains many traces of those who made their names
famous. Epworth has not much left in it to remind one of
the Wesleys, nor Olney of Cowper and Newton and Scott,
nor Haworth of Grimshaw, nor Everton of Berridge, nor
Madeley of Fletcher, but King's Cliffe reminds one of Law
at every step ; and it may be added that those who may
be so fortunate as to gain access will find in more than one
of the houses at Cliffe still more interesting memorials of
the departed saint.

It is not necessary to transcribe here information about
King's Cliffe which may be found in a directory. I shall
therefore only add that the whole valley, on an acclivity of
which Cliffe (hence the name) lies, formerly belonged to
the Forest of Rockingham, and that one of the walks of
that forest is called Morehay. There, in an interesting old
house still standing, lived William Law's eldest brother,
George, who was a sort of ranger or bailiff for the Earl of

---

[1] Since this sentence was written, the old dress has, alas ! been improved
off the face of creation. It is no part of the present work to discuss the
arrangement of the schools ; but I may remark, as a matter of fact, that any
education, not based on distinctively Church principles, would have been
utterly abhorrent to the feelings of William Law.

Westmoreland. Enough, it is hoped, has now been told to
enable the reader to realise what sort of a place it was in
which Law was born and bred and where he passed the
last twenty years of his life.

In the year 1744 this curious family circle was settled
in the Hall Yard, and no time was lost by them in carrying out their benevolent designs. It has been already
mentioned that William Law had, seventeen years previously, founded a school for the education and full clothing
of fourteen poor girls. In 1745, Mrs. Hutcheson founded
a similar school for eighteen boys, and in 1756 increased
the number to twenty, and directed that every boy who
should have stayed out his full time in the school, with
good behaviour, should be put to some trade. She then
bought a school-house for the master, and built a school and
four small tenements adjoining it ' for the separate habitation of four ancient and poor widows, chosen out of the Town
of King's Cliffe.' William Law also built a school-house
and school, and also two small ' tenements adjoining to the
school, to be inhabited separately by two ancient maidens
or widows of the Town of King's Cliffe.' The ' widows ' in
Mrs. Hutcheson's alms-houses, and the ' ancient maidens or
widows ' in Mr. Law's ' are to have two shillings and sixpence paid them on every Saturday throughout the year,
and ten shillings to each of them every Lady-day to help
them to firing.'

It would be wearisome to the general reader if all the
laws of these excellent charities were here inserted. It will
suffice to mention two or three which are most characteristic of W. Law's spirit and intention. With regard to the
' widows and ancient maidens ' it is provided that ' none
are to be looked upon as qualified to be chosen merely because they are old and poor, but only such old and poor
women as are of good report for their sobriety, industry,

and Christian behaviour in their several stations. The
want of these virtuous qualifications is not to be dispensed
with ; it being our desire and intention by these provisions
to reward the virtue and merit of such ancient women, and
prevent their falling to the straitness of a parish allowance in
the time of their age and infirmities. If, therefore, in any
after times any ancient women of ill manners, of unchristian behaviour, who have had the character of idle, gossiping, or slothful persons should be nominated, such disregard of virtuous qualifications would be as great a viola-
tion of the nature and design of these charities, as if young
women, or persons of another parish, were chosen in them.'
The same strict regard for virtue and religion is shown in
the case of the schools :—' If a master or mistress be not
of a perfectly sober, decent, and Christian behaviour, and
of good example to the children, the trustees are earnestly
requested not to suffer the continuance of such a master
or mistress, a more pious and virtuous education of the
children than that of a common school being the one
great end chiefly intended by these foundations.' And as
an indication of the particular form of Christianity in which
W. Law desired the children to be trained, and the ancient
maidens and widows to be cherished, the following provisions may be quoted :—' The Rector of King's Cliffe for the
time being is always to be a trustee. As soon as he is
inducted into the living of King's Cliffe, and enters upon
his first residence, he has a right to claim admission into
the trust. No other person of King's Cliffe is ever to be a
trustee ; be he who he will, or of what degree soever, he is
utterly incapable of being admitted or chosen into any
share of this trust.' The Trustees are always ' to be chosen
out of the neighbouring gentry and clergy not more than
four miles distant from King's Cliffe.' ' Every boy and
girl at their going out of the school are to have a new

Bible, and Book of Common Prayer distinct from it, given
to them.' The holidays are to be only at the times of the
three great Church festivals—Christmas, Easter, and Whit-
suntide—' but in harvest time the children are allowed to
glean in the fields for their parents, after having said each
of them one lesson early in the morning.' 'The master at
his first entrance into the school in the morning is to pray
with the children, and again at 12 o'clock, except on those
days when they go to church, and again at their breaking
up in the evening.'

The other provisions are mostly of a business nature,
sensible, but not generally interesting ; but the above extracts are quoted to show that what Law most of all
desired was that the children should be so trained that they
might grow up to be good Christians, and good churchmen
and churchwomen. When Law became a mystic he did
not cease to be a churchman.

These points are more strikingly brought out in the
following ' Rules to be observed by girls,' which were evidently drawn up by Mr. Law himself, and which are so
interesting in their touching simplicity, that I trust there is
no need to apologise for quoting from them at some length.
After some excellent injunctions about teaching the girls to
pray, to behave courteously, to learn certain lessons, &c.,
they provide :—

(7) Every girl, as soon as she can say the whole catechism in a ready manner shall have a shilling given her,
before them all, with commendation and exhortation to go
on in her duty.

(8) Every girl shall have sixpence given her, as soon
as she can say by heart the morning and evening prayer.

(9) Every one that shall get by heart the 5th, 6th, 7th,
18th, or 25th chapters of S. Matthew, or the 6th or 7th of
S. Luke, or the 18th or 19th of S. John ; or the 15th

chapter of 1 Cor. from the 20th verse, shall have for every
such chapter, a shilling given her, in the presence of all the
rest, with commendation and exhortation to love and practise
the Word of God. They shall also ever after repeat these
chapters, one at a time, once every week, in a plain and
distinct manner ; at which time every other girl shall leave
off her work, and quietly listen to the chapter that is repeating. At the end of which chapter they shall all say, ' Glory
be to Thee, O Lord, for this thy holy word,' and, making
a curtsey, every one shall sit down in their proper seat.

(11) Every girl that gives the lie to any other girl, or
to any person, or that calls another, fool, or uses any rude or
unmannerly word, shall, the morning afterwards, as soon as
they are all there, be obliged to kneel down before her mistress, and in the presence of them all, say in a plain and
distinct manner, these words :—' Our blessed Saviour, Jesus
Christ, hath said that "Whosoever shall say, thou fool,
shall be in danger of hell fire." I, therefore am heartily
sorry for the wicked words that I have spoken to my fellow Christian ; I humbly beg pardon of God, and of all
you that are here present, hoping and promising, by the
help of God, never to offend again in the like manner.'
Then shall the girl she had abused come and take her
from her knees, and kiss her ; and both turning to their
mistress, they shall make a curtsey, and return to their seats.

(12) Any girl that shall be found to have told a lie, to
have cursed or swore, or done any undutiful thing to her
parents, or to have stolen anything from any other girl,
shall stand chained a whole morning to some particular
part of the room by herself, and afterwards, in the presence
of them all, shall, upon her knees, repeat these words :—
' The word of God teaches us that if we confess our sins,
God is faithful and just to forgive us our sins, and to cleanse
us from all unrighteousness. I, therefore, a wicked child,

humbly confess before God, and all you that are here present, that I have grievously sinned against God, in lying
[or cursing, swearing, or stealing, as the case may be]. I
am heartily sorry for this great sin, and humbly on my
knees, beg of God to forgive me. I desire you all to pray
for me and to forgive me, and I promise by God's grace
never to commit the like fault.' Then shall the mistress
say this prayer: 'Almighty God, who art always more
ready to hear than we to pray, who desireth not the death
of a sinner, but rather that he should turn from his sins, and
be saved ; we beseech Thee to have mercy upon this child,
who hath confessed her sins unto Thee, and grant that both
she, and all of us here present, may, by the assistance of
thy Holy Spirit, be preserved from all sin, strengthened in
all goodness, and serve Thee faithfully all the days of our
life, through Jesus Christ our Lord. Amen.' Then shall all
the girls rise, and making a curtsey, return to their seats.

(13) Any girl that continues to commit these faults,
after the third time, Mr. George Law shall be called in, and
he shall turn her away.

(14) Every girl when she walks in the street shall make
a curtsey to all masters and mistresses of families, and to
all ancient people, whether rich or poor. They shall also
make a curtsey when they enter into any house, and at
their coming out of it.

(16) Every girl shall be constant at church at all
times of divine service, as well on the week-days as on
Sundays. They shall all learn to sing the psalms, and to
get them by heart that are most commonly sung. They
must always go to church at all funerals, and placing themselves at those times together, all of them join in singing the psalm that shall then be appointed.

These rules, and others which it is unnecessary to quote,
are all corrected in Mr. Law's own handwriting. Then

there are prayers for all the canonical hours, private prayers
for the children, and a short ' prayer on entering into the
church,' which is so beautiful that I cannot forbear quoting
it :—' Lord, receive me, I beseech thee, in this thy holy
house of prayer, and grant that I may worship and pray
unto thee, with as much reverence and godly fear, as if I
saw the heavens open, and all the angels that stand round
thy throne.   Amen.'   The other prayers are too long to
quote, but they are so spiritually and elegantly expressed,
that if we had no other evidence (which we have) than
internal evidence, we might be quite sure that they were
the composition of none other than Mr. Law himself.   In
fact, the settlement of these charities occupied a good deal
of Mr. Law's time during the first three years of his residence with Mrs. Hutcheson and Miss Gibbon in the Hall
Yard ; and indeed the attending to them seems to have
constituted one of his chief outward employments during
the remainder of his life.

The life spent by this worthy trio was not an eventful
one ; but, for its literal fulfilment of the precepts of the
Sermon on the Mount, it was perhaps without a parallel in
England, at least during the eighteenth century.   Law
had described in the ' Serious Call,' the sort of life a Christian, in his opinion, ought to live ; and that life he strove
to live himself to the very letter, without the slightest
abatement or reserve.   A few details of his mode of doing
so will, it is hoped, not be uninteresting to the reader.

It will be remembered that in the ' Serious Call ' great
stress is laid upon the duty of early rising.   Accordingly,
Mr. Law himself rose about five o'clock every morning, and
spent of course the first hours of the day in private devotion and study.   At nine o'clock the whole household
assembled for devotion, of which the collects and psalms
for the day invariably formed part.   Then Mr. Law retired

to his study, but not to a sanctum where he was liable to no interruption.   His window overlooked a courtyard, and every mendicant knew that if he appeared before that window and preferred his claim for relief, that claim would secure Mr. Law's instant and careful attention, no matter how busily he might be engaged.   As there was, no doubt, the same freemasonry among beggars in the eighteenth as there is in the nineteenth century, we can readily believe that Mr. Law rarely spent a ' quiet morning ' without holding a sort of ragged levee ; and as he always made a point of inquiring into every applicant's peculiar wants, and seeing them supplied with his own eyes, no small amount of his time must have been thus taken up.   The family dined at noon in summer, and at one in winter ; immediately after dinner the whole household was again assembled for devotion.   Then Mr. Law again retired to his study until tea-time, when he descended into the parlour and entered into cheerful conversation with the ladies, not, however, sitting down and partaking of the meal, but standing and eating a few raisins.   The whole household was then again assembled for devotion, the servants reading a chapter of the Bible in turn and Mr. Law explaining it.   Law then took a brisk ' constitutional,' and after another frugal meal and a final assembling of the whole family for devotion, retired to his room, smoked one pipe and drank a glass of water, and retired to rest at nine o'clock.

This was the ordinary routine of every day when there was no church service ; but on Wednesdays and Fridays, as well as, of course, on Sundays, the whole family went to church, and also often entertained some of the neighbouring gentry, whom they probably invited on those days for the express purpose of getting them to accompany them to God's house.   The Hon. Misses Finch Hatton used to dine with them every alternate Friday, and after service the whole party used to go out for an airing, Mrs. Hutcheson and the guests in a carriage (no doubt, Mrs. Hutcheson's, for Byrom speaks of ' Mrs. Hutcheson's coachman '), and Mr. Law and Miss Gibbon on horseback.

Such was the quiet and regular life which Law led at King's Cliffe. It may add vividness to the picture to mention one or two of his little habits which are thoroughly characteristic of the mingled simplicity, oddity, kindliness, and at the same time beautiful Christian ideas of the man.

1. Law held that the outward employment of every day ought to commence with an act of charity. Accordingly, after his early devotions and studies, his first act daily was to distribute with his own hands among his poorer neighbours all the milk (except the little that was required for the family use) derived from four cows which he kept for this very purpose.

2. Wood turnery was then, as now, the staple trade of King's Cliffe. Law, therefore, always ate out of a wooden trencher, in order to encourage the local trade. Some say that he adopted this habit, because it was the ancient college fashion ; others, because he thought that plates injured knives ; but, besides that the evidence for the former reason is stronger, it is also far more like the man, and therefore may safely be adopted.

3. In order that he might not give to others what he would not thankfully receive himself, Law always made a point of wearing on his own person the coarse linen shirts which he had made for the poor ; they were then washed, and distributed as occasion required.

4. For the same reason, he made a point of tasting the soup which was concocted regularly every day for the poor ; and it is said that the only occasions on which his constitutional irascibility ever showed itself were, when, on making a sudden raid upon the kitchen, he found that the soup

was not strong enough, or that room was not at once made upon the kitchen fire for a mendicant's vessel.

5. Law was very humane to dumb animals. When he saw a bird in a cage, he always felt an irrepressible desire to open the cage door and give the captive a chance of escape—a doubtful kindness in the case of such birds as canaries, who, if they took advantage of the chance offered them, would only fly away to die. This, by the way, was not the only mistaken kindness which Mr. Law showed, as we shall see presently.

6. Law was exceedingly fond of music. Whether he had any great musical power himself, does not appear ; probably not, for if he had, he would hardly have maintained the paradox that everybody could sing. But to listen to music, and to sing himself, after a fashion, was his delight. Of course, like everything else in Law's view, music was to be made subservient to religious purposes. It was probably at his request that the Psalms were always sung at King's Cliffe Church ; it was certainly at his suggestion that a large music-room was built in the Hall Yard, and an organ placed there, on which Miss Gibbon used to perform sacred music. Singing also formed a regular and frequent employment at the schools of which Law was the presiding genius.

7. Law loved little children, and, like many men of his temperament, seems to have lost all his austerity when he had to do with them. The large space which he devoted to the right training of the young in his 'Practical Treatises,' the money which he spent, and, still more, the time and trouble which he gave to the management of his charity schools are a sufficient indication of this partiality. And he loved to have little ones about him. He was always delighted to see his nephew's children, and encouraged them to visit the Hall Yard as often as possible. A pretty pic-

ture has been left us by an eye witness, of this grave, stern man playing with his great-nephews and nieces, and giving them ' rides on his foot.'

One almost instinctively speaks of Law as a grave and stern man, partly because his works—especially those written in his ante-mystic period—give one that impression, and partly because a tradition of the kind has been handed down ; but there were others besides little children, on whom Law left anything but an impression of sternness and gravity. Perhaps this is as convenient a place as will be found for saying a few words on Law's personal appearance and manners.

Very characteristically, but very inconveniently for his biographer, Law steadily refused the entreaties of his friends that he should sit for his portrait. He would not allow any sketch of any kind to be made of him ; he is thus, perhaps, the only celebrity of the eighteenth century of whose outer man we have no authentic picture. The consequence is that we have some very conflicting accounts of his personal appearance, varying, no doubt, according to the various impressions which he made upon those who, to use a vile modern term, ' interviewed ' him. The expression is used advisedly ; he was literally ' interviewed,' that is, visited with the same purpose with which ' Our own Correspondent ' visits great personages at the present day, to make a report of what he sees. Law strongly objected to the process ; and we can well understand his not making a very favourable impression upon some of his interviewers. The biographer of Mr. Charles Wesley writes : ' Mr. Law is said to have been a tall, thin, bony man, of a stern and forbidding countenance, sour and repulsive in his spirit and manner, resembling, in this respect, the religion which he taught.'[1] This is written in reference to a visit paid by

[1] Jackson's *Memoirs of the Rev. Charles Wesley*, p. 52.

Charles Wesley in September, 1737, to 'this eloquent but
erring man, then resident at Putney.' Dr. Jackson does not
inform us by whom this was said, but one can quite believe
that it would be the sort of tradition about Law that would
be handed down from generation to generation of Methodists. And not altogether without reason. For Law,
though he was frequently dubbed a Methodist, had in reality but very little sympathy with them ; he did not do
justice to their good points, and he was keenly alive to
their weaknesses ; [1] therefore he did not show himself, perhaps he did not even desire to show himself, at his best to
them. We have seen that even the first and greatest of
them, John Wesley himself, had to complain of Law's 'sour
and morose behaviour ; ' and, if John Wesley was not altogether to Law's liking, most certainly others, who belonged,
broadly speaking, to the same school, were still less so.
One of the sisters of the Wesleys, who had an interview
with Law, described him, as 'the very model of the law
itself for severity and gravity.' This is the way in which
Peter Böhler describes an interview he had with Law. On
the introduction of John Wesley, ' I began speaking to him
of faith in Christ. He was silent. Then he began to speak
of mystical matters again. I saw his state at once ; ' and
the good man is pleased to add, ' it was a very dangerous
one.' It is curious to compare with this, Law's own account
of the same interview ; but without attempting to reconcile
the discrepancies between the two accounts, of this we may
be sure, that Böhler was just the sort of man before whom
Law would shut himself up in his shell. As a proof of this
here is a graphic description in Law's own words of the
way in which the London Moravians, of whom Böhler was

---

[1] For instance, he wrote to his friend Langcake, ' These men of zeal,
whether of the Foundry, the Tabernacle, or elsewhere, seem to have a fire
that has as much of nature as of grace in it,' and as such he treated them.

a shining light, impressed Law, and the way in which he
treated them. 'Mr. Gambold was with me both before and
after he was a Moravian. At first he came with six or
seven of his fellow Methodists from Oxford ; he only then
hung down his head, spoke now and then a word or two,
with much show of humility, meekness, &c. I said to one
of them, whom I had been more acquainted with, that I
could not tell what to make of Mr. Gambold, or why he
should come to me. He said it was his great modesty that
made him act in this manner. When I afterwards saw him
by himself, and he was more open, I could see nothing in
him but that same kind of soft, humble, and meek language,
that had nothing else in it. He afterwards consulted me
by a letter from Oxford, in which he desired me to consider
him as one that had been deeply experienced in all that
the mystics had written in every age. And yet his letter
was a full demonstration of quite the contrary. Two or
three of the chief Moravians made attempts upon me in the
same show of meek, humble, and mighty deliberate language.
This may, perhaps, have much helped forward Mr. Gambold's uniting with them, for what they say has nothing to
recommend it but their manner of saying it. What a folly
for a man to say he has read Behmen and the mystics, who
can talk no better about them than Mr. G. has done.' [1] As
Law was the very last man in the world to conceal his real
sentiments, as he was outspoken almost to a fault, we can
well conceive that he would show his rough side to men of
whom he wrote after this fashion.

But he had another side which he showed to his friends,
on whom his outward appearance made a very different
impression from that which it made upon Methodists and
Moravians. Mr. Richard Tighe visited Cliffe at the begin-

---

[1] This was written in 1757, probably to Mr. Langcake.

ning of the present century for the express purpose of ac-
quiring all the information he could respecting William
Law. He must therefore have conversed with several who
remembered him personally ; and, in fact, one of his in-
formants was Law's great-nephew and heir, one of those
very children whom Law had danced on his knee half-a-
century before. Mr. Tighe thus describes Law's appearance
and habits. 'Mr. Law was in stature rather over than
under the middle size ; not corpulent, but stout-made, with
broad shoulders ; his visage was round, his eyes grey ; his
features well proportioned, and not large ; his complexion
ruddy, and his countenance open and agreeable. He was
naturally more inclined to be merry than sad. In his
habits he was very regular and temperate ; he rose early,
&c.'[1] And again, ' By those persons now dwelling at Cliffe
who knew Mr. Law, it was reported that he was by nature
of an active and cheerful disposition, very warm-hearted,
unaffected, and affable, but not to appearance so remarkable
for meekness as some others of the most revered members
of the Christian Church are *reported* to have been'[2]—a hit,
of course, at the Methodists. A correspondent of the
' Gentleman's Magazine' for October 1800, writes : ' Concerning that good and truly great man, the Rev. W. Law,
commonly called the mystic divine, give me leave to observe, that many years since I was acquainted with some
of his admirers, from whom I understood that Mr. Law was
a bachelor all his life-time, that in person he was a well-set
man, and rather of a dark complexion, though remarkably
cheerful in his temper.' And that most indefatigable inves-
tigator of everything relating to William Law, the late Mr.
Walton, after repeating, but with fuller detail, the account

---

[1] *A Short Account of the Life and Writings of the late Rev. William Law,*
by Richard Tighe, p. 30-1. There is a portrait in the possession of Miss Law
which is supposed to have resembled William Law, and it tallies with this
description. [2] *Ibid.* p. 12.

of Mr. Tighe, adds: 'His (Law's) general manner was lively and unaffected, though his walk and conversation among his friends was that of a sage. Perhaps the gravity of his looks and demeanour was a little heightened by the soberness of his dress, which was usually a clerical hat, with the loops let down, black coat, and grey wig.' It would be alien to the spirit of Law to dwell longer upon a matter of which he himself made so light account, but there can be no doubt that, in the eyes of his friends, he was a man of prepossessing appearance and agreeable manners.

And Law's friends were many. He was fond of retirement, but was by no means an unsociable man. Mr. Hartley, the Rector of Winwick, and therefore a neighbour, though rather a distant one, of Law's, repels with some indignation a charge which Bishop Warburton brought against Law on this head. 'Upon my knowledge,' he writes, 'I can affirm as to Mr. Law, that he lived in a market-town, and was a gentleman of a free conversation. He resided many years before his death at King's Cliffe in Northamptonshire, where he often received company.'[1] And the same writer speaks quite with rapture of Law's 'warm and loving heart,' and 'that excellent man's universal charity.' The bishop, like many others, seems to have jumped at the conclusion that mysticism necessarily implied asceticism. The very reverse is the case. The mystic has no need of those outward austerities which to the anchorite are essential to devotion. That was the mistake into which Madame Guyon fell before she was set right by the good Franciscan. The true mystic finds all that he requires within ; he can retire within himself at any time and in any place ; he can therefore well afford to converse with the world with the utmost freedom ; his inner life is hid with Christ in God,

---

[1] 'A Short Defence of the Mystical Writers,' appended to *Paradise Restored,* p. 466, note.

but his outer life may, with perfect consistency, be passed in friendly and sociable relations with his fellow-creatures, for, as Mr. Hartley rightly observes, 'the term mystic does not imply any separation from society, like hermit or anchoret ; the distinction relates to the inward state of the person, and not to the outward circumstances of his abode.'[1] This was certainly William Law's theory and practice. His asceticism, so far as he *was* an ascetic, was the asceticism of the author of the 'Serious Call' (to the sentiments of which book he never ceased to adhere), not of the 'Spirit of Love.' His severity and asceticism were toned down, not aggravated, by his mysticism.

A curious illustration of the mistaken idea of the results of mysticism may be found in the common description of William Law's study. When we read of it as 'a little cell, about four feet square, furnished only with a chair, a writing-table, the Bible, the works of Jacob Behmen, and a few other mystic writers,' there is conjured up in the mind's eye as uncomfortable an abode as the most self-mortifying of hermits need desire. As a matter of fact, Law's sanctum was as comfortable a retreat as a literary man could hope for. The 'cell' is really part of a most commodious bedroom, being parted off from it merely by a thin wainscoting, with a large door in it, which was in all probability, generally open. It was well-lighted by a large window, well-warmed, and altogether a most convenient little snuggery, which many a student of the present day would envy.

A kindred error has prevailed respecting Law's employments in this cruelly maligned little recess. In his very graphic and appreciative sketch of Law's life, Mr. Leslie Stephen quotes, with a very natural sense of the absurdity of the account, the description of Law 'prostrating himself,

[1] 'Short Defence of the Mystical Writers,' p. 467.

R

body and soul, in abyssal silence, before the interior central throne of Divine revelation ; and, according to his high supersensual science, presenting the now passive, desireless, resigned, mirror-eye of his purified will, &c. &c. &c. ;' but it should be remembered that this is not Law's own account of his doings, but only that of a rather weak admirer. Law, no doubt, employed his time in his study, like the sensible, rational man that he was. He was a most indefatigable student. He had a very extensive library. It is said that 'boxes upon boxes' of volumes were disposed of to a London bookseller after Miss Gibbon's death ; and in the small but well-selected library which yet remains, the books show evident traces of having been carefully read (many of them underlined and annotated) by William Law. They were all, no doubt, of a strictly theological or religious character, for Law thought it positively wrong to read any other kind of book, and most of them were of a more or less mystic tendency ; but no one who is at all acquainted with the extent and nature of mystic literature will have any difficulty in realising that Law might find ample range for the exercise of his favourite pursuit, and that, without reading anything that was unworthy of the attention of an able and cultured man. It should be remembered that Law possessed the key to unlock many treasures which were hidden from the majority of his countrymen. He was an excellent linguist, being perfectly familiar with Latin, Greek, Hebrew, French, German, and Dutch, and having besides some little knowledge of Spanish and Italian ; and he would certainly find as many works to his taste in one or other of these languages as in his native tongue. As an illustration of his sedentary habits it may be noted that the hearthstone of his room was worn away in two places by the rubbing of his feet, which, owing to his long sittings at study, were subject to cold. This hearthstone, by the way, is in the bed-room, not in the recess, and seems to show, what one would naturally expect, that Law used the whole apartment, not merely the so-called closet, for his study. Let it be remembered also, that Law, what with his extensive correspondence, and his works for publication, which, if not very numerous, all indicate great thought and much pains bestowed upon them, was a diligent writer as well as reader. Let it also be borne in mind that much of Law's time must have been taken up with his outer pursuits ; he had his little pupils to attend to at the schools, and his great pupils at home, for Mrs. Hutcheson and Miss Gibbon used to write exercises every day under the careful supervision of their spiritual director ; he had his regular pensioners to look after at home, and his occasional, but doubtless very frequent, mendicants from abroad ; he had his Church to attend, his exercise to take, his friends to entertain, the frequent family devotions to conduct. Surely, with all these unquestionable calls upon his time, there is no need to have recourse to the perfectly gratuitous ' abyssal silence ' theory to account for the way in which Law spent his days.

It would be wearisome and unnecessary, even if we had materials for doing so, to trace day by day, the course of this quiet and regular life. But one little episode, which tended to ruffle the usually smooth and tranquil course of Law and his two companions must be noticed.

The charity of the worthy trio was almost boundless. Out of a joint income of not less than three thousand pounds a year, only about three hundred pounds were spent upon the frugal expenses of the household, and the simple, personal wants of the three inhabitants. The whole of the remainder was spent upon the poor ; for not one penny of the income was ever saved ; this was made a matter of principle.

One naturally asks, how was this very large sum, amounting to at least two thousand five hundred pounds annually, distributed ? Charitable organisations were then few and far between ; and those that did exist do not appear to have been known, or, at any rate, taken advantage of, at King's Cliffe. The vast charities at the Hall Yard seem to have been distributed in the most indiscriminate fashion among the resident poor of the village and the chance mendicants whose name was legion. If a dim notion ever entered Law's head that he was doing more harm than good by helping a scoundrel, who was a more proper subject for a magistrate than for an almoner to deal with, he silenced the thought by reflecting that the donor meant well, and that if the recipient was unworthy, his blood would be upon his own head. The inevitable result of this sort of almsgiving was that the worthy trio were shamefully imposed upon. Stories are told of impostors changing their better clothing behind the buttresses of the Church hard by, for rags, and then appearing again before the well-known window, and claiming relief, and receiving it.

But this was not the worst. King's Cliffe became demoralised ; the respectable inhabitants complained that the village was swamped with a parcel of vagabonds who were attracted thither by the injudicious kindness of the guileless Christians of the Hall Yard. Foremost among the complainants was the Rev. Wilfred Piemont, who, as his epitaph informs us, was ' for thirty-three years the pious, faithful, diligent, and allways resident Rector of the Parish ;' and there is nothing, so far as I am aware, to lead us to suppose that he was undeserving of any of these epithets. There appears to have been no intimacy between the Rectory and the Hall Yard, but this may be easily accounted for without laying any blame upon Mr. Piemont. For Law was quite out of sympathy with the mind—especially with the clerical mind—of his day. And in the little fracas which occurred between him and his rector, a parochial clergyman can hardly help feeling some sympathy with the rector. For he knows that that Bashi-Bazouk sort of charity, particularly when exercised by churchmen without the direction of the chief churchman in the place, who, if he does his duty, must know best the wants of the poor under his charge, is a very embarrassing thing in a parish. Perhaps Mr. Piemont did not take the kindest or most judicious course, when he made use of the vantage ground which his pulpit gave him, to condemn the indiscriminate alms-giving of Law and his friends. But it must be remembered that Law was a formidable antagonist to meet, face to face ; and one can quite understand, if one cannot quite approve of, the policy of his clergyman in giving Law a piece of his mind, where he was safe from retort. Matters, however, came to a crisis in the following letter, which explains itself. It is dated ' King's Cliffe, February 21, 1753,' and is headed :

' A Letter to the writer and subscribers of a certain paper presented to George Lynn, Esq., and the neighbouring Justices of the Peace, praying for justice and judgment against us, in behalf of this parish, as being, amongst other things, the occasion of the miserable poverty of the said parish.'

It runs thus : ' We observe that great part of this paper contains an idle narrative of such matters as the justices can administer no relief to. And, therefore, we must believe that they are related only as an occasion of preferring a complaint against us, and to prevent that gratitude which is due to us from the parish.

' Ever since we came to this place, full of good will to do all the good in it that we could, we have been railed at from the pulpit in the most outrageous manner ; and scarce a Sunday has passed without edifying the people with some or other the most reproachful reflections cast upon us. Nobody can be a stranger to this, but he who is a stranger to the church.

'But this treatment from the pulpit we were determined to bear with, for the sake of that good which we so much wished to the parish, looking upon it as unreasonable that tne town should suffer for the unchristian behaviour of its rector. But since so many considerable inhabitants of the town have thought it proper, in conjunction with their minister, to set their names to the truth and justice of this complaint against us, as helping to increase the poverty of the town, we have also thought it proper to make known to all the parish that we will no longer do them this injury, but grant them all that relief ourselves for which they have applied to the justices. We will immediately put a stop to everything that we have set on foot, and stay no longer here, than till we can conveniently remove. And though it is our intention, by the grace of God, never to make any other use of our fortunes than as we have done here, yet as to this place, all is at an end, unless such reasons should arise for our staying here, as do not yet appear to us. And we make no doubt that every gentleman in the neighbourhood, whether he be a Justice of the Peace or not, and every person of sense and goodness, will approve of this our resolution. Your hearty friends and well-wishers,—ELIZ. HUTCHESON, HESTER GIBBON, WILLIAM LAW.'

Then follows a postscript, desiring the parish officers to call a public meeting before which the letter might be read, and expressing an intention of drawing up a memorial of all that had been done, to be presented to the bishop and gentry of the neighbourhood.

Happily, however, the affair seems to have blown over. The good people did not execute their threat of removing ;

in the very next year we find the name of the rector among the trustees of Mrs. Hutcheson's newly-founded charity, and we hear of no more troubles at Cliffe. The charities still went on ; and if the dispute caused a little more discrimination to be shown, good came out of evil. Mr. Piemont died two years before Law, and was succeeded by a Mr. Howard, who married Mr. Law's great-niece ; we may therefore hope that at the close of his life, Law's relations with the ecclesiastical authorities of the place were more satisfactory.

Here we must pause in the account of Law's outer life. Other matters connected with it, such as his relations to his friends and opponents, as well as to the various sects with which he was more or less brought into contact, cannot be properly understood, until we have considered what Law's system of theology was in his later years. This, therefore, will be the subject of the next chapter.

CHAPTER XIV.

LAW'S LATER THEOLOGY.

ALTHOUGH William Law is now best known as the author of ' The Serious Call,' and although he is admitted to have been almost without an equal as a controversial writer in his day, still his most remarkable works are those which will now come under our notice. For both in his practical and his controversial treatises he only did what others were doing. He did his work better indeed than most of his contemporaries ; but the difference is one of degree rather than of kind. As an English mystic he is unique. Of course there were others in England both before and after him who held similar views ; but hardly one, at least in the eighteenth century, who had any pretensions to be called an English classic.

The fascination which Jacob Behmen's writings exercised over Law's mind has already been referred to. It remains for us to consider what he wrote when that spell was upon him ; that is, from about the year 1734 to almost the day of his death in 1761.

But as Law's peculiar sentiments are repeated in almost all his later works with little variation, it will be the best plan to give a summary of those sentiments generally before proceeding to consider his separate compositions in detail.

A caution seems necessary at the outset. When Law's ' later theology ' is spoken of, in contrast with his earlier system, it must not be supposed that he diverged, con-

sciously at least, a hair's breadth from any one of the doctrines to which he was bound as a clergyman of the Church
of England. If he had done so, there can be no manner
of doubt that he would at once have renounced his Orders.
For of all the characteristics, both of Law's moral, and also
of his intellectual nature, none is more conspicuous than
his thorough and downright honesty. He was totally incapable of any quibbling, moral or intellectual. One sees
this in every step of his career. He warmly advocated the
doctrines of Divine right, passive obedience, and the rest of
the Jacobite programme, at the time when these doctrines
were fashionable; and when they became unfashionable, he
never hesitated one moment in his adherence to them, at
the expense of all his worldly prospects. His part in the
Bangorian controversy was simply the carrying out to their
logical results of principles which others who had advocated
them were not prepared, as Law was, to put forward so openly
at a time when they were extremely unpopular. He took
the Sermon on the Mount quite literally; and, in every action of his life, no less than in his 'Serious Call,' he showed
that he was bent upon carrying out every precept of it
thoroughly, without the slightest compromise. In fact, as it
has been well said, 'his sensitiveness to logic was as marked
as his sensitiveness to conscience.'[1] And this sensitiveness
is distinctly shown in his mystic phase. There is no sort of
difficulty in reconciling his Behmenism with his position
as an Anglican priest. If we take the three Creeds of the
Church as a full exposition of the doctrines of Christianity,
it would not be enough to say that there is not one single
article in those Creeds to which Law to the day of his death
could not give his most cordial adherence[2]; more than that,

---

[1] Leslie Stephen's *English Thought in the Eighteenth Century*, vol. ii.
p. 396.

[2] Law's eschatology in no wise affected his acceptance of the Athanasian
Creed in its most literal sense.

the denial of any one of their articles would be a distinct denial of one of the very bases on which Law built his system.

Indeed, it seems to me, that it was this very sensitiveness to logic and conscience which caused him to embrace enthusiastically the views which are now to be described. This will be seen at once when we begin to investigate what those views were.

'God is Love, yea, all Love, and so all Love, that nothing but Love can come from Him.'[1] This doctrine, repeated in various forms a thousand times in Law's mystic works, is the very hinge on which the whole of his system turns.[2] Or, perhaps, it would be more correct to say that Law held this doctrine before he became a Behmenist, and that he embraced Behmenism, because he found in that system what seemed to him a satisfactory explanation of all the disorders of nature, in harmony with this great fundamental truth ; and this was the reason why I said above that it was Law's sensitiveness to logic and conscience which led him to adopt his later system.

Starting then from this axiomatic truth, that God is Love, and then characteristically insisting that His dealings not only with men, but with the whole universe, must be

[1] *The Grounds and Reasons of Christian Regeneration*, Works, vol. v. (2) p. 46. It may here be explained that the figure in brackets (2) is inserted necessarily, because in the common edition of Law's works which I have used, two or more separate treatises, each with a separate pagination, are often very inconveniently bound up in the same volume. This will be the meaning of the bracket whenever it occurs in references to Law's works.

[2] See, *inter alia*, *Works*, vol. v. (2) 49, vi. (2) 30, vii. 26, 29 (2), 99, 127, viii. 5 (2), 5, &c., &c. 'Law's theological system,' writes Bishop Ewing, 'may be said to rest upon one only basis, viz. that God is Love—from eternity to eternity Love—abyssal love, ordering all his counsels, working all his works, regulating all events, governing all creatures according to the rules and measures of love alone ; every sentiment antagonistic to love being absolutely foreign to the Divine nature, and existing not in the creator, but in the creature.'—' Present Day Papers,' p. 16.

reconciled with this principle, Law was naturally led to ask, how could any evil, any disorder, arise in that universe which was framed and governed by One who was ' nothing but an Eternal Will to all goodness?' This was the reason why Law's system must begin before the foundation of the world, even with that mysterious subject, the Fall of the Angels. It was not because Law loved mysteries, not because he loved to pry with morbid curiosity into profound subjects beyond the ken of finite men ; such feelings were quite foreign to his character, which was essentially a plain, clear-sighted, and humble character. But it was also a very logical character, one that could not slur over difficulties ; and here was a difficulty at the outset ; how *could* evil and misery ever find a place in the universe of the all-loving God ? Behmen suggested an answer to this question, and Law did not so much repeat that answer as assimilate and make it his own, and present it to his readers in his own nervous and luminous style. The answer was briefly this : ' All qualities are not only good, but infinitely perfect as they are in God. But the same qualities, thus infinitely good and perfect in God, may become imperfect and evil in the creature ; because in the creature, being limited and finite, they may be divided and separated from one another by the creature itself.' This was how the angels fell. ' They broke off from the Heavenly Light and Love of God.'[1] Law illustrates his meaning by an instance in the natural world ; or rather, he shows an example of precisely the same process in a lower form ; for in his view, evil in every part of the universe—in a vegetable, as in an angel— was one and the same thing. ' If,' he says, ' a delicious, fragrant fruit had a power of separating itself from that rich spirit, fine taste, smell, and colour, which it receives from

---

[1] *Appeal to all that Doubt, &c.,* Works, vol. vi. (2) 24.

the virtue of the sun, and the spirit of the air, ; or, if it
could in the beginning of its growth turn away from the
sun, and receive no virtue from it, then it would stand in
its own first birth of sourness, bitterness, and astringency,
just as the devils do, who have turned back into their own
dark root, and rejected the Light and Spirit of God.'[1] And
so neither the Angels' fall nor their punishment was any
derogation to the love of God. For 'no Hell was made for
them, no new qualities came into them, no vengeance or
pains from the God of Love fell upon them ; they only stood
in that state of division and separation from the Son and
Holy Spirit of God, which by their own motion they had
made for themselves,'[2] and that was misery unspeakable,
for 'by their revolt from God, they lost the Divine Light,
and awakened in themselves, and the region in which they
dwelt, the dark, wrathful fire of Hell.'[3]

But then how was it possible that they *could* thus
separate themselves from God ? In this very possibility
Law saw only another proof of the love of God. God gave
them a free will, 'an offspring or ray derived from the will
of God.'[4] 'And herein consisteth the infinite goodness of
God, in the birth of all intelligent creatures ; and also the
exceeding height, perfection, and happiness of their created
state ; they are descended from God, full of Divine power ;
they can will and work with God, and partake of the Divine
happiness. They can receive no injustice, hurt, or violence,
either from nature or creature ; but must be only that
which they generate, and have no evil or hurt but that
which they do in and to themselves.'[5] But then the possession of this great gift rendered it possible that they

---

[1] *Appeal to all that Doubt*, Works, vol. vi. (2) p. 28.   [2] *Ibid.* p. 29.
[3] *Spirit of Prayer*, Works, vol. vii. (2) 26.
[4] *Appeal to all that Doubt*, Works, vi. (2) 106.
[5] *Way to Divine Knowledge*, Works, vii. (3) 141.

might abuse it ; this they did, and so they fell. 'They fell, not because God ceased to be an infinite open fountain of all good to them, but because they had a will which must direct itself.'[1] They 'renounced their Heavenly life, and therefore raised up a kingdom that was not Heavenly.'[2]

Where and what was this kingdom ? 'It was,' said Law, ' the very place or extent of this world, as is plain for two reasons ; (1) because the place of this world is *now* their habitation. For we must by no means suppose that God brought them from some other region into this world only to tempt man, and make this life dangerous ; but they are here now, because they were created to dwell here. (2) Because the whole extent of this world, everything in it, must be dissolved and pass through a purifying fire. Therefore all these things are polluted, and have in them some grossness and disorder from the Fall of the Angels.'[3]

And here was shown again the boundless love of God in the creation of this world. ' When the angels had, by their rebellion against God, lost the Divine Life *within* themselves, and brought their *whole outward* kingdom into darkness, grossness, wrath, and disorder, so that, as Moses speaketh, " Darkness was upon the Face of the Deep," that is, the whole deep, or extent of the place of this world ; then at the Fall of the Angels, and in the place where they were fallen, and out of the materials of their ruin'd angelical kingdom, did God begin the creation of this present, material, temporary, visible world.'

' In the beginning, saith Moses, God created the Heaven and the Earth ; here, at this instant, ended the Devil's power over the place or kingdom in which he was created. As soon as the whole of his outward, disordered

---

[1] *Appeal to all that Doubt*, Works, vi. (2) 105.
[2] *Ibid.* p. 117.
[3] *Answer to Dr. Trapp*, Works, vol. vi. p. 28-9.

kingdom was thus *divided* into a created Heaven and
Earth, all was taken out of his hands, he was shut out of
everything, and he and his hosts became only poor prisoners
in their lost kingdom, that could only wander about
in chains of darkness, looking with impotent rage and
anger at the created Heaven and Earth, which was sprung
up in their own place of habitation, and which they could
not rule over, because their nature had no communion with
their new created Heaven and Earth.'

' Thus was this outward kingdom, of the whole extent of
this world, taken out of the hands of Lucifer and his angels;
all its wrath, darkness, grossness, disharmony, fire, and disorder, were by the six days' creation, changed into a temporary state, restored to a certain, but low resemblance of
its first state, and put into that form and order of sun, stars,
fire, air, light, water, and earth, in which we now see it.'

' Into the world thus created out of the ruins of the kingdom of the fallen angels, and made paradisical, by the
goodness of God, was man introduced on the sixth day of
the creation, to take his place, as Lord and Prince of it, to
have power over all outward things, to discover and manifest the wonders of this new created world, and to bring
forth such a holy offspring, as might fill up the places of
the fallen angels.   And when that was done, and certain
periods of time had produced these great effects, then
this whole frame of things was, by the last purifying fire,
to have been raised from its paradisical state, into which it
was put at the creation, into that first heavenly brightness,
and high degree of glory, in which it stood before the Fall
of Lucifer.'[1]

How did this glorious being fall from his high estate ?·
and how could he be restored to it ?

[1] *Answer to Dr. Trapp,* Works, vol. vii. p. 28-30.

The answers to these two questions embrace, in Law's view, the whole scheme of Christianity; and both are equally illustrative of Law's central thought, the infinite love of God. For Law found in man's capability of falling, as in that of angels, only a fresh proof of this blessed truth Man was capable of falling, because God gave him that noblest of gifts, a free will, 'a spark of the Divine omnipotence,' for he could not be an Angel of Light with less freedom.[1] 'Thus, from the creation of Adam, through all the degrees of his Fall, to the mystery of his Redemption, everything tells you that God is Love. Nay, the very possibility of his having so great a Fall gives great glory to the goodness and love of God towards him. (1) He was created an angel, and, therefore, had the highest perfection of an angel, which is a freedom of willing. (2) He was created to be the restoring angel of this new creation. Now, these two things, which were his highest glory, and greatest marks of the Divine Favour, were the only possibility of his falling. Had he not had an angelic freedom of will, he could not have had a false will; had he not had all power given unto him over this world, he could not have fallen into it; it was this Divine and high power over it, that opened a way for his entrance or falling into it.'[2]

. To understand this expression, ' falling into it,' we must consider more closely what Law's view of the nature and results of the Fall was. He differs widely from the popular notions in many respects, but he grounds his theory upon what he holds to be the strictly literal interpretation of Holy Scripture.

'This,' says Law, 'and this alone, is the true nature and degree of the fall of man. When he was created in his original perfection, the Holy Trinity was his Creator; the

---

[1] *Answer to Dr. Trapp,* Works, vol. vi. p. 32.
[2] *Spirit of Prayer,* Part II. Works, vol. vii. (2) p. 99.

" breath of lives," which became a living soul, was the
Breath of the Tri-une God ; but when man began to will
and desire contrary to the Deity, then the life of the Tri-une
God was extinguished in him ; he fell into or under the
light and spirit of this world ; that is, of a Paradisical man,
enjoying union and communion with Father, Son, and Holy
Ghost, and living in earth in such enjoyment of God as the
angels live in Heaven, he became an earthly creature, subject to the dominion of this outward world, capable of all
its evil influences, subject to its vanity and mortality, and
as to its outward life stood only in the highest rank of
animals.'[1]

This account seemed to Law to explain many passages
of Scripture, which he thought otherwise inexplicable, and
also to harmonise with his favourite doctrine of the boundless love of God. For instance, God expressly said, " *In
the day* that thou eatest thereof, thou shalt surely die ; "
and Law contended that it was quibbling with Scripture to
say that this merely meant that he should be subject to
death, as it must mean if this death refers to the death of the
body ; for in this sense, Adam did not die on the day of his
fall, but lived many hundred years after it. But, according to
Law's theory, Adam *did* 'die the very day of his transgression ; he died to all the influences and operations of the
kingdom of God upon him, as we die to the influences of
this world when the soul leaves the body ; and, on the other
hand, all the influences, operations, and powers of the elements of this life became opened in him, as they are in
every animal at its birth into this world.'

Again, Scripture assures us, that after the Fall, 'his
eyes were opened.' ' I suppose,' says Law, ' this is a proof
that before the Fall they were shut. And what is this but

---

[1] *Appeal to all that Doubt*, Works, vol. vi. (2) p. 37.

saying in the plainest manner, that before the Fall the
life, light, and spirit of this world were shut out of him, and
that the opening of his eyes was only another way of saying
that the life and light of this world were opened in him?'

Again, when his eyes were thus opened, Scripture tells
us that 'he was immediately ashamed and shocked at the
sight of his own body, and wanted to hide it from himself,
and from the sight of the Sun.' 'But now, what was this sad
state and condition of his body? What did Adam see in
it? Why he only saw that he was fallen from his Paradisiacal glory to have the same gross flesh and blood as the
beasts of this world have. There was nothing else in his
outward form that he could be ashamed of, and yet it was
his outward form that filled him with confusion. And is not
this the greatest of all proofs that before his fall his body
had not this nature and condition of the beasts in it? Is
it not the same thing as if he had said, " This body which
now makes me ashamed, and which I want to hide, though
it be only with thin leaves, because it brings me down
amongst the animals of this world, is not that first body of
glory, into which God at first breathed the breath of lives,
and in which I became a living soul." '[1]

But there was another point which commended this
view of the Fall to Law, even more than its harmony with
the Mosaic account; it seemed to him to harmonise
thoroughly with that great fundamental truth that God is all
Love. It has always been a common objection of unbelievers that the sin of Adam in disobeying an apparently
trifling and arbitrary command was inadequate to the terrible punishment that was inflicted upon him and his innocent posterity for untold generations. But on Law's theory
this objection fell of itself to the ground. 'Herein lay the

---

[1] *Appeal to all that Doubt,* 'Works,' vol. vi. (2), p. 41.

ground of Adam's ignorance of good and evil; it was because his outward body and the outward world (in which
alone was good and evil) could not discover their own
nature, or open their own life within him, but were kept
inactive by the power and life of the celestial man within
it. And this was man's first and great trial; a trial, not
imposed upon him by the mere will of God, or by way of
experiment, but a trial necessarily implied in the nature of
his state.'[1] And thus, 'the command of God, not to lust
after, and eat of the forbidden tree, was not an arbitrary
command, given at pleasure, or as a mere trial of man's
obedience, but was a most kind and loving information
given by the God of Love to his newborn offspring, concerning the state he was in with regard to the outward
world; warning him to withdraw all desire of entering into
a sensibility of its good and evil, because such sensibility
could not be had without his immediate dying to that
divine and heavenly life which he then enjoyed.'[2] And
thus 'the misery, distress, and woful condition which Adam
by his transgression brought upon himself and all his posterity was not the effect of any severe vindictive wrath in
God, no more than if Adam had broken both his legs and
put out both his eyes, it could be said that God had
punished him with lameness and blindness. In fact, Adam
had no more hurt done to him at his fall than the very
nature of his own action brought along with it upon himself.

Again, this view of the Fall explained to Law satisfactorily all the difficulties connected with the doctrine of
Original Sin. The question was not, as it was often put,
'How can it consist with the goodness of God, to impute
the sin of Adam to all his posterity?' but, 'How was it
consistent with the goodness of God, that Adam could not

---

[1] *Spirit of Prayer,* 'Works,' vol. vii. p. 8.
[2] *Ibid.* p. 21.

generate children of a nature and kind quite superior to himself?'—a question, says Law, whose absurdity confutes itself. For the only reason why sin is found in all the sons of Adam is, because Adam of earthly flesh and blood cannot bring forth a holy angel out of himself, but must beget children of the same nature and condition with himself.

And, once more, Law's theory of the Fall accounted for the existence of this noxious tree in the Paradise of the all-loving God. Had Adam always willed what God willed, ' no evil would have been known either in plant, or fruit, or animal, nor could have been known, but by the declining will and desire of man calling it forth. The earth, as now, had then the natural power of bringing forth a tree of its own nature, viz. good and evil ; but Paradise was that heavenly power which hindered it from bringing forth such productions ; but when the *Keeper* of Paradise turned a wish from God and Paradise, after a bad knowledge, then Paradise lost some of its power, and the curse or evil hid in the earth could give forth a bad tree. But see now the goodness and compassion of God towards this mistaken creature ; for no sooner had Adam, by the abuse of his power and freedom, given occasion to the birth of this evil tree, than the God of Love informs him of the dreadful nature of it, commands him not to eat of it, assuring him that Death was hid in it, that Death to his angelic life would be found in the day that he should eat of it. A plain proof, if anything can be plain, that this tree came not from God, was not according to His own will and purpose towards Adam, but from such a natural power in the earth as could not show itself till the strong will and desire of Adam, beginning to be earthly, worked with that which was the evil hid in the earth.'[1]

[1] *Spirit of Prayer,* ' Works,' vii. (2), p. 95.

It will be gathered from the above that Law regarded the Fall as a gradual process. He did. He thought that, ' if the first sin had been only a single act of disobedience, instead of being unpardonable, it would have been more worthy of pardon than any other sin, merely because it was the first, and by a creature that had as yet no experience.' But, in Law's view, the eating of the tree was only the climax of a process that had been going on long before. ' His first longing look towards the knowledge of the life of this world was the first loosening of the reins of evil ; it began to bear life, and a power of stirring, as soon as his desire began to be earthly. The first degree of his lust towards this world had some stop put to it by the taking his Eve out of him ; that so his desire into the life of this world might be in some measure lessened.'[1] We need not dwell longer on this last curious notion. All that need be added on the subject of the Fall is that, from beginning to end, Law saw, on the part of God, only ' a gradual help administered by God to this falling creature, suitable to every degree of his falling.' From beginning to end, *He* showed Himself as nothing but one boundless abyss of love, ' till at last, in the fulness of man's fall, an *universal* Redeemer of him and his posterity was given by a Second Adam, to regenerate again the whole seed of Adam the First.'[2]

This leads us to the other cardinal division of Law's theology—the *Redemption*. Man fell through the loss of his life in God. How could he be restored ? Obviously, said Law, only by a revival—that is, renewal of life ; and, as all life comes from a birth, therefore it must be by a *new birth*—in the most literal sense of the term—in him of the life which was lost. ' If,' he asks, ' we want to be re-

[1] *Spirit of Prayer,* ' Works,' vii. (2), p. 94.
[2] *Ibid* p. 97.

deemed or regenerated only because Adam died in Paradise, must not regeneration be only and solely the bringing forth again that first birth in the human nature?'[1] Therefore, 'the one great doctrine of the Christian religion, and which includes all the rest, is this: that Adam, by his sin, died to the kingdom of heaven, or that the divine life was extinguished in him; that he cannot be *redeemed*, or restored to its first divine life, but by having it kindled or regenerated in him by the Son and Holy Spirit of God.'[2]

And this redemption was universal. After dwelling upon the utter impossibility of human nature by itself 'putting off all that which the Fall had brought upon it,' Law proceeds, in a fine passage, 'But let us now change the scene, and behold the wonders of a *new creation*, where all things are called out of the curse and death of sin, and created again to life in Christ Jesus; where all mankind are chosen and appointed to the recovery of their first glorious life, by a *new* birth from a second Adam, who, as an *universal* Redeemer, takes the place of the first fallen father of mankind, and so gives life, and immortality, and heaven, to all that lost them in Adam. God, according to the riches of His love, raised a Man out of the loins of Adam in whose mysterious Person the *whole* humanity and the Word of God were personally united; that same Word which had been reserved and treasured up in Adam at his fall, as a secret bruiser of the serpent and *real beginning* of his salvation, so that, in this second Adam, God and man were one Person. And in this union of the divine and human nature lies the foundation and possibility of our recovery. For thus the holy Jesus became qualified to be the second Adam, or universal Regenerator of all that are born of Adam the first; for being Himself that Deity,

---

[1] *Answer to Dr. Trapp,* 'Works,' vol. vi. p. 33.
[2] *Appeal to all that Doubt,* vol. vi. (2) p. 70. See also vol. v. p. 170.

which as a seed or spark of life was given to Adam, thus
all that were born of Adam had also a birth from Him,
and so stood under Him, as their common Father and
Regenerator of a heavenly life in them. And it was this
Word of Life, which was preserved and treasured up in
Adam, that makes all mankind to be the spiritual children
of the second Adam, though he was not born into the
world till so many years after the Fall ; for, seeing the
same Word that became their perfect Redeemer in the
fulness of time, was in them from the beginning, as a
beginning of their redemption, therefore He stood related
to all mankind as a fountain and deriver of an heavenly
life into them, in the same *universal manner* as Adam was
the fountain and deriver of a miserable mortality unto
them.'[1] It will be observed that Law took those memorable words about ' the seed of the woman ' not merely as
a promise for the future, but as a declaration of a fact
which should immediately take place. This, in fact, was
the keynote of this part of his system, and he recurs to it
over and over again in all his mystic works.[2]

At the same time, he was far too clear-sighted not to
perceive that this theory of redemption would suggest
many difficulties. For instance, it would be asked—

1. If Christ was the common Saviour of all mankind,
what was the difference between Christians and non-
Christians ?

In answer to this question Law makes a distinction
between Gospel Christianity and ' that original, universal
Christianity which began with Adam, was the religion of
the patriarchs, of Moses and the prophets, and of every
penitent man, in every part of the world, that had faith
and hope towards God to be delivered from the evil of this

---

[1] *Appeal to all that Doubt*, vol. vii. (2), p. 187, 188.
[2] See vol. v. pp. 168, 181, &c., &c.

world.' 'When,' he says, 'the Son of God had taken a
birth in and from the human nature, had finished all the
wonders that belonged to our redemption, and was sat
down at the right hand of God in heaven, then a heavenly
kingdom was set up on earth, and the Holy Spirit came
down from heaven, or was given to the flock of Christ in
such a degree of birth and life as never was, nor could be,
given to the human nature till Christ, the Redeemer of the
human nature, was glorified. But when the humanity of
Christ, our Second Adam, was glorified, and become all
heavenly, then the heavenly life, the comfort, and power,
and presence of the Holy Spirit was the gift which He
gave to His brethren, His friends and followers, which He
had left upon earth. The Holy Ghost descended in the
shape of cloven tongues of fire on the heads of those that
were to begin and open the new powers of a *Divine life*
set up among men. This was the beginning and manifestation of the whole nature and power of *Gospel Christianity*,
a thing as different from what was Christianity before as
the possession of the thing hoped for is different from
hope, or deliverance different from the desire or expectation of it.' [1]

2. If this 'seed of a Divine life,' this 'inspoken word
of grace,' this 'treader or bruiser of the serpent,' was implanted in Adam immediately after the Fall, and if this
was the 'Holy Jesus, the Second Adam,' what becomes of
the historical Christ who was born of the Virgin Mary?

'It may be said,' replied Law, 'in a true and certain
sense, that from that time [the Fall] the incarnation of the
Son of God began, because He was *from that time* entered
again into human nature, as a seed or beginning of its
salvation, hidden under the *veil* of the Law, and not made

---

[1] *Way to Divine Knowledge*, 'Works,' vol. vii. (3), p. 77, 78. See also
vol. v. p. 182.

manifest till he was born in the holy and highly blessed
Virgin Mary.'[1] This was what was meant by Christ's own
words, 'I am the Light *of the World*,' and S. John's words,
'That was the true Light which lighteth *every man that
cometh into the world*'—two of Law's favourite texts, which
he constantly quoted.[2] But Law emphatically, and almost
indignantly, repudiates the charge that this doctrine in any
way lessened his belief in the Christ of history. 'Let no
man,' he exclaims, 'think to charge me with disregard to
the holy Jesus, who was born of the Virgin Mary, or
with setting up an inward Saviour in opposition to that
outward Christ whose history is recorded in the Gospel.
No ; it is with the utmost fulness of faith and assurance
that I ascribe all our redemption to that blessed and
mysterious Person that was then born of the Virgin, and
will assert no inward redemption but what wholly proceeds
from, and is effected by, that life-giving Redeemer who
died on the cross for our redemption.' Then, drawing an
analogy, as he loved to do, between the natural and the
spiritual world, he illustrates his meaning by what, as we
shall see presently, was, in his view, more than an illustration, an actual representation, of the same process. 'Was
I to say,' he asks, 'that a plant or vegetable must have the
sun *within* it, must have the life, light, and virtues of the
sun incorporated in it, that it has no benefit from the sun
till the sun is thus *inwardly* forming, generating, quicken-
ing, and raising up a life of the sun's virtues in it,—would
this be setting up an inward sun in opposition to the
outward one ? Could anything be more ridiculous than
such a charge ? For is not all that is here said of an
inward sun in the vegetable so much said of a power and
virtue derived from the sun in the firmament ? So, in

[1] *Answer to Dr. Trapp*, 'Works,' vol. vi. p. 36.
[2] See vol. v. p. 181.

like manner, all that is said of an inward Christ, inwardly formed and generated in the root of the soul, is only so much said of an *inward life* brought forth by the power and efficacy of that blessed Christ that was born of the Virgin Mary.'[1]

3. 'If redemption be equivalent to the restoration of the Divine life in the soul, is not the scriptural doctrine of the Atonement virtually excluded from such a system?'

On the contrary, said Law, 'this doctrine of the Atonement made by Christ, and the absolute necessity and real efficacy of it to *satisfy* the righteousness, or justice, of God, is the very ground and foundation of Christian redemption, and the life and strength of every part of it.'[2]

From the popular view of the Atonement, particularly in the gross form in which it was apt to be presented in the eighteenth century, Law shrank with something like horror. It seemed to him perfectly shocking ' to suppose the wrath and anger of God upon fallen man to be a *state* of mind in God Himself, to be a political kind of *just indignation*, a point of *honourable resentment* which the Sovereign Deity, as Governor of the world, ought not to recede from, but must have a sufficient satisfaction done to His offended authority before He can, consistently with His sovereign honour, receive the sinner into His favour.' ' Neither reason nor Scripture,' he said, ' will allow us to bring wrath into God Himself, as a temper of His mind, who is only infinite, unalterable, overflowing Love.' The ' wrath of God ' of which Scripture speaks ' was not *such* a wrath as when sovereign princes are angry at offenders, and will not cease from their resentment till some political satisfaction or valuable amends be made to their slighted authority. No, no; it was such a wrath as God Himself

---

[1] *Spirit of Prayer*, ' Works,' vol. vii. p. 49.
[2] *Spirit of Love*, ' Works,' vol. viii. (2), p. 87.

hated, as He hates sin and hell ; a wrath that the God of
all nature and creature so willed to be removed and
extinguished, that, seeing nothing less could do it, He
sent His only begotten Son into the world that all mankind might be saved and delivered from it.   He spared
not the precious, powerful, efficacious blood of the holy
Jesus, because that alone could extinguish this eternal
wrath of death and hell, and rekindle heaven and eternal
life in the soul.'[1]   Law then goes on to show why 'without
shedding of blood there could be no remission ;' but his
arguments on this point are too long to be even recapitu-
lated here.   Law's views on the Atonement were more
obnoxious to his contemporaries than any other of his
peculiar sentiments.   It is no part of a biographer's duty
either to defend or to controvert those views ; but, whether
he explained the doctrine rightly or not, it is at any rate
certain that he held it, in his own sense of it, with all the
tenacity of the most intense conviction, and that he firmly
believed that he had the Bible on his side.   'When sin,'
he writes, ' is extinguished in the creature, all the wrath
that is between God and the creature is fully atoned.
Search all the Bible, from one end to the other, and you
will find that the atonement of that which is called the
Divine wrath, or justice, and the extinguishing of sin in the
creature, are only different expressions for one and the
same individual thing.'[2]   'The Apostle says, " Christ died
for our sins."   Thence it is that He is the great Sacrifice for
sin, and its true Atonement.   But how and why is He so ?
The Apostle tells you in these words : " The sting of death
is sin.   But thanks be to God, who giveth us the victory
through our Lord Jesus Christ."   And therefore Christ is
the Atonement of our sins when, by and from Him living

---

[1] *Appeal to all that Doubt*, 'Works,' vol. vi. (2), p. 181, 182.
[2] *Spirit of Love*, 'Works,' vol. viii. (2), p. 88, &c.

in us, we have victory over our sinful nature.' 'The whole
truth of the matter is plainly this : Christ given *for us* is
neither more nor less than Christ given *into us*. And He is
in no other sense our full, perfect, and sufficient Atonement
than as His nature and spirit are born and formed in us,
which so purge us from our sins that we are thereby in
Him, and by Him dwelling in us, become new creatures,
having our conversation in heaven. As Adam is truly our
defilement and *impurity* by his birth in us, so Christ is our
Atonement and *Purification* by our being born again of Him,
and having thereby quickened and revived in us that first
Divine life which was extinguished in Adam ; and therefore, as Adam *purchased* death for us, just so, in the same
manner, in the same degree, and in the same sense, Christ
purchases life for us ; and each of them solely by their *own
inward life within us.*' [1]

Those who desire to understand more fully Law's views
on this topic must be referred to the 'Spirit of Love,' where
they will find the subject most thoroughly worked out.
To the same treatise (one of the latest and most finished
of all Law's mystical works) must be referred those who
desire to see a full statement of the Behmenist doctrine of
the Seven Properties of Nature. It is simply impossible to
condense this part of Law's works, and equally impossible
to cull satisfactory extracts from them. Law has been
termed by a thoughtful modern author 'the most continuous writer in our language, each of his sentences and
paragraphs leading on naturally and, as it were, necessarily, to that which follows.' [2] The perfect truth of this
description I have felt most painfully while endeavouring
to select specimens which might give the reader the best

---

[1] *Spirit of Love*, 'Works,' vol. viii. (2), p. 99, &c.
[2] Rev. F. D. Maurice, in his *Advertisement to the Remarks on the Fable of the Bees.*

insight into Law's tenets. And on this most difficult subject, the seven properties of nature, Law could not be done
justice to without transferring bodily all that he has written
on it to these pages. It must suffice to say that Law
plunges into these depths (for depths they are) not from
a mere love of theorising, but for a really practical purpose.
It seemed necessary to him, in order to vindicate his central thought, the abyssal love of God, to explain what evil
was in itself, and what place it could find in a system which
was created and upheld by an omnipotent Being who was
all Love. The elucidation of this difficulty Law found in
Behmen's ' Seven Properties of Nature,' the mere statement
of which will probably cause the reader to cry, ' Hold,
enough !' The first three are Attraction, Resistance, and
Whirling ; the fourth is Fire ; the fifth, Light and Love ; and
the sixth, Sound, or Understanding. These latter three
' only declare the gradual effects of the entrance of the
Deity into the three first properties of nature, changing,
or bringing their strong wrathful attraction, resistance, and
whirling into a life and state of triumphing joy and fulness
of satisfaction, which state of peace and joy in one another
is called the *seventh property*, or state of nature. And this
is what Behmen means by his *Ternarius Sanctus,* which
he so often speaks of as the only place from whence he
received all that he said and writ. He means by it the
holy manifestation of the Triune God in the seven properties
of nature, or kingdom of heaven.' [1] Not to pursue this mysterious subject further, it may be stated in a word that evil
in every part of the universe is simply the first three properties of nature separated from the next three ; in other
words, it is nature alone, separated from the manifestation
of God in nature.

[1] *Spirit of Love,* ' Works,' vol. viii. pp. 36–39 and *passim.*

Hitherto, Law has been presented to us in this chapter rather as a theosopher than as a mystic proper. On every point, however, on which the true mystics insisted, Law expressly and repeatedly avows his concurrence with them. His mysticism appears most distinctly when we turn from his theosophical speculations to his practical application of them to the Christian's life and conduct.

Man's fall being simply a breaking off from his true centre in God, and a consequent loss of the Divine life, and man's redemption being simply a new birth in him of the life which he has lost, what is man himself to do with a view to his recovery ?

In seeking an answer to this question in Law's writings, we are led at once to all the familiar doctrines and precepts of mysticism.

1. We have seen that the doctrine that 'the Divine Word is instilled into all men' is the starting-point of all mysticism.[1] And so it is with Law. 'Thou needest not,' he says, 'run here or there, saying, "Where is Christ ?" thou needest not say, " Who shall ascend into heaven, that is, to bring down Christ from above ? " or, " Who shall descend into the deep, to bring up Christ from the dead ? " For behold the Word, which is the wisdom of God, is in thy heart. It is there as a Bruiser of thy serpent, as a Light unto thy feet and Lanthorn unto thy paths ; it is there as an Holy Oil, to soften and overcome the wrathful, fiery properties of thy nature, and change them into the humble meekness of Light and Love ; it is there as a speaking Word of God in thy soul, and, as soon as thou art ready to hear, this eternal, speaking Word will speak wisdom and peace in thy inward parts, and bring forth the birth of

[1] See *supra*, p. 142.

Christ, with all His holy nature, spirit, and tempers, within thee.'[1]

2. We have seen that the complete union of the soul with God, through Jesus Christ, is the goal of all Christian mysticism.[2] And so it is with Law. 'There is,' he says, ' but one salvation for all mankind, and the way to it is one ; and that is, the Desire of the soul turned to God. This desire brings the soul to God, and God into the soul ; it unites with God, it co-operates with God, and is one life with God. Oh, my God ! just and good, how great is Thy love and mercy to mankind, that heaven is thus everywhere open, and Christ thus the common Saviour to all that turn the desire of their hearts to Thee ! Oh, sweet power of the Bruiser of the serpent, born in every son of man, that stirs and works in every man, and gives every man a power and desire to find his happiness in God ! O holy Jesu, heavenly Light, that lightest every man that cometh into the world, that redeemest every soul that follows Thy light, which is always within him ! O holy Trinity, immense Ocean of Divine Love, in which all mankind live, and move, and have their being !—None are separated from Thee, none live out of Thy love ; but all are embraced in the arms of Thy mercy, all are partakers of Thy Divine life, the operation of Thy Holy Spirit, as soon as their heart is turned to Thee.'[3]

3. We have seen that the mystics held that the means by which this union is to be effected are faith and love. And so did Law. For that 'desire of the soul turned to God' spoken of in the preceding paragraph is only another term for faith. 'When,' he says, 'the Seed of the new

---

[1] *Spirit of Prayer,* 'Works,' vol. vii. p. 69. See also vol. v, pp. 200, 203. '*In Him* we live, and move, and have our being,' was a favourite text of Law's ; he understood it quite literally.

[2] See *supra,* p. 142.

[3] *Spirit of Prayer,* 'Works,' vol. vii. pp. 98, 99.

birth, called the inward man, has faith awakened in it, its faith is not a notion, but a real, strong, essential hunger, an attracting or magnetic desire of Christ, which, as it proceeds from a seed of the *Divine* nature in us, so it attracts and unites with its *like* ; it lays hold on Christ, puts on the Divine nature, and in a living and real manner grows powerful over all sins, and effectually works out our salvation.'[1] And as to the importance, nay, the necessity, of love.in effecting this union, it is the whole burden of the ' Spirit of Love ' to set forth this truth. ' No creature can have any union or communion with the goodness of the Deity till its life is a spirit of Love. This is the one only bond of union betwixt God and His creature.'[2]

4. We have seen that, according to the mystic theory, this union must be sought by looking, not without, but within. And so taught Law. ' Awake ! thou that sleepest, and Christ, who from all eternity has been espoused to thy soul, shall give thee light. Begin to search and dig in thine own field for this Pearl of Eternity that lies hidden in it. It cannot cost thee too much, nor canst thou buy it too dear, for it is all ; and when thou hast found it thou wilt know that all which thou hast sold or given away for it is as mere a nothing as a bubble upon the water.'[3]

5. We have seen that in seeking this union with God the mystic taught that all thoughts of self must be abandoned, and that thus humility was his cardinal virtue. And such was Law's teaching. ' Poor mortals !' he exclaims, ' what is the one wish and desire of your hearts ? What is it that you call happiness and matter of rejoicing ? Is it not when everything about you helps you to stand upon

---

[1] *Grounds and Reasons of Christian Regeneration, &c.,* ' Works,' vol. v. (2), p. 71.

[2] *Spirit of Love,* ' Works,' vol. viii. p. 8.

[3] *Spirit of Prayer,* ' Works,' vol. vii. p. 60.

higher ground, gives full nourishment to *self-esteem,* and gratifies every *pride* of life ? And yet *life* itself is the *loss,* unless pride be overcome. Oh, stop awhile in contempla- tion of this great truth ! It is a truth as unchangeable as God ; it is written and spoken through all nature ; heaven and earth, fallen angels and redeemed men, all bear witness to it. The truth is this : pride must die in you, or nothing of heaven can live in you. Under the banner of this truth give up yourselves to the meek and humble spirit of the holy Jesus, the overcomer of all fire, and pride, and wrath. This is the one Way, the one Truth, the one Life. There is no other open door into the sheepfold of God ; everything else is the working of the devil in the fallen nature of man. Humility must sow the seed, or there can be no reaping in heaven. Look not at pride only as an unbecoming temper, nor at humility only as a decent virtue ; for the one is death, and the other is life ; the one is all hell, and the other is all heaven. . . . . He who alone can redeem the world has plainly shewn us wherein the life and spirit of our redemption must consist, when He saith, " Learn of Me, for I am meek and lowly of heart." Now, if this lesson is unlearnt, we must be said to have *left* our Master, as those disciples did " who went back, and walked no more with Him." ' [1]

6. The mystics taught that love must be pure and disinterested, without any regard to reward. And so taught Law. ' The spirit of Love,' he says, ' does not want to be rewarded, honoured, or esteemed ; its only desire is to propagate itself and become the blessing and happiness of everything that wants it.' [2] One whose ' heart was truly touched by such a pure and perfect love,' would say, ' My

---

[1] *Spirit of Prayer,* ' Works,' vol. vii. (2), p. 53, 54.
[2] *Spirit of Love,* ' Works,' vol. viii. p. 7.

religion consists in living wholly to my Beloved, according to *His* satisfaction, and not *my own.* What God wills, that I will ; what God loves, that I love; what pleases God, that pleases me. I have no desire to know anything of myself, or to feel anything in myself, but that I am an instrument in the hands of God, to be, to do, and suffer according to His good pleasure. I am content to know that I love and rejoice in God *alone,* that He is what He is, and that I am what He pleases to make of me and do with me.' [1]

7. The adherence of Law to the mystic doctrine of passivity is hinted at in the above passage. It is more plainly advocated elsewhere. ' All,' he says, ' depends upon thy right submission and obedience to the speaking of God in thy soul. Stop, then, all self-activity, listen not to the suggestions of thy own reason, run not in thy own will ; but be retired, silent, passive, and humbly attentive to this new-risen Light within thee ; ' and much more to the same effect.[2]

8. The mystic ' prayer of silence ' is of course closely connected with this passivity ; and, in Law's view, ' the last state of the spirit of prayer ' is when ' the soul is now come so near to God, has found such union with Him, that it does not so much pray to as live in God. Its prayer is not any particular action, is not the work of any particular faculty, not confined to times, or words, or places, but is the work of its whole being, which continually stands in fulness of faith, in purity of love, in absolute resignation, to do, and be, what and how its Beloved pleaseth.' [3]

---

[1] *Grounds and Reasons of Christian Regeneration,* 'Works,' vol. v. (2), p. 86.

[2] *Spirit of Prayer,* 'Works,' vol. vii. pp. 77, 78, 83, &c.

[3] *Ibid.* (2), p. 172. See also p. 183. In fact, the whole tenor of this part of the treatise is directly or indirectly concerned with the prayer of silence.

9. Least of all must we omit to notice that essential part of Law's system which, in one shape or another, entered into the scheme of all mystics, viz. the analogy between the visible and the invisible worlds, and the priority and far greater reality of the latter than of the former. This view may perhaps be more correctly termed idealism than mysticism ; it was held by many who were not mystics, but not rejected by any who were. Every mystic is an idealist, though every idealist is not necessarily a mystic. It is the theory which was so finely set forth by Plato in many passages, notably in his magnificent allegory of the cave.[1] It was clothed in a Christian garb by S. Augustine ; it was gracefully and luminously set forth by Malebranche, and reproduced in an English dress by Norris of Bemerton.[2] But it found a far more powerful and original expositor than Norris in William Law.   Norris was a mere echo of Augustine and Malebranche ; but Law was never content to be a mere echo of anyone — no, not even of the 'blessed Jacob.'

'The invisible things of Him from the creation of the world are clearly seen, being understood by the things that are made ' (Rom. i. 20).   This was Law's pivot text, and it seemed to him to prove that 'this outward world was not created out of nothing, but out of the invisible things of God ; so that the outward condition and frame of visible

---

[1] In the Seventh Book of the *Republic*.   For the benefit of the unlearned reader I quote Dr. Jowett's analysis of the allegory.   ' Imagine human beings living in a sort of underground den which has a mouth wide open towards the light, and behind them a breastwork, such as marionette players might use for a screen, and there is a way beyond the breastwork along which passengers are moving, holding in their hands various works of art, and among them images of men and animals, &c. &c.   The cave is the world of sight, the fire is the sun, the way upwards is the way to knowledge, and in the world of knowledge the idea of God is last seen,' &c.   Those who only see the world of sight do not even see ' the shadows of reality, but only the shadows of an image.'

[2] See his *Theory of an Ideal World, passim.*

nature is a plain manifestation of that spiritual world from whence it is descended. For, as every outside necessarily supposes an inside, and as temporal light and darkness must be the product of eternal light and darkness, so this outward visible state of things necessarily supposes some inward· invisible state, from whence it is come into this degree of outwardness. Thus, all that is on earth is only a change or alteration of something that was in heaven, and heaven itself is nothing else but the first glorious out-birth, the majestic manifestation, the beatific visibility of the one God in Trinity.'[1]

So far, Law only wrote what Platonists of every shade had written in effect before him ; but, with characteristic thoroughness, he followed up this analogy—one might almost say this adunation—of the spiritual and the natural worlds into the closest details, some of which, when barely stated, apart from their context, sound almost grotesque. Thus, life and death are the same things throughout the universe ; therefore 'the beginnings and progress of a perfect life in fruits, and the beginnings and progress of a perfect life in angels, are not only like to one another, but are the very same thing, or the working of the very same qualities, only in different kingdoms.'[2] 'Look at life in an angel, and life in a vegetable, and you will find that life has but one and the same form, one and the same ground in the whole scale of beings. No omnipotence of God can make that to be life which is not life, or that to be death which is not death, according to nature ; and the reason is, because nature is nothing else but God's own outward manifestation of what He inwardly is and can

---

[1] *Appeal to all that Doubt,* ' Works,' vol. vi. (2), p. 22. See also p. 116, and vol. v. (2), p. 80.
[2] *Ibid.* vol. vi. (2), p. 69, &c.

do.' And therefore, also, 'eternal death in an angel is the same thing, and has the same nature, as the hard death that is in a senseless flint.' [1]

All those Scriptural expressions which speak of fire, and light, and air, and darkness, and seed, &c., in reference to spiritual things, Law took not in a metaphorical, but in a perfectly literal sense. Thus, 'there is but one fire throughout all nature and creature, standing only in different states and conditions. That fire which is the life of our bodies is the life of our souls ; that which tears wood in pieces is the same which upholds the beauteous forms of angels ; it is the same fire that burns straw that will at last melt the sun ; the same fire that kindles life in animals that kindled it in angels.' [2] So, too, earthly light was not a type, but a lower form of heavenly light. 'The heaven in this world began when God said, " Let there be light," for so far as light is in anything, so much it has of heaven in it, and of the beginning of a heavenly life. This shows itself in all things of this world, chiefly in the life-giving power of the sun, in the sweetness and meekness of qualities and tempers, in the softness of sounds, the beauty of colours, the fragrance of smells, and richness of tastes, and the like ; as far as anything is tinctured with light, so far it shows its descent from heaven, and its partaking of something heavenly and paradisaical.' [3] 'When God said, " Let there be light and there was light," it could not be the present light of this world which now governs the night and the day ; for the sun, the moon and stars were not created till the

---

[1] *Appeal to all that Doubt*, 'Works,' vol. vi. p. 78. It is hardly fair to take such assertions as these simply as they stand, detached from their context, which explains them. But space does not allow more ; therefore the reader must be referred to Law's own works for their explanation. They are quoted simply as illustrative of the thoroughness with which Law accepted the my ic theory of the close relationship between the spiritual and the material worlds.

[2] *Ibid.* (2), p. 171.
[3] *Ibid.* p. 145.

fourth day. But the light which God then spake forth, was a degree of heaven, that was commanded to glance into the darkened deep, which penetrated through all the depth of the chaos, and intermixed itself with every part ; . . . it was God's baptizing the dead chaos with the spirit of life, that it might be capable of a resurrection into a new creation ; for darkness is death and light is life ;' or, which in Law's view would come to the same thing, 'the darkness is the evil and the light is the good that is in everything ; darkness is natural, essential, and inseparable from hell ; light is natural, essential and inseparable from heaven ; it belongs only to heaven, and, wherever else it is, it is only there as a gift from heaven.'[1] The effects of the sun on this world,[2] the exact analogy between the birth and growth of the seed of a vegetable and of the heavenly seed in the soul,[3] the law of attraction which governs all bodies, ' from vegetables to angels,'[4] and many other points on which Law traced the closest correspondence between the worlds of matter and of spirit, cannot here be described without taking up too much space. It must suffice to add that, as a necessary consequence of these views of the oneness throughout all nature, Law took a much wider view of the purposes of redemption than the popular one. 'All the design of Christian redemption,' he says, 'is to remove everything that is unheavenly, gross, dark, wrathful, and disordered from every part of this fallen world ; and when you see earth and stones, storms and tempests, and every kind of evil, misery, and wickedness, you see that which Christ came into the world to remove, and not only to give

---

[1] *Spirit of Prayer*, ' Works,' vol vii. (2), pp. 29-31.

[2] See *Grounds and Reasons of Christian Regeneration*, ' Works,' vol. v. (2), p. 69 ; *Appeal to all that Doubt*, vol. vii. (2), pp. 73, 140 ; *Spirit of Prayer*, vol. vii. (2), p. 16 ; *Spirit of Love*, vol. viii. (2), p. 42.

[3] See *Appeal to all that Doubt*, vol. vi. (2), p. 79 ; *Spirit of Prayer*, vol. vii. (2), p. 146, &c.

[4] See *Appeal to all that Doubt*, vol. vi. (2), pp. 32, 33, 65

a new birth to fallen man, but also to deliver all outward
nature from its present vanity and evil, and set it again in
its first heavenly state.'[1]   This first heavenly state is called
in the Revelation of S. John a 'glassy sea,' as being the
nearest and truest representation of it that can be made to
our minds.   On this 'glassy sea' Law loves to descant ;
but we must not dwell upon it, at any rate in this place,
where the object is simply to show how thoroughly Law
was at one with the mystics.   Enough, it is hoped, has now
been said to show this ; but, if more be needed, let us hear
his own eloquent vindication of them.   'Writers,' he says
to Dr. Trapp, 'like those I have mentioned[2] there have
been in all ages of the Church ; but, as they served not the
ends of popular learning, as they helped no people to figure
and preferment in the world, and were useless to scholastic
controversial writers, so they dropt out of public use, and
were only known, or rather unknown, under the name of
mystical writers, till at last some people have hardly heard
of that very name ; though, if a man were to be told what
is meant by a mystical divine, he must be told of something as heavenly, as great, as desirable as if he was told
what is meant by a real, regenerate, living member of the
mystical body of Christ ; for they were thus called for no
other reason than as Moses and the prophets, and the
saints of the Old Testament, may be called the "spiritual
Israel," or the true "mystical Jews."   These writers began
their office of teaching as John the Baptist did, after
they had passed through every kind of mortification
and self-denial, every kind of trial and purification,
both inward and outward.   They were deeply learned

---

[1] *Spirit of Love,* 'Works,' vol. viii. p. 21.

[2] Law had just mentioned S. Cassian, 'a recorder of the lives, spirit, and
doctrine of the Holy Fathers of the desart,' Dionysius the Areopagite, Rusbrochius, Thaulerus, Suso, Harphius, Johannes de Cruce, J. Behmen, Fénélon,
Guion, and M. Bertot.

in the mysteries of the kingdom of God, not through
the use of lexicons, or meditating upon critics, but
because they had passed from death unto life. They
highly reverence and excellently direct the true use of
everything that is outward in religion; but, like the
Psalmist's king's daughter, they are all glorious within.
They are truly sons of thunder, and sons of consolation;
they break open the whited sepulchres; they awaken the
heart, and show it its filth and rottenness of death; but
they leave it not till the kingdom of heaven is raised up
within it. If a man has no desire but to be of the spirit of
the Gospel, to obtain all that renovation of life and spirit
which alone can make him to be in Christ a new creature,
it is a great unhappiness to him to be unacquainted with
these writers, or to pass a day without reading something
of what they wrote.'[1] What Law preached, that he practised; no day passed without his reading something of
what the mystics wrote, and all his later writings show how
thoroughly saturated he was with their spirit.

[1] *Works*, vol. vi. (2), pp. 320, 321.

CHAPTER XV.

LAW ON THE SACRAMENTS.

THE first work which Law wrote in his mystic stage is
entitled ' A Demonstration of the Gross and Fundamental
Errors of a late Book, called "A Plain Account of the
Nature and End of the Sacrament of the Lord's Supper." '
The reputed author of the ' Plain Account ' was Law's old
antagonist Bishop Hoadly, now advanced to the wealthy
see of Winchester. The Bishop never claimed the authorship of the work, but he never disclaimed it, and internal
evidence is decidedly in favour of his authorship, for both
the style and sentiments are very similar to those of his
avowed writings. Moreover, it is pretty clear that the
younger Hoadly, who must have been acquainted with the
facts of the case, was of opinion that it was his father's
work.[1]

[1] He inserts it in full in his edition of Bishop Hoadly's works (1773), but
without asserting that it was his father's composition. In his preface he quotes
without comment the following passage from the *Biographia Britannica* (Art.
' Hoadly '), the last sentence of which, it will be seen, plainly implies that
Bishop Hoadly was the author. ' He [Bishop Hoadly] was the reputed author
of *A Plain Account, &c.* As this masterly performance rationally limited the
nature and effects of this *positive* rite to the words and actions of our Lord
Himself, and to those of S. Paul afterwards (the only certain inspired accounts of it), it was consequently unfavourable to the commonly received
opinions of its peculiar efficacies and benefits, and accordingly met with a very
warm, though weak opposition. . . . A new edition (the fifth) was printed off
when Bishop Warburton's *Rational Account, &c.*, was published in 1761, and
the publication was some time deferred, as the author designed to have added
a postscript on that occasion, but his death prevented it, and we are informed
no papers remain on the subject.'— *Preface*, pp. xxii. xxiii.

The article on ' Hoadley ' in the *Penny Cyclopædia* says : ' His *Plain Ac-*

It seemed for awhile as if the slumbering flames of the Bangorian controversy were about to be revived. Pamphlet after pamphlet, and letter after letter, were issued from the press, in rapid succession, on both sides of the question ; but the predominant feeling was unquestionably one of deep indignation that so unworthy a view of the highest act of Christian worship could be even suspected of having come from the pen of a Christian prelate. In fact, the question of authorship created at least as much interest as the contents of the work itself. But in vain was the Bishop challenged or allured to avow or deny his connection with the book. More than one enterprising gentleman boldly took the bull by the horns, and dedicated their attacks or defences of the ' Plain Account ' to the Bishop of Winchester himself. ' Never,' wrote one, ' was a book more likely to please, nor less likely to reform, the present times. The author must have had the propagation of irreligion and vice prodigiously at heart. What he preaches has been for some time generally practised. It has reduced the most pernicious practice to theory. Next to the wickedness and folly of its author is the malice of those who would make us think it the work of so great and excellent a man as the Bishop of Winchester. What a scandalous and uncharitable age is this that can ascribe such a work of darkness to an apostolical messenger of light ! to a bishop ! to a servant and successor of our Saviour !—an imputation that would fix one of the worst books that ever was wrote on one of the best bishops that ever adorned ours or any other Church.'[1] The last part of this is evi-

count, &c., shows how rational was the view which he took of Christianity,' &c. Bishop Van Mildert unhesitatingly attributes the work to Hoadly. See *Life of Waterland*, pp. 161-3.

[1] *A Vindication of the Right Reverend the Lord Bishop of Winchester against the malicious aspersions of those who uncharitably ascribe the book intituled ' A Plain Account, &c.,' by the author of the ' Proposal for the Revival of Christianity,'* 1736.

dently ironical ; for the author goes on to hit at Hoadly's
ample income, and his share in the silencing of Convocation.   His 'best of bishops' is something like Junius'
'best of kings.'   Another writer, who dedicated his work
to Bishop Hoadly, and addressed him as 'Your lordship,
the reputed author,' commences : 'It is now, from my own
writing this; little more than a month since I could first
allow myself to take the 'Plain Account' into my hands.
Popular clamour had made me apprehensive that, possibly,
the very touch might be infectious ; but to be sure that I
could not give it the reading, without running the utmost
risque of making shipwreck of some principles of faith, and
sacrificing the answer of a good conscience.'[1]   Bishop Van
Mildert mentions, among 'a host of eminent writers who
controverted the " Plain Account,"'[2] the names of Warren,
Wheatly, Whiston, Ridley, Leslie, Law, Brett, Johnson, and
Stebbing ;[2] but the weightiest of all the authorities which
were ranged against the work was that of the great Waterland himself, who, though he did not enter the lists on his
own account, sent 'his humble service and thanks to Dr.
Warren for the great service he had done to our common
Christianity,' and complimented Wheatly for 'detecting the
Socinianism of the " Plain Account," and for opening the
eyes of some ignorant admirers.'   Dr. Waterland is evidently of opinion that Hoadly was the author ; for he
speaks of Dr. Warren 'having girded *the great man* closer
than anyone before,' and adds, 'I am persuaded *the
principal man* will write no more on that argument, for
fear of exposing himself further.'   The mysterious allusions
to 'the great man,' and ' the principal man,' point clearly
to Hoadly, who was at that time (1735–6) one of the most

---

[1] *A Defence of the ' Plain Account, &c.,* 1748.
[2] *Life of Waterland,* prefixed to vol. i. of his 'Works,' p. 163.

influential men at court.[1] The 'Plain Account' created an
excitement immediately on its publication, and it was immediately attributed to Hoadly ; for it was only published

[1] See Waterland's *Letters*, 'Works,' vol. vi. pp. 448, 449, also 418–20 (Van
Mildert's edition) Dr. Hunt (*Religious Thought in England*, vol. iii. p. 56)
mentions Waterland alone by name among the writers against the *Plain Account*, but, except in the letters quoted in the text, I cannot find that Waterland wrote *expressly* against it, though, no doubt, he had it in his eye when he
wrote his *Review of the Doctrine of the Eucharist, &c.*, in 1737. Dr. Hunt
attributes, without doubt, the *Plain Account, &c.* to Hoadly.

The following list of some, and only some, of the writings which the *Plain
Account* called forth, will give the reader some idea of the interest it awakened : –

1. *Answer to Hoadly's ' Plain Account &c.' in Three Parts*, by Dr. Rd.
Warren, Fellow of Jesus Coll. Cambridge, &c., 1735.

2. Appendix to the above, 1736–7.

3. *Christian Exceptions to the ' Plain Account, &c.,' with a Method proposed for coming at the true Apostolical sense of that Holy Sacrament*,' published
anonymously, but known to have been written by Mr. Wheatly, 1736.

4. *The ' Plain Account, &c.' vindicated from the misrepresentations of Dr.
Warren, &c.* (Anonymous), 1737.

5. *The Winchester Converts, or a Discovery of the Design of a late Treatise
entitled a ' Plain Account, &c.,'* 1735.

6. *A Proper Answer* to the above, 1735.

7. *Reply to the Winchester Converts*, attributed to Mr. Ayscough of
C. C. C. Camb.

8. Brett (Dr. F.), *A True and Scriptural Account of the Nature and
Benefits of the Holy Eucharist.*

9. Bowyer's *True Account of the Nature, End, and Efficacy of the Sacrament, &c.*, 1736.

10. *A Testimony of Antiquity concerning the Sacramental Body and Blood
of Christ, in answer to the ' Plain Account, &c.,'* 1736.

11. *Letters on Baptism*, to the author of the *Plain Account*, 1757.

12. *The ' Plain Account ' not drawn from or founded on Scripture*, 1738.

13. *The ' Plain Account ' contrary to Scripture*, being a second part to the
above.

14. *The Lord's Supper not a Sacrifice, or, The Doctrine of a Material
Sacrifice in the Lord's Supper not founded on Scripture, being a Defence of the
' Plain Account,'* by T. Wingfield, Vicar of Yalmeton (? Yealmpton), Devon,
1739.

15. *The Sacrament of the Altar against the ' Plain Account '* (Anon.).

16. *Remarks on a Book entitled a ' Plain Account,'* by the Rev. Mr.
Lamb, 1739.

17. *A Letter to Mr. Lamb, occasioned by his ' Remarks, &c.'* (Anon.), 1740.

18. *A Defence of the ' Plain Account, &c.'* See *supra*, p. 282, note, 1748

19. *A Vindication of the Bishop of Winchester, &c.* See *supra*, p. 281
note.

20. *Defence of a late Book intituled ' A Plain Account, &c.,' in Reply*

in June 1735, and on July 6, 1735, Waterland wrote to Mr. Loveday, 'There is an odd piece upon the Sacrament lately published, and supposed to come from a great hand, which makes much noise.'

The biographer of Law, however, should be the last person in the world to spend time in discussing the question whose the 'great hand' was which produced the 'Plain Account ;' for, at the commencement of his 'Demonstration,' Law very characteristically rebukes the idle curiosity which was rife at the time he wrote. 'Who,' he says, 'this nameless author is, neither concerns the truth, nor you, nor me, and therefore I leave that matter as he has left it.'

But the fact that the 'Plain Account' roused so much indignation is interesting historically, as tending to show that the higher and nobler view of the Holy Eucharist was more prevalent in the middle of the eighteenth century than is commonly supposed ; and Law's own contribution to the controversy is particularly interesting to us, as showing that his Churchmanship was only modified, not lost, when he became a mystic. Here we have him volunteering his sentiments on a crucial point ; and on this point he evidently holds as distinctly High Church views as he did when he measured swords with (probably) the same antagonist twenty years earlier.

It must be remembered that when Law published his first mystic work (1737) he had been for at least three years a diligent student and ardent admirer of Behmenism, for which he had been previously prepared by a long course of study of the mystic writers, and, though his Behmenism is not quite so prominently brought forward in this as in

---

several *Answers to it*, as Dr. Brett, Dr. *Warren*, Mr. *Bowyer*, &c., by Thos. Buttenshaw, Rector of Addington, 1747.

21. Whiston (W.), *The Primitive Eucharist Revived, occasioned by the 'Plain Account, &c.,'* 1736.

his subsequent writings, still he was evidently to all intents and purposes settled in that belief which he maintained with increasing clearness to the very end of his life. This belief was plainly not inconsistent with his holding the highest view of the Christian Sacrament, as we shall see by a short examination of the contents of this work.

The key of the position of Law's opponent was this: that the bare words of Christ in the institution of the Sacrament, interpreted according to the common rules of speaking in like cases, tell us all that can be known about the nature, end, and effects of that Sacrament.

This position Law assails with all his accustomed logical acumen and racy wit. The author laid down that the words of institution must be interpreted 'according to the common rules of speaking in like cases.' 'But pray, sir,' asks Law very pertinently, 'where must a man look for a like case ? Does the world afford any case like it ? Have the speaker, or the things spoken, any things in common life that are alike to either of them ? Take the words of the institution alone, as the Apostles first heard them, when they knew not what person their Saviour was, or how He was to save them, or what their salvation itself implied — take them thus understood only according to the common rules of speaking—and then there is nothing in them but that poor conception which they had of them at that time, and such as did them no good ; and then, also, we have that knowledge of this institution which this author pleads for. But take the same words of the institution, understood and interpreted according to the articles of the Christian faith, and seen in that light in which the Apostles afterwards saw them, when they *knew* their Saviour, and then everything that is great and adorable in the redemption of mankind, everything that can delight, comfort, and support the heart of a Christian is found to be centred in this holy Sacrament.   There then wants nothing but the wedding garment to make this holy Supper the marriage feast of the Lamb.'

Again, the words of the institution, ' Do this in remembrance of Me,' imply to the Christian, ' Let this be done as your confession and acknowledgment of the salvation that is received through Me.'   But this is altogether unintelligible to any man who is left (as this author would leave him) solely to the bare words of the institution ; they would signify no more to him than they would to a heathen, who had by chance found a bit of paper in the fields with the same words writ upon it.

The principle which the author recommended for interpreting this Sacrament was precisely the principle on which the Jews interpreted the Scripture, and in consequence, rejected the Messiah.   *They* placed all in the letter of Scripture, as this author does ; *they* understood that letter only according to the common rules of speaking amongst men, as this author does ; *they* looked upon and understood all the institutions of their religion, as this author looks upon and understands the Sacrament ; *they* saw just as far into the Law as he does into the Gospel ; *they* had his degree of knowledge, and he has their degree of ignorance. It was precisely on this author's principle that the letter-learned Pharisee thought that the whole nature and end of a sacrifice was fully observed when he had slain an ox, and not cut off a dog's head.   In short, if you ask the true reason why the religion of the scribes and Pharisees was so odious in the sight of our blessed Saviour—why He cast so many reproaches upon it—why He denounced so many woes against it—it was because they stood on the outside of the Law, just as this author stands on the outside of the Gospel, and were content with such a '*plain account*' of their sacrifices and circumcision as he has given us of the

Sacrament. When our Saviour said, in the 6th of S. John, that 'His flesh was meat indeed, and His blood was drink indeed,' and His disciples asked, 'How can this Man give us His flesh to eat?' He did not reply, as on this author's principle He should have done, 'Consider My words only according to the common rules of speaking, and then you will know *all* that is to be known of them,' but He replied, 'The words that I speak unto you, they are spirit, and they are life;' and, if the words of the Sacrament are also 'spirit and life,' then this author's contrivance is as unfit for the purpose as an iron key would be to open the gate of the kingdom of heaven. If they are spirit and life, then to seek for the sense of such words in the common forms of speaking is truly to seek the living amongst the dead.

It is not necessary to follow Law in his demonstration that the word remembrance does not, as his author asserts, necessarily imply absence; that the Sacrament is more than a mere positive duty (reminding one, in this part of his work, of Dr. Waterland's reply to Dr. Clarke); that the Sacrament can be rightly understood only in the light which the after events of Christ's death, resurrection, and ascension, and, above all, the coming of the Holy Ghost, shed upon it; and that the making it a bare act of memory makes it to be an act with no more religion in it than the act of a parrot. But one very grave charge which Law makes against his author must be noted. When Christ said, 'Do this,' He meant, Do it as your act of faith in Me as your Saviour, that is, as a real atonement for your sins, and a real principle of life within you; and the foundation and possibility of Christ's being all this was His Divine nature. 'If the author will declare without any equivocation that he fully believes these great truths, no further a recantation of his whole book need to be desired.' In fact, Law is of opinion that the real cause of all his author's errors is that he does not believe that Jesus was truly and essentially God, as well as perfect man. Socinianism was, in Law's view, closely connected with Deism, or natural religion as opposed to revealed ; and, accordingly, against this tendency, which was very prevalent when Law wrote, he directs the whole of the remainder of his treatise. As Law's views on this question will be discussed later on, they need not be dwelt on here. Let us conclude with a passage which shows us what Law's view of the Holy Communion was after he became a mystic. 'You must consider,' he says, 'the Sacrament purely as an object of your devotion, that is to exercise all your faith, that is to raise, exercise, and inflame every holy ardour of your soul that tends to God. It is an abstract or sum of all the mysteries that have been revealed concerning our Saviour, from the first promise of a " seed of the woman to bruise the serpent's head " to the day of Pentecost. Jacob's ladder, that reached from earth to heaven, and was filled with angels ascending and descending between heaven and earth, is but a small signification between God and man, which this holy Sacrament is the means and instrument of. Whatever names or titles this institution is signified to you by—whether it be called a *sacrifice*, propitiatory or commemorative—whether it be called an *holy oblation*, the *Eucharist*, the *Sacrament* of the *body* and *blood* of Christ, the Sacrament of the *Lord's Supper*, the *heavenly banquet*, the *food of immortality*, or the *Holy Communion*—all these names are right and good, and there is nothing wrong in them but the striving and contention about them ; for they all express *something* that is true of the Sacrament, and therefore are every one of them, in a good sense, rightly applicable to it ; but all of them are far short of expressing the whole nature of the Sacrament, and therefore the help of all of them is wanted.'

(2.) '*The Grounds and Reasons of Christian Regeneration.*'

As the preceding work gave us Law's sentiments on
one of the Sacraments of the Gospel, so the title of this
would lead us to expect that he would here give us his
sentiments on the other. And we are not disappointed.
It might seem at the first glance that Law's mystic views
were plainly inconsistent with the doctrines taught in the
Church Catechism and the Baptismal Service. If Christ
be literally 'the light which lighteth *every* man that
cometh into the world;' if 'all men, as sons of Adam,
are by the free grace of God made sons of the second
Adam,' and as such 'have a seed of life in them from
Him ;' if 'this seed of a new birth, or light of life, is the
general and *preventing* grace of God,' so that 'all mankind
may, in a certain and good sense, be said to be sharers of
this regeneration'—and these sentiments are affirmed in
various forms over and over again in Law's mystic works,
and especially in the treatise now before us—what becomes
of the doctrine that children, 'being by nature born in sin
and children of wrath, are by baptism made the children
of grace'?

An answer to this question will at once be found when
it is remembered that Law drew a marked distinction between what he called 'original Christianity' and 'Gospel
Christianity.' All are partakers of the new birth, inasmuch as all are partakers of original Christianity—the
'Christianity as old as the creation,' in which Law believed
as firmly as Tindal himself, though what he understood by
it was as different from the Deist's meaning as light is from
darkness. But of the new birth of Gospel Christianity,
Law held that Holy Baptism was not only the sign and

pledge, but actually the vehicle. In his mystic, as in his earlier days, it was still to him the Sacrament of Regeneration. ‘ Our baptism,’ he says in this treatise, ‘ is to signify our seeking *and obtaining* a new birth ; and our being baptized in, or into, the “ name of the Father, Son, and Holy Ghost,” tells us in the plainest manner what birth it is that we seek, namely, such a new birth as may make us again what we were at first, a living, real image or offspring of the Father, Son, and Holy Ghost. It is owned on all hands that we are baptized into a renovation of some Divine birth that we had lost ; and, that we may not be at a loss to know what that Divine birth is, the form in Baptism openly declares to us that it is to regain that first birth of Father, Son, and Holy Ghost in our souls, which at the first made us to be truly and really images of the Holy Trinity in Unity. The form in Baptism is but very imperfectly apprehended till it is understood to have this great meaning in it. Baptism is the appointed Sacrament of this new birth ; and how finely, how surprisingly, do our first and our second birth answer to and illustrate one another ! At our first birth it is said thus : “ Let us make man in our Image, after our own Likeness.” When the Divine birth was lost, and man was to receive it again, it is said, “ Be thou baptized into the name of the Father, Son, and Holy Ghost,” which is saying, “ Let the Divine birth be brought forth again in thee,” or “ Be thou born *again* such an image of Father, Son, and Holy Ghost as thou wast at first.” ’

In the following passage he shows still more clearly how he reconciles his doctrine of an universal redemption, or regeneration (for in Law’s view these expressions mean the same thing), with the belief which he unquestionably retained in ‘ baptismal regeneration.’ ‘ The mystery,’ he says, 'of an inward power, of a salvation *hidden* in all men, has had just such degrees of obscurity and manifestation as the nature, and birth, and person of the Messiah have had ; that is, as the nature and person of Jesus Christ, as an Atonement, Saviour, and Redeemer of mankind, were for several ages of the world only obscurely pointed at and typified by the religion of the Jews, so this end of a new birth, or saving power of Christ hidden in the souls of all men, was through the same ages under the same veil and obscurity. . . . When Jesus Christ came into the world declaring the *necessity* of a new birth, to be owned and sought by a Baptism in the name of Father, Son, and Holy Ghost, this was not a *new* kind or power of salvation, but only an *open* declaration of the *same* salvation, that had been till then only *typified*, and veiled under certain figures and shadows, as He Himself had been.'

In a word, if Law held clearly that 'all men had in them a seed of life that is contrary to their corrupt nature, which seed they partake of as heirs of the first grace granted to Adam in the *ingrafted Word*,' he also held quite as clearly that 'all Christians are in a *higher* and *further* state of regeneration by the grace of Baptism in the name of the Holy Trinity.' [1]

This short treatise, besides giving us the clearest indication which we possess of Law's views, as a mystic, on the initial Sacrament of the Christian life, is also interesting and important as giving, in a concise form, a very complete statement of Law's mystical sentiments generally. Law himself regarded it as a sufficient exposition of his views ; for he constantly refers his reader to it in his later works,

---

[1] See *Works*, vol. v. (2) pp. 28, 61, 64, 75, and *passim*. This treatise being very short, it did not seem necessary to indicate the exact page from which each quotation was made.

and in one passage declares that, if he could afford it, he would have 'this little book sent gratis into all parts of the kingdom.'[1] As the reader is already familiar with Law's views, there is no need to dwell further on this abstract of them.

[1] See *Works*, vol. vi. p. 46.

CHAPTER XVI.

'ANSWER TO DR. TRAPP,' AND 'APPEAL TO ALL THAT DOUBT, &C.'

As in the last two works we were reminded that we were
still under the guidance of the writer of the 'Three Letters
to the Bishop of Bangor,' so in the work now to be considered we are reminded that we are still under the guidance
of the author of the 'Serious Call.' Law's mysticism no
more changed his asceticism than it did his catholicism.
It modified both; but that was all. As he was still the
High Churchman in point of doctrine, so he was still the
Puritan in his estimate of the Christian's relation towards
'the world.' A discourse, therefore, 'on the folly, sin, and
danger of being righteous overmuch,' would naturally call
forth a refutation from him, even if he had not been personally attacked, as he was, by Dr. Trapp. But if on such
a subject Law still held Puritan sentiments, they were entirely free from Puritan sourness. The first paragraphs of
the 'Earnest and Serious Answer to Dr. Trapp' give us the
true key to the understanding of the spirit in which Law
wrote. 'Might I,' he writes, 'follow the bent of my own
mind, my pen, such as it is, should be wholly employ'd in
setting forth the infinite love of God to mankind in Christ
Jesus, and in endeavouring to draw all men to the belief
and acknowledgment of it. . . . It is so difficult to enter
into controversy without being, or at least *seeming*, in some
degree unkind to the person that one opposes, that it is

with great reluctance that I have enter'd upon my present undertaking, having nothing more deeply riveted in my heart than an universal love and kindness for all mankind, and more especially for those whom God has called to be my fellow-labourers in promoting the salvation of mankind.'

There is not one word in this treatise which belies this fair profession. An earnest, tender care for the welfare of all mankind, and especially for that of his brethren in the sacred ministry, breathes through every line of it. One feels, as one reads, that every word comes from the heart— and that a very large, noble, and generous heart. Above all, his appeal to the clergy on their duty in the sad state of religion which was confessed on all sides, is singularly touching and affectionate. 'However unwilling,' he said, 'yet I find myself obliged to consider and lay open many grievous faults in the doctor's discourse, and to show to all Christians that the dearest interests of their souls are much endanger'd by it;' and it is manifest on the face of it that nothing but an intense conviction of the truth of this assertion would have led him to write as he did. He might have said of this, as he did of a previous work, ' My stile is the stile of love and zeal for your salvation ; and if you condemn anything but love in it, you condemn something that is not there.'[1]

At the same time, it would be a great injustice to Dr. Trapp to judge him simply by the impression which this treatise of Law's leaves upon the mind. It has been remarked before, that Law, in spite of his temperateness, had an extraordinary knack of putting his adversary in the wrong. Perhaps it would be more correct to say 'in consequence of his temperateness'; for intemperate language

---

[1] On the ' Plain Account, &c.,' *Works*, vol. v. p. 195.

always recoils upon its author. The fact is, Mr. Law and
Dr. Trapp looked upon life from such entirely different
standpoints that it was impossible for either to appreciate
the other. Dr. Trapp was a very incarnation of eighteenth-
century feeling ; Law in the eighteenth century was an
anachronism, A few words on Dr. Trapp's life and writings will bring out clearly the contrast between the two
men. He was born in 1679, and was therefore seven years
older than Law. In 1704 he was elected Fellow of Wad-
ham College, Oxford ; and, in 1708 (the year in which
Law took his degree), was appointed the first Professor of
Poetry at Oxford.[1]   Trapp, like Law, was a distinct High
Churchman, acting as manager for Dr. Sacheverell in his
trial in 1709, and subsequently contributing his quota to
the Bangorian controversy on the same side as Law. But,
unlike Law, he was more attracted by the political than by
the theological aspect of High Churchmanship ; and, unlike
Law, he did not suffer his High Church opinions to carry
him to their logical result, and so become a nonjuror. He
became what was called a Hanoverian Tory, and took an
active part in political disputes on the Tory side. He was
then made Rector of Christ Church, Newgate Street, and
S. Leonard's, Foster Lane, and held the somewhat thank-
less office of chaplain to Viscount Bolingbroke, whom he
always regarded as his patron. But it is rather unfair to
suggest, as has been done,[2] that Bolingbroke's contemptuous opinion of the clergy was to any extent based on the
estimate which he had formed of his chaplain. In point of
fact, there seems to be no reason to doubt that Dr. Trapp
was a worthy man, according to his lights ; but those
lights were certainly not Law's lights. Like many of the
eighteenth-century clergy, he had a strong lay element

---

[1] His portrait is still to be seen in the Bodleian.
[2] See *The Life and Times of Selina, Countess of Huntingdon*, vol. i. p. 179.

in his composition. He was an active-minded man, and a voluminous writer on a most heterogeneous mass of subjects. Many of his writings Law would have regarded as sheer waste of time, if not something worse. According to Law's rigorous sentiments, it was bad enough for a clergyman to translate Virgil into English blank verse, to describe foreign countries, to write on exclusively political subjects. All these things the doctor did ; but even these were not all. As a crowning enormity, Dr. Trapp actually wrote a tragedy ; thus, according to Law's views, directly helping on the devil's own work.[1] It need hardly be said that Dr. Trapp was a violent and uncompromising opponent of the Methodists. But here, again, it is hardly fair to affirm, as has been done, that his opposition arose ' from a mistaken notion that he was thereby recommending himself to his ecclesiastical superiors.'[2] He only took the part

[1] The following is a list of Dr. Trapp's works, so far as I have been able to trace them :

1. *Prælectiones Poeticæ, in schola naturalis philosophiæ, Oxon. habitæ.*

2. *Preservative against Unsettled Notions and Want of Principle in Religion.* Two vols. of sermons.

3. *Popery Truly Stated and Briefly Refuted.*

4. *Explanatory Notes on the Four Gospels.*

5. *The Doctrine of the Trinity.*

6. *Thoughts upon the Four Last Things—Death, Judgment, Heaven, and Hell.* A poem.

7. *Mesech and Kedar.*

8. The whole of *Virgil* translated into English blank verse.

9. *A Single Combat* (on Whitefield), and several other works against the same man.

10. *The Character of the Present Set of Whigs.*

11. *The Spirit of the Nunnery.* A tale from the Spanish.

12. *Pean.* A poem (dedicated to Lord Bolingbroke).

13. *A Picture of Italy.* Translation.

14. *Abra-Mule.* A Tragedy.

15. *The Nature, &c., of being Righteous Overmuch, &c.*

16. Various Papers in the *Examiner.*

17. A translation of *Anacreon* into Latin verse.

18. Milton's *Paradise Lost* translated into Latin verse.

[2] *Life of Lady Huntingdon*, vol. i. p. 179.

which the vast majority of his order took, and, though we
may consider them mistaken, we have no right to consider
them insincere. But few clergy attracted so much attention by their opposition to the Methodists as Dr. Trapp.
Loud and many were the invectives which he thundered
forth from the pulpit, and afterwards issued from the press,
against these new disturbers of the peace ; and one of the
most notorious of these effusions now comes before us in
connection with William Law.

'The Discourse on the Nature, Folly, Sin, and Danger of
being Righteous Overmuch,' is, as it stands in Dr. Trapp's
printed works, the substance of four discourses rolled into
one.[1] Considering the universal complaint in George II.'s
reign that all classes were righteous overlittle, we might
certainly agree with the comment of a noble lady, who to
a certain extent favoured Methodism, on the sermon. 'It
is a doctrine,' she says, 'which does not seem absolutely
necessary to be preached to the people of the present age.'[2]
Dr. Trapp, however, thought otherwise ; but it is only fair
to him to state that he deals with this very obvious objection at the outset of his discourse. 'Righteous overmuch ? may one say' (thus he commences) ; 'is there
any danger of that ? Is it even possible ? Can we be too
good ? Or, if that might be, is there any occasion, however, of warning against it in these times, when the danger

---

[1] It is entitled, *The Nature, Folly, Sin, and Danger of being Righteous Overmuch, with a particular view to the doctrines and practices of certain modern
enthusiasts; being the substance of four discourses lately preached in the parish
churches of Christ Church and S. Lawrence Jewry, London, and S. Martin's-
in-the-Fields, Westminster. By Joseph Trapp, D.D.* 1739.

[2] The Countess of Hertford, afterwards Duchess of Somerset. She contrasts this discourse of Dr. Trapp's with the great tenderness and moderation
with which the Bishop of London [Gibson] treated the Methodists personally,
though he had thought it necessary to write a pastoral letter to warn the people
of his diocese against being led away by them. See *The Life and Times of
Selina, Countess of Huntingdon*, vol. i. p. 197.

is manifestly on the contrary extreme; when all manner
of vice and wickedness abounds to a degree almost un-
heard of? I only answer at present that to be righteous
overmuch is itself, very often at least, one sort of vice and
wickedness, and a bad sort too.' After having set aside
the exposition of those who would have the words to be
spoken not in the person of Solomon himself, but in that
of a carnal and corrupt reasoner persuading men to indifference and neutrality in religion, and having admitted
that 'there can be no such thing, properly speaking, as
being righteous overmuch, but that the expression is owing
to the imperfection of language,' the doctor proceeds to
explain what he means by being righteous overmuch. His
doctrine is simply the old Aristotelian doctrine of the mean :
'When vertue rises beyond its due bounds, it loses its nature,
and degenerates into vice ; and since it loses its nature, it
ought to lose its name.' Thus, courage degenerates into
foolhardiness, temperance into abstinence, and so forth.
Then the doctor defines more explicitly his position. 'To
be righteous overmuch is to place much religion (where
there is really none, but the contrary) in extraordinaries,
in new inventions, and striking out into bye-paths.'

This, of course, is a hit at the Methodists; and among
them the chief offenders were George Whitefield and
William Law, the latter of whom he evidently regards as
the *fons et origo mali.* On the appearance of the 'Christian Perfection' and the 'Serious Call,' Dr. Trapp had
'prophesied they would do harm, and so it had happened,
for shortly afterwards up sprung the Methodists.' It is
true that William Law and George Whitefield had little in
common, except an intensely earnest spirit of piety ; on
almost every other point they differed as widely as two
men could do. But it was not to be expected that Dr.
Trapp could recognise these minor shades of distinction ; it

was enough for him that they both were tainted with that most hateful thing, enthusiasm. No ; we must beg Dr. Trapp's pardon. These 'righteous overmuch' men were bad enough ; but not quite so bad as that—only on the highroad to it. 'Another mischief,' says the doctor, 'is that *it tends*, at least, to that baneful plague ENTHUSIASM ! It is itself somewhat enthusiastical, at best, and tends, as I said, to downright enthusiasm. I do not say that all righteous overmuch are enthusiasts ; but I do say that in all ages enthusiasts have been righteous overmuch. They began with the last-mentioned and ended with the other.'

Dr. Trapp's sentiments are so exactly the antipodes of those of William Law that they help, by their very contrast, to illustrate the subject of this biography ; they represent the very spirit which Law consecrated his whole life to thwart. Perhaps he fell into the other extreme, particularly in the earlier stage of his life. Dr. Trapp, alluding especially to the 'Christian Perfection,' declares that 'it dejects and perplexes persons truly and sincerely religious, making them think they do not do their duty, when they really do ; and, on the other hand, it hardens the wicked and prophane, making them explode the Christian religion, as being impracticable and, by consequence, irrational.' Whether this be so or no, Dr. Trapp took a very different view of Christianity ; and, as that view was by no means an uncommon one in the eighteenth century, it is worth while to consider a few more of his sentiments, as illustrating very fairly that spirit of the age with which Law was so utterly out of sympathy.

Dr. Trapp, then, would have men go to church, 'even upon ordinary days, as often as their necessary business will permit ;' he would have them 'practise all Christian vertues ;' but he differed *in toto* from Law in his view of what Christian virtues are. 'These men,' he says, with a

special reference to Law (for he quotes a passage from the
'Christian Perfection' to illustrate his meaning), tell us that,
according to the spirit and genius of the Christian religion,
we must absolutely renounce all the possessions and enjoy-
ments of the world, and have nothing to do with them. No
sort of gayety or expensiveness in dress is permitted to any
person whatsoever. And yet,' asks the doctor, ' was not
our Lord present at weddings, feasts, and entertainments?
nay, at one of them worked a miracle to make wine, when
it is plain there had been more drank than was absolutely
necessary for the support of nature, and consequently something had been indulged to pleasure and chearfulness?'
Some of Christ's rules were, he thinks, ' only intended for
the early Christians ;' the Sermon on the Mount contains
many ' hyperbolical phrases.' 'And surely,' he argues,
'some Christians not only may, but must, admit of pomps,
otherwise what would become of sovereignty and magis-
tracy? And all Christians must have to do with some
vanities, or else they must needs go out of the world
indeed ; for the world is all over vanity.' Charity is all
very well, but it may be recommended to ' the ruin of a
man's wife and children ; and does not the Scripture tell
us that he who provideth not for his own household hath
denied the faith, and is worse than an infidel '? As to pre-
tending to have ' the Spirit of God, some way or other, and
this made known in a particular and extraordinary manner,'
it was nothing but a ' revival of the old fanaticism of the
last century.' This doctrine of a ' light within is sheer
Quakerism.' Therefore, ' go not after these impostors ;
shun them as you would the plague.'

No one who has followed so far the course of Law's
life needs to be told that such sentiments as these would
be utterly abominable in his eyes. In fact, considering the
extreme repugnance he must have felt against them, it is

perfectly wonderful to see how calm and moderate he is in his reply. Others answered Dr. Trapp in a very different spirit, as the mere titles of their works show. One is called ' Dr. Trap Vindicated from the Imputation of being a Christian ; ' another, ' The Anti-over-righteous Trap.' But Law never forgets that such a work required an ' earnest and serious ' answer. The subject is too solemn for him to show any of his wonted racy humour in dealing with it. Earnestness and seriousness breathe through every line of the ' Earnest and Serious Answer.'

On one point alone does he show anything like wrath. He cannot brook the thought that the doctor should have attempted to enlist the Blessed Saviour Himself on his side. ' O holy Jesus,' Law exclaims, with a burst of eloquence, in which righteous indignation is mingled with a most touch-ing pathos, ' that Thy Divine life should, by a preacher of Thy Gospel, be made a plea for liberties of indulgence ! O holy Jesus ! Thou didst nothing of Thyself, Thou soughtest only the glory of Thy Father, from the beginning to the end of Thy life ; Thou spentest whole nights in prayer in mountains and desart places ; Thou hadst not where to lay Thy head ; Thy common, poor fare, with Thy disciples, was barely bread and dried fish ; Thy miraculous power never helped Thee to any dainties of refreshment, though ever so much fatigued and fainted with labour. But yet, because this holy Jesus came into the world to save all sorts of sinners, therefore He entered into all sorts of companies. But why did He do so ? It was that He might reprove and convert sinners at their own tables.

' It is said that wherever the King is, there is the court ; but with much more reason may it be said that wherever our Saviour came there was the Temple, or the Church. He came to feasts and entertainments with the same spirit, for the same end, and in the same Divine power as He went to raise a dead corpse ; namely, to show forth the glory of God. Wherever He came, it was in the spirit and power of the Redeemer of mankind ; everything He did, was only to destroy the works of the devil. It made no difference to Him whether He did this in the Temple, or in the streets ; at a feast, or at a funeral. As He was everywhere God, so every place became holy to Him.'

And so Law goes on to 'vindicate our Saviour's holy life and example from the shocking misapplication the doctor has made of it.' It is not necessary to enter here into Law's somewhat whimsical explanation of the miracle at Cana of Galilee, in reply to what he calls the doctor's ' horrid account' of it ; but the above passage seemed worth quoting, not only for its intrinsic beauty, but also because it is highly characteristic of the man. Law suffered his adversary to abuse *him* as much as he pleased, and never gave one angry word in reply ; but when the doctor seemed to reflect upon Law's Divine Master, *then* he spoke out— more in sorrow than in anger, but with some touch of anger nevertheless.

In the same spirit he vindicates S. Paul from what he considered Dr. Trapp's misinterpretation of the Apostle's famous saying to Timothy.

But when he deals with the doctor's strictures upon his (Law's) own early writings, he writes with a calmness and temperateness very rare in controversial divinity in the eighteenth century. On several points he shows plainly that the doctor had misrepresented his meaning ; but there is not one word of personal bitterness. And when he turns from this old minister of the Gospel to his younger brethren in the ministry, his appeal is so tender and touching that I cannot refrain from quoting a few passages, especially as Law is generally thought to have been a severe man by those who did not know what an affectionate heart was beating under that somewhat stern exterior. 'I beseech you,' he writes, ' for your own sakes, for the Gospel's sake, for the sake of mankind, to devote yourselves *wholly* to the love and service of God. As you are yet but beginners in this great office, you have it in your power to make your lives the greatest happiness, both to yourselves and the whole nation. You are enter'd into Holy Orders in degenerate times, where trade and traffic have seized upon all holy things, and it will be easy for you, without fear, to swim along with the corrupt stream, and to look upon him as an enemy, or *enthusiast*, that would save you from being lost in it. But think, my dear brethren, think in time what remorse you are laying up for yourselves if you live to look back upon a loose, negligent, unedifying life, spent among those whose blood will be required at your hands. Think, on the other hand, how blessedly your employment will end if by your voices, your lives, and labours, you put a stop to the overflowings of iniquity, restore the spirit of the primitive clergy, and make all your flock bless and praise God for having sent you among them ; ' and much more in the same loving and earnest spirit.

Many of Dr. Trapp's charges had no application to Law, for they were levelled at practices and doctrines of the Methodists, in which Law took no part, and with which probably, as a High Churchman, he had no sympathy. Law never alludes to this in his answer. As against Dr. Trapp, he was certainly on the side of the Methodists, and therefore this was not the occasion to emphasise his differences with them.

In one passage there might seem, at first sight, to be a touch of personality. It is that in which he describes an ideal Bishop of Winchester, who brought up his children, 'one a carpenter, in which business our Saviour is

said to have labour'd in his youth ; another a maker of
tents, the trade of the great Apostle ; and the rest in the
like manner ;' and, when he died, 'left only 20*l.* a year
amongst them,' only to be used by them ' as sickness and
age made them stand in need of it;' 'and will the doctor,'
asks Law, with a little touch of humour, 'say that this
Bishop has ruin'd his wife and children, has denied the
faith, and is worse than an infidel ?' Now the real Bishop
of Winchester was Bishop Hoadly, Law's old antagonist,
whose life was framed on a rather different model. Did
Law mean to say in effect, ' Look on this picture and then
on that'? Many of his readers could hardly help doing
so, but it would not be in accordance with Law's general
spirit to suppose that the contrast was intended. It is
more likely that he selected Winchester simply because it
was one of the richest bishoprics.

In quite a different connection, however, Law *does* refer
to Bishop Hoadly. At the close of his treatise he mentions
the fact that the then Bishop of Bangor had not answered
the three letters Law had written to him twenty-three years
earlier, without one word to indicate that he regretted or
desired to retract anything he had written in those letters.
Does not this again confirm the theory that Law's mysticism did not make him altogether drift away from his old
moorings ? Indeed, in this very treatise he reaffirms in a
modified form the same high conception of the Christian
ministry, to defend which he wrote his famous letters in
1717.

_____

The 'Answer to Dr. Trapp' appeared in the early part
of 1740. Later in the same year Law published one of
the most comprehensive and important of all his mystic
works. It is entitled in full, 'An Appeal to all that
Doubt or Disbelieve the Truths of the Gospel, whether they
be Deists, Arians, Socinians, or *nominal* Christians. In

which the true Grounds and Reasons of the whole
Christian Faith and Life are plainly and fully demonstrated.' The title is an ambitious one, but Law performs
what he promises. Other works bring out particular points
in his system more fully and distinctly; but none takes so
full a sweep of the *whole* system as the 'Appeal.' For this
reason it has been more largely quoted in Chapter XV. of
this book than any other of Law's works. There is, therefore, the less need to dwell upon it in this chapter. But
the last ten pages deserve special notice, as furnishing a
remarkable instance of the link—or rather one of the
links—which bound together Law the High Churchman
and Law the mystic.

If one might sum up the contents of the 'Appeal' in
one single word, that word would be 'nature.' And in
these last pages, Law shows how closely the mystic view
of nature harmonised with the high conception of the
Christian sacraments which he always held. He had been
explaining on that principle of extreme literalism, which,
though quite contrary to the popular idea of mysticism,
really forms a most striking feature in its system, how 'the
blood of Christ is the life of this world, because it brings forth
and generates from itself the paradisiacal, immortal flesh and
blood, as certainly, as really, as the blood of fallen Adam
brings forth and generates from itself the sinful, vile, corrupti-
ble flesh and blood of their life.' And then he asks, 'Would
you farther know what blood this is, that has this atoning,
life-giving quality in it? It is that Blood which is to be
received in the Holy Sacrament. Would you know why it
quickens, raises, and restores the inward man that died in
Paradise? The answer is from Christ himself. " He that
eateth my Flesh and drinketh my Blood, dwelleth in Me,
and I in him."' After having elucidated these points in
detail, he sums up: 'Here, therefore, is plainly discovered

X

to us the true nature, necessity, and benefit of the Holy
Sacrament of the Lord's Supper ; both why, and how, and
for what end, we must of all necessity eat the Flesh, and
drink the Blood of Christ. No *figurative meaning* of the
words is here to be sought for ; we must eat Christ's Flesh,
and drink His Blood in the *same reality* as He took upon
Him the *real flesh and blood* of the Blessed Virgin : We
can have no real relation to Christ, can be no true members
of His mystical body, but by being real partakers of that
same kind of Flesh and Blood, which was truly His, and
was His for this very end, that through Him the same
might be brought forth in us: All this is strictly true of the
Holy Sacrament, according to the plain letter of the expression, which Sacrament was thus instituted, that the
great service of the Church might continually show us, that
the whole of our Redemption consisted in the receiving the
Birth, Spirit, Life, and Nature of Jesus Christ into us, &c.
. . . . This is the adorable height and depth of this Divine
Mystery, which brings Heaven and Immortality again into
us, and gives us power to become sons of God.' 'And
woe,' he exclaims, in a strain which almost reminds us of
some old Hebrew prophet, ' Woe be to those who come to
it with the mouths of beasts, and the minds of serpents !
who, with impenitent hearts, devoted to the lusts of the
flesh, the lusts of the eyes, and the pride of life, for worldly
ends, outward appearances, and secular conformity, boldly
meddle with those mysteries that are only to be approached
by those that are of a pure heart, and who worship God in
spirit and in truth.'

It is quite clear that Law held the doctrine of a Real
Presence, not only in the hearts of the worshippers, but in
the Elements, a doctrine to which his mystic views would
only tend to give a deeper and more vivid meaning. The
sacred significance which mysticism gives to all outward

nature would render it perfectly congruous that the Holy
Jesus should impart Himself through the bread and wine ;
and, therefore, considering the 'sacramental view of nature'
to which Keble so well draws attention, it is no wonder
that Law should set forth his views of sacramental grace
far more distinctly in his mystic than in his earlier works.
The last words which he would have to linger in the minds
of the various unbelievers and misbelievers to whom he
addressed his 'Appeal,' were an emphatic reiteration of this
doctrine of the Real Presence. 'And thus,' he concludes
the appeal, 'is this great sacrament, which is a continual
part of our Christian worship, a continual communication
to us of all the benefits of our Second Adam ; for in and
by the Body and Blood of Christ, to which the Divine nature
is united, we receive all that life and immortality and
redemption, which Christ as living, suffering, dying, rising
from the dead, and ascending into Heaven, brought to
human nature ; so that this great mystery is that in which
all the blessings of our redemption and new life in Christ
are centered. And they that hold a sacrament short of
this *reality* of the true Body and Blood of Jesus Christ,
cannot be said to hold that sacrament of *eternal life*, which
was instituted by our Blessed Lord and Saviour.'

Appended to the 'Appeal' and published together with
it, is an interesting tract entitled, 'Some Animadversions
upon Dr. Trap's Reply.' Dr. Trapp had certainly not followed the example of Christian courtesy which Law had
set him in his 'Answer.' The 'Reply' is full of the most
violent abuse, a few choice specimens of which Law quotes
in his 'Animadversions ;' and these quotations from the
doctor's own words really form the only severe part of
Law's tract. No provocation could tempt him to return
railing for railing. 'As I neither have,' he says, 'nor (by
the grace of God), ever will have, any personal contention

with any man whatever, so all the triumph which the doctor has gained over me by that overflow of contempt which he has let loose upon me I shall leave him quietly to enjoy.'

Law was as good as his word. Not one single syllable unworthy of a Christian gentleman can be found in the 'Animadversions.' At the same time he cannot retract any of the assertions of his former work. Dr. Trapp declared that a ' Quaker or infidel ' could not well have reflected with more virulence upon the clergy than Law had done, but he could not deny the facts which Law alleged. Those facts Law here reiterates, but there is sincerity on the very face of his emphatic denial of aught but love towards his brethren in the ministry. 'If it was a thing required of me,' he says, ' I know no more how to raise in myself the least spark of rancour, or ill-will towards the clergy, as such, than I know how to work myself up into a hatred of the light of the sun. It is as natural to me to wish them all their perfection as to wish peace and happiness to myself both here and hereafter ; and when I point to any failings in their conduct, it is only with such a spirit as I would pluck a brother out of the fire.' No unprejudiced reader can read what Law has written to and of the clergy in any of his works, without feeling that what he here says is literally true ; there is, therefore, no need to follow him as he answers, point by point, but with the utmost courtesy, the doctor's angry vituperations. Many interesting points are touched upon incidentally in this tract,[1] some of which have been already referred to, and others will be by-and-by, in connection with Law's life.

But we must not pass over this tract without noting

---

[1] E.g. his remarks on the Romanists, on the Quakers, on Sir I. Newton Behmen, on the mystical divines, &c. See *supra*, pp. 129–

that in it Law ventured to write in defence of that hated bug-bear of the eighteenth century—enthusiasm. Nothing shows more clearly both his moral courage and his antagonism to the spirit of his age than this defence. There were many who were called, and with very good reasons, enthusiasts, but most of them denied the charge. Law boldly accepts it, and defends a character which had certainly very few friends in *his* day. Those alone who are acquainted with the literature of the eighteenth century can appreciate the courage which it required to make such remarks as the following : ' To appropriate enthusiasm to religion is the same ignorance of nature as to appropriate love to religion ; for enthusiasm is as common, as universal, as essential to human nature as love is. . . . No people are so angry at religious enthusiasts as those that are the deepest in some enthusiasm of another kind. He whose fire is kindled from the divinity of Tully's rhetoric, who travels over high mountains to salute the dear ground that Marcus Tullius Cicero walked upon.; whose noble soul would be ready to break out of his body, if he could see a desk, a rostrum, from whence Cicero had poured forth his thunder of words, may well be unable to bear the dulness of those who go on pilgrimages only to visit the sepulchre whence the Redeemer of the world rose from the dead, or who grow devout at the sight of a crucifix, because the Son of God hung as a sacrifice thereon ! He whose heated brain is all over painted with the ancient hieroglyphics ; who knows how and why they were this and that, better than he can find out the customs and usages of his own parish ; who can clear up everything that is doubtful in antiquity, &c. &c., may well despise those Christians, as brain-sick visionaries, who are sometimes finding a moral and spiritual sense in the bare letter and history of Scripture facts. . . . Even the poor species of fops and beaux have a right to be placed among enthusiasts, though capable of no other flame than that which is kindled by tailors and peruke-makers.

'The grammarian, the critick, the poet, the connoisseur, the antiquary, the philosopher, the politician are all violent enthusiasts, though their heat is only a flame from straw, and therefore they all agree in appropriating enthusiasm to religion. . . . Enthusiasts we all are, as certainly as we are men. You need not go to a cloyster, the cell of a monk, or to a field-preacher to see enthusiasts ; they are everywhere : at balls and masquerades, at court and the exchange. Enthusiasm is not blameable in religion when it is true religion that kindles it.' Then, after defending this position at some length, he thus sums up the character of the true religious enthusiast, in whom we still see the mystic and the High Churchman blended. 'Every man, as such, has an open gate to God in his soul ; he is always in that temple, where he can worship God in spirit and truth ; every Christian, as such, has the firstfruits of the Spirit, a seed of life, which is his call and qualification to be always in a state of inward prayer, faith, and holy intercourse with God.' So far the mystic. Now observe in the passage which immediately follows the High Churchman : 'All the ordinances of the Gospel, the daily *sacramental* service of the Church, is to keep up, and exercise, and strengthen this faith ; to raise us to such an habitual faith and dependence upon the Light and Holy Spirit of God, that by thus seeking and finding God in the *institutions* of the Church, we may be habituated to seek Him and find Him, to live in His Light, and walk by His Spirit in all the actions of our ordinary life. This is the enthusiasm in which every good Christian ought to endeavour to live and die.' [1]

---

[1] It is interesting to compare with this passage Wesley's sermon on 'Enthusiasm' (see his *Sermons*, vol. i. serm. xxxvii). Of course Wesley agrees with Law in defending those whom the world calls 'enthusiasts,' but, unlike

The reflection which the reading of such a passage as this calls up must be, Is it possible that this man could have lived in the eighteenth century ? This defender of pilgrimages and crucifixes in an age when anti-Popery was rampant ? This depreciator of ' grammarians, criticks,' and the rest, in an age when reason was triumphant ? This apologist for enthusiasm in an age which, when it had labelled a man 'enthusiast,' thought that it had put him under an universal ban ? Could William Law really have been the contemporary of the Warburtons, the Hoadlys, and the Trapps, ay, or even of the Butlers and the Sherlocks ?   .

Law, he gives up the name: 'As to the nature of enthusiasm, it is undoubtedly a disorder of the mind,' &c.   Wesley is far more of an eighteenth century man than his quondam mentor ; hence, in part, the far wider influence which he exercised.

CHAPTER XVII.

'THE SPIRIT OF PRAYER' AND 'THE SPIRIT OF LOVE.'

IF the 'Appeal to all that Doubt, &c.,' is the most comprehensive of all Law's mystic works, the two treatises which
are the subject of this chapter are certainly the most
attractive, and also the most exhaustive in their explanation of particular points. They were written after Law's
mysticism had excited much attention and much opposition ; and therefore he adopts a method which gave him
an opportunity not only of elucidating his own views, but
also of answering possible and actual objections to those
views. That method was, in both cases, first, to unfold his
own sentiments without interruption, and then to intro-
duce speakers who comment upon them ; that is, to give
first an essay, and then some dialogues upon it.

The first part of the ' Spirit of Prayer' was published in
1749. It is an essay of about one hundred pages, written
in a most fascinating style, and describing on the principles
of Behmenism the progress of 'the Soul Rising out of the
Vanity of Time into the Riches of Eternity.' This, indeed, is
its alternative title, and a very proper one, according to
Law's view ; for he understands the word ' prayer' in the
same sense as he did in the two practical treatises ;[1] that is,
not merely as the offering up of petitions to God, nor even
as holding communion with God, but as synonymous with
a *life* of devotion in the strictest sense of the term.

[1] See the *Christian Perfection* and *Serious Call, passim.*

The second part was not published till 1750, because, it is said, Law wished to observe the reception of the first part, and to be in some measure guided by it as to the construction and contents of the remainder. It is, as has been already observed, in the form of dialogues ; and these dialogues are singularly characteristic of the writer's own mind and position.

The speakers are *Academicus, Rusticus,* and *Theophilus,* with the addition of a dummy, who is called *Humanus.* Theophilus represents Law's own views, and is completely master of the situation, as Law himself always was ; he is an adept in the art of shutting-up, as Law also certainly was ; but there is an earnestness, a tenderness, and a thorough reality about him which attract far more than his occasional asperity repels us, and in these respects he exactly resembles Law. Academicus is a professing and, according to his lights, a sincere Christian, but he is so hampered by his 'letter-learning,' that he finds many obstacles to the reception of Christianity according to Behmen. He is, therefore, continually laying himself open to severe snubs from Theophilus ; and is still more often being set right by Rusticus, who, being unable to read or write, is in a far better position to receive the truth in its fulness and simplicity. Humanus is a learned unbeliever, a friend and neighbour of Academicus, who is admitted into the company only on the express condition that he is never to open his mouth—a condition which he strictly fulfils in the first two dialogues.

The ' Way to Divine Knowledge' was published in a volume by itself in 1752, 'as preparatory to a new edition of the works of Jacob Behmen, and the right use of them.' So far as it had this object in view, it may be regarded as a separate work ; but in other respects it is, to all intents and purposes, merely a continuation of the ' Spirit of

Prayer,' the same speakers taking up the thread of their discourse just where they left it at the end of the preceding dialogue. It opens with a full confession of his errors by the long tongue-tied Humanus, who owns that his objections to Christianity had been due simply to the wrong tactics of its defenders. ' I had frequently,' he says, ' a consciousness rising up within me that the debate was equally vain on both sides, doing no more real good to the one than to the other ; not being able to imagine that a set of scholastic, logical opinions about history, facts, doctrines, and institutions of the church, or a set of logical objections against them, were of any significance towards making the soul of man either an eternal angel of heaven, or an eternal devil of hell. . . . You have taught me that Christianity is neither more nor less than the goodness of the Divine Life, Light, and Love living and working in the soul !' This to some extent represents Law's own experience. Not that he had ever for one moment the slightest temptation to join the ranks of the unbelievers to which Humanus belonged. But it is obvious that Humanus' conclusion may be reached as well from the Christian as from the un-Christian side. In fact it *was* so reached by Academicus, whose long account of his experience is well worth quoting, both as a specimen of Law's quiet humour, and as a vivid picture, *mutatis mutandis*, of Law's own mental history.

' When,' he says, ' I had taken my degrees, I consulted several great divines to put me in a method of studying divinity. Had I said to them, " Sirs, what must I do to be saved ? " they would have prescribed hellebore, or directed me to the physician as a vapoured enthusiast. It would take up near half a day to tell you the work which my learned friends cut out for me. One told me that *Hebrew* words are all ; that they must be read without points, and then the Old Testament is an open book ; he recommended to me a cartload of lexicons, critics, and commentators upon the Hebrew Bible. Another tells me, the *Greek* Bible is the best; that it corrects the Hebrew in many places; and refers me to a large number of books learnedly writ in the defence of it. Another tells me that *Church history* is the main matter; that I must begin with the first fathers, and follow them through every age of the Church; not forgetting to take the lives of the *Roman* emperors along with me, as striking great light into the state of the Church in their times. Then I must have recourse to all the councils held, and the canons made, in every age; which would enable me to see with my own eyes the great corruptions of the Council of Trent. Another, who is not very fond of antient matters, but wholly bent upon *rational* Christianity, tells me, I need go no higher than the *Reformation*; that Calvin and Cranmer were very great men; that Chillingworth and Locke ought always to lie upon my table; that I must get an entire set of those learned volumes wrote against Popery in King James's reign; and also be well versed in all the discourses which Mr. Boyle's and Lady Moyer's Lectures have produced; and, then, says he, you will be a match for our greatest enemies, which are the Popish priests and modern Deists. My tutor is very liturgical; he desires me, of all things, to get all the collections I can of the antient liturgies, and all the authors that treat of such matters, who, he says, are very learned and very numerous. He has been many years making observations upon them, and is now clear, as to the time when certain little particles got entrance into the liturgies, and others were by degrees dropt. He has a friend abroad, in search of antient manuscript liturgies, for, by-the-bye, said he, at parting, I have some suspicion that our Sacrament of the Lord's Supper is *essentially* defective, for want of a little water in the wine. Another learned friend tells me the *Clementine Constitutions* is the book of books, and that all that lies loose and scattered in the New Testament, stands there in its true order and form ; and though he will not say that Dr. Clarke and Mr. Whiston are in the right, yet it might be useful to me to read all the *Arian* and *Socinian* writers, provided I stood upon my guard, and did it with caution. The last person I consulted advised me to get all the histories of the rise and progress of heresies, and of the lives and characters of heretics. These histories, he said, contract the matter, bring truth and error close in view, and I should find all that collected in a few pages, which would have cost me some years to have got together. He also desired me to be well versed in all the casuistical writers and chief schoolmen ; for they debate matters to the bottom ; dissect every virtue and every vice into its many degrees and parts ; and show how near they can come to one another without touching, And this knowledge, he said, might be useful to me when I came to be a parish priest. Following the advice of all these counsellors as well as I could, I lighted my candle early in the morning, and put it out late at night.' This labour he continued for many years, when (to cut a long story short) the unlearned Rusticus appeared and taught this learned scholar to find the true way to Divine knowledge, ' and let the dead bury their dead.'

These two passages seem to me to furnish the right clue to the explanation of Law's change of opinions—so far as there *was* a change—when he became a mystic. It must be remembered that, just before his lighting upon Behmen, Law had plunged into the thick of the controversy which was then everywhere raging. Deism was the fashionable topic of the day. In coffee-houses and in drawing-rooms, by men of pleasure and by ladies, as well as by grave divines, from the Court of Queen Caroline down almost to the very kitchen, profound questions concerning natural and revealed religion were being glibly discussed on all sides ; and the saddest feature of all was that practical piety seemed to be in inverse ratio to theological speculation. Law's last two ante-mystic writings were the ' Case of Reason,' against the Coryphæus of the Deists, and the ' Letters to a Lady inclined to enter into the Communion of the Church of Rome.' In both instances it is evident that his mind was painfully impressed with the weariness and unprofitableness of religious disputings. To a spiritually minded man like Law, both the Deistical and the anti-Deistical literature must have seemed sadly wanting in spirituality ; while the ' restless, inquisitive, self-seeking temper,' which he is so constantly rebuking in his lady correspondent, showed him another phase of the harm which this spirit of dispute did to the soul. No one can read these two last works of Law's earlier career without perceiving how thoroughly ripe he was when he wrote them for some such influence as that which Behmen exercised over him. ' Bury all your reasonings and speculations, all your doubts and distrusts, in such resignation, such faith and confidence in the love and goodness of God, and then all trials and temptations will but increase your safety, and give you a more confirmed repose in God.'[1] These were the last words of Law that have been published, before the ' illuminated Jacob ' comes upon the scene to do for him the office which Rusticus did for Academicus. How ready Law must have been when he wrote them to echo Behmen's

---

[1] The concluding words of his last letter to the lady inclined to enter the Church of Rome, written May 29, 1732. It has sometimes been doubted whether these letters or the ' Case of Reason ' were published first, but that question is quite cleared by the original first edition of the ' Case of Reason,' of which I have been fortunate enough to gain possession ; the date of its publication is 1731. The first letter to the lady is dated May 24, 1731, so this possibly may have been written before the ' Case of Reason,' but the last, dated by Law himself, May 29, 1732, could not have been.

appeal : 'O thou poor confounded soul in Babel, what dost thou do ? Leave off all opinions, by what name soever they are called, in this world ; they are all no other than the contention of reason ; you must forsake all in this world (let it be as glistening as it will), and enter into yourself, and only gather all your sins (which have captivated you), together on a heap, and cast them into the mercy of God, and fly to God, and pray to Him for forgiveness, and the illumination of His Spirit ; there needs no longer disputing, but earnestness, and then heaven must break asunder, and hell tremble. . . . Turn away your heart and mind from all contention, and go in very simply and humbly at the door of Christ, into Christ's sheepfold ; seek that in your heart,' &c.[1] How ready to hear about the 'bright crown of pearl, brighter than the sun,' that was 'so very manifest, and yet so very secret, that among many thousand in this world it was scarcely known of any one, and yet carried about in many that knew it not.'[2]

It must not, however, be for one moment supposed that because Law would have men turn from the dust of debate into the green pastures which the 'spiritual writers' (as he always call the mystics) offered to them, that his frame of mind resembled in the very least degree that suggested by Pope's hackneyed couplet—

> For modes of faith let graceless bigots fight,
> He can't be wrong whose life is in the right.

Theophilus, who represents Law, had a very distinct mode of faith, for which he was prepared to fight to the death; and it was just because their varied culture and scholarship led them away from the 'faith once delivered unto the saints' into all sorts of irrelevant issues, that Academicus

---

[1] *Threefold Life of Man*, Behmen's 'Works,' vol. ii. ch. vii. p. 70, &c.
[2] *Ibid.* ch. vi. p. 89.

and Humanus went astray ; while Rusticus found less difficulty, not because his faith was *less* but because it was
more definite, inasmuch as he was not tempted to turn
aside into the by-paths of heathen learning nor to lean
upon that bruised reed, carnal reason.

It must be confessed, however, that Law in this treatise
presses his favourite theory of the worthlessness of learning
to the verge of absurdity. It really would seem as if one
of the morals taught by the ' Spirit of Prayer ' was the inestimable blessing of being unable either to read or write.
Rusticus was in that happy condition, and looked down,
as from an eminence, on Academicus and Humanus, who
were trammelled by those two unfortunate accomplishments.
But it is rather amusing to find Rusticus, in spite of his
blissful ignorance, talking and arguing as none but an accomplished scholar could do. The fact is, Rusticus is an
utterly impossible rustic ; Law had very little knowledge
of the poor except as recipients of his bounty.

From one very common fault of dialogues written for
a purpose, the ' Spirit of Prayer ' is entirely free. Law's
mind was far too logical and too honest to allow his supposed objectors to state their objections weakly. Like his
great contemporary, Bishop Butler, Law always does his
adversary's case complete justice : the giants which he
slays are real giants, not windmills.

The first part of the ' Spirit of Love ' was published in
the same year as the ' Way to Divine Knowledge.' It is
dated by Law himself, ' King's Cliffe, June 16, 1752,' being
in the form of a letter to a friend who had been deeply
affected, as well he might be, by the spirit of love that
breathed in all Law's writings. He finds, however, two
objections often rising in his mind ; the first is that old
objection which Bossuet and his party had raised against

Fénélon and Madame Guyon in the preceding century, viz.
that the doctrine of pure and universal love was too refined
and imaginary for practical purposes ; the other, that the
description of the Deity as a Being that is all love seemed
inconsistent with those passages of Holy Scripture which
speak of a righteousness and justice, a wrath and vengeance
of God that must be atoned and satisfied.

The answer to these objections forms the subject of this
singularly beautiful treatise ; the first of them being answered in the first part, the second in the dialogues that
follow.   For the ' Spirit of Love' is composed on the same
principle as the ' Spirit of Prayer ;' we have first a continuous essay, and then a series of conversations.

How Law would answer both of his friend's objections
the reader will anticipate for himself.   It is only necessary
to observe that in the first part of the ' Spirit of Love,' he
brings out more distinctly than elsewhere that striking
feature of the later mysticism, its intense realisation of the
analogy between the natural and the spiritual world.   It is
because they have lost the blessed spirit of love which
alone makes the happiness and perfection of every power
of nature, that not only all intelligent creatures, but all
inanimate things, are in disorder.   It is the spirit of love
which must ' rectify all outward nature, and bring it back
into that glassy sea of unity and purity in which S. John
beheld the throne of God in the midst of it.   For this
glassy sea which the beloved apostle was blessed with the
sight of, is the transparent, heavenly element, in which all
the properties and powers of nature move and work in the
unity and purity of the one Will of God, only known as so
many endless forms of triumphing Light and Love.   For
the strife of properties, of thick against thin, hard against
soft, hot against cold, &c., had no existence till the angels
fell—that is, till they turned from God, to work with nature.

This is the original of all the strife, division, and materiality
in the fallen world.' And this glassy sea, this heavenly
materiality shall one day be seen again. 'The last universal
fire must begin the deliverance of this material system, and
fit everything to receive that Spirit of Light and Love
which will bring all things back again to their first glassy
sea, in which the Deity dwelleth, as in His throne. And
thus, as the earthly fire turns flint into glass, so earth will
become heaven, and the contrariety of four divided elements
will become one transparent brightness of glory, as soon as
the last fire shall have melted every grossness into its first
undivided fluidity, for the light and love and majesty of
God to be all in all in it. How easy and natural is it to
suppose all that is earth and stones to be dissolved into
water, the water to be changed into air, the air into æther,
and the æther rarefied into light ! Is there anything here
impossible to be supposed ? And how near a step is the
next, to suppose all this changed or exalted into that
glassy sea, which was everywhere before the angels fell ! '

Whether every reader will find it so easy to conceive
all this as Law supposed, may well be a question. To
some it may appear all very wild and dreamy, while to
others the thought may be suggested, that there are more
things in heaven and earth than are dreamt of in their
philosophy. But surely, whether we can follow Law in all
his details or not this idea of the connection between the
natural and the moral world, and especially of the salvation
of Christ being applicable to both is a very grand and suggestive one ; and if such texts as that which Law loved to
quote, ' The whole creation groaneth and travaileth in pain
together,' taken in connection with its context, are to be
understood literally, the general theory has more scriptural
authority than some are apt to imagine.

The second part of the ' Spirit of Love ' was not pub-

lished until 1754, the delay being probably owing to a
temporary weakness of eyesight from which Law was at
this time suffering, and to which he alludes in several
letters. It was written, as has been said, in the form of
dialogues, the speakers being our old acquaintance, Theophilus, Theogenes (who represents the friend in answer to
whom Law wrote the whole treatise), and Eusebius, ' a very
valuable and worthy curate of my neighbourhood,' says
Theogenes. It deals more fully than any other of Law's
works with the doctrine of the Atonement—a doctrine
which, it must be again repeated, formed a very corner-
stone of Law's system. It was only against one particular
theory of the Atonement—a theory which, to say the least
of it, has certainly not been the universally accepted theory
of the Catholic Church—that Law objected. There was
not one single expression in the Bible, or in the creeds of
the Church, or in the liturgy, or articles, or any of the
formularies of the Church of England, on the subject of the
Atonement, to which Law would not have given his most
unfeigned and hearty adherence. But as this question has
been fully discussed in a preceding chapter,[1] nothing
further need be said.

[1] See Ch. XIV. of this work.

CHAPTER XVIII.

LAW ON WARBURTON'S 'DIVINE LEGATION.'

MORE than three years elapsed before Law again appeared in print. During the interval he seems to have been a good deal occupied with the final settlement of the foundation of the schools and almshouses at King's Cliffe ; moreover, he may have thought it desirable to spare his eyes until some really important occasion called for the use of his pen. And, very characteristically, he did not consider that an attack made upon himself personally was such an occasion ; but he *did* consider that an attack upon his friend was. Wesley's pamphlet of 1756 was unanswered by Law, partly because Law thought that it answered itself, partly because he did not desire to be brought into antagonism with one who was trying, and trying success-fully, to stem the torrent of vice and irreligion that was flooding the land, and partly because he always disliked defending himself personally. But it was a very different matter when his old friend Bishop Sherlock was attacked by men whose doctrines traversed Law's most deeply cherished convictions. Accordingly, in the spring of 1757, appeared 'A Short but Sufficient Confutation of the Rev. Dr. Warburton's Projected Defence (as he calls it) of Christianity, in his Divine Legation of Moses. In a Letter to the Right Reverend the Lord Bishop of London.' The work which called forth this letter was not the 'Divine Legation' itself, but a defence of it, by an anonymous author, against Bishop Sherlock, entitled, ' A Free and Candid Examination of the Bishop of London's Sermons, &c.' Law, however, soon leaves the subordinate for the principal, and attacks, with marvellous keenness and vigour, the main positions of Warburton's famous work.

The debate, he declares, was betwixt Dr. Warburton on the one side, and the whole Christian Church of all ages on the other;[1] and he undertakes to prove ' that (1) there is not in all the New Testament one single text which, either in the letter or the spirit, proves, or has the least tendency or design to prove, that the immortality of the soul, or its perpetual duration after the death of the body, was not an universal commonly received opinion, in and through every age of the world, from Adam to Christ ; and (2), that this doctrine or belief of a future state was not designedly secreted, or industriously hidden, from the eyes of the people of God by Moses, neither by the types and figures of the law, nor by any other part of his writings.'

It was no wonder that Law took up the subject warmly ; because, if Warburton established his point, it is obvious that Law's whole system must fall to the ground. So much has been already said of Law's views on the Fall

---

[1] For the convenience of the unlearned reader it may be well to state that the argument of the ' Divine Legation ' is stated by Warburton himself in the following syllogisms :—

I. Whatsoever Religion and Society have no future state for their support must be supported by an extraordinary Providence.

The Jewish Religion and Society had no future state for their support.

∴ The Jewish Religion and Society was supported by an extraordinary Providence.

II. It was universally believed by the ancients, on their common principles of legislation and wisdom, that whatsoever Religion and Society have no future state for their support must be supported by an extraordinary Providence.

Moses, skilled in all that legislation and wisdom, instituted the Jewish Religion and Society without a future state for its support.

∴ Moses, who taught, believed likewise that *this* Religion and Society was supported by an extraordinary Providence.

and the Redemption that it is hardly necessary to point
out how violently antagonistic to them Dr. Warburton's
theory was. But Dr. Warburton, like Law, professed to
find a confirmation of his theory in Scripture. Law therefore begins by pointing out the misapprehension of the
true meaning of the texts on which Warburton founded
his notions. The life and immortality, Law maintained,
which was brought to light by the Gospel was not that
natural immortality which was common to all men, and
even to fallen angels, but it was that new immortality,
' that immortal, heavenly nature, which was purchased for
us by the precious blood and merits of Christ,' ' by the
blessed Jesus being and doing what He was and did in our
poor immortal nature that had lost its God.' The death
which Christ abolished was not natural death, but the
deadly nature of sin in our souls, which is rightly called
death, for ' to be carnally minded is death.' After mar-
shalling a vast array of texts to show that this use of the
terms ' life ' and ' death ' was thoroughly scriptural, Law
goes on to show that the Old Testament and the New took
precisely the same course in regard to immortality, in
the ordinary sense of that term. ' It is as much secreted
in the one as in the other—in the Gospel as in the
books of Moses : it is never expressly mentioned, but
always necessarily implied. The Mosaic history and types
just hide it in the same manner as the Gospel hides it—
that is, not at all ; and they fully prove it, in the same
manner as the Gospel proves it, by doctrines which absolutely require it, in the first conception of them.'

Of course the eleventh chapter of the Hebrews was a
favourite chapter with those who, like Law, held the
higher and nobler view of the aspirations of the Old Testament saints. ' And, therefore, Dr. Warburton,' says Law,
with an odd touch of his almost morbid contempt for

'pagan learning,' 'is so out of humour with this whole chapter that he gives it the heathenish name of the *Palladium of the cause* which he had undertaken to demolish, and he accordingly attacks it with a number of critical inventions that may as truly be called heathenish, for they are in direct opposition to all Christian theology.'

After vindicating the Messianic character of the faith of the old Fathers, Law sums up thus: 'For to live by faith always was and always will be living in the kingdom of God ; and to live by reason always was and always will be living as a heathen under the power of the kingdom of this world. To live by faith is to live with God in the spirit and power of prayer, in self-denial, in contempt of the world, in Divine love, in heavenly foretaste of the world to come, in humility, in patience, long-suffering, obedience, resignation, absolute trust and dependence upon God, with all that is temporal and earthly under their feet. To live by reasoning is to be a prey of the old serpent, eating dust with him, grovelling in the mire of all earthly passions, devoured with pride, embittered with envy, tools and dupes to ourselves, tossed up with vain hopes, cast down with vain fears, slaves to all the good and evil things of this world, to-day elated with learned praise, to-morrow dejected at the unlucky loss of it ; yet jogging on year after year, defining words and ideas, dissecting doctrines and opinions, setting all arguments and all objections upon their best legs, sifting and defining all notions, conjectures, and criticisms, till death puts the same full end to all the wonders of the ideal fabric that the cleansing broom does to the wonders of the spider's web so artfully spun at the expense of its own vitals. The old serpent was the first reasoner, and every scholar, every disputer of this world, has been where Eve was, and has done what she did, when she sought for wisdom that did not come from God. All libraries of the world are full proof of the remaining power of the first sinful thirst after it ; they are full of a knowledge that comes not from God and therefore proceeds from that first fountain of subtilty that opened her eyes.'

And so the old man (he was now in his seventy-first year) goes on, pouring forth his invectives against his old enemy, human reasoning. We may smile at his extravagance, but we cannot help admiring his intense earnestness of purpose, his strong faith, and his vigour and raciness, both of thought and diction, which old age had not in the least degree diminished.

But Law was not so far carried away in his crusade against 'reasoning' as to forget to deal with what was really the strong point of Dr. Warburton's argument. Law never shirks a difficulty. He admits, therefore, the full force of the doctor's position, 'That the sanctions of the Mosaic law, its rewards and its punishments, were all of a temporal nature,' but he denies that this unquestionable fact really touched the point at issue. For ' the law no more belonged to the *true religion* of the Old Testament than of the New ; it was purely and merely on the *outside* of both, had only a temporary, external relation of service to the true religion, either before or after Christ, but was no more a *part* or *instead* of them *for a time*, than the hand that stands by the road directing the ignorant traveller is itself a part of the road, or can be instead of it to him.' Not that Law thought lightly of the Mosaic law. No. ' The law and its theocracy was not only most divinely contrived to preserve the faith of the first holy patriarchs and guide them to the time and manner of receiving the promises made to their fathers, but it was all mercy and goodness to the rest of the world, being no less than one continual, daily, miraculous call to them to receive blessing and protection, life and salvation, in the knowledge and worship of the one true God of heaven and earth. But in its whole nature it was but a temporal covenant of outward care and protection, and the utmost care was taken by the Spirit of God that, to eyes that could see, and ears that could hear, enough should be shown and said to prevent all carnal adhesion to temporal and outward things, and bring forth a spiritual Israel full of that faith and piety in which their holy ancestors had lived and died, devoted to God, in hope of everlasting redemption from the fall of Adam.'

Yes ; Dr. Warburton had proved that the doctrine of a future state did not make part of the Mosaic dispensation ; but 'to prove that a state *beyond* time and this world did not make a part of a state that is confined to time and this world, is as easily and as vainly done as to prove that the Garden of Eden is not to be found in a part of a map that is confined to England. And to infer that the Israelites had no notion or belief of an immortality because it was not a part of their ritual, is no better than to infer that the people of England can have no notion or belief about the Garden of Eden because nothing of it is to be seen in the map of this country.'

'Let us make man in our image, after our likeness.' This is the first text on which Law dwells to vindicate Moses from the grovelling view which Warburton took of him. This leads Law to state his views on the nature of the soul ; and a casual remark of Dr. Warburton brings Law face to face, as it were, with the great man who was really the inspirer of all that school of thought to which Law, from the beginning to the end of his career, was most opposed. The only antagonists with whom Law was fundamentally at variance were those who, directly or indirectly, derived their inspiration from *John Locke.* His

differences from others were only on the surface, or, at
most, on mere side issues ; but with Locke, and the school
of Locke, his differences were radical and irreconcilable.
How could there be any harmony of sentiment between
two men, one of whom held that the soul is originally
like a blank sheet of paper, the other that it is originally
an emanation from, and image of, the Deity ? between
two men, one of whom was known as a theologian chiefly
because he strove to prove the ' Reasonableness of Christianity,' while to the other, the very terms ' Reason ' and
' Reasonableness,' as applied to Christianity, acted like a
red rag to a bull ?   It was not merely that Lockism was
the arch-enemy of all mysticism.   It was so ; but the differences between Locke and Law lay deeper than that, and
it was against one of these deeper differences that Law
took up his parable in this treatise.   ' Vain,' he exclaims,
' and entirely to be rejected is that principle published to
the world by a celebrated philosopher of the last century,
namely, that the soul in its first created state has nothing
in it, but is a mere " Rasa Tabula," or blank paper—a
fiction that is contradicted by all that we know of every
created thing in Nature.'   ' If the essay upon human understanding has produced a metaphysicks, in many points
dangerous to religion, and greatly serviceable to false and
superficial reasoning, it is not to wondered at, since so
eminent an error is the fundamental principle on which it
proceeds.'   And then he goes on to descant, on the true
mystic principle, upon the dignity of all created things.

If every ' clod of earth was a mystery of almost infinite
powers,' was it likely that ' the two-legged animal, who is
the disputer of this world,' whom Dr. Warburton alone
could understand, really represented what Moses meant by
' the image and likeness of God in man ? '   ' He might as
well,' says Law, with one of his racy similes, ' search for

that Paradise of which Moses writes in the Hundreds of
Essex or in the Wilds of Kent.' Then Law states his
own well-known views of the ' Divine man who died the
very day that he did eat of the forbidden tree, and of the
Christ within who was to restore him.' In a noble passage,
which is too long to quote, Law protests against Warburton's explanation of the creation of man, as if God
had merely 'formed dust and clay into a dead lumpish
figure of a man, and then breathed life into it.' Law's
own theory is already familiar to the reader,[1] who will at
once perceive how widely he differed from Warburton.
After re-stating it he concludes, ' Had not man an eternal
spirit in him, as the offspring of the eternal God, he could
no more want to have any intercourse with the eternal
world than a fish can want to be out of the water. He
could no more be taught religion than a parrot could.
" Let us eat and drink for to-morrow we die," would be
the highest and truest philosophy, if there is no more
of a Divine life or heavenly nature in man than in the
chattering swallow.'

Not only Law's sense of the dignity of the human
soul, but also his reverence for the inspired writer was
outraged by Dr. Warburton's account. It was a 'most
horrible doctrine' that Moses designedly and industriously
secreted from God's chosen people all thought and apprehension of any eternal relation that they had with God.
' If he really taught them that they had nothing to enjoy
or hope for but the good things of this life, he did all that
well could be done to make them an earthly, covetous,
stiff-necked, and brutal people.'

Nor was Moses the only sacred penman who was
debased by Dr. Warburton's account. Law was, if possible,
even more indignant at his attempting to enlist David in

---

[1] See Ch. XV. of this work, *passim.*

his cause. It will be remembered that the chanting of the
Psalms of David formed an essential part of the Christian's
devotion in the ' Serious Call,' and it is interesting to find
the old man vindicating the favourite of his youth and
middle age from the charge of confirming Warburton's
theory of the suppression of the doctrine of immortality.
' Holy David's case,'· writes Law, ' is sufficient to have
deterred the doctor from a hypothesis which has obliged
him to place this Divine, sweet singer of Israel amongst
those who had not the least sense or thought of any
eternal relation they had to God. This holy David, the
man after God's own heart, the type of Christ, the royal
prophet who foretold the resurrection of Christ, who was
thus deep in the counsels of God, whose inspired Psalms
are and have been chanted in all ages of the Christian
Church as the pious breathing of the Holy Spirit ; this holy,
spiritual, typical, prophesying David, to be crowded among
those who had nothing to hope from God or thank Him
for but the blessings of a temporal life, till death put the
same end to the _All_ of David as it did to those few sheep
that he had once kept ! This David, appealed to as giving
evidence against all happiness but that of this life, and represented in his Divine transports as setting forth the
wisdom of believing that the life of man ends like that of a
rotten sheep, in a death that brings him into the dark land
of forgetfulness, singing gloriously, " The dead praise not
the Lord, neither any that go down into silence," &c. ! '
Law then vindicated such expressions as these in the
Psalms from an interpretation which made them ' mere
heathenish songs,' instead of being, as they are, ' as full of
heavenly devotion, as flowing with Divine love, as if composed by an angel.'

Once more. Not only was Warburton's general theory
as well as his incidental proofs of it abhorrent to Law ; the

doctor's method of proving it was equally objectionable. We have seen that in Law's view there was but one way to Divine knowledge ; the turning of the soul to God in gentleness, humility, and resignation. Human learning could do nothing here. The somewhat ponderous and elaborate display of knowledge, 'de quolibet ente et quibusdam aliis,' which Warburton showed in his colossal work grated upon Law's feelings terribly. ' The Doctor,' he says, ' has, by strength of genius and great industry, amassed together no small heap of learned decisions of points, doctrines, as well heathenish as Christian, much the greatest part of which the Christian reader will find himself obliged to drive out of his thoughts, as soon as he can in right good earnest say with the jaylor, "What must I do to be saved?"' Law did not doubt the sincerity of Warburton's intention to defend Christianity against the Deists, but he thought such a defence was 'not more promising than a trap to catch humility.' The spirit and the language in which alone unbelievers could be effectually addressed must be ' the spirit and the language of that Love and Goodness in whose arms the defender should long to see them embraced.'

Yet deeply as Warburton shocked and grieved Law both by his matter and his manner, Law never once descends to personal scurrility in reply ; he is severe against his doctrine, never against the man. How Warburton met him in return we shall see in a future chapter.

Here we may fitly close our examination of what Law wrote with a view to publication.[1] He wrote yet two other treatises before his death ; but the first of these, entitled,

---

[1] It seemed right to word this clause thus, rather than to say 'Law's printed works,' because his letters were published, but they were not written with a view to publication.

'A Dialogue between a Methodist and a Churchman,' is too slight a performance to require a separate notice ; it will be referred to when we treat of the connection between Law and the Methodists. The other, entitled 'An Address to the Clergy,' was written when Law was all but a dying man, and will be best considered in connection with his death.

To some it may appear that too much has already been said about Law's writings in a work which purports to be a life of the man. But the fact is, we see the man *in* his writings. Law thought very little, and said very little, directly, about himself. Egotism and vanity are the very last faults with which he can be charged. Nevertheless, a man of great force of character, who throws his whole soul into his works, who always writes with intense earnestness of purpose, always with a view to the edification, never to the amusement, hardly ever to the instruction, of his reader, cannot help stamping all that he writes with his own marked individuality. When Miss Gibbon was asked to write a life of Law, she replied, ' His life is in his books.' This is so far true, that a biographer would be neglecting to work a mine rich in illustrations of his subject if he did not thoroughly sift these books ; and this must be the apology for having dwelt so long upon them.

CHAPTER XIX.

LAW AS A CORRESPONDENT.

THERE are two species of composition which one expects to find, as a matter of course, largely quoted in every biography —at any rate in every religious biography—belonging to the eighteenth century, viz. the diary and the correspondence. When a man became seriously impressed, his first impulse appears to have been to write a diary.[1] Sometimes he went further still, and wrote a regular autobiography. But Law's biographer could expect to find no such godsends. Happily for him, Law's friend Byrom differed from his master in this respect ; but then, Byrom lived a very different life from that of Law ; his contact with the outer world at many points afforded him ample material for that amusing journal which has been and will be so largely utilised in the work. But if Law had kept a diary, what could he have put into it ? His outer life was a singularly uneventful one ; and he was the last man in the world to keep a record of his ' frames and feelings and religious experiences,' all which things' he heartily distrusted. ' The desire of the soul turned to God in humility, gentleness, and resignation '—that was the one frame of the Christian, and it did not admit of any substantial variation. Law was no more likely to have left us any word-painting of

---

[1] Thus, when Charles Wesley became very seriously concerned about spiritual things, he wrote to his brother John, ' I would willingly write a diary;' and then consults him as to what he should put into it. See *Memoirs of the Rev. Charles Wesley*, by T. Jackson, p. 7.

his mental phases, than to have left us any portrait of his bodily features. Knowing the man, it would be unreasonable to look for either the one or the other. But letters Law *did* leave behind him, and these will form the subject of the present chapter.

In the eighteenth century the art of letter-writing reached its perfection. At no other period of English history have there been so many really good letter-writers. In an earlier age the English style was not sufficiently easy and flexible to admit of excellence in an art which, of all things, requires ease and flexibility. In a later, the penny post, the electric telegraph, and the general rush and hurry of life, have, among them, well-nigh improved letter-writing off the face of the land. Men make known their wants, express their sentiments, and so forth, to their friends in writing, but they no longer write letters. In these degenerate days an average letter hardly contains as many lines as in the last century it contained pages.[1] *Then* almost every able man left behind him many more or less good specimens of this delightful branch of literature.

Law, however, cannot be ranked among the best letter-writers of the eighteenth century. Neither the bent of his mind nor the circumstances of his life were conducive to his excelling in this kind of composition. A good letter must be the outpouring of one mind to another on perfectly equal terms. But Law's correspondence was not of this character; it was, for the most part, simply the imparting by post of advice to those who could not come and sit at the master's feet and hear the same advice delivered *vivâ voce*. Again, a certain degree of ' abandon,' and, in the inoffensive sense of the word, of levity, is, perhaps, essential

---

[1] This was written before I had seen Mr. Goldwin Smith's *Life of Cowper*. Similar remarks have been made in that work ; and in Mr. W. Bagehot's *Literary Studies*, ' On Cowper,' which I had also not read when I wrote the above.

to the perfect letter. But this frame of mind was not
Law's. He had abundance of wit and humour, and those
of the raciest kind. But they were always held in check.
His mind rarely unbent itself from its natural gravity.
The playfulness of Cowper, that most charming of all letter-
writers ; the raillery of Horace Walpole ; the easiness of
Venn ; the vigorous, if somewhat elephantine, gambolling
of Warburton ; which constitute respectively the charms of
the correspondence of these eminent men, were all wanting
in Law. Or, to compare his letters with those of John
Newton, to which they bore, from the circumstances which
called them forth, the closest resemblance, there is a softness about the 'Cardiphonia' which Law, as a rule, does
not show.

A collection of Law's letters was published with his consent about a year before his death, at the request and through
the instrumentality of his friends, Mr. Langcake and Mr.
Ward. The first of them is addressed to his old friend Bishop
Sherlock, and is interesting as an independent testimony
to the merits of that very able man, from one who never
flattered, and who could have no interested motive for
writing as he did. Against the random aspersions of such
men as Horace Walpole and John, Lord Hervey,[1] may be
fairly set Law's opinion that the name of Sherlock was
'justly venerable to much the greatest and most worthy
part of the whole English Church,' and that his 'life had
been manifestly serviceable in the most trying times, to
the good of this part of the Christian Church.'

The next letter, addressed to 'Mr. J. L.' (probably John
Lindsay), is worth noticing, because it touches slightly
upon a subject on which Law, as a rule, was very reticent,
viz. the relations between Church and State. The reasons

---

[1] See Walpole's *Letters* and Lord Hervey's *Memoirs of the Court of
George II.*, both of which give an unfavourable account of Bishop Sherlock.

for his reticence are obvious. He had no wish to stir up
the troubled waters of ecclesiastical politics. ' Private
Christians,' he says, ' have no power or call to govern the
world, or set up thrones according to the principles of truth
and righteousness ; but are by the spirit of the Gospel
obliged to submit to, and be contented with, that state of
government, good or bad, under which the providence of
God has placed them.' At the same time, they are not to
call evil good, and good evil, nor ' to imagine that evil loses
its evil nature, and may be called right and good, as soon
as Providence has suffered it to become successful.' And,
therefore, since Law appears to have been called upon by
his correspondent to express his views on the influence of
the civil power upon the Church, he does not hesitate to
declare what he thinks.

It must be remembered that when Law wrote, the
blighting effects of Sir R. Walpole's ecclesiastical policy
were only too conspicuous ; and perhaps Law was a little
too ready to draw a general induction from a particular
case. At any rate, he asserts roundly that ' where the
Church and the State are incorporated, and under one and
the same power, all the evil passions, corrupt views, and
worldly interests, which form and transform, turn and over-
turn, all outward things, must be expected often to come
to pass, as well in the Church as in the State to which it is
united ;' and much more to the same effect. The whole
tenor of the letter, which is a long one, shows that Law
was by no means disposed to join in the jubilant strain in
which the many optimists of his day spoke of ' our happy
establishment in Church and State.' And as he tried
every mode of worship by the standard of the Primitive
Church, we can hardly be surprised to find that he was not
perfectly satisfied with the Church arrangements of the
eighteenth century. For the matter of that, the nine-

teenth century would in some points have been equally objectionable to him. One is reminded of the troubles of poor John Wesley in Georgia, just fresh from the influence of Law, as one reads in this letter of 'the Scripture baptism of the whole body under water' being 'only, as it were, mimicked, by scattering a few drops of water on a new-born child's face.' Law, if he were living, might still see this custom; and he might still hear what he terms 'prayers for the destruction of our Christian brethren, called our enemies, and thanksgiving for the violent slaughter and successful killing of mankind.' Many other points he specifies which he would like to see altered, especially in the 'outward form and performance of the two sacraments;' but he comforts himself (though it is rather a cold comfort, one must confess) with the thought that 'all that is inwardly meant, taught, or intended by them, as the life, spirit, and full benefit of them, is subject to no human power, but is wholly transacted between God and myself.' And, therefore, he never ceased to be a regular worshipper in his own parish church; and this was the uniform tenor of his advice to all who, like his present correspondent, consulted him on the subject.

Of the remaining letters in the published collection, several are written to clergymen in answer to questions, some doctrinal, some practical, on which they had asked Mr. Law's advice. The wide extent of Law's reputation as a spiritual adviser appears from the mere titles of these letters. One is 'to a clergyman of Bucks;' another 'to a clergyman of Westmoreland;' another 'to a clergyman in the north of England;' another to 'the Rev. Mr. S.'— that is, probably, Mr. Shirley; another, in 'answer to a scruple,' was written to one who was then in training for holy orders at Oxford, and who afterwards became a very eminent clergyman—the good Bishop Horne. Three more,

though not addressed to clergymen, are all about clergymen. They are headed, 'To a person of quality,' the person
of quality being none other than the pious Selina, Countess
of Huntingdon. The first of them is evidently in answer
to a letter which the good Countess had written to him at
the request of one of her clerical *protégés*, who desired
Law's advice on the subject of expounding the Scriptures ;
the second is the famous letter on the subject of John
Wesley's pamphlet (to be noted hereafter) ; and the third
refers to a letter which the Countess had received from 'a
pious and very excellent clergyman,' who thought that
'Mr. Law had gone half a bow-shot too far,' because by
his mysticism 'he had touched the heart-string of all sys-
tematical divinity.' Then we have a long and very loving
letter 'to a person burdened with inward and outward
troubles.' This person was, I have very little doubt, Mr.
Langcake himself, one of the editors of the letters ; and to
him and to his co-editor, Mr. George Ward, all the rest of
the letters, under the headings of 'To Mr. T. L.' and 'To
G. W.,' are addressed.

The letters in this printed collection were not published
in the exact form in which they were originally written ;
therefore, although the alterations and interpolations were
made with the concurrence of the writer, they are not the
most satisfactory specimens which are at hand of Law's
correspondence. For, happily, besides this published collection, and the numerous short notes from Law which
Byrom has inserted in his journal, there is still a large
number of Law's letters extant.[1]

From the nature of his position, Law had necessarily
an extensive correspondence in his later years. For King's
Cliffe was not so accessible as Putney ; and, therefore, the

---

[1] See *Notes and Materials for an adequate Biography of the celebrated Divine and Theosopher, William Law*, passim.

little knot of disciples who looked up to him as a spiritual
director were forced, in default of a personal interview, to
have recourse to the post to obtain counsel ; and moreover,
besides his regular disciples, Law had several occasional
and even anonymous correspondents (some being personally unknown to him), who rarely failed to obtain from
him the advice they needed.   It will be quite unnecessary,
however, to swell the bulk of this volume by quoting at
any great length from these letters.   The tenor of them
all is the same—Law had but one tale to tell.   Death to
self, and absolute resignation to the will of God, in gentleness, humility, and love—that was his one panacea for all
the ills of life, the one method of cultivating the heavenly
seed, that it might be fitted in God's due time to blossom
in the Paradise above.   Besides this, ' all was push-pin,' as
he once expressed it.   Less even than Wesley or Whitefield, or the good men of the Evangelical school, who were
coming into prominence as his life was waning, did Law
take any interest in what was going on in the outer world.
Politics, literature, and even theology itself were matters in
which he cared little to intermeddle.   What could any of
them do to help the inner, spiritual life, which to him was
all in all ?   A typical specimen of his style in writing to
correspondents of various classes will suffice for these pages.

It has been seen that Law's natural character was somewhat stern and unbending ; but grace had softened nature
much, and some of his letters are written with an ex-
quisite tenderness, which, if foreign to the natural man,
was the natural outpouring of that spirit of love which had
become the very breath of his life.   Let us take the following, dated October 12, 1757, as an example :—

' My unknown friend in Christ Jesus,—I am glad that
you are so heartily affected, and so deeply instructed in

the things of God. It is a happiness that no one knows, or can know, but he that is possessed of it. One of the surest signs of Divine light and true regeneration, is an in-expressible tenderness, an unfeigned love, an unchange-able compassion towards all that are under any hardness of heart, blindness, or delusion of our fallen nature. This is the necessary effect of regeneration; it brings forth nothing but the nature of Christ in the soul. All that Christ was towards sinners, is in its degree found in the truly regenerate man. He cannot murmur or complain, though he sees foxes have their holes, birds their nests, but he hath not where to lay his head. He must turn the other cheek to the smiter ; he cannot revile the reviler ; is as free from censure, and judging his brother, as a new-born infant. As all that he has to rejoice in is the unmerited free love and compassion of God towards his own once wretched state, so he has no eyes but those of love and compassion towards those who are only as blind and dead as he was, till the Giver of life and light did that for him which He did for Lazarus lying in the grave. All the concern that he has for the outward state of things, whether in Church or State, is discharged in these words : " Hallowed be Thy name ; Thy kingdom come, Thy will be done on earth, as it is in heaven ;' and, as for those who oppose this king-dom, he only thinks and speaks of them in the spirit of its King: " Father, forgive them, for they know not what they do." Wishing you all increase of light and life in Christ Jesus, is the best proof I can give you of my being your hearty friend, WM. LAW.'

The following letter of condolence is worth quoting, among other reasons, on account of the interest which attaches to the subject of it. Lady Elizabeth, or, as she was commonly called, Lady Betty Hastings, was one of ' the

excellent of the earth,' whose merits extorted the admiration of people who were by no means inclined to follow
her strict and unworldly mode of life. In her youth she
was immortalised in the 'Tatler.' It was to her that the
chivalrous Steele paid what has been well termed 'the
finest compliment to a woman that perhaps ever was
offered '[1] : 'To love her is a liberal education.' Congreve
drew a portrait of her under the singularly inappropriate
name of 'Aspasia' ; and, after having described her perfections in rapturous, though somewhat stilted and conventional terms, he thus concludes : 'This character is so
particular, that it will very easily be fixed on her only by
all that know her ; but I dare say she will be the last that
finds it out.'[2]

Law was not given to paying compliments to young
ladies ; but, thirty years later, when this saintly woman
had just gone to her rest, he took occasion to pay a fine
tribute to her memory in his 'Answer to Dr. Trapp ;'[3] and
in the same year (1740) he wrote to her sister in a strain
which is at once tender and respectful, but dignified withal,
and utterly free from that tone of servility in which the
great were then too often addressed. His letter runs thus :—

[1] Thackeray's *English Humourists* : Steele. By a slight but important
alteration, Thackeray, in his quotation, makes it appear as if Steele himself
had loved her, which the original does not justify. Steele does not say 'to *have
loved* her,' but 'to love her is a liberal education,' which he thus ingeniously
explains : 'for, it being the nature of all love to create an imitation of the
beloved person in the lover, a regard for Aspasia naturally produces decency
of manners and good conduct of life in her admirers.' If such were the result, it would perhaps have been well, if the simple and kindly, but very frail,
writer *had* been one of the lovers. See *Tatler*, No. 49.

[2] *Tatler*, No. 42. With extremely questionable taste, Congreve wrote,
'Methinks I now see her walking in her garden like our first parent, with unaffected charms, before beau'y had spectators, and bearing celestial conscious
virtue in her aspect.' In the 8vo. edition of the *Tatler* of 1797, the annotator
remarks on this with delightful *naïveté*, 'This fine lady's character seems to
have been superior to that of our first parent ! '

[3] See Law's *Works*, vol. vi. (2), p. 281.

'January 19, 1740.

'Madam,—As I seldom see the newspapers, so I did not hear of the death of Lady Elizabeth Hastings, of blessed memory, till some time after the public had been informed of it. For two or three post days after this I had a strong impression upon my mind to write to your Ladyship, which I continually resisted ; and the next post I had the honour of your kind and obliging letter. This made me look upon it as something very providential. My intention in writing to your Ladyship was to desire you to draw up an Historical Account of that blessed Lady's spirit, life, and virtues, from the first knowledge you had of them, that a memorial of her virtues might be communicated to the world. I have very lately by accident discovered that that good Lady had wrote several letters to me without a name, and I can't help thinking with some trouble that I did not then know I had such a correspondent.[1] The use that your Ladyship is to make of this great event of your life is to exercise the highest acts of love and gratitude to God, for having blessed you with such a near relation, whose virtues have been so eminent and highly edifying to this part of Christendom. This peculiar circumstance of your happiness ought to fill you with the greatest comfort, and inflame your heart with the sincerest ardours of love to God. Looking at the high character of a piety so endeared to you, raised up out of your own flesh and blood, you are thereby called to make an absolute donation of yourself to the glory and praise of God, to desire nothing but that His will may be done in you, that all you are, all that you have and are able to do, may be a sacrifice and service of love and devotion to Him that has thus called you. God has called you to stand in the place

---

[1] The letter from Bishop Wilson of Sodor and Man, to Lady Elizabeth Hastings, quoted above, p. 49, shows the interest which she took in Law.

of your blessed sister, to keep up her spirit, life, and virtues
in the world. . . .[1] Your Ladyship is, I hope, directed by
God to choose the retirement which you mention. The
visits you speak of I can by no means advise you wholly
to forbear ; for since you make them not as self-gratifica-
tions, but as prudential condescensions to the order of
human life, they will do your piety no hurt, and may
have better effects than generally happens. At least, it
will be time enough to forbear them when they appear
to have ill effects. Good and edifying conversation is not
always to be had, and yet your Ladyship may edify where
you are obliged to say nothing. . . . I am, with hearty
prayers to God to make you a true successor to the piety
of your blessed sister, your Ladyship's most dutiful, obliged,
and obedient servant,

'W. LAW.'

Law's correspondents came from all classes of society,
and from all varieties of sinners as well as saints. Let us
now turn from the wealthy, high-born lady, of unimpeach-
able character, to a poor ' servant, who cannot marry without entailing beggary and misery upon himself,' who is
constantly sinning grievously and repenting bitterly, and
then sinning and repenting again. His name would convey no information to the reader, and therefore, though it
is now before me, it will be better suppressed. He writes
to Law, a perfect stranger, because he had been deeply
impressed by his writings, and was sure he should receive
nothing but his pity and his prayers. He states his most
piteous case. In his childhood the seeds of piety had been
sown in his mind. He went out into the world ' to get his
living in the prime of giddy youth,' and fell a victim to the

---

[1] The paragraphs omitted are a repetition of Law's peculiar sentiments,
which are already well known to the reader.

temptations of the town. His downward career was arrested by 'hearing one Mr. Wesley' preach ; but only for a time. The lusts of the flesh again got the better of him, and then he was again conscience-stricken on reading some of Law's works ; but lust again got dominion over him, and, 'as it was, so,' he says, 'it continues to be, the very pest and perplexity of my life. And what shall I do ?' he exclaims in utter misery. 'Oh, dear Sir, consider my case ! Excuse this long broken account, and, if your wisdom can suggest to you the reason of my miserable situation, I hope your compassion will prompt you to favour me with good council.'

The poor backslider had not mistaken his man. Law, with all his strictness and hatred of sin, had nothing but love and compassion for the sinner. This is his reply to the heart-rending letter : 'Poor honest man, whom I much love and esteem, your letter has been lost amongst a multiplicity of papers, and is but just found by me. I am not without hopes but God and time may have done that for you in a better way than it would have been done by me. To be left in distress is oftentimes the only way to be delivered from it ; and, when help seems farthest off, then are we nearest to the place where it can only be had. Happy is that desolation, wheresoever it comes, that forces us to see no glimpse of relief but in giving up ourselves blindly, implicitly, and wholly to the redeeming power and goodness of God, without the least thought or conceit of having any other or more goodness than what His holy nature and spirit bring forth in us.' Then follows an eloquent description of that faith which 'draws Divine virtue from the hem of a garment, can remove mountains, pluck up whole trees of sin by the roots, make lepers clean, and raise the dead to life.' But Law was too sensible a man to think that these generalities would be sufficient to meet the case of his poor unknown friend ; so he goes on to give him the good practical advice to 'have a strict eye upon his outward life, to be temperate in everything, and, as much as he can, to avoid temptation.' And then, having recommended constant prayer, he actually takes the trouble to compose a prayer for his constant use—a prayer which, like everything that Law wrote, is full of beauty both of thought and expression, but which was perhaps a little too high-flown for his humble friend. 'One Mr. Wesley' would probably have dealt with the very distressing case more effectually, for he knew the mind of the poor and half-educated far better than Law did ; but neither he nor any other man could have dealt with it more tenderly or more earnestly.

But while Law's letters to the ignorant and erring breathe nothing but tenderness and love, he can also, on occasion, administer a very severe snub by post. Witness the following specimen. It is addressed to a Mr. William Briggs, a subordinate officer of the Customs in London, who had written several letters to Mr. Law on the subject of his works, for which he professed a great admiration, but, at the same time, felt called upon to criticise on various points. The first of these letters, written in 1746, Law had answered fully ; but to the rest he had not thought it necessary to send a reply, until March, 1751, when he finally disposed of his irrepressible correspondent in a long letter, the tenor of which may be gathered from the following extract :—

'My dear Friend,—I thank God it is neither through age nor infirmities, nor any indisposition to serve you, that I have not answered your letters ; but from a just sense of the unreasonableness of employing both you and myself in such a manner. Be patient, and receive in the spirit of meekness what follows ; and remember that *love* is my God and *wrath* my devil, and then

you may reap the fruits of Love from the following letter,
though written in a way and manner so contrary to your
expectation.

'There is hardly anything more hurtful to true spirituality (the life of God in the soul) than a talkative, inquisitive, active, busy, reasoning spirit, that is always at
work with its own ideas, and never so content as when
talking, hearing, or writing upon points, distinctions, and
definitions of religious doctrines. This may as truly be
called an earthly, worldly spirit, and as great an enemy to
conversion from darkness to light, from flesh to spirit, as
that of the old Athenians who spent all their time, as
S. Paul tells us, in telling or hearing some new thing. To
be trained up in the school of *reason*, and to have learnt
from Locke or Le Clerc, and such like masters, how to be
reasonable Christians, is to be taught how to be content
with eating dust and serpent's food instead of the tree of
life.'

Then follows one of Law's favourite diatribes against
'reasoning,' which, among its other misdeeds, had produced
'Deists, Arians, and Socinians.' Then Law proceeds to
operate, in his most caustic fashion, upon the unfortunate
Mr. Briggs' lucubrations, turning them inside out, and
showing their absurdity. One is tempted to ask why it
was thought necessary to crush this poor little butterfly on
so powerful a wheel ; but the answer is obvious. Law saw
that there was real good in the man, and, seeing this, he
very characteristically did not grudge the expenditure of
some time and labour in setting him right once for all.
'Bear,' he says, 'with patience, my dear friend, this great
and useful truth, viz. that all your letters to me are, from
the beginning to the end, of the same kind with the passages I have here remarked : mere hasty, needless, fruitless
words, brought forth by a talkative spirit, which is the

spirit you want to have cast out of you. You must have seen, in common life, that when a man has this turn he is neither wise nor useful in his discourse ; he becomes tiresome to everybody, and never talks to the purpose, because always talking. I take you to have good parts, and an awakened sense of piety ; but neither sense nor piety can bring forth their proper fruits when under the power of a talkative spirit. You tell me that the " greatest part of my Second Part of 'The Spirit of Prayer' gave you great consolation ; that it contains that pure and Christian philosophy which leads the fallen man to find eternity in himself, and Jesus Christ the source of all true happiness." Oh, Sir ! is it possible for you to see and know this, and yet make no better use of it ? What has the heart to wish or seek from men and books after such a philosophy as this is found ? But now, instead of saying to yourself, as you should have done, " It is enough ; the mystery of salvation is here opened ; in this light will I thankfully give up myself to God for the remainder of my life "—instead of thus thinking, my book had not been published a week before you sent me word of a great fright you were in lest a certain notion there advanced should " give occasion to the enemy not only to cavil, but to blaspheme." But, my dear friend, this is again mere talk. You have no such fear ; for, if you had this fear in the smallest degree, how could you possibly ask my leave to publish this very notion in a newspaper? In my book, grounded, guarded, and supported as it is, there is no room to be afraid of anyone's seeing it ; but for a serious person to remove it out of its place, where it stands supported by a pure Christian philosophy, to place it among the trash and babble of a newspaper, is as wise a contrivance to preserve it from the ill use of the enemy as if it were to be placed at the end of a play-book.'

Law then condescends to explain at great length the point at which Mr. Briggs had stumbled, and concludes his long letter thus: ' But I have done, and shall only desire you not to be offended at any freedom used in this letter ; for it is a letter of true love to you, written in the same style I should have spoke to you had you been with me. I embrace you in the ardour of Christian love ; I esteem you much, and should be heartily glad to cherish the good spark of Divine life that I know is in you. The activity of your nature will perhaps be still for making replies, and giving way to farther doubts. But choose *silence*, the handmaid to Divine wisdom, and give yourself to the spirit of *prayer*, and then the perfection both of the first and Second Adam will be opened in you, and become your song of praise to-day, to-morrow, and to all eternity. Dear friend, adieu. W. LAW.'

Mr. Briggs appears to have taken the significant hint contained in the last sentences of this letter, for we hear no more of him. In justice to Law it should be added that he very rarely mingled the vinegar with the oil in his correspondence ; but, when he did, it was uncommonly pungent.

CHAPTER XX.

LAW'S FRIENDS IN HIS LATER YEARS.

WHEN Mr. Law retired finally to King's Cliffe, he necessarily saw less of those friends who had been wont to visit
him at Putney, and also formed a new circle of acquaintances. It is now purposed to describe briefly a few of the
good people who were brought into contact with Law in
his later years.

His fellow-inmates of the Hall Yard claim our first
attention.

Of Mrs. Hutcheson, the elder of the two ladies who
shared their house with him, little is known. She was
twice a widow, and both her husbands were well connected
and held a good position in life. The latter had been
M.P. for Hastings. From one source or another Mrs.
Hutcheson was in possession of a handsome income—
about 2,000*l.* a year—and thus she contributed by far the
largest share towards the frugal expenses and sumptuous
charities of the simple household. But there does not
appear to have arisen the slightest difficulty about the
disproportionate share of her contribution. As a true
disciple of Mr. Law she would of course feel that, whatever her income might be, she was bound to devote the
surplus, after the necessaries of life were supplied, to
charitable objects ; if she possessed more than the other
inmates, she would of course devote more, and there was
an end of the matter. Her noble foundations of schools
and almshouses have been already described. Tradition

states that she was of a very gentle and lovable disposition; and this tradition is borne out by a letter from Mr.
Langcake, who knew her well. Writing to Miss Gibbon,
upon the death of Mrs. Hutcheson, he speaks of the ' dear
departed saint in whose countenance, when living, childlike simplicity and Divine love sat smiling.' She lived to
the great age of ninety. In her will she particularly recommended to Miss Gibbon (whom she left as trustee for
several benevolent bequests) ' my god-daughter Elizabeth
Law, and the rest of that family, out of the respect and
regard which I bear to the memory of my late worthy
friend the Rev. William Law.' It was at the sole expense
of Mrs. Hutcheson that the imperfect but costly edition of
Behmen's works, of which Law is erroneously said to have
been the editor, was published.

The individuality of the other inmate of the Hall
Yard, Miss, or, according to the custom of the time, Mrs.,
Hester Gibbon, is far more distinctly marked. The
mere fact of her relationship to the greatest of English
historians lends an interest to her which her own personal
character would perhaps have scarcely commanded. We
have, moreover, two or three graphic touches from the
historian's own pen which bring his aunt vividly before
us. ' A life,' he says, ' of devotion and celibacy was the
choice of my aunt, Mrs. Hester Gibbon, who, at the age of
eighty-five, still resides in a hermitage at Cliffe, in Northamptonshire, having long survived her spiritual guide and
faithful companion, Mr. William Law, who, at an advanced
age, about the year 1761, died in her house.'[1] Mr. Law
died in his own house; it did not become Miss Gibbon's
until after Law's death, when she received it as a bequest,
or rather a trust, from him; but this is of little importance.
In 1774 (some twelve years before Gibbon wrote the above)

[1] *Memoirs of my Life and Writings*, by E. Gibbon, p. 14.

he met his pious aunt in London, and described the meeting in a letter to his step-mother, in the following terms : 'Guess my surprise when Mrs. Gibbon, of Northamptonshire, suddenly communicated her arrival. I immediately went to Surrey Street, where she lodged ; but, though it was no more than half-an-hour after nine, the Saint had finished her evening devotions, and was already retired to rest. Yesterday morning (by appointment) I breakfasted with her at eight o'clock ; dined with her to-day, at two, in Newman Street, and am just returned from setting her down. She is, in truth, a very great curiosity. Her dress and figure exceed anything we had at the masquerade ; her language and ideas belong to the last century. However, in point of religion she was rational ; that is to say, silent. I do not believe that she asked a single question or said the least thing concerning it. To me she behaved with great cordiality, and, *in her way*, expressed a great regard.'[1] The sneer at 'the saint having finished her devotions' is not only irreverent, but rather low ; and the whole description is in very questionable taste. But Gibbon's step-mother, who was connected with the Mallets, and had come indirectly or directly, as we shall see presently, into collision with Miss Gibbon, would perhaps relish the allusions. Fourteen years later we find Gibbon writing to his aunt herself in a very different strain—a strain, however, which reminds one rather painfully of certain passages in the 'Decline and Fall.' It appears that his aunt had refused to see him, on the ground of his religious opinions, but had expressed some 'kind anxiety at his leaving England.' 'But I need not remind you,' writes Gibbon, 'that all countries are under the care of the same Providence. Your good wishes and advice

[1] *Letters to and from Edward Gibbon, Esquire,* No. LII. Gibbon's 'Miscellaneous Works,' vol. i. p. 484.

will not, I trust, be thrown away on a barren soil ; and, whatever you may have been told of my opinions, I can assure you, with truth, that I consider religion as the best guide of youth and the best support of old age, that I firmly believe there is less real happiness in the business and pleasures of the world than in the life which you have chosen of devotion and retirement.' May we hope that the historian's views had undergone a change since he wrote to his step-mother ? May he have been influenced by reading the works of Law himself, for whose character and abilities he expressed a very warm and evidently sincere admiration, and whose 'theological writings,' he tells us, 'our domestic connection has tempted me to peruse' ? Possibly. But one cannot shut one's eyes to the fact that Gibbon had very strong reasons for keeping in the good graces of his wealthy and pious aunt, who was at the time evidently approaching her end. Not only was he her nearest heir, but he had also strong additional claims upon her from the fact that his grandfather had, as he tells us, 'enriched his two daughters, Catherine and Hester, at the expense of Edward his only son [the historian's father], with whose marriage he was not perfectly reconciled.' [1]

One can scarcely be surprised that the 'Decline and Fall' should not recommend the writer to the favour of a lady who had sat at the feet of Mr. Law ; and, accordingly, when that great work was in its mid-course, we find her insinuating a wish to Lord Sheffield that her 'nephew would let publishing alone.' To this, Gibbon's faithful friend replied, ' He finds his works a very necessary pecuniary resource ; but you may be assured that he will publish nothing in future in the least disrespectful to the Christian religion. The continuation of his history may

---

[1] *Memoirs of my Life and Writings,* p. 14.

lead him to mention the establishment of the Mahometan
religion, which he may do without offence.'   Whether this
assurance was justified by the result need not here be
discussed ; any way, one is glad to find that Miss Gibbon
did leave the bulk of her property to her nephew.

Gibbon and his friends seem to have been rather alarmed
lest his aunt should be led by the great influence which Mr.
Law exercised over her to leave her property to some of
the Law family instead of to her own kinsman.   But they
little knew the character of Law when they suspected this.
' We seek not yours, but you,' might have been said as truly
by Law as by S. Paul.

From the letters of Miss Gibbon which are still extant,
and other incidental notices, she appears to have been an
imperfectly educated and rather narrow-minded lady, who,
with the best intentions, did not, perhaps, recommend in
the happiest way her religion to the outer world.   One
instance may be quoted.   A violent rupture took place
between Miss Gibbon and the only daughter of her sister
Catherine, in consequence of the formation of an intimacy
between that young lady and the family of the Mallets, a
relation of whom Mr. E. Gibbon, the historian's father,
afterwards married for his second wife.   However much
Miss Gibbon might have disapproved of this connection,
she surely ought, under the circumstances, to have expressed her disapproval delicately.   This she does not
appear to have done ; an explosion took place during a
visit in town, and on her return to King's Cliffe she received the following letter from her niece :—

> ' Putney, June 12, 1755.

' Madam,—As I suffered you to go out of town without
wishing you a good journey, I think myself bound to
give you some reason for such behaviour.   No respect
from me to you should have been wanting, had not you

yourself first given cause for it by what you thought proper
to say of *my friends*, . . . The injurious expressions you
made use of towards them, especially to Mrs. Mallet, I
could not to your face have answered as I ought, but now
the contradiction will be much stronger as you will have it
under my hand ; and if it was the last sentence I should
speak, these would be my words, " that the aspersion was
false as heaven is true, &c." '

In reply to this Miss Gibbon concocted the following
extraordinary epistle :—

'If Miss Elliston had not lost all sense of duty, both
to God and man, she would not treat in such a saucy and
contemptable [*sic*] manner *her* who is the nearest female
relative she has, and the only surviving sponsor at her baptism, and for no other reason than for acting as suitable
as I could to these relations I bear to her, and this she
may (if she pleases) remember I told her when we conversed
last together ; and if ever her heart comes to be softened
with prayer, and turned to God in true humility, she will
then be shocked at this epistle which she has earnestly
desired me to treasure up, though it must be deemed a
monument of *shame* to all *sincere sober-minded* Christians
that read it. That you may begin the preparation for a
happy eternity, and be speedily loosed from the *bands* of
blasphemy, hypocrisy, and infidelity is the right hearty
prayer of—Your real affectionate aunt.'

This letter was not sent. It was submitted to Mr.
Law for approval, and he dictated in its place a letter which
was more grammatical, but not less severe. Law had as
great a horror of the tenets of the friends among whom
Miss Elliston had fallen as her aunt could possibly have.
There is hardly a work of his in which he does not find
room for a protest against what he regarded as the soul-

destroying doctrines of the Deists. It shocked him, therefore, quite as much as it did Miss Gibbon, to hear of her
niece, and the granddaughter of his benefactor, being 'shut
among infidels, rejoicing in their friendship, and thankful
for having a seat where dead Bolingbroke yet speaketh.'[1]
'Their friendship,' he makes Miss Gibbon write, 'is of no
better a nature than that which kindly gave thirty pieces
of silver to Judas Iscariot, and both you and your unhappy uncle sooner or later must find that falseness, base-
ness, and hypocrisy make the whole heart and spirit of
every blasphemer of Jesus Christ.'[2] The 'unhappy uncle,'
it must be remembered, was Law's old pupil, to whom and
of whom he naturally felt privileged to speak plainly without being guilty of impertinence. How the letter was
received we know not, but if the young lady had any discernment she must have perceived that though the handwriting was her aunt's the composition, both in thought
and diction, was the product of a far more powerful mind.
The hands might be Esau's hands, but the voice was,
rather too obviously, the voice of Jacob.

There is a tradition that Mrs. Hutcheson and Miss
Gibbon did not harmonise very well together, and that the
strong hand of Mr. Law was necessary to keep the peace
between them. After his death the breach of course was
widened, and the story goes that the odd position of the
graves, still to be seen in Cliffe churchyard, is due to the
fact that the two ladies would not be buried side by side ;
hence Mrs. Hutcheson is laid at the feet of Mr. Law, where
she had often sat, figuratively speaking, when living.

But in whatever else the ladies may have disagreed,

---

[1] The point of this allusion will be apparent when it is remembered that
Mr. Mallet was the editor of Lord Bolingbroke's posthumous works, which
had lately been published when this letter was written.

[2] The three letters are quoted in *Notes for a biography of W. Law*, by Mr.
Walton.

they were perfectly agreed in regarding Mr. Law with the utmost veneration. There appears never to have been the slightest hitch in his relationship with either of them. Neither Mrs. Hutcheson nor Miss Gibbon has left any traces to show that she understood much of the profound mysteries of Behmenism, but they could both appreciate the beauty of a perfectly consistent and holy life, such as Law lived, and the unbounded influence which he evidently exercised over them—as indeed he did over almost all the few people with whom he was personally brought into contact—was all for good. They were his docile pupils, and, at his direction, copied out daily for their own spiritual edification passages of mystic lore which probably flew far above their heads. But the atmosphere they breathed, as everyone must have breathed who lived with William Law, was an atmosphere as like that of heaven as one can hope to find on this poor earth. Law was their oracle while he lived, and, when he died, the memory of the departed saint was always a hallowed one in both their hearts.

The next in order of intimacy with Law at King's Cliffe is our old friend, John Byrom. The personal intercourse between these good men after Law left London was to some extent interrupted, but this in no way affected the relationship between them ; there is just the same reverent admiration on the one side, and good-humoured affection on the other as ever there was. The only difference is, that instead of constant meetings, Byrom had to content himself with making excursions, at rare intervals, to King's Cliffe, to drink in wisdom at the fountain head.[1] His first

---

[1] It seemed necessary to state this point, because it has been strangely misrepresented. For instance, in the sketch of Byrom's life in Chalmers' edition of the *English Poets* (vol. xv.), the following confused account of his mental phases is given : 'At first he appears to have been rather a disciple of the celebrated Mr. Law, zealously attached to the Church of England, with strong prejudices against the Hanoverian succession, and a strong opponent of the divines termed latitudinarians. Afterwards he held some opinions

visit appears to have been in 1743, when, as we have seen,
'he light at the "Cross Keys,"' found 'Mr. Law at his
house by the church,' and 'rid with him over his brother's
grounds,' and had a long conversation with him on Behmen
and the mystics, and also on the famous anonymous
treatise, "Christianity not Founded on Argument," about
the tendency of which men's minds were at that time much
exercised. The last sentence in the account of this visit
is curiously illustrative of the ascendency which the mentor
still maintained over his modest pupil. 'Mr. Law said
that I might make some hymns.' It is unnecessary to
describe the different visits, which are all duly chronicled
in the 'Journal.'[1] The 'good Doctor' was quite as welcome to the ladies as to Law, and he is desired to make
'King John's House, not the "Cross Keys," his inn.' Byrom
appears to have taken King's Cliffe on his way to or from
Cambridge, whenever he paid a visit to his old University.

Law's affection for Byrom increased as years rolled on;
his letters become more and more full of the most affectionate expressions. In fact he evidently regarded Byrom
as the dearest of all his friends, and no wonder. Byrom's
was exactly the sort of character to attract a man like
Law. Simple as a child, yet not without ability, deeply
religious, yet without a vestige of cant, gentle and yielding,
yet by no means of a colourless character, he was eminently
a loveable man. The defects which most of all roused
the natural impatience of Law's temper, self-conceit and
unreality, were entirely foreign to Byrom's composition.

usually termed methodistical, but was opposed to Hervey's doctrine of imputed
righteousness and predestination.' Of course, his opposition to Calvinism, as
well as to Latitudinarianism, was inspired by Law; and his own journal shows
conclusively that instead of being *at first* a disciple of Law and afterwards
drifting away, he was more and more attached to Law's doctrines, the longer
he lived. A far better authority, Miss Wedgwood (*Contemporary Review*),
seems to intimate that the two became estranged by other circumstances besides
distance, but I can find no trace of the estrangement.

[1] See the *Journal* for May 1743, February 1747-8, May 1749.

On the other side, Law was just the sort of friend that Byrom wanted ; a strong character, who could well fulfil the office of ' Magnus Apollo ' with which Byrom invested him. Byrom once said of the relation of his verse to Law's prose, ' It wants to cling like an ivy to an oak.' [1] The remark would be more appropriate to the personal relationship between the two friends. Byrom, the ivy, required the oak to cling to for support ; and Law, the oak, had his sternness softened by the ivy twining round him.

But though we can well believe in the personal sympathy between Law and Byrom, it is not so easy to understand the admiration which each had for the other's writings. On the one hand, one would hardly have anticipated that a simple, transparent mind like that of Byrom would be attracted by the profound subtleties of Behmenism, even as expounded in the luminous style of Law. It is true that Byrom's admiration for Behmen was like that of the old Scotchwoman for her favourite preacher ; he admired, but ' wadna presume ' to understand. ' I have a respect,' he says, ' for a man that honestly understands a valuable author, though never so difficult to myself; Jacob Behmen I believe to be such an one.' [2] When Charles Wesley showed him some letters from his brother John on mysticism, ' I thought,' he remarks, ' that neither of the brothers had any apprehension of the mystics, if I had myself—which query.' [3] But, with his usual modesty, he scarcely does himself justice, for his poems show that he had very fairly caught Behmen's meaning.

Still more difficult is it to understand the high appreciation which Law had of Byrom's literary powers. He certainly

---

[1] *Journal,* ii. (2), 521.
[2] *Ibid.* ii. (1), 313. See also the odd poem entitled, *Socrates' Reply concerning Heraclitus' Writings.*   [3] *Ibid.* ii. (i.) 181-2.

regarded Byrom as a most valuable ally. He remonstrates
with him half-angrily, half-mournfully, for delay in the fulfilment of his promise to versify his prose;[1] he is afraid
that it is too much like self-seeking to ask for such invaluable aid, 'and therefore,' he says, 'I renounce it as
such. An assistance that comes in unlooked and unsought
for I can rejoice in as coming from God ; but I have the
fullest confidence that I ought to be as fearful of desiring
to be assisted as of desiring to be esteemed.'[2] He is 'too
interested a person to give judgment upon them' (that is,
Byrom's precious verses, for the aid came after all), and is
also 'afraid of himself, lest he should be too much pleased
with the honour that Byrom did him.'[3]

Now what possible advantage could arise from trans-
muting Law's nervous and luminous prose into such verses
as these?

> *Academicus:* So then I must, as I perceive by you,
> Renounce my learning and my reason too,
> If I would gain the necessary lights
> To understand what Jacob Behmen writes, &c.
> *Theophilus:* Why really, Academicus, the main
> Of all that Rusticus so bluntly plain
> Has here been saying, though it seems so hard,
> Hints truth enough to put you on your guard.

After many more verses of the same calibre, Theophilus
ends thus:

> This matter, Academicus, if you
> Can set in a more proper light - pray do.[4]

---

[1] 'It is now just two years,' he writes, 'since you have failed of your
promise. I am much at a loss to guess at the reason of it. If you repent of
having put your hand to the plough, I should be glad to know why. The
"Appeal" is making its way in the world, and if you give some assistance,
your labour is not likely to be lost. I hope you will not leave me in any
longer uncertainty about this matter, nor make me any promises that you will
not strictly perform.'—Quoted in Byrom's *Journal* for Oct. 3, 1751.

[2] From Byrom's *Journal* for May 1749. The whole letter is in the same
strain.

[3] From Byrom's *Journal*, ii. (2), 548.

[4] Byrom's *Poems* in Chalmer's English Poets, vol. xv. 'A dialogue be-

It seems to an outsider as if this was just the way to make the whole thing ridiculous. To render it more absurd, Byrom sometimes adopted the ambling 'Haunch of Venison' metre—an admirable metre for Goldsmith's playful letter to Lord Clare, but singularly ill-suited for the profound subjects on which Byrom wrote. To most people who have read Law's noble passages on 'the Wrath of God,' it will seem little short of profanation to twist them into such verses as these :

> All wrath is the product of creaturely sin ;
> In immutable love it could never begin ;
> Nor indeed in a creature, till opposite will
> To the love of its God had brought forth such an ill,
> To the love that was pleas'd to communicate bliss
> In such endless degrees, through all nature's abyss ;
> Nor could wrath have been known, had not man left the state
> In which nature's God was pleas'd man to create.'[1]

And so on, and so on, to an interminable length. Byrom's mind was a sort of philosopher's stone which turned everything it touched, not into gold, but rhyme. The most unlikely subjects, passing through that crucible, came out in a metrical shape. For instance, it would hardly have occurred to everyone that the 'Prayer for all sorts and conditions of men' was a promising subject for a poem. But Byrom was equal to the occasion. Among his poems appears a paraphrase of this beautiful prayer, beginning,

> It will bear the repeating again and again
> Will the prayer for all sorts and conditions of men, &c.

Nay, he can versify the very rubric. Thus :

> This short supplication, or Litany read,
> When the longer with us is not wont to be said, &c.[2]

---

tween Rusticus, Theophilus, and Academicus on the nature, power, and use of human learning in matters of religion. From Mr. Law's *Way to Divine Knowledge.*

[1] See Byrom's *Poems,* 'On the Meaning of the word Wrath as applied to God in Scripture.'

[2] Byrom's *Poems,* 'A Paraphrase of the Prayer used in the Church Liturgy, for all Sorts and Conditions of Men.'

Law, however, was by no means singular in his admiration of Byrom's poetry. John Wesley says of it :—'Read Dr. Byrom's poems. He has all the wit and humour of Dr. Swift, together with much more learning, a deep and strong understanding, and above all a serious vein of piety. A few things in the second volume are taken from Jacob Behmen, to whom I object. But setting these things aside, we have some of the finest sentiments that ever appeared in the English tongue ; some of the noblest truths expressed with the utmost energy of language, and the strongest colours of poetry.'[1] Warburton treated Byrom with a respect which he rarely showed to his antagonists, and said of him in a letter to Hurd : 'He is certainly a man of genius, plunged into the rankest fanaticism. His poetical epistles show him both.' Byrom's poem on the 'Fall of Man,' 'reminded' his first biographer 'strongly of Pope's celebrated essay.' Now we may have our own opinion about the true poetry of the 'Essay on Man,' but it is impossible to deny the brilliancy and polish of the versification ; and it is difficult to conceive any one being reminded of that finished work of art (not to call it a poem), by such slip-shod lines as these :—

> Language had surely come to a poor pass
> Before an author of distinguished class
> For shining talents could endure to make
> In such a matter such a gross mistake,

and so forth.

In justice to Law and Byrom's other admirers it is fair to add that the good doctor had now and then gleams of inspiration, and wrote in a very different style from that of the specimens quoted above. The poem on enthusiasm is spirited and well-sustained throughout. So also is the poetical paraphrase of 'Law's Prayer from the Spirit of

[1] Wesley's *Journal* for 1773.

Prayer.' So also is the poem on the 'Origin of Evil,' which, also, unlike many of Byrom's poems, is written in a metre suited to the subject.

But, after all, Byrom's lucid intervals are rare (that is to say in this department ; some of his hymns are good) ; the residuum of true poetry in his metrical essays is nearly drowned amid the grotesque and prosaic doggrel by which it is surrounded. And the admiration in which his verses were held by men of undoubted ability can only be accounted for by the fact that Byrom wrote in an age singularly barren in poetic genius. Pope was dead, and Cowper had not yet begun to sing. Men had no high living standard to judge poetry by, at any rate poetry of the nature of Byrom's, for Young and Thomson were poets in a very different department. Lockism, the dominant philosophy of the day, was ill-calculated to foster a poetical frame of mind. ' Public taste,' wrote Warburton to Hurd in 1749, ' is the most execrable imaginable.' And really, considering the opinion he expressed of Byrom's poetry, he might have added, ' Take my own, for example.' As for Law himself, though he was full of noble thoughts, which in the highest sense of the word were eminently poetical, yet, in the technical sense of the term, he had not a spark of poetry in his composition. ' I am not a bit of a vir-tuoso,' he wrote to Byrom ; he never himself perpetrated a line of verse in his life ; and he probably read no verses except hymns ; for, with his very strict notions, he looked upon the study even of Milton as waste of time. There is, therefore, little wonder that in his eyes the goose, whom personally he dearly loved, should have appeared a verit-able swan.

Beneath a somewhat austere and awe-inspiring exterior, a very warm heart beat in William Law, and as his strict views of the duty of clerical celibacy prevented him from

ever forming the closer ties of marriage, his affectionate
nature attached him all the more strongly to his friends.
Next to Dr. Byrom, a Mr. Thomas Langcake was the
most valued friend of his later years.   He is the ' T. L.' to
whom ten out of the twenty-eight published letters are
addressed, and Law wrote to him many letters besides, in
all of which he expresses himself in the warmest terms of
affection.   'I love to hear from you,' ' I cannot tell you
how much I love you,' 'Talk no more of obtruding upon
me with your letters.   Everything that comes from you is
welcome,' ' Much pleasure always comes with every letter
that has your name to it,' 'The friendly salutation of this
house waits upon my best beloved friend,' ' Je vous porte
dans mon cœur,' and innumerable other such expressions
from one who never said or wrote more than he felt, argue
a very deep attachment on the part of Law to his somewhat obscure friend.   And he writes in the same loving
strain *of* him as *to* him.   'I like,' he writes to Mr. Ward,
' everything that my Langcake does, and have no corner of
my heart that I would conceal from him.'   Langcake on
his side cannot find language strong enough to express his
enthusiastic devotion to Law.   He 'never met with so
much strength of genius, penetrating judgment, divine wisdom, exalted piety, solid comfort, and compassionate goodness to all mankind in any other author.'   Law's writings
are ' an heavenly panacea of sovereign efficacy to calm agi-
tated spirits.'   Law is 'this exalted author,' ' a resplendent
luminary, newly arisen in the intellectual and spiritual
world.'   Law 'teaches both learned and unlearned the
momentous truths of Salvation with a noon-day clearness,
divine energy, and irresistible conviction,' ' his vast, comprehensive mind soared into the Heaven of Heavens,' &c., &c.'

---

[1] See ' A Serious and Affectionate Address to all Orders of Men, adapted
to this awful crisis, in which are earnestly recommended the works of that great

He consults Law, not only on spiritual, but on temporal matters. Now we find Mr. Law permitting him to learn French, but he is 'to proceed very leisurely in it, and as it were by the by,' for 'to learn and love the language of the internal speaker is more than to learn and love the tongues of men and angels;' now he advises him about his health, 'not to be too abstemious, not to be too fond of a milk diet,' to 'tamper with no physicians, but content himself with that share of health which a regular and good life called him to,' and much more to the same effect. One of the last, if not the very last letter which Law wrote, dated March 27, 1761, was to Langcake; and it is to the same friend that we owe the interesting account of Law's last Easter-day on earth. He was Law's confidential agent in London, and when Law died, he helped to draw up his epitaph.

One would like to know a little more about a man who was so closely connected with and so dearly loved by William Law;[1] but all that can be ascertained is, that he was a clerk in the Bank of England and an enthusiastic Behmenist; an odd combination, for Threadneedle Street is not exactly the spot on which one would have expected mysticism to flourish. We are sorry to find from a not very delicate allusion in one of Miss Gibbon's letters, that he was subsequently in straitened circumstances;[2] however, the good lady made amends by remembering him in

and good man, Mr. Law.' The work is published anonymously, but internal evidence, with which it is unnecessary to trouble the reader, makes it absolutely certain that the writer was Mr. Langcake.

[1] Curiously enough, Byrom seems to have known nothing of Law's friendship with Langcake. One of the last entries in which Law's name occurs in Byrom's *Journal* is this: 'J. Wesley said it was Mr. Langcot, a gentleman of the Temple, that Mr. Law wrote letters to in the collection. I said I did not know Langcot, but Lindsay, a friend of Mr. L.'

[2] 'I did not think that Mr. Langcake's circumstances would admit of entertainments, &c.' Letter from Miss Gibbon to Mr. Fisher, of Bath, in 1789.

her will. There is a touching letter from Langcake to
William Law the younger,[1] written many years after the
great William Law's death, which is worth quoting:—
' Bristol, Dec. 11th, 1790. Dear Sir,—It gave me great
pleasure to see the much beloved name of *William Law*
subscribed to your letter, and what made it doubly agreeable was, its informing me that Mrs. Gibbon had kindly
remembered me in her will. . . . . Pray, dear Sir, are you
and your sister the happy favourites, whom my dear and
reverend friend used often to sport and play with, in great
sweetness and simplicity after dinner? If you are, I
remember you as well as your sister, and that he tossed
you both up and down upon his foot. I recollect I said
upon the occasion, that you were formed for to live eighty
years ; he replied, " Yes, if you did not hurt your constitution." I long to make one more visit to beloved King's
Cliffe before I die.' Prefixed to an edition of the ' Serious
Call,' of 1797 is a short account of the life of William Law
which, though published anonymously, was beyond a
doubt[2] the work of Mr. Langcake, who thus expresses his
devoted admiration for Law :—' Thrice happy departed
saint ! whose sublime genius and comprehensive mind were
excelled by nothing but the unbounded goodness of thy
heart. Blessed soul ! a pleasing remembrance of the happy
friendship which I enjoyed with thee, while thou wast in
the body, constrains me to offer this very feeble tribute of
praise, love, and gratitude to thy sacred memory.'

If Mr. Langcake is to us little more than a shadow,
still more shadowy is his co-editor of Law's letters, Mr.
George Ward. That he was an intimate friend of Law's,

[1] I.e. Law's great-nephew and heir. See *Notes for a biography of W. Law.*
[2] I say 'beyond a doubt' because the anonymous author inserts in the
account some letters addressed by Law to him, which can be identified with
letters addressed to Mr. Langcake.

that he was a devoted Behmenist, that he lived in Hackney
Road—an atmosphere, one would fancy, not more congenial to mysticism than Threadneedle Street—that he is
described after his death as 'a great and good man, and an
eminent Christian,' is about all we know of him. He and
Langcake were Law's confidential agents in London, and
saw most of his later works through the press. Their aid,
however, was more than mechanical ; Law expressly asserts
that it was in compliance with the judgment of Mr. Ward,
that he republished his 'Case of Reason' in 1755. Mr.
Ward was also the principal editor of the imperfect edition
of Behmen's works, which was published at Mrs. Hutcheson's expense.

From a bank clerk to a countess, from Threadneedle
Street and Hackney Road to the park at Ashby, is a long
step to take. But religion bridges over wide social intervals ; and there were others besides Law who could associate alike with a pious tradesman and a pious countess,
though few could equally well maintain their dignity in
both societies. It is not very easy to determine the degree
of intimacy which subsisted between the inmates of the
Hall Yard and the good Selina, Countess of Huntingdon.
That Lady Huntingdon held for some years a not infre-
quent correspondence with Mr. Law, a correspondence suggested possibly in the first instance by the high opinion in
which that good man was held by the saintly Lady Betty
Hastings, half-sister to the Countess's deceased husband, is
quite clear. But there is a letter in Lady Huntingdon's
Life which implies a closer intimacy. It purports to have
come from Miss Gibbon to her ladyship, and runs thus :—

'King's Cliffe, May 29, 1750.

'My dear Madam,—Your excellent physician, and our
worthy and respected friend, Dr. Stonhouse, about a month

since, was so kind as to inform us of your ladyship's illness, and the alarming state of debility to which you were reduced. At our particular wish Mr. Law requested good Mr. Hartley to visit Ashby, and report to us the result of his observations; but the duties of his parish prevented his leaving home at that time, and we were not able to learn any tidings of your ladyship till the other day, when we were delighted with the sight of your valuable chaplain, Mr. Whitefield. Oh, my dear madam, how have we prayed and wrestled with the great Author of Life and Light for the preservation of your invaluable existence! Precious above estimation is the prolongation of such a life as yours. We mourned, we wept, we prayed, and each returning day your case was presented on our family altar. Thanks, eternal thanks to Him with whom are the issues of life and death, for your restoration and subsequent amendment. My dear Mrs. Hutcheson has not been quite well for some time, and good Mr. Law's advanced stage of life precludes our leaving our beloved retreat, or we should do ourselves the gratification of personally congratulating you on your recovery. Present our united thanks and good wishes to Lady Ann Hastings for her kind remembrance of us. We hope, now that your ladyship is so much better, she will pay us her long promised visit. Best compliments to Lady Frances, and all your amiable circle, in which good Mr. Law most cordially unites.—I am, my dear madam, very sincerely, and with Christian affection, your faithful friend,

'HESTER GIBBON.'

This letter is a puzzle. Mr. Law and the two ladies were, no doubt, on visiting terms with all the aristocracy of the county, and there is no reason why the family at Ashby should not have been among the number of their friends. But the letter itself is suspicious. The style is not like that of Miss Gibbon, which was peculiar, and, to say the truth, not very grammatical. Still less is it the style of Mr. Law, who frequently revised Miss Gibbon's effusions, and would have been extremely likely to have done so in the case of a letter written to a lady of great eminence in Christian society. But the fact of his being twice referred to as 'good Mr. Law' is a conclusive proof that he himself had no hand in the composition. Moreover, there is an unctuousness about some of the sentences which was totally foreign to the sentiments which Law held and taught his fellow inmates to hold.

Again, I should much doubt whether Lady Huntingdon's position in the religious world would have been rated so highly by Mr. Law as it appears to be in this letter ; and, if not by Mr. Law, then certainly not by Miss Gibbon ; for she and Mrs. Hutcheson took their cue entirely from Mr. Law. And once more, did ' good Mr. Law's advanced stage of life preclude' all the family ' from leaving their beloved retreat ' so early as 1750?[1] That would be making Law a premature old man, while on the contrary he was extraordinarily hale and active for his years, even to the very last.

That devoted Law-worshipper, Mr. Walton, whose information about everything which concerned his hero is most extensive, ' very much doubts the authenticity of the letter.' But is it possible that ' a member of the houses of Shirley and Hastings,' as the anonymous author of Lady Huntingdon's life proudly calls himself, should have deliberately concocted a letter, with the date, address, and signature of Miss Gibbon all complete ? It is a puzzle, and that is all that can be said.

---

[1] Five years later Law wrote to his friend Langcake, 'Mrs. Hutcheson and Mrs. Gibbon are in a town for a few days.'

The Mr. Hartley mentioned in the foregoing letter was an intimate acquaintance, if not a friend of Mr. Law. He was a neighbour, though a somewhat distant one, being the Rector of Winwick, at the other end of the county, and appears to have been a pretty frequent visitor at the Hall Yard. Like most people who were brought into close contact with William Law, he entertained the deepest respect for his character, and writes quite rapturously of ' that excellent man's universal charity,' ' warm and loving heart,' and so forth.

Mysticism in general, and Behmenism in particular being commended to him by one whom he reverenced so highly, Mr. Hartley was naturally inclined to regard the system with a favourable eye ; and he therefore appended to his strange work entitled ' Paradise Restored ' one of the most interesting and rational defences of Mysticism, and especially of the mystic Law, which is extant. At the same time he and Mr. Law must have differed very widely on many points ; for Hartley was at one time in agreement with his neighbour James Hervey, and with Whitefield, which Law never was ; and subsequently he became an enthusiastic and prominent Swedenborgian, which would be still more out of accord with Law's opinions ; these later views, however, he did not adopt in their fulness until after Law's death. At any rate, Law's friendship with him continued to the end. For within half a year of his death we find Law giving directions as to whom copies of his last work, which he never lived to see in print, are to be sent, and he particularly adds, ' Do not forget Mr. Hartley.'

The rest of Law's friends need not detain us long.

Mr. Henry Brooke, of Dublin, nephew to the author of the well-known work ' The Fool of Quality,' Mr. Symes, Rector of St. Werburgh and friend of Hannah More, Mr.

Edward Fisher of Bath, the preserver of many MSS. of Law and Freher, Mr. Payne, the editor of the 'Imitation of Christ,' and the reproducer of Law's later views in an inferior form, Mr. Lindsay, a correspondent of Byrom, were all slight acquaintances but deep admirers of Law among his contemporaries. One name only deserves a longer notice. It is that of Mr. Francis Okely, a graduate of St. John's College, Cambridge, and afterwards a preacher among the 'United Brethren' at Northampton. Like many others he had been deeply impressed in his early years by reading the 'Serious Call' and the 'Christian Perfection ;' but though he had long lived in the same county with Law, he did not make his acquaintance until a few months before Law's death. He then made bold to propose to Law that he should visit him at King's Cliffe for the purpose of conversing with him on spiritual matters. Law's reply to this request is so thoroughly characteristic that it is worth quoting :—

'As to your intention,' he wrote, 'of a visit here, I can say nothing to encourage it ; and though my countenance would have no forbidding airs put on by myself, yet as old age has given me her own complexion, I might perhaps bear the blame of it. But my chief objection against a visit of this kind, is the reason which you give for it, viz., for my instructive conversation on the Spiritual Life. An appointment for religious conversation has a taking sound, and passeth for a sign of great progress in goodness. But with regard to myself, such a meeting would rather make me silent, than a speaker in it.' Then he gives his reasons, which the reader who has followed Law's course so far, can anticipate for himself, and concludes : 'Rhetorick and fine language about the things of the Spirit, is a vainer babble than in other matters ; and

he that thinks to grow in true goodness by hearing or
speaking flaming words or striking expressions, as is now
much the way of the world, may have a great deal of talk
but will have but little of his "conversation in heaven." I
have wrote very largely of the Spiritual Life ; and he that
has read it and likes it, has of all men the least reason to
ask me any questions or make any visit on that subject.
He understands not my writings, nor the end of them, who
does not see that their whole drift is to call all Christians
to a God and Christ within them, as the only possible life,
light, and power of all goodness they can ever have ; and,
therefore, they turn my readers as much from myself as
from any other, " Lo here ! or Lo there !" I invite all
people to " the Marriage of the Lamb," but no one to myself.—Your humble servant, W. L.'

Undeterred by this very unpromising reception of his
proposal, Mr. Okely paid his visit to Law nevertheless,
and ' was indulged with an ample and intimate conversation
with him upon the present state of religion in our time and
nation, and on many other most interesting subjects.' He
went away enraptured with Law, ' regarding,' he tells us,
' this visit as a favour of God bestowed upon him, and which
he would not have been without on any consideration.'
But it is rather amusing to observe that the specimen he
gives us of the conversation which passed between them is
of the same tenour as the letter Law wrote to him. ' Sir,'
said he (Law), ' I am not fond of religious gossiping ; my
best thoughts are in my works, and to them I recommend
you. If I should seem to you a positive old fellow, I cannot help it, well knowing the ground from which I write.'
However the visit was so satisfactory that it was repeated ;
and it is to one of these two visits that we are indebted for
the account of the way in which Law first met with Behmen.

Before dismissing Mr. Okely it should be added that he afterwards became a voluminous writer ; and that he took every opportunity in his writings of recommending Law's works. It is to be feared that if Law had lived to see his admirer's lucubrations, he could not have returned the compliment, for there were certainly many things in them of which he would have strongly disapproved. It is doubtful, too, whether Mr. Okely's praises were likely to recommend Law's writings to the world at large. This is the way in which he sums up a rapturous account of Law's mystic works ;—' Now, courteous reader, if thy spiritual stomach doth not loath such sweets, know that this great author's works are like so many honeycombs by him assiduously collected, formed, digested, and filled during a long life out of all the spiritual writers, or *mystic flowers*, ancient and modern. And if the translator [1] has any degree of spiritual judgment, and may be allowed to express his poor opinion, the very last book of this *mystical* bee is like *quintessential* clarified honey itself, collected out of all the rest.' Okely shared Byrom's extraordinary infatuation (or rather derived it from Byrom, for ' my late friend, Mr. Byrom, of Manchester, first pointed out this way to me,') that Law's good prose might be improved by being put into bad rhyme ; and accordingly he set about, with some misgivings, the task of versifying various passages of Law's mystic works. ' Sacred poetry,' he says, ' ought, like the true daughters of Abraham and Sarah (1 Pet. iii. 3–6), never to be tricked up in the gaudy and tawdry manner of the daughters of this world.' At the same time ' a regard due to my very important subject, my reader's edification, and my own usefulness, has put me upon the exertion of my

---

[1] The passage occurs in Okely's *Translation of the Life, Death, Burial, and Wonderful Writings of Jacob Behmen*, published 1780.

very best talents.' The exertion of his very best talents resulted in such verses as these :—

A PLAIN VERSION OF AN UNPOPULAR AUTHOR.

(From the *Way to Divine Knowledge*.)

Before we part, I'll in your presence trace
Christianity's true nature and firm base.
'Tis Gospel Christianity I mean
God's masterpiece; distinguishable clean
From the Christianity original
By grace first introduc'd on Adam's fall.
The old religion of the patriarchs
And that which Moses and all prophets marks, &c.

The reader may have thought that this curious kind of literary work had reached its nadir in some of Byrom's verses ; but he will now see that in the lowest depths there is yet a lower. Byrom's friend out-Byroms Byrom.

A dim consciousness seems to have possessed Mr. Okely that, though such sacred poetry as that which has been quoted [1] was certainly like the true daughters of Abraham and Sarah in being free from all ornament, it still might not have reached the acme of perfection. And therefore he modestly adds, ' Being, after all, not insensible that the execution has not always answered the design, I take this opportunity of inviting some better disposed and more

---

[1] Lest it should be thought that an unusually bad specimen has been selected, here are two more taken quite at hap-hazard:

From the *Appeal to all that Doubt, &c.*

And now to us it clearly will appear
Why our dear Lord so much must do and bear,
If we but him as second Adam view,
Who is, what wrong the first did, to undo.
For he must enter into ev'ry state
Which of fall'n nature one might term the fate.

From the *Short Confutation of Dr. Warburton.*

Men in two ways, one may quite plainly see,
Attach themselves to Christianity.
One's with conviction as a sinner poor,
The other as a scholar and no more, &c.

competent person to go on.' Moreover, it occurs to him as
just within the bounds of possibility that Law will be more
acceptable to some people in his own dress than in Okely's,
Byrom's or anybody else's, and so he makes this kind con-
cession :—' Should any one, whether before acquainted
with Mr. Law, or now by this means first made so, prefer
the original prose to this metrical, or even to the very best
poetical version, I shall have no reason to regret the inclination of either.'

The general impression which one gathers from the
accounts of Law's friends is that, though they all belonged
to what are called the educated classes, they were (*exceptis
excipiendis*) but a feeble folk. And it is distinctly a misfortune to Law in more ways than one that this was the case.
Law himself is in danger of being compromised by such absurdities as those which have been quoted ; his strong sense,
his good judgment, and his intellectual powers generally
would never be suspected by those who regarded him through
the distorting medium in which some of his injudicious
friends have presented him. And then it is never wholesome
for a man to be always king of his company ; the friction of
equal minds is necessary to bring out a man's brightness ;
Law seldom or never had the benefit of such friction. And
once more, a certain peremptoriness of tone was constitutional to Law ; at bottom he was the humblest man living ;
but his humility does not always appear upon the surface ;
it was not good for him always to be bowed down to, always
to be made an oracle of. In short, it would have been well
for him if he had sometimes been brought into personal
communication with men of the calibre of some of those
who will be noticed in the next chapter.

CHAPTER XXI.

LAW'S OPPONENTS.

IN the admirable essay 'On the Mysticism attributed to the Early Fathers,' in Tract 89 of the 'Tracts for the Times,' the writer (Mr. Keble), observes :—'Mysticism is not a *hard* word, having been customarily applied to such writers as Fenelon and William Law, whom all parties have generally agreed to praise and admire.' So far as William Law is concerned this remark is only applicable to his personal character. No one could help admiring *that*. The thorough reality of the man, his ardent piety, his splendid intellectual powers were undeniable ; and with very few exceptions, his warmest opponents did homage to them. But, just in proportion as they admired the man, they abominated all the more the opinions which seemed to them to spoil so fine a character. 'The person I greatly reverence and love. The doctrine I utterly abhor.' These words of one of the most distinguished of Law's opponents express the pretty general feeling among them all.

In fact, instead of 'praise and admiration,' few writers (*quâ* writers) have met with so much abuse from so many different quarters as Law did in his later years. It could hardly be otherwise. The eighteenth century was, of all periods, that in which popular sentiment was most unfavourable to anything which savoured of enthusiasm, mysticism, idealism — whatever vague term best expressed the pet

abhorrences of the day. All men, it is said, are born Aristotelians or Platonists. If there had been a registry of births
on this principle, there would have been found an enormous
preponderance of Aristotelians in the period we are speaking
of. Perhaps at no other period could such an utterance have
been made as that which Voltaire—the very incarnation of
eighteenth century feeling in its most unspiritual form—
made when he called Locke 'the English Plato, so far
superior to the Plato of Greece,' nor as that which Gibbon
made when he unhesitatingly declared his preference for
Xenophon over Plato, as an exponent of Socrates. But
the opponents of Law were not men of the stamp of Voltaire and Gibbon. They were, for the most part, orthodox
divines of the Church of England, thoughtful men and
well read in theological literature. And, really, one cannot wonder that such men should have taken exception to
many of Law's sentiments, and, still more, to many of his
incidental expressions. Law's later works certainly breathe
the spirit of earnest piety ; they are full of beautiful thoughts,
beautifully expressed ; they deal in a very striking and
suggestive way with difficulties which press upon the minds
of thoughtful men in all ages ; but, on the other hand, they
are certainly full of strange theories and interpretations ;
they cannot, to say the least of it, bear to be judged by
the '*quod semper, quod ubique, quod ab omnibus*' standard.
His views on the Atonement, on the Wrath of God, on the
creation of the world, on the state of the universe before the
creation, and on many other points, range beyond the
beaten track of theology, to put it in the mildest form.
His speculations on the 'glassy sea,' on the universal fire,
on the Pearl of Eternity, &c., are curious and fascinating,
but often very wild and fanciful. His admiration of Behmen almost amounted to an infatuation ; and his violent
diatribes against 'human learning' were not unnaturally

offensive to a church which has always taken a reasonable pride in having a learned clergy.

One of the best types of an opponent to Law on these grounds was Mr., afterwards Bishop Horne. He had been an ardent admirer of Law's earlier works, and had ' conformed himself' (his biographer tells us), ' in many respects to the strictness of Law's rules of devotion.'[1] But Law's later theology shocked him. Speaking of Law's Behmenism, ' We have seen,' he says, ' one of the brightest stars in the firmament of the church (oh! lamentable and heartbreaking sight), falling from the heaven of Christianity.' Briefly but very pointedly he states his objections to each of Law's peculiar views ; and though he is sometimes rather too violent, and sometimes misunderstands Law's real meaning, yet on the whole his treatise is a weighty and useful one. It would swell the bulk of this volume too much to quote it in detail ; it must therefore suffice to cite one very reasonable remark :—' Mr. Law,' he says, ' is injudicious in condemning all human learning ; though all that tends not to the knowledge of God deserves the censure which he bestows in a very masterly manner. But I see not why time is not as well spent in the writings of the noble army of saints and martyrs and confessors, as in those of Jacob Behmen, much better than in searching for truth in the inward depth and ground of the heart, which is indeed deceitful above all things—who can know it ?'[2]

Another opponent of Law on similar grounds was Bishop Horne's friend, chaplain, and biographer, Mr. Jones of Nayland. He too had a very high opinion of Law's earlier works. His praise of the ' Letters to Bishop Hoadly ' has already been quoted, and he valued equally

---

[1] *Life of Bishop Horne*, prefixed to his ' Works,' in 6 vols., by Rev. W. Jones (of Nayland), i. 68.

[2] See Horne's *Cautions to the Readers of Mr. Law.*

Law's practical treatises. He had, moreover, a deep admiration for Law's personal character ; but, for these very reasons, he was all the more opposed to his later views ; for he was 'sensible how easy it was for many of those who took their piety from Law, to take his errors along with it,'[1] and therefore he felt it his duty to lift up his testimony against one 'who, after writing so excellently upon the vanity of the world, and the follies of human life (on which subjects he has no superior), has left us nothing to depend upon but imagination, &c.'[2]

We next come to our old friend Bishop Warburton, who assailed Law repeatedly in true Warburtonian language. Warburton has been accused of waiting till Law's death before he ventured to attack him ;[3] but the imputation is an unjust one ; for, in point of fact, he attacked him pretty freely during his lifetime. Whatever Warburton's faults may have been, cowardice was not among the number ; the antagonist of Lowth and Gibbon cannot be fairly charged with shrinking from strong adversaries. It is true that Warburton's bitterest invectives were not uttered until after Law's death ; but then it must be remembered that Law's strictures on the Divine Legation were written within a short period of his death, and his further strictures on Warburton when he was actually a dying man. Still, if there is anything in the 'de mortuis, &c.' rule, Warburton certainly violated it most grossly. Indeed, whether he had been writing of the dead or the living, such language as the following was rather strong :—'The late Mr. Law obscured a good understanding by the fumes of the rankest enthu-

---

[1] Jones, of Nayland, *Life of Bishop Horne,* p. 68.

[2] Jones' *Catholic Doctrine of the Trinity,* p. xiii. 'To the Reader.' See also his *Letters to a Lady on Jacob Behmen's Writings, passim.*

[3] Thus Okely writes to Byrom, 'Some of my friends think he (Warburton) would not have ventured to attack Mr. Law had he been alive.' See also Hartley's *Defence of the Mystic Writers* appended to his *Paradise Restored.*

siasm, and depraved a sound judgment still further by the prejudices he took up against all sobriety in religion. . . . The poor man, whether misled by his fanaticism or his spleen, has fallen into the trap which his folly laid for his malice.'[1] 'I have the honour to be plentifully though *spiritually* railed at by Mr. Law. Rash divines might be apt to charge this holy man, so meek of spirit, with enthusiasm, with a brutal spite to reason, and with more than Vandalic rage against human learning. If human reason can argue no better than Mr. Law, I am ready to deny her too.' 'The leader of the sect [of Behmenists] amongst us, though manifesting an exemplary abhorrence of all carnal impurity,[2] has fallen into the lowest dregs of spiritual. When I reflect on his [Law's] wonderful infatuation, who has spent a long life in hunting after, and with an incredible appetite devouring the trash dropt from every species of mysticism, it puts me in mind of what travellers tell us of a horrid fanaticism in the East, where the devotee makes a solemn vow never to taste of other food than what has passed through the entrails of some impure or savage animal. Hence their whole lives are passed (like Mr. Law's among his ascetics) in woods and forests, far removed from the converse of mankind.'[3]

The coarseness of this last paragraph needs no comment; but even this is not so objectionable as the sneer against 'the holy man of so meek a spirit,' language common enough among the baser opponents of the Methodists, but happily unique from the pen of a Christian bishop.

Still, even Warburton, violently as he disagrees with

---

[1] Warburton's *Doctrine of Grace*, Book I. ch. v. p. 565.

[2] The Bishop had just been speaking of the carnal impurity of the *Brethren of the Free Spirit*, 'a vagabond crew of miscreants' whom he puts into the same category with Law and the Behmenists.

[3] *Doctrine of Grace*, Book I. pp 705-7.

Law's *mode* of religion, gives one the impression that Law
was a truly religious man. And it is the same with most
of Law's opponents. With most but not with all. One,
and, so far as I am aware, only one, hints in a vague sort of
way, and without giving the slightest shadow of a proof of
any kind, that Law's life would not bear close inspection.
Alexander Knox wrote a strong letter to Mr. David Parken
on the dangers of mysticism generally, and on William Law's
presentment of it in particular.[1] He was perfectly justified
in doing so; but he was *not* justified in writing such a sentence as the following in his answer to Mr. Parken's reply:
' I think you are perfectly right in making a marked distinction between Fenelon and William Law ; I intended
strongly to convey this idea ; Fenelon's errors were as
innoxious to him as such errors could be ; one may therefore examine his case without pain ; but I should not wish
to analyse the character of William Law ; his temper, first
to last, is of a questionable complexion.'[2]

Mr. Knox was not a contemporary of Law, and the
distance of time which elapsed between Law's death and the
writing of the above words really seems to be the only explanation that can be given of them. The tradition of
Law's true character may have passed away when Knox
wrote thus. It is almost needless to say, in the words of
Bishop Ewing, ' if he had made the analysis from which he
shrank, he might have formed a different judgment, or at
least expressed himself in different language.'[3] Law's

---

[1] See Alex. Knox's *Remains*, vol. ii. ' Letter to D. Parken, Esq., on the
Character of Mysticism,' *passim*.

[2] *Ibid.* p. 373. Mr. Knox was rather prone to make vague insinuations
of this kind without giving the slightest proof. He says of Cowper's friend,
Lady Austen, in his correspondence with Bishop Jebb, that ' he had a severer
idea of her than he should wish to put into writing for publication, and that
he almost suspected she was a very artful woman.'

[3] *Present-Day Papers*, edited by Bishop A. Ewing.

temper [1] was certainly not 'of a questionable complexion ;' it was as Christ-like a temper as one could hope to find in this poor world ; and one is sorry to see a really good man making so unworthy an imputation without any grounds whatever.

It has been suggested by Bishop Ewing that Alexander Knox's dislike of William Law may have arisen from his friendship with John Wesley. But if so, it would have been well if he had followed more closely the example of Wesley, who must again appear before us as an opponent, but a very honourable opponent of William Law. It will be remembered that the last correspondence between Law and Wesley took place in 1738. After this they appear to have gone on their respective ways, holding no intercourse with one another. But in 1756, Wesley, after eighteen years' silence, felt bound to give expression to his disapproval of Law's more pronounced development of mysticism, especially as it appeared in the 'Spirit of Prayer' and the 'Spirit of Love.' This he did in the form of a letter or pamphlet addressed to Mr. Law, but published for the benefit of Christians generally. This pamphlet has been very severely condemned. Whitefield characterised it to Lady Huntingdon as 'a most unchristian and ungentlemanly letter.' Dr. Byrom, on more than one occasion,[2] roundly took Wesley to task, urging him to 'repent of that wicked letter,' and on Wesley's promise to soften some of his expressions about Law, quoted the line :—

Multæ non possunt, una litura potest.

But the letter was not 'wicked,' nor 'unchristian,' nor 'un-

---

[1] I assume that by 'temper' Mr. Knox means what is now more generally termed 'temperament '; Law had no doubt naturally an irascible 'temper' in the popular sense of the term, but it seems nonsense to talk of temper, in this sense, as of 'a questionable complexion' or as something which a man would shrink from analysing.

[2] On August 1, 1757, and April 2, 1761. See *Journal.*

gentlemanly,' nor did it deserve the '*una litura*,' the entire
obliteration, which Byrom suggested. From Wesley's own
point of view it was a very natural one ; and it was written,
like everything that was written by that great and good
man, from the purest motives ; nor is it difficult to see
what those motives were. To do reasonable justice to
Wesley we must remember that he was an eminently practical man. The question with him would be, Is such
teaching likely to do my people practical harm ? And
remembering that he had seen what had been the practical
effect of the sort of diluted mysticism of the London Moravians upon his people, we can hardly wonder that he concluded that harm would be done. Hence this well-meant,
if not very judicious attempt to counteract the evil. Law
characterised it (in a private letter, however, not intended
for publication), in his own incisive language, as ' a juvenile
composition of emptiness and pertness, below the character
of any man who had been serious in religion but half a
month.' And regarding it purely as an intellectual performance, perhaps Law was not very far wrong. Wesley
had obviously a very imperfect acquaintance with Behmenism. While condemning Law, he strongly praised Byrom's
poems, which are really nothing more than a reproduction
of Law in verse ; and he actually reprinted for the use of
his disciples Law's answer to Warburton which is Behmenish to the very core, evidently not detecting the Behmenism
which it contained. The fact is, such speculations were
entirely out of Wesley's line, and in this pamphlet he laid
himself open to a crushing retort which no one could have
administered more effectually than Law. But Law was not
the man to do it. Men who wrote from obviously Christian
motives were not the men whom Law ever chose to attack.
' Wish them well in all that is good,' was his advice to a
friend who censured the Methodists, in reference to this very

pamphlet. This was the reason—and not, as Wesley supposed, contempt for the writer—which kept Law silent.
Law could hit a very hard blow when required ; but Wesley was not the man to whom he would deal it. We may
well follow his example with regard to this letter. Those
who wish to read it may find it in ' Wesley's Works,' vol. ix.
All that need be said further is that amid all his vehement
abuse of the sentiments, Wesley still showed his deep
respect and love for the piety and abilities of the man who
uttered them. Witness the preface of his letter:—

' Rev. Sir,—It will easily be allowed by impartial judges,
that there are few writers in the present age who stand in
any competition with Mr. Law, as to beauty and strength of
language, readiness, liveliness, and copiousness of thought ;
and (in many points), accuracy of sentiment. And these
uncommon abilities you have long employed, not to gain
either honour or preferment, but with a steady view to
promote the glory of God, and peace and goodwill among
men. To this end you have published several treatises,
which must remain as long as England stands almost un-
equalled standards of the strength and purity of our language, as well as of sound practical divinity. Of how great
service these have been in reviving and establishing true,
rational, scriptural religion, cannot fully be known, till the
author of that religion shall descend in the clouds of heaven.'

And again :—' It may indeed seem strange not only
to you, but to many, that such an one as I should
presume thus to speak to you, a person superior to me in
so many respects, beyond all degrees of comparison.'
And even in the midst of his abuse of mysticism, he
interrupts himself constantly to utter such apologies as
these :—' I would not speak, but I dare not refrain.' ' I

would greatly wish to forget who speaks, and simply consider what is spoken.' 'The person I greatly reverence and love.' 'I have used great plainness of speech, such as I could not have prevailed upon myself to use, to one whom I so much respect, on any other occasion.' It is true that there are other occasions on which Wesley writes as though he were well aware of Law's infirmities, his peremptoriness, dictatorial character, and so forth ; but no one can read all that Wesley has said about Law, without feeling that if the founder of Methodism was an opponent he was a very generous opponent of his former mentor, for whom, in spite of fundamental differences, he had the very highest possible esteem, reverence, and love.

With the exception of Wesley, the Methodists, properly so called, do not seem to have come into collision with Law. Their converts were, for the most part, won from the lower and lower middle classes ; and, in spite of Law's incessant depreciation of human culture, his mystic works were, though unconsciously, addressed solely to the cultured classes. But to the rising evangelical school Law's sentiments were naturally very offensive. The good men of this school were moderate Calvinists ; and Calvinism in every shape and form was an abomination in the eyes of Law. To his logical mind the doctrine of reprobation presented itself in all its force ; and that doctrine seemed to him entirely to overthrow the central truth of his system that ' God is Love, yea, all Love, and so all Love that nothing but Love can proceed from Him.' Possibly if Law had lived to see the immense amount of practical good which the Calvinists undoubtedly did, he would have modified some of the sweeping censure he levelled against their system. That censure was scattered through all his works ; but his penultimate work was the only one which was exclusively directed to the subject. It was entitled,

'Of Justification by Faith and Works: a Dialogue between a Methodist and a Churchman.' The Methodist took as a sort of text a passage from the letters of Mr. Berridge, the pious but eccentric Vicar of Everton ; and his first sentence is a sufficient specimen of his style :—' Say what you will, sir, I must still stand to it, that almost all the sermons of your bishops and curates for the last hundred years have been full of a soul-destroying doctrine.' Law, in the character of the Churchman, defends the Church against the Methodist's sweeping assertion. He was jealous for the honour of the Church of which he was a sincere and attached member, though his Jacobitism, prevented him from taking an active part in her ministry.[1] Looking back at the nomenclature from the stand-point of history, we see of course that it was not correct ; for as a matter of fact, it was chiefly the Church side in the Evangelical revival which took the Calvinistic, and the Methodist side which took the (so-called) Arminian view. Taking, however, a wider range than that of the mere position of parties in the eighteenth century, we shall see that Law was quite right in the distinction which he made. He was a thoroughly well-read man, and he knew perfectly well that ' the Church,' as Dr. Mozley has pointed out in his essay on Luther, ' has always admitted good works into a regular place in the process of man's justification.'[2] This was all that Law contended for, and it is unnecessary to specify in detail the arguments which he used in doing so. The Calvinistic controversy of the eighteenth century is not edifying reading, and Law's contribution to it is not a very remarkable one.

---

[1] There is a gentleman's ring in the possession of a member of the Law family, containing a portrait which is evidently that of the son of James II. The ring is reported to have been worn regularly by Mr. Law. If the tradition be true, it is a further proof that Law cherished deeply his loyalty to the exiled dynasty.

[2] Mozley's *Essays*, vol. i. p. 337.

It is not even relieved by any of those brilliant strokes of
wit and satire which are found in most of his writings.
The only point worth noting is that he hit off rather neatly
the hot positiveness and wilfulness which in truth characterised the combatants on both sides in this unhappy dispute, though Law put them only into the mouth of the so-
called Methodist. But Law himself had not a very high
opinion of this work ; for he told his friend Langcake that ' he
over-rated the dialogue, which was written, by one who was
grown very old, in much haste, amid various interruptions.'

This work of course met with much opposition, but
none of the works written against it deserve notice, except,
perhaps, a pamphlet addressed to Lady Huntingdon,[1] and
that only on account of the personal relationship between
Law and the good Countess. ' It can be no pleasure,'
writes the author, ' to your Ladyship to find the admired
Mr. Law an opponent of the Methodists.' This anonymous
gentleman—who calls himself ' a hearer of the Apostles,' and
' a Member of the New Testament Church, which yet enjoys
the apostles as their instructors in the Gospels, Sermons,
and Epistles, because they admit no successors to supply
their place '—would of course object to Law's churchmanship generally, and to his belief in the apostolical succession in particular, quite as much as to his anti-Calvinism.
He therefore writes very violently against him.[2] But it is
interesting to observe that he is obliged to pay an involun-
tary tribute to Law's high repute as a pious Christian ; he

---

[1] *The Doctrine of our Lord and his Apostles cleared from the false glosses
and misrepresentations of the Rev. William Law in his Dialogue between a
Methodist and a Churchman, addressed to the Countess-Dowager of Huntingdon
by a Hearer of the Apostles*, 1761.

[2] E.g. ' Mr. Law's mind and conscience are defiled and stand in need of
that circumcision which is by the spirit and truth of the Gospel.' ' Mr.
Law's corrupt and abominable language.' ' What but the evil treasure of Mr.
Law's heart could bring forth this evil thing ?' ' Mr. Law gives a very heathenish
account of faith in Christ's blood.'

does so by warning the Countess that 'Our Lord, speaking to men as seemingly devout, pious, and zealous of what they call good works as Mr. Law, and who had much the same expectation from their personal goodness as Mr. Law, calls them a generation of vipers.' What the good Countess—a Calvinist of the Calvinists—thought of this performance of her correspondent at King's Cliffe, we do not know.

To some it may appear strange to find the Methodists ranked among the opponents of Law. For were they not, it may be asked, his spiritual children? Did not Bishop Warburton declare that William Law begot Methodism? Did not Dr. Trapp prophesy, when the 'Serious Call' appeared, that 'harm would come of the book, and so it happened, for shortly afterwards up sprang the Methodists'?

No doubt, in the sense in which Warburton and Trapp used the term, Law was a Methodist of the Methodists. If we understand Methodism according to the literal meaning of the word, and, indeed, according to its original application to the Wesleys, that is, as a living strictly according to rule or method, then Law's Methodism is undeniable. Or, if we look upon Methodism as a sort of revival of Puritanism, in its rigorous condemnation of all worldly amusements and in its proscription of all studies which did not directly tend to religious edification, then, again, Law was undoubtedly a Methodist. Or, once more, if we regard Methodism as a species of what was branded in the eighteenth century as 'enthusiasm,' or, as a revival of the belief in the direct and continual acting of the Spirit of God upon the spirit of man, in contradistinction to such views as of those of Lavington and Warburton, and, a little earlier, of South, on the nature of the Holy Spirit's influence, again Law was assuredly a Methodist.[1]

[1] But also as assuredly a Churchman. He could point out, as he did in his reply to Bishop Warburton, that the church puts into the mouth of her

But, in spite of these points of agreement, it is quite clear that Law did not, in any period of his career, sympathise with the peculiar sentiments of any section of the (so-called) Methodists, Calvinist or Arminian, Wesleyan or Evangelical. In modern language there was always much of the High Churchman about him, and not a little of the Broad Churchman, but nothing at all of the Low Churchman. [1]

Those clergymen, therefore, who disapproved of Methodism, but admired Law's writings, were perfectly justified in claiming the author as on their side ; though it is rather amusing to observe the curious way in which they sometimes refer to the charge of Methodism, as if it were something which must not be mentioned to ears polite. Thus a clergyman writing from Scarborough in 1772, who signs himself 'Ouranius,' says of Law :—'This worthy clergyman has been accused (by those lukewarm Christians who ridicule all degrees of piety that are above the common standard), of * * * * * * ; a charge which is utterly false. I say not this as my own private opinion, but from the testimony of several gentlemen of undoubted credit, who are acquainted with his manner of life and conversation. Indeed, this is sufficiently demonstrated in many parts of this

---

ministers over and over again expressions quite as strong on the immediate influence of the Spirit on the Christian's soul, as any he himself used : e.g., 'Almighty God unto whom all hearts be open . . . cleanse the thoughts of our hearts by *the inspiration of Thy Holy Spirit*,' &c. In fact, as Wesley, I think, said, 'The clergy often contradicted in the pulpit what they said in the desk when they preached against the direct influence of the Holy Spirit on the soul as enthusiasm.'

[1] Mr. Lecky accurately describes Law's position : 'His opinions were of a High Church type, much tinctured with asceticism, and latterly with mysticism' (*England in the Eighteenth Century*, i. 548). So does Mr. Gladstone when he says, 'Law's successors were Hook and Keble' (*British Quarterly Review*, July 1879). Law defined his own position in his reply to Dr. Trapp : 'Doctrines of religion I have none, but what the Scriptures and the first-rate Saints of the Church are my vouchers for.' This, be it remembered, was written long after he became a mystic.

author's works . . . , all which evidently declare the reverend author to be an orthodox divine, and an indefatigable labourer in the Lord's vineyard.'

The six mysterious stars do not stand, as the uniniated might suppose they do, for 'murder,' or any unmentionable crime, but simply for 'Methodism.' And they were quite understood by the initiated ; for a month or two later, we find another clergyman, who signs himself 'Theophilus,' writing in reply to 'Ouranius' :—'The charge of * * * * * * I never heard insinuated against him, and could proceed only from those who must be unacquainted with any among the writings of our able defender of Church discipline and authority, and especially of the last, except one, 'On Justification by Faith and Works.' [1]

Similarly, the Methodists and Evangelicals are quite correct in disclaiming William Law as their spiritual father. It is true that most of the leaders of both sections of the Evangelical movement were stimulated in their Christian ardour by the 'Christian Perfection,' or the 'Serious Call,' or both ; but then the same may be said of many others who were neither Methodists nor Evangelicals. Of the great revival of religion which took place in the middle of the eighteenth century Law was unquestionably one of the earliest and most important instruments ; but with the particular form or forms which it subsequently took he had literally no connection whatever. On the contrary, he expressly avowed his disagreement with the mode of stating those two great doctrines, the New Birth and Assurance, which, under the preachings of the Wesleys and Whitefield produced such marvellous effects.[2] Still less did he agree with the distinctive tenets of the Calvin-

---

[1] The letters both of 'Ouranius' and 'Theophilus' appeared in *Lloyd's Evening Post.* They are also quoted in a biographical sketch of Law prefixed to the 20th edition of the *Serious Call*, 1816.

[2] See Law's treatise on *the Grounds and Reasons of Christian Regeneration, or the New Birth*, 'Works,' v. (2), 76.

istic section of the Evangelical movement. We have, therefore, the best of reasons for placing these good men among Law's opponents ; as we shall see when we consider what some of their chief leaders wrote and said about him.

Let us take first Law's rather distant neighbour, Mr. James Hervey, of Weston Favel. It is somewhat curious that the two most popular authors of devotional books in the eighteenth century should have both belonged to the same county. It has been said with perfect truth that Hervey's ' Meditations ' and ' Theron and Aspasio ' to some extent superseded the ' Christian Perfection ' and ' Serious Call ' as popular reading among the pious.[1] If we regard the compositions simply from an intellectual point of view, the charge does not say much for the taste of our great-grandfathers. For the two authors stand respectively almost at the zenith and the nadir of literary merit. In regard of strength of reasoning, depth and beauty of thought, purity and elegance of style, the earlier works are so immeasurably superior, that they hardly even admit of comparison with the later. But it is obvious that works of this class must not be judged merely by an intellectual standard. Of course, one can quite understand a man of strong mind like Dr. Johnson being profoundly impressed by Law, and contemptuously parodying Hervey's admired performance, in his ' Meditations upon a Pudding.' But then the majority of mankind are not strong-minded ; and the preference given to Hervey over Law may be admitted without implying any reflection upon the taste of the latter half of the eighteenth century above other periods. Some very popular works of our own day show that we too like vapid declamation, fine writing, and ' sesquipedalia verba.' This sort of thing Law certainly did not give his readers, and

---

[1] In the *Christian Observer* for February 1877, a ' The Writings of William Law.'

Hervey did. Law supplied, perhaps, too strong food
for the popular taste of any generation. But this is
not all. Law, in his practical treatises, was very stern ;
he made the task of living the Christian life almost a
hopeless task for ordinary humanity. There is too little
of 'the Gospel,' the good news of God, in the 'Serious
Call.' Hervey was more tender, more sympathetic—in
the truest sense of the word, more 'Evangelical'—than
his predecessor. And then, again, Hervey's works came
into notice on the wave of a great popular movement :
Law stood alone, or rather ran counter to every popular
sentiment. A comparison between the two Northamptonshire worthies naturally suggested itself, and, accordingly,
our old friend Byrom drew such a comparison *more suo* in
rhyme :—

> Two diff'rent painters, artists in their way,
> Have drawn religion in her full display ;
> To both she sat, one gazed at her all o'er ;
> The other fix'd upon her features more ;
> Hervey has figur'd her with every grace
> That dress could give ; but Law has hit her face !

This is not very valuable as a literary criticism, in fact
it is not very easy to attach any definite meaning to it at
all ; but it seemed worth quoting, as showing that Law
and Hervey presented themselves as natural objects of
contrast to a contemporary.

The gentle Hervey could not be a virulent opponent
of any one, least of all of one whose genuine piety he
respected, though he deplored his errors ; but, in a mild
sort of way, he was a very decided opponent of Law.
Such opposition was rather injudiciously forced upon him.
Law's humble friend, John Spanaugle, desired Mr. Hervey
to read 'his neighbour's writings '—a piece of advice about
as likely to be acceptable as if a friend were to recommend
to Mr. Spurgeon the Pope's last Pastoral as agreeable and

profitable reading. Hervey, of course, replied, 'I am so
far from admiring my neighbour's writings (Mr. Law's, I
suppose you mean) that I think it my duty to disclaim his
notions.' And he *did* disclaim them in ' Theron and Aspasio.' The latter part of the Second Dialogue in that
once popular work has especial reference to Law, and the
' Ouranius,' whose opinions are confuted in the middle of
the Seventh Dialogue, is Mr. Law himself. But, though
Hervey felt bound to express his very strong disagreement
with the mystic and anti-Calvinistic sentiments of Mr. Law,
whom he terms 'a most remarkable legalist,' he still pays
a generous tribute to the 'eminent devotion ' of the man.
Weston Favel was too near King's Cliffe for the vicar of
the former place not to have known the saintly character
of the devotee at the latter.

In fact, Hervey laid too much stress upon Law's piety
to suit some of his Evangelical friends. ' You see,' writes
the anonymous author of a tract entitled ' A Full and
Compleat Answer to the Capital Errors contained in the
Writings of Rev. W. Law, in a Letter to a Friend '—' You
see how genteelly my late friend, Mr. Hervey, has treated
Mr. Law. I'll allow with him that "Ouranius" may be
eminently devout, and so may a Mahometan Dervise, or
an Indian Brachman.' But, though he allows Mr. Law's
devoutness (in the grudging fashion quoted above), he can
by no means allow his Christian humility. ' Mr. Law
delivers his own sayings as oracles. This is the humble
Mr. Law!' Here there is some truth in the premisses, if
not in the implied conclusion. Law certainly writes as he
spoke, like one who was not accustomed to be contradicted ;
and one can quite understand a reader, who did not know
what the man really was, supposing that meekness was not
his strong point. But another argument which the writer
uses, tending to the same conclusion, seems to me to be

utterly fallacious. After quoting Law's sentiments on the
Divine Birth within—sentiments with which the reader, it
is hoped, is now thoroughly familiar—he adds : ' Mr. Law
may be a man of an humble deportment, but this does not
look like an humble opinion.' Now just as a general confession of human depravity is, as we all know, quite consistent with personal pride, so a general belief in the dignity
of human nature, or rather, in the God within, is quite
consistent with personal humility. On the whole, Law's
personal character evidently does not appear to this
writer in an amiable light, and its darker shades were, he
thinks, deepened by his mysticism. ' It had been good for
Mr. Law if he had not looked into the writings of this
people [the Quietists]. He has a gloomy turn of mind, and
they have proved too hard for him.'

I have dwelt the longer on this not very important
pamphlet because the anonymous author was probably a
man of eminence in the Evangelical world. The author
of the Preface to it certainly was ;[1] viz., the Rev. Martin
Madan, favourably known as a hymn-writer and preacher,
not so favourably as a defender of polygamy on Old Testament principles. Mr. Madan was a decided opponent of
Law's later views. ' Mr. Law's writings,' he says, in this
Preface, ' are full of the grossest absurdities and most dangerous errors, yet cordially received and held almost sacred
by many.' At the same time Mr. Madan, like most of
Law's opponents, had a profound admiration for Law's
talents. ' It must be confessed,' he says, ' that Mr. Law
had a masterly pen, and there are some strokes in his per-
formances that are exceeded by no writer I ever met with.'

---

[1] I have a shrewd suspicion that the avowed author of the preface and the
anonymous author of the pamphlet were one and the same person, viz., Mr.
Madan. This mild sort of pious fraud was not uncommon in the eighteenth
century. Thus ' Junius' and ' Philo-Junius,' who defends Junius, were obviously identical.

But there were more notable representatives of the Evangelical school than Mr. Madan who must be ranked among Law's opponents. There was the excellent Mr. Henry Venn, Vicar of Huddersfield, and author of the 'Complete Duty of Man.' Like so many earnest men in the eighteenth century, he had been deeply impressed with Law's practical treatises ; and when the 'Spirit of Prayer' was in the press, 'no miser,' wrote Venn's biographer, 'waiting for the account of a rich inheritance devolving on him, was ever more eager than Venn was to receive a book from which he expected to derive so much knowledge and improvement. The publisher was importuned to forward it to him without delay ; but when it came, his disappointment was as bitter as his expectation had been eager.' Of course, Law's views on many subjects, but especially on that of the Atonement, would be utterly at variance with Mr. Venn's. Bishop Ewing thinks that 'he either failed to appreciate, or else he misunderstood Law's, that is, in other words, the Pauline, doctrine of reconciliation.'[1] But I cannot agree with this. Venn knew perfectly well what *he* meant ; and he also knew perfectly well that Law not only did not agree with him, but strongly and directly repudiated the theory of the Atonement held by the Evangelical school.

John Newton, too, must be counted among the opponents of W. Law, but an opponent of the most gentle and courteous kind. In the 'Sequel to the Cardiphonia,'— (happily chosen title ! for if ever words were the utterance of the heart, they were the words of this much-misunderstood man)—all the fourteen letters addressed to 'the Rev. Dr. * * * *'[2] were more or less directed against the later views of Law, whom he frequently mentions by name. I

[1] *Present-Day Papers.*
[2] See Newton's *Works* (Cecil's edition), vol. vi. from p. 201 to p. 249.

am inclined to think that 'the Rev. Dr. * * * *' was Dr. Dixon, Principal of St. Edmund's Hall, Oxford, who was certainly a correspondent of Newton ; and Newton's reference in the first of these letters to 'your learning, your years, and your rank and character in the University' seems to tally with this supposition. Be this as it may, it is clear that the Doctor was deeply fascinated with Law's speculations, and that he was a man of learning and culture. Newton evidently felt that, in dealing both with his correspondent and with Law, he was dealing with men of no ordinary stamp ; every sentence that he wrote breathes the spirit of true Christian modesty, no less than of firm, Christian conviction. 'In every other point,' he writes, 'I hesitate and demur (and it becomes me to do so), when I differ from persons of learning and years superior to my own. But I think that the views which constrain me to differ from Mr. Law and many other respectable names, would embolden me to contradict even an angel from Heaven, &c.' Newton's differences from Law are manifold. Among other things he of course strongly disapproved of Law's doctrine of the 'inner light ;' but his mode of expressing his disagreement is touchingly humble. 'Every one,' he writes, 'must speak for themselves : and for my own part, I cannot ascribe my present hopes to my having cherished and improved an inward something within me, which Mr. Law speaks of ; but, on the contrary, I know I have often resisted the motions and warnings of God's Spirit ; and, if He had not saved me with a high hand, and in defiance of myself, I must have been lost.' But it is needless to specify particular points. The whole of Law's system was at variance with his own, and so he tells his correspondent, decidedly, repeatedly, but very modestly, and recognising fully the fascinations which Law possessed. 'Though the scheme of the Quakers, as set forth with some supposed improvements by Mr. Law, is in your view very amiable, to me it appears much otherwise;' and then he gives his reasons, and is careful to add, 'I allow, in some respects and upon a superficial view, Mr. Law's scheme may appear more agreeable to what we call reason and the fitness of things than St. Paul's. But this to me is an argument against it, rather than for it.' Then, having explained what he means, he sums up with a touch of that quaint humour which constitutes one of his many charms: 'I would no more venture my soul upon the scheme which you commend, than I would venture my body for a voyage to the East Indies in a London wherry.'

Newton's arguments do not seem to have convinced the doctor, who, on the contrary, appears to have desired the good man to reconsider his opinion about Law; for in the next letter we find Newton declaring, 'I cannot retract the judgment I passed upon Mr. Law's scheme,' and then he expresses a wish that 'we could all be freed from an undue attachment to great names and favourite authors.' This reference to 'great names, &c.,' is very characteristic of the way in which Law was often referred to; as if he exercised a mysterious influence, or cast a spell upon his disciples against which they ought to struggle. From the last letter of the series it seems that Newton had himself been once under the charm; he had sent the 'Olney Hymns,' just published, as a sort of olive-branch to the doctor; they had been favourably received; and this is the bright, kindly way in which he concludes the little controversy:—'Methinks my late publication comes in good time to terminate our friendly debate. As you approve of the hymns, which, taken altogether, contain a full declaration of my religious sentiments, it should seem we are nearly of a mind. If we agree in rhyme, our apparent differences in prose must, I think, be merely verbal, and cannot be very important. And, as to Mr. Law, if you can read his books to your edification and comfort (which I own, with respect to some important points in his scheme, I cannot), why should I wish to tear them from you? I have formerly been a great admirer of Mr. Law myself, and still think that he is a first-rate genius, and that there are many striking passages in his writings deserving attention and admiration.'

It would be easy to multiply instances of the opposition which Law's later writings met with, especially among the Methodists and Evangelicals.[1] But this is quite unnecessary, especially as Law did not consider pious Christians who differed from him on the subject of mysticism as his opponents at all. It should never be forgotten that Law regarded Behmenism simply as of the ' *bene* esse,' not as of the 'esse' of Christianity. This is clearly implied in all his mystic works, and is distinctly stated, and indeed largely dwelt upon in one of them.[2] It was said of others

---

[1] Among others may be mentioned good Mr. Adam, of Wintringham, author of the once popular devotional book, ' Private Thoughts.' His biographer tells us that ' he received his first impressions of a serious kind from the writings of the mystics, particularly from the works of Mr. Law ; ' but ' while he continued a disciple of Mr. Law, though growing in a conviction of his sinfulness and becoming more strict and serious, yet still he could gain no solid peace of conscience.' That peace he found under the teaching of the evangelicals; and when the ' Spirit of Prayer ' was published, he expressed his disapproval of it. See Life of the Author, by J. Stillingfleet, of Hotham, prefixed to *Private Thoughts.*

[2] *The Way to Divine Knowledge.* ' Theophilus ' (i.e. Law) points out the dangers of making a wrong use of Behmen's works. Upon this ' Academicus ' asks whether it would not have been better if these deep matters had not been communicated to the world, since it was so natural to man to make a wrong use of them? ' Theophilus,' after showing that the same question might be asked with regard to the Scriptures, proceeds, ' If I knew of any person, who stood in the faith and simplicity of the first Christians, &c., to such an one I could freely say, this mystery was needless. And this may pass for a good reason why this mystery was not opened by God in the first ages of the Church ; since there was then no occasion for it.' After much more to the

besides Warburton, that they postponed their attacks upon
Law until after his death, and then came forth with impunity to kick the dead lion ; I doubt whether the insinua-
tion is true, but if it be, the precaution was quite unnecessary ; had they known it, they might with equal impunity
have attacked the living lion ; for, do what they would, he
was not to be provoked.

It would be difficult to find a word in any of Law's
works which could be construed into a retort upon those
who assailed him simply on the score of his Behmenism ; in
fact, he hardly ever refers to such writers.   There is indeed
one short passage in one of his private letters, which was
never intended for publication, though he afterwards
allowed it to be published, which indicates that he had not
a very high opinion of his neighbour's literary work at
Weston Favel :—' You tell me, my friend,' he writes, ' that
the seraphic Aspasio is quite transported with the thought
of the imputation of Christ's righteousness to the sinner,
&c.   It may be so.   Transport seems to be as natural to
Aspasio as flying is to a bird.   My friend, let any old
woman preach to you rather than these doctors.'

With this exception, and it is hardly an exception, I
know of no passage in any one of Law's works, which shows
that he regarded his opponents *as* opponents simply because they disagreed with his peculiar views about Behmen
and the mystics.

The assailants of revealed religion, including Deists,
Arians, Socinians, and Free-thinkers generally, were Law's
real adversaries.   Against these he *does* wage internecine
war.   There is scarcely one of his works in which he does
not hit them severely ; they are the only writers in whose

same effect, he adds, ' Let not the genuine, plain, simple Christian, who is
happy and blessed in the simplicity of Gospel-faith, take offence at this mystery,
because he has no need of it.'

case he transcends the bounds of that measured language which has been so justly praised in his general method of conducting controversy. But even in the case of these, his arch-foes, it is always the writings, not the writers, that he attacks. It was no empty boast, but simple truth, when he said :—' I neither have, nor (by the grace of God) ever will have any personal contention with any man whatever,'[1] and of these special adversaries in particular, ' The deists and unbelievers have a great share of my compassionate affections, and I never can think or write of the infinite blessings of the Christian redemption, without feeling in my heart an impatient longing to see them the happy partakers of them.' Hatred of the opinions, but love for the men, or rather hatred of their opinions *because* of his love for the men, is conspicuous in all the hard things he wrote against unbelief in its various forms.

And among these various forms he included all who did not accept the divinity of Christ in its fullest sense. ' A true and full confession of the Holy Trinity in Unity ' was an essential part of his Christianity, though Behmenism was not. ' Let,' he says, ' Arians, semi-Arians, and Socinians, who puzzle their brains to make paper images of a Trinity for themselves, have nothing from you but your pity and your prayers ; ' but he could not have added, let them be regarded by you as Christians.

These, then, were Law's real opponents. Let us take one out of many specimens of the way in which he deals with their sentiments.

The following passage cannot be appreciated in its full significance, unless it be remembered that it was written in the memorable year 1750 ; that year in which all England was thrown into consternation by the shock of an earthquake which was to be the precursor of another earthquake

<hr />

[1] *Some Animadversions upon Dr. Trap's Reply,* ' Works,' vi. (2), 216.

that was to swallow up London. Then it was that Law's friend, Bishop Sherlock, issued a pastoral on the subject, of which not less than 100,000 copies are said to have been sold ; then it was that Romaine sounded his famous ' Alarm to a Careless World,' that Charles Wesley ' preached for hours almost without intermission,' that Whitefield, in the blackness of that very night in which the doomed city was to fall, ' took his stand in the middle of Hyde Park, preaching to a dense mass of awestruck and affrighted hearers upon the judgments of the Lord.' [1] But I doubt whether any—prelate or field-preacher—poured forth a more splendid burst of eloquence than Law did, when he took occasion from the panic [2] to warn his country-men against the spread of impiety and unbelief which he appears to attribute mainly to the writings of those whom I have ventured to call his only real opponents.

' O Britain, Britain,' he exclaims, ' think that the Son of God saith unto thee, as he said to Jerusalem, " O Jeru-salem, Jerusalem, how often would I have gathered thy children, as a hen gathereth her chickens under her wings, and ye would not ! Behold, your house is left unto you desolate." And now let me say, What aileth thee, O British earth, that thou quakest, and the foundations of thy churches that they totter ? Just that same aileth thee as ailed Judah's earth, when the Divine Saviour of the world, dying on the Cross, was reviled, scorned, and mocked, by the inhabitants of Jerusalem ; then the earth

---

[1] See Lecky's *History of England in the Eighteenth Century*, vol. ii. ch. ix. p. 596.

[2] Law makes no direct allusion to the panic, nor has it, so far as I am aware, ever been remarked that the passage quoted was written with reference to the earthquake, but I think, when read in the light of history, the allusion will be obvious to the reader. It reminds one of the references to the terrible tempest which swept over England in 1703, in Addison's ' Campaign,' which Lord Macaulay was, I believe, the first to point out —

Such as of late o'er pale Britannia passed, &c.

quaked, the rocks rent, and the sun refused to give its light.
Nature again declares for God ; the earth and the elements
can no longer bear our sins ; Jerusalem's doom for Jerusalem's sin may well be feared by us. O ye miserable pens
dipt in Satan's ink, that dare to publish the folly of believing in Jesus Christ, where will you hide your guilty heads,
when Nature dissolved shall show you the Rainbow, on
which the crucified Saviour shall sit in judgment, and
every work receive its reward ?   O tremble ! ye apostate
sons that come out of the schools of Christ to fight Lucifer's battles, and do that for him which neither he nor his
legions can do for themselves.[1]   Their inward pride, spite,
wrath, malice, and rage against God and Christ, and human
nature, have no pens but yours, no apostles but you. They
must be found to work in the dark, to steal privately into
impure hearts, could they not beguile you into a fond
belief that you are Lovers of Truth, Friends of Reason,
Detectors of Fraud, Great Geniuses, and Moral Philosophers,[2] merely and solely because you blaspheme Christ
and the Gospel of God.   Poor deluded souls, rescued from
Hell by the Blood of Christ, called by God to possess the
thrones of fallen Angels, permitted to live only by the
mercy of God, that ye may be born again from above, my

---

[1] This may be, in part, an allusion to those of the clergy who verged on
Arianism or Socinianism, systems which Law considered as hostile to Christianity as Deism itself.   It must, however, be remembered that the Deists
themselves still professed to be Christians, and so might be said to ' come out
of the schools of Christ.'   Tindal, Chubb, Collins, &c., all called themselves
' Christian Deists,' and even Lord Bolingbroke, the most virulent of all, drew
a marked distinction between what he calls ' the religion of the schools,' and
' true Christianity as it came from its founder,' of which latter he professes to
be a devoted advocate, though it would be difficult to name a single distinctive doctrine of Christianity which he does not ridicule or attack.   Even
Gibbon veils his attack on Christianity under the most painfully elaborate expressions of regard for it.

[2] All who are acquainted with the Deistical literature will recognise in
these expressions, phrases of constant occurrence in the Deists' writings ; they
show that Law was well acquainted with his opponents' works ; the *Moral
Philosopher* was the title of one of the latest, that of Dr. Morgan.

heart bleeds for you. Think, I beseech you, in time, what mercies ye are trampling under your feet. Say not that reason and your intellectual faculties stand in your way ; that these are the best gifts that God has given you, and that these suffer you not to come to Christ. For all this is as vain a pretence, and as gross a mistake, as if ye were to say that you had nothing but your feet to carry you to Heaven.'[1]

The advocates of natural, as opposed to revealed religion, disgusted Law all the more, because their system appeared to him to be a sort of hideous parody of some of his own most cherished sentiments. The doctrine of an universal Saviour was a cardinal point of his scheme. As he expressed it, ' Heathens, Jews, and Christians differ not thus, that the one have a Saviour, and are in a redeemed state, and the other are not ; or that the one have *one* Saviour, and the other have *another* ; for the one Judge of all is the one Saviour of all. But they only differ in this, that one and the same Saviour is *differently* made known to them, and differently to be obtained by them. The heathens knew Him not as He was in the numerous types of the Jewish law ; they knew Him not as He is gloriously manifested in the Gospel ; but they knew Him as He was the God of their hearts, manifesting himself by a light of the mind, by instincts of goodness, by a sensibility of guilt, by awakenings and warnings of conscience. And this was their *Gospel*, which they received as truly and really in, and by, and through Jesus Christ, as the Law and Gospel were received through Him. Therefore it is a great and glorious truth, enough to turn every voice into a trumpet, and make heaven and earth ring with praises and hallelujahs to God, that Jesus Christ is the Saviour of all the world, and of

---

[1] From the *Spirit of Prayer*, 'Works,' vii. (2), 160 2.

every man, of every nation, kindred, and language.' And
then he quotes, very appositely, and with evident rapture,
Rev. v. 9 and vii. 9, 10.

But then, was not this the very thing that the friends
of natural religion were contending for ? Was not this the
very 'Christianity as old as the Creation' of their ablest
exponent ? Law anticipates the question, and answers it
fully. 'I must,' he writes, 'before I proceed further, put in
here a word of caution. If you are touched with modern
infidelity, having your reason set upon the watch to guard
you against the Gospel, it may here do its office, and will
perhaps tell you that what I have here said in favour of
the general light, or seed of life, that is in all men, is much
the same thing that you say in defence of natural reason,
or religion, only with this difference, that I mention it as
coming from Christ, and you consider it as the bare light
of nature. . . . To prevent all misapprehension, I now
declare to you, and will show you in the most explicit
manner, that that which I call the light of men, or the
seed of life sown into all men by Jesus Christ, is as wholly
different from that which you call *natural reason* as light
is different from darkness ; and that they stand in that
same state of contrariety to each other, both as to their
original, their nature, and qualities, as our Saviour and
Pontius Pilate did. I must therefore asssure you that,
as I fear God, and wish your salvation, so I can no more
say a word in favour of what is now called the religion of
natural reason than I would recommend to you the ancient
idolatry of heathens.'[1]

Law is as good as his word, and *does* show the distinction 'in the most explicit manner' ; but, unfortunately, he
takes sixty pages to do so. It is, of course, impossible to
transcribe them ; and as Law is, as has been said, the

----

[1] See *Works*, v. 185.

most consecutive of writers, it is equally impossible to condense his arguments without doing him grievous injustice. It must, therefore, suffice to add that Law shows unanswerably his perfect consistency in adhering to his literal interpretation of his favourite text on 'the Light which lighteth every one that cometh into the world,' and yet warning his reader to 'cast away this religion of nature from him with more earnestness than he would cast burning coals out of his bosom'; 'for,' he adds, 'could it only destroy your body, I should have been less earnest in giving you notice of it.'

Considering Law's reluctance to take up any personal quarrel, we have perhaps lingered too long on the subject of this chapter. But, whether he would or no, Law's opponents occupied too conspicuous a place in relation to his biography to allow his biographer to ignore them ; and even yet there is more to be said on the subject, as the next chapter will show.

CHAPTER XXII.

LAW ON SYSTEMS KINDRED TO MYSTICISM.

WE have seen that there were several systems which hung, as it were, on the outskirts of mysticism. With these, Law's position necessarily brought him into contact ; and his relation to them must now be briefly noticed.

From the wild extravagances which characterised some of these semi-mystic schemes, Law was saved not merely by his strong sense and clear judgment, but still more by his firm adherence to the creeds of the Church. He might be a ' rank enthusiast ' ; but the rankest enthusiasm cannot go far beyond the bounds of sound spirituality so long as it is chastened and corrected by the well-weighed and deliberate judgments of the Church Catholic, as expressed in the symbols of her faith. Those who depreciate the value of creeds would do well to ponder on the contrast between the enthusiasts who let their fancy run riot, scorning to be bound by such trammels, and the enthusiast whose speculations, wild and dreamy as they sometimes were, were always held in check by his regard for the utterances of the Church. This contrast will, it is hoped, be brought out in strong colours in the following brief sketch.

1. *The Philadelphians.*

In the year 1697 a short-lived society was formed under the name of the ' Philadelphian Society,' the object of which was 'to cultivate spiritual and practical piety founded on the study of Jacob Behmen.' Its leading spirits were Mrs. Joanna Lead, who was the intimate friend of Dr. Pordage, a nonjuring clergyman, and afterwards a physician, the learned and excellent Francis Lee, who married Mrs. Lead's daughter, Lot Fisher, also a physician, and Thomas Bromley, also a physician, the author of the 'Sabbath of Rest.' The society, however, was not content with Behmenism pure and simple, but regarded Mrs. Lead as an inspired prophetess, and accepted her visions almost as articles of faith. The society was broken up long before Law became a mystic, having 'completed its public testimony,' and consequently dissolved itself, in 1703./ But, as a Behmenist, Law was naturally led to give his opinion about these earlier admirers of the illuminated Jacob. When accused of 'reading Jacob Behmen, Dr. Pordage, and Mrs. Lead, with almost the same veneration and implicit faith that other people read the Scripture,' he replied, ' Two of these writers I know very little of, yet as much as I desire to know.'[1] And from a private letter we find, what, indeed, we might have anticipated from the general tone of Law's writings, the reason why he desired to know no more of Dr. Pordage and Mrs. Lead. ' In the beginning,' he writes, ' of this century, a number of persons, many of them of great piety, formed themselves into a kind of society, by the name of Philadelphians. They were great readers, and well versed in the language of Jacob Behmen, and used to make eloquent discourses of the mystery in their meetings. Their only thirst was after *visions, openings*, and *revelations*. And yet nowhere could they see their distemper so fully described, the causes it proceeded

---

[1] See *Works*, vi. (2), 313.

from, and the fatal consequences of it, as by J. B.'[1] On another occasion he stigmatised Mrs. Lead as a 'seeker of visions,' a character of which, the reader need hardly be told, Law highly disapproved.

But though Law had little sympathy with the Philadelphians generally, and the visions of their prophetess in particular, he was deeply interested in the writings of Francis Lee, who was really a man of learning and culture, as well as of piety. Lee was a fellow of St. John's, Oxford ; but, like Law, lost his fellowship on account of his conscientious adherence to the Stuart dynasty. He then became a physician, and, like so many others who practised physic, was imbued with mystical notions. The affinity between mysticism and the medical profession probably arose from the deep, spiritual view of nature which the mystics took. There certainly was no class of minds to which mystic schemes were so attractive as those which studied the human body. Lee thus belonged to the first generation of nonjurors, as Law belonged to the second ; but, unlike Law, he was not isolated when he declined to take the oaths. The earlier nonjurors hung closely together, as a small party naturally does ; and Lee became an intimate friend of Nelson, Dodwell, Hickes, and the other good men who suffered for conscience' sake.[2] It has been said that Lee reversed the process which Law went through, having first been a mystic and then a High Churchman, whereas Law's progress was *vice versâ*. But this is not quite accurate ; at any rate, the statement requires very large modification.

---

[1] 'The Philadelphian Society,' writes Dr. Blunt, 'contributed largely to the spread of that mystical piety which is so conspicuous in the works of the good and learned William Law, and which affected in no small degree the early stages of Methodism.'—*Dictionary of Sects, Heresies, Ecclesiastical Parties, and Schools of Religious Thought*, by J. H. Blunt.

[2] See Mr. Abbey's chapter on Robert Nelson and his friends in *The English Church in the Eighteenth Century*.

For, in the first place, a wide distinction must be drawn between the so-called mysticism of Lee and that of Law. Both were mystics, and something more—Law as a Behmenist, Lee as a Philadelphian—but the apologist for Mrs. Lead's visions diverged far more widely from mysticism proper than Law ever did. Again, it is not quite correct to say that Law changed from High Churchism to mysticism. His mysticism very largely modified his Churchmanship; but that was all. When he became a mystic he did not cease to be a Churchman, nor even a High Churchman, if it is necessary to use that epithet to distinguish his Churchmanship from that of Hoadly and Warburton, on the one side, or of Hervey and Berridge on the other. And, once more, Lee did not cease to be a mystic when he ceased to be a Philadelphian, while he could hardly have been other than a High Churchman *before* he became a mystic ; for there is a correspondence—interesting, but of portentous length—between him and Dodwell which clearly implies as much. To no other than a High Churchman would the uncompromising Dodwell have written as he did in his first letter to Lee :—

'Shottisbrook : Oct. 12, 1697.'[1]

'Worthy Sir,—I was at once both troubled and surprised to hear that so good and so accomplished a person as you are should be engaged in a new division from that Church for whose principles you had so generously suffered ; and I hope you will excuse me if the love of our late common excellent cause, as well as of a common brother and common assertor of it, encourage me to hope that so new a change has not altogether alienated you from hearing an affectionate expostulation concerning it. . . . You, who

---

[1] Shottisbrook was the residence of the excellent Francis Cherry, a country gentleman who kept open house for the ejected nonjurors.

know what it is to reason accurately, I hope, will not venture your soul on luscious fancies, or warm, unaccountable affections, which would be more excusable in a person of meaner education.' [After having argued at great length against Mrs. Lead's pretensions, the writer concludes] 'Return to your deserted brethren, and contribute not to the further divisions and ruin of that small number to which we are reduced, that I may again be able to justify, by principles, the subscribing myself,

'Your most affectionate brother,

'HENRY DODWELL.'

In course of time, Lee *did* return to his deserted brethren, and wrote strongly against that very enthusiasm which led him to uphold his mother-in-law's claims.[1]   In fact, his Philadelphianism was simply an episode in the middle of his mental career, the beginning and ending of which was simply that of a good Churchman tinged with a strong flavour of mysticism.[2]

Law was evidently much interested in the numerous works which Lee wrote.   He borrowed from Lee's daughter many of her father's MSS., and took the trouble to copy several of them out with his own hand.   Lee's works were some of the very few books which were honoured with a constant place in his sanctum at King's Cliffe.   One would have thought that Lee's writings would have been too fanciful and too verbose for Law's taste ; for instance, besides his numerous expositions of, and apologies for, Mrs. Lead, one of his tracts is entitled, 'A Dialogue between Lazarus and his Sisters after his Return from the Dead' ; another

[1] See his *History of Montanism, passim.*

[2] See his edition of à Kempis' *Christian Exercise,* &c., published long after he had ceased to be a Philadelphian.   He also influenced his friend, Robert Nelson, who speaks of the mystical theology as 'the most perfect essence of the Christian religion,' &c.,—another proof of the attraction which mysticism possessed for High Churchmen.

is, 'On Naval Architecture, as Applied to Noah's Ark,
showing how it was Accommodated to Live in a Tempest
of Waters.' I must, however, frankly confess that I have
shrunk from the formidable task of mastering Lee's
voluminous and, in many places, obscure writings ; but
a cursory perusal of some of them has been sufficient to
show me that the author was a man of deep devotion, and
also of great learning and culture.[1] Indeed, one might
guess this from the mere fact that Lee was a favourite
writer with Law ; for, in spite of Law's incessant depreciation of learning, it is quite clear that no author was ever
a favourite with him unless he was a man of literary merit.
Piety was the first recommendation of a writer to Law.
He would probably have said and thought that this was
the only *sine quâ non* ; but, as a matter of fact, he never
cared about studying any writer who did not bear the
strong impress either of genius, like Behmen, or of culture,
like Lee ; and it may be added that he was a remarkably
good judge of what *did* bear the traces of genius or culture.
He never wrote a sentence that was feeble or vapid himself, and he could not tolerate feebleness or vapidness in
other writers.[2]

---

[1] See, *inter alia*, 'Ἀπολειπομένα or *Dissertations*, by Francis Lee, M.D.,
2 vols., 1751. In the memoir of the author prefixed to these volumes, the
anonymous writer (I imagine Lee's daughter, Mrs. De La Fontaine) says,
' As there has been some inquiry made after the exposition of the seven visions
of Esdras ; they, with all the papers that I entrusted the late Dr. Thos. Haywood with at the death of Dr. Lee, are in the hands of the Rev. Mr. William
Law, together with his life written by Dr. Haywood.' In another place,
' There is now a controversial piece against the " Sleep of the Soul," with
several others, most of which are imperfect, in the hands of the Rev. Mr.
William Law.' See also i. 145, *note*. For fuller information about Dr. Lee,
see Secretan's *Life of the pious Robert Nelson*, esp. pp. 270-3.

[2] The reader will perhaps think this a contradiction to what has been said
above about his admiration of Byrom's feeble poetry. But it was *only* Byrom's
versification that was feeble, not his sentiments. These were Law's own, and
his greatest enemies will hardly accuse them of feebleness, whatever their
faults may be.

2. The Cambridge Platonists.

Those who regard Plato as 'the Father of Mysticism,' 'the great Idealist,' and so forth, might naturally expect to find some references to him in the works of the English mystic. It might also have been expected that Law would have cited Plato as an illustrious instance of the truth that Christ is 'the Light which lighteth every man that cometh into the world,' inasmuch as the great philosopher is thought to have approached very nearly to some of the distinctive doctrines of Christianity. Similarly, it might have been supposed that Law would have found in the school of English Platonists—in one sense, a mystic school, beyond doubt [1]—spirits kindred to his own, and that their writings would have been frequently quoted by the mystic of the next generation. And all the more so, when that mystic was not only a Cambridge, but also an Emmanuel, man, for Emmanuel College may be looked upon as almost the cradle of Cambridge Platonism, three out of the four most prominent leaders of the little band having been trained in that college.

All such expectations, however, would be disappointed. I cannot remember one single passage in Law's works in which the name of Plato is mentioned. But so far from being surprised at the omission, it seems to me highly characteristic of the man. And for this reason : Law never said a truer word about himself than when he declared, ' I never wrote upon any subject till I could call it my own, till I was so fully possessed of the truth of it, that I could sufficiently prove it in my own way.' [2] It was part of the thoroughness, the reality, the intellectual honesty of the man to act thus. And it was, I believe, because he

---

[1] Kingsley, in his review of Vaughan's *Hours with the Mystics*, (*Miscellanies*, p. 356), says of the Platonists, 'in one sense all are mystics, and of a very lofty type.'   [2] *Works*, vi. (2), 319.

acted thus, that he scrupulously abstained from making
any mention of Plato. For those who are at all intimately
acquainted with Plato's writings know full well that it is a
dangerous thing to quote him in support of *any* doctrine.
You never know when you have the real Plato. His dialogues abound in splendid images and most suggestive
thoughts, but those who expect to find in them a complete
and coherent system of philosophy, still more of theology,
will certainly be disappointed.[1] It is easier to quote Plato
(especially at second-hand) than to understand him. And
as Wilkes said he was never a Wilkite, so assuredly might
Plato have said he never was a Platonist—in the later sense
of the word. No doubt it is quite easy to cite passages
from Plato which harmonise with the tenets both of idealists
and mystics, but then it is equally easy to cite passages
which are directly at variance with both. In short, we
must carefully distinguish between what Coleridge by a
neat alliteration calls ' Plotinism and Platonism.' For
with all due deference to Dr. Taylor, I must adhere to what
he calls ' the iniquitous opinion '[2] that the later Platonists

---

[1] *Ex uno disce omnes.* The doctrine of ideas is from one point of view
the pivot-doctrine of Platonism. It was the very point of divergence between
Plato and Aristotle. It is set forth with remarkable force and singular beauty
in the ' Timæus' and the ' Republic.' And yet turn to the ' Parmenides,' and
you will find the whole doctrine completely refuted ! In which is the real
Plato speaking?

[2] *The Commentaries of Proclus on the Timæus of Plato,* translated from
the Greek by Thos. Taylor. Introd. p. v. The silence of Law happily ab-
solves his biographer from the thorny task of discussing the connection of
Plato and the Alexandrian Platonists with Christian mysticism. Those
who desire to investigate the difficult subject may be referred to Jowett's
Plato, especially the ' Introduction to the Timæus,' vol. ii. p. 468, and the
Preface, vol. i. ; to Lewes' *History of Philosophy,* especially i. 197, 217, 222,
224, 261, and for the opposite view to Taylor, quoted above, and to Enfield's
abridgement of Brucker's *Historia Critica Philosophiæ,* especially i. 229-232.
See also Grote on Plato in his *History of Greece, passim,* and Hallam's
Literature of Europe, especially i. 146 and 195, ii. 4-13, and iii. 303 ;
Charles Kingsley's *Alexandria and her Schools, passim* ; Matter's *History of
the Schools of Alexandria.*

were not followers of Plato. Be this as it may, it is quite clear that Platonism, and neo-Platonism, and Christian Platonism, or Platonic Christianity, were all something very different from what Law meant by mysticism ; it is no wonder, therefore, that he rarely, if ever, refers to any of them.

For the same reason he naturally has very little to say about the Cambridge Platonists, who simply translated Plato into the language and ideas of the seventeenth century, and had much more affinity with the Platonism of Alexandria than with the Platonism of the Academy. But there were other causes which repelled Law from this school. The very names by which they were called are sufficient to show how thoroughly out of harmony they were with his sentiments. Anything would seem to him to come in a most questionable shape which came from men who could be called with any justice ' Latitudinarians,' ' Latitude men,' ' Gentlemen of a wide swallow,' and ' Rational Theologians '—terms which convey to the mind the very ideas to the confutation of which every one of Law's works more or less directly tended. It is curious to note how opposite Law's course was to the traditions of his college. Emmanuel was a Puritan foundation ; Law was a distinct High Churchman. Emmanuel was a home of the Rational Theologians ; nothing savouring of Rationalism found favour in Law's eyes.

The only one of the Cambridge Platonists who came into any sort of relation to Law was Dr. Henry More. We learn on the highest authority[1] that ' Mr. Law was

---

[1] I.e. the authority of Mr. Langcake, who, I have no doubt, wrote ' Some Account of the Life of Mr. William Law,' prefixed to an edition of the *Serious Call* of 1797, but copied, of course, from an earlier edition, because Mr. Langcake died before 1797. In this, as in many other cases, it will be observed that I have assumed the authorship of anonymous works. I have

particularly fond of reading the instructive life of the learned and pious Dr. Henry More.' And no wonder, for a beautiful and fascinating life it was. Scarcely twenty years had passed since More had died at Christ's—the college in which he had spent nearly half a century, reading, and writing, and meditating, and doing acts of charity— when Law went to reside at the neighbouring college of Emmanuel. Traditions of the pious and gentle recluse, about whose whole life there was an air of repose, poetry, unworldliness that contrasted strangely with the prosaic, common-sense and common-place life of the eighteenth century, must still have been lingering about Christ's and have reached its next-door neighbour, Emmanuel. It was just such a life as one could fancy Law living himself, and but for that unlucky Abjuration Oath, the thoughtful, recluse Fellow of Emmanuel might have been the counterpart of the thoughtful, recluse Fellow of Christ's a generation before. Not that Law and More were alike, except in their deep piety and their love of retirement and study. More was a softer man than Law, both in the complimentary and the uncomplimentary sense of the term ' softer.' There was more tenderness, and grace, and poetry in the elder, but infinitely more power in the younger man. But though the points of contrast between the two were even more marked than the points of resemblance, one can quite understand Law's thorough appreciation of the beauty of More's life and character.

But the life and character were one thing, the opinions quite another. Because Law was fascinated with the man,

never done so without absolute certitude, but then this certitude has been gained through a chain of evidence which would have to be cited in its entirety or not at all ; and this would have swelled the bulk of this volume with very tedious and uninteresting matter. At the risk, therefore, of being charged with making assertions on my own *ipse dixi*, I have ventured to spare the reader the premisses on which the conclusions have been founded.

that was no reason why he should have been fascinated with the opinions, and he has left us unequivocal proof that he was not. In answer to a correspondent who had asked his opinion about More, Law wrote : ' Many good things may be said of Dr. More, as a pious Christian, and of great abilities. But he was a Babylonian philosopher and divine, a bigot to the Cartesian system, knew nothing deeper than an hypothesis, nor truer of the nature of the soul than that which he has said of its pre-existence, which is little better than that foolish brat descended from it, the transmigration of souls. I know no other name for his "Divine Dialogues" than a jumble of learned rant, heathenish babble, and gibberish, dashed or heated here and there with flashes of piety. What you have seen of his severity against the light within (which is, in other words, *God within*), is sufficient to determine his character with you.' [1]

In this severe judgment Law shows plainly enough that he had read and thoroughly mastered his author,—he never *did* express a judgment about an author without having read and thoroughly mastered him. The points he mentions are just those points on which More was most at variance with Law. The ' Babylonian' philosophy and divinity of Descartes, Law condemned in one of his printed works.[2] The doctrine of the pre-existence of souls was one result of what More termed ' bringing back the Church to her old loving nurse, the Platonic philosophy.' It was a mystical doctrine in one sense, but utterly at variance with Law's mysticism. More's views on the ' Light Within ' may be gathered from one single sentence, the gist of which was constantly repeated in all his works : ' The Divine Logos cannot otherwise be said to lighten all men,

---

[1] See *Notes, &c., for an adequate biography of W. Law.*

[2] It should be added that in his later life More utterly changed his opinion about Cartesianism, and wrote his *Enchyridium Metaphysicum* expressly to refute it.

than so far as He may be said to have implanted the notions
of Good and Evil by creation,'[1] which Law would have
assuredly regarded as a most inadequate and erroneous
explanation of his favourite text. But of the 'Divine
Dialogues,' Law surely shows a strange want of appreciation. There is a humour and a certain weird fascination
about them which, one would have thought, every man of
taste would have recognised. But the fact is, Law's rugged
and essentially masculine nature revolted from the somewhat feminine delicacy of More. Let us take one example
out of many. In one of his dialogues More recounts a
vision he had of an old man who gave him a silver key
with a motto on it, 'Claude fenestras, ut luceat domus,' and
a golden key with the motto, 'Amor Dei Lux animæ,'
and then he was awoke by the braying of two asses, one
on each side of him. Now the interpretation of this
allegory would be quite in accordance with Law's views.
He, too, believed that you must 'shut the windows of the
soul that the house may be enlightened.' He, too, believed
that 'the love of God was the light of the soul.' He, too,
had had quite enough experience of the babble and folly of
the world to appreciate the humorous allusion to the
awakening by the braying of the two asses. But then he
would not like the way in which More sets forth these
truths. Whatever Law had to say he said in plain and
unmistakeable terms, not under the form of allegories and
visions. He had plenty of humour, but it was of a different
kind from More's ; it was racy rather than delicate. There
were many other points in which Law would disagree with
More, and still more with the other Cambridge Platonists,

---

[1] See More's *Philosophical Works*, i. 96 (Latin edition). Also i. 533,
where he calls Behmen 'haud ita contemnendus scriptor ;' and 537-540,
where he gives a catalogue of Behmen's errors. Also ii. 18, 25, 468, where he
praises and exalts human reason. All these passages and many others would
of course be an abomination in the eyes of Law.

but he says so little on the subject that it is unnecessary to specify these.[1]

3. *The Quakers.*

Nothing shows more strikingly the vagueness with which the term 'mystic' is used than the fact that it is applicable in a very real sense to people of such different views as William Law and the Quakers. It is hardly necessary to dwell upon the various points on which Law disagreed *in toto* from this so-called mystic sect. Law, to the very end of his life, held the highest views of the two Sacraments of the Gospel; the Quakers objected to the very word Sacrament, which 'was not found in Scripture but borrowed from the heathen'; and, as to the thing, they held that the 'outward signs in the Sacraments were of no avail.'[2] Law held the highest views of the Christian ministry; in none of his mystic works does he ever retract what he wrote on the grace of orders and the apostolical succession in his 'Three Letters to the Bishop of Bangor;' on the contrary, he distinctly refers to them as expressing his sentiments twenty years later. The Quakers thought that 'the outward ceremony of laying-on of hands or ordination was not necessary.'[3] Law never missed a service in his parish church. The Quakers thought that carnal ordinances were unnecessary. Law's views on the Holy Trinity were strictly those of the Athanasian Creed. The Quakers objected to the word 'Person' as applied to the Godhead.[4] On these and many other points Law was as

---

[1] An interesting sketch of Dr. Henry More's life and opinions will be found in Dr. Tulloch's *Rational Theology and Christian Philosophy in England in the Seventeenth Century.* See vol. ii., the chapter on 'The Cambridge Platonists.'

[2] See Barclay's *Apology for the True Christian Divinity*, p. 389.

[3] *Ibid.* p. 282.

[4] See Sewel's *History of the Quakers*, and Howitt on the Quakers in the *Encyclopædia Britannica*, and Barclay's *Apology for the True Christian Divinity*.

much at variance with the Quakers as his brother non-juror, Charles Leslie himself.

Nor was it only in doctrine that he disagreed with them ; he equally objected to their practice. The Quakers in the eighteenth century were a very prosperous, well-to-do people ; being debarred by their principles from many of the excitements of the outer world, they found excitement in the acquisition of wealth, and were suspected, though very unjustly, of being worldly-minded.[1] Law was as much an ascetic when he wrote the ' Spirit of Love ' as when he wrote the ' Serious Call,' and this money-getting spirit was of all spirits the most distasteful to him.[2]

On the other hand, Law of course agreed with the Quakers on many points on which they were at variance with the popular religious feeling of the eighteenth century. He believed with them in the ' inner light ' ; *their* favourite text (' That was the true light,' &c.) was *his* favourite text ; *their* sentiments on the Fall of Man,[3] on the uselessness of Logic and Philosophy and School Divinity,[4] on the unlawfulness of war, on the inexpediency of Christians going to law, on the literal interpretation of the Sermon on the Mount generally, were *his* sentiments. But then, just in proportion as Law felt the truth and importance of these

---

[1] See Cunningham's *History of the Quakers*, p. 218.

[2] See Byrom's *Journal* for April 17, 1737.

[3] ' In the day that thou eatest thereof,' &c. ' This death could not be an outward death or the dissolution of the outward man ; for as to that, Adam did not die yet many hundred years after ; so that it must needs respect his spiritual life and communion with God.'—Barclay's *Apology for the True Christian Divinity*, p. 91.

[4] ' If ye would make a man a fool to a purpose that is not very wise, do but teach him logic and philosophy, and whereas before he might have been fit for something, he shall then be good for nothing but to speak nonsense. School divinity is a monster made up of some scriptural notions of truth and the heathenish terms and maxims. It is the devil darkening and veiling the knowledge of God with his serpentine and worldly wisdom.'—Barclay's *Apology for the True Christian Divinity*, pp. 295-6.

points, he was all the more annoyed at their being mixed
up with other points which he considered erroneous. It is
not to be wondered at, therefore, that the little which Law
wrote and said about the Quakers was not in their favour.
At the same time he did not approve of much that was
written against the Quakers, because it seemed to him to
be in reality equally written against all divine and spiritual
influences.[1] For this reason he was himself very guarded
in what he said and wrote on the subject of Quakerism,
because he felt that it was so liable to be misunderstood.
His friend Byrom was much interested in this matter,
having a young-lady cousin and other friends who were
tempted to turn Quakers, and so he constantly tried to
draw out Law on the subject, and generally received a
snub for his pains. He *did*, however, persuade Law to
write five letters to dissuade the young lady from leaving
the Church of England. These letters I have not seen,
but the few allusions in Law's printed works to those
whom, in spite of their differences, one must regard as his
brother mystics, only show that Law was ready to recognise good even when it was found in men with whom he
disagreed—in a George Fox as in an Ignatius Loyola.[2]

In one respect Law might certainly with advantage
have taken a lesson from the Quakers, whose judicious and
systematic method of spending their wealth on carefully-
considered schemes of philanthropy contrasted favourably
with the too reckless and indiscriminate alms-giving which
went on at King's Cliffe.

---

[1] Law told Byrom that ' the writers against Quakerism were not proper
persons, for they writ against the Spirit in effect, and gave the Quakers an
advantage.' Byrom's *Journal* for April 1737.

[2] See Law's *Works*, vi. (2) 285, &c. and vii. 191-2.

4. *The Moravian Brethren.*

Moravianism has an obvious affinity to mysticism. The Moravian 'stillness,' which gave so much offence to John Wesley, bore, at least a superficial resemblance to the passivity of the mystics ; and there are other points of connection which it is unnecessary to specify. Law was brought into frequent contact with the Moravians. His interviews with Peter Böhler, Wesley's 'extraordinary good young man,' Mr. Gambold, a Methodist who turned Moravian, and Mr. Okely, a distinguished preacher among the United Brethren, have already been noticed. He also studied, with evident interest, the writings of the Brethren, and he shared with them the general imputation of en-thusiasm. Bishop Warburton, for instance, groups the Moravians and the Behmenists, and particularly William Law, 'the leader of the sect amongst us,' in one sweeping condemnation, expressed in true Warburtonian language.[1]

In point of fact, however, Law had very little sympathy with the Moravians ; indeed, he hardly did justice to their good points. His mind was formed in a very different mould from that of those to whom Moravianism would naturally prove attractive. His was essentially a robust and masculine character, and there seemed to him to be a certain degree of effeminacy in the mental calibre of the Moravians. The position, moreover, of Count Zinzendorf among his people was peculiarly repugnant to the ideas of Law, who loved to quote the text 'Call no man Rabbi,' though, much against his will, he was often, in effect, called Rabbi himself. One can quite understand that many of the doctrines of the Moravians would appear to Law to be quite subversive of his own system, and that many of their expressions would be grievously offensive to his pure and cultivated taste. We need not, therefore, be surprised to find him writing thus, in 1753 : ' My dear Langcake,—I had a volume of Count Zinzendorf's ser- mons. I was prepared to find such things in them as would surprise me ; but I could hardly persuade myself to read them through. The Moravians may, for aught I know, have many good people among them, as every denomination hath ; but their form is quite sectarian, full of inventions, and wholly attached to a particular opinion or rather, to a particularity of expression, concerning the blood and sufferings of Christ.' And again, in 1757 : ' What they [the Moravians] say has nothing to recom- mend it but their manner of saying it. The first thing to be done with any Moravian is to show him the necessity of confuting what has been laid to their charge, and taken from their own books, by Rimius, the German ; he has no title to be talked with till this is done.' This allusion to Rimius shows that Law had read the most ruthless ex- posure of the ' Herrnhuters ' (Rimius will not allow them the title of Moravians) that ever was published.[1] But it hardly needed this exposure to put Law out of love with the Brethren.

5. *The Swedenborgians.*

Bishop Horne entitled his tract, which has been noticed in the preceding chapter, ' Cautions to Readers of Mr.

---

[1] See *A Candid Narrative of the Rise and Progress of the Herrnhuters*, by Henry Rimius, esp. p. 12, where he contends that they were not, as they pro- fessed, ' a sprig of those Bohemian and Moravian Brothers, who a long time before Luther lived separated from the Romish Church.' His quotations from some of Zinzendorf's sermons, if correct, are highly objectionable, while some of the hymns quoted are positively filthy. Warburton called the ' Moravian's open hymn-book a heap of blasphemous and beastly nonsense,' and their practices in regard to marriage ' unspeakably flagitious,' but he had not the slightest ground for mixing up Law with them, as he seems to do. See *Doctrine of Grace,* p. 627.

Law, and, with very few variations, of Swedenborg.' But, in point of fact, the resemblance between the doctrines of Law and Swedenborg is more apparent than real. There is this fundamental difference between Behmenism and Swedenborgianism. The whole system of the latter hinges on the fact of a new revelation being given to Baron Swedenborg, who saw visions and conferred with spirits in the spiritual world. Nothing of this sort was claimed by Behmen. As Behmen is never tired of telling us, nor Law of repeating, it was no vision or revelation from without, but simply an 'opening' within him, which Behmen professed to have experienced. To one who, like Law, had already been charmed with the writings of the mystics, we can quite understand that this would be the great recommendation of Behmenism ; and, for the same reason, such a person would be repelled by Swedenborgianism. On many points, of course—notably on the doctrine of correspondences between the spiritual and the natural, the visible and the invisible worlds—the two systems would more or less agree ; but all these are minor points when compared with the great point of difference. How far Law was acquainted with Swedenborg's writings, or Swedenborg with Law's, is, in spite of much that has been written on the point, very uncertain. There is a tradition that Swedenborg's mind was first turned to spiritual subjects by reading Law's 'Appeal,' and his other early mystical writings. There are also two letters extant, which are supposed to have been addressed by Law to his friend and neighbour Mr. Hartley, of Winwick, both commenting most unfavourably on Swedenborg's doctrines ; but the external proofs of the genuineness of these letters are inadequate, and their style is not, to my mind, the style of Law. Then, again, Mr. Hartley was an enthusiastic admirer of

Swedenborg, the first translator of parts of the Baron's works into English, and a distinct Swedenborgian. Now, if Law had expressed himself so strongly to Mr. Hartley against Swedenborg, is it likely that Mr. Hartley would have so strongly recommended Law's sentiments to his readers as he has done ? We can quite understand his admiring Law's character,—*that* no good man could help doing ; but it *does* seem strange that he should have also admired his opinions, if he had known that they were so antagonistic to those of his oracle. The only piece of evidence which, in my opinion, can be thoroughly relied upon as to Law's estimate of Swedenborg, is an expression in a letter of Mr. Langcake, who ' was told by a friend that Law said Swedenborg was very voluminous, and that was not his worst fault.' That sounds like Law all over, and Mr. Langcake is always to be trusted ; but it does not tell us much, and the little that is told only comes at second hand. It is useless, therefore, to speculate further on the subject.

6. *The Universalists.*

The term ' Universalist' was not coined, nor the sect so called formed, until a little after Law's time ; but there were in his day individuals who held the doctrine, and they not unnaturally expected to find a sympathiser in William Law. Even before his mystic period he had been consulted on the subject by the ' lady inclined to enter the Church of Rome,' whose domestic circumstances prompted her to seek some comfort in the thought that there might be hope beyond the grave. Law's reply was so sensible and judicious that I am tempted to quote a few sentences from it. ' Discourses,' he writes, ' about the restoration of all things are about something that we have not the least knowledge of,

nor any faculties or foundation for such knowledge ; we have
nothing certain or plain within ourselves about it, and so
have nothing to oppose to anything that is told us. We
are, therefore, easily taken by every writer that has parts
and abilities to form an agreeable scheme of it. Again,
the irrecoverable state of men, or angels, is a dreadful
thought to us ; our sense of misery, tenderness, and
compassion for our fellow-creatures makes us wish that
no creatures might fall into it, and we are unable to show
how such a state should result from the infinite wisdom,
goodness, and perfection of God : and so we are mightily
prepared to think every scheme to be rational and well
grounded that puts an end to such a state. But then we
must consider that we are here governed by our passions
and weakness, and only form a God according to our own
conceptions ; . . . to pretend to know what God *must* do,
in the vast compass of futurity, with regard to His fallen
creatures, is as absurd as to pretend to be infinitely wise
ourselves.' After many more excellent remarks, which
space forbids me to quote, he sums up : ' For my own
part, this one saying, " Shall not the Judge of all the earth
do right ? " is a stronger support to my mind, and a better
guard against all anxiety, than the deepest discoveries that
the most speculative, inquisitive minds could help me to.
With this one assurance of the infinitely infinite goodness
of God, I resign up myself, my friends, relations, men, and
angels, to the adorable and yet incomprehensible disposal
of His wisdom,' &c.

When Law became a mystic, the subject was, of course,
still more urgently pressed upon his attention. The foundation of his mystic teaching was that ' God was one
boundless abyss of Love, from whom nothing but endless
streams of Love could flow upon all His creatures.' Was
it consistent with this fundamental doctrine that God should

suffer any of His creatures to perish finally? Now Law was the very last man to shirk the logical results of his teaching; but then, just in proportion as he realised the love of God, he also realised the heinousness of sin, and the certainty and fearfulness of its punishment hereafter, if unrepented of and unpardoned here; and, therefore, he particularly guarded himself against saying anything which might be taken hold of as an excuse by those who had strong personal reasons for hoping that future punishment might in any way be mitigated. He *did* believe, strongly and fully,'in the purification of all human nature, either in this world or some after ages;' he did not altogether despair about the restoration of the fallen angels. But for all practical purposes, he believed that the future retribution of the wicked would be so terrible—not from the vindictive wrath of an angry God, but from the very nature of sin—that it should be as much dreaded as if it were literally eternal. And, therefore, he considered it a most dangerous and mischievous thing to preach or teach the restoration of all things, as it was sometimes done. He constantly alludes to the certainty and awfulness of the future state of punishment; but hardly ever to its possible limitation, and then in the most guarded terms, so as to preclude the possibility of its being turned into a pretext for sin. The 'terrors of the Lord' were as vividly realised by him as the 'love of the Lord.' It is only in his last 'Address to the Clergy,' which, being a *concio ad clerum*, he probably thought less liable to abuse, that he dwells at any length on the doctrine of Restoration, and then it is in such terms as would alarm rather than lull the sinner into a false security; for he speaks of 'long and long ages of fiery pain and tormenting darkness,' of the 'black lakes, bottomless pits, ages of a gnawing worm, and fire that never ceases to burn between the poor

sinner that dies without Adam's repentance and a kingdom of God afar off.'

The fact is, Law thought that the discussion of so
mysterious a subject as this was always profitless, and
might be perilous. That the punishment of the wicked
would be unspeakably awful was enough for man to know,
and therefore he systematically discouraged all further
prying into the question. Mrs. Lead was fond of pro-
pounding theories upon the mystery ; and Law certainly
did not approve of Mrs. Lead. His friend Langcake also
showed much curiosity upon the point, and wrote to Law
telling him that a certain Mr. S. 'called him [Law] blind
and ignorant, because he had not a self-evident knowledge
of the salvation of devils.' 'Dear L., son of my love,'
writes Law, with even more than his usual affection for
his friend, ' I do not know that ever I wasted my spirits
in writing or thinking in the manner of this letter before,
and trust I never shall again. But love towards you, and
a hearty zeal for your true growth in the spiritual life,
have compelled me into this wrangle. Put away all needless
curiosity in Divine matters ; and look upon everything to
be so but that which helps you to die to yourself, that the
spirit and life of Christ may be found in you.'

It is so difficult to compress what Law has written in
his mystic works on the subject of a future state, that I
must be content with referring the reader to the works
themselves.[1]

7. *Pantheism.*

All mysticism has a sort of tendency to Pantheism in
some sense. The step from the recognition of the Divine

---

[1] See *Appeal to all that Doubt*, 'Works,' vi. (2),pp. 88-92; *Way to Divine
Knowledge*, ' Works,' vii. (3), pp. 63-65 ; *Spirit of Love*, viii. (2), pp. 111-115;
Letter II. to a Lady inclined to enter the Church of Rome and Letter XIII. in
printed collection, ' Works,' ix. (3), pp. 163-8.

element in outward nature, and in the soul of man, to the
absorption of all nature in God, is an easy one ; and the
rapturous expressions which the more extravagant mystics,
such as Eckart and Ruysbrock, were wont to use respecting
God and nature, often seem to go to the full lengths of
Pantheism. But Pantheism is a vague word—almost as
vague as mysticism itself. Wordsworth, the pious poet of
nature, has been called a Pantheist ; and, in this sense,
Pantheism might even be predicated of him who wrote as
the conclusion of his truly mystic hymn—

> Thou who hast given me eyes to see
> And love this sight so fair,
> Give me a heart to find out Thee,
> And read Thee everywhere.

Now Law dwelt very largely upon these two aspects of
mysticism, the Divine element in outward nature, and the
Divine Seed in man ; and. therefore, it is no wonder that
his enemies charged him with Pantheism. But the charge
was brought against him by one enemy in its most objectionable form ; he was accused by Warburton of Spinozism,
that is, of confounding nature with God. Whether this
Spinozism was really the doctrine of Spinoza, is not now the
question. It was in this sense that Spinozism was understood in the eighteenth century, and by Law himself. No
charge wounded him more deeply. As a rule, he made
very light of the accusations that were brought against
him ; but this touched him to the quick. It seemed to
him not only untrue, but a most mischievous perversion
of the truth ; for he contended that Behmenism (the exposition of which laid him open to the charge) was not only
free from Pantheism, but that it was the only system which
explained the real distinction between God and nature.
' The charge,' he wrote, ' of Spinozism, brought against
me by Dr. Warburton, has all the folly and weakness that

can well be imagined ; for, as Spinozism is nothing else
but a gross confounding of God and nature, making them
to be only one and the same thing, so the full absurdity
and absolute impossibility of it can only be fundamentally
proved by that doctrine which can go to the bottom of the
matter, and demonstrate the essential, eternal, and absolute distinction between God and nature—a thing done
over and over, from page to page, in those books from
which the doctor has extracted Spinozism.' Law then
goes on to show that Behmen alone set forth 'the why,
the how, and in what God and nature were essentially
different.'• We need not follow him in detail ; but, whether
we agree or not with the *positive* part of his argument, it
must be owned that he fully proved the *negative* part. Law
was no Spinozist. God was to him a true, personal Being,
absolutely distinct from all His creatures, who were, at
most, but the image, the dim, faint reflection of the Creator.
No unprejudiced reader can possibly be led even to the
verge of that Pantheism which practically amounts to
Atheism by anything that Law ever wrote.

These were the principal schools of thought with which
Law's mysticism brought him into contact, or rather,
collision, for he agreed with none of them.

THE last work which Law wrote is entitled 'An Humble, Earnest, and Affectionate Address to the· Clergy.' The title is rather misleading, for the work does not deal with matters exclusively clerical ; but Law gives us the explanation of his choice of a title for his last utterance in its opening paragraph. ' The reason,' he says, ' of my humbly and affectionately addressing this discourse to the clergy, is not because it treats of things not of common concern to all Christians, but chiefly to invite and induce them, as far as I can, to the serious perusal of it, and because whatever is *essential* to Christian salvation, if either neglected, overlooked, or mistaken by them, is of the saddest consequence both to themselves and the churches in which they minister. I say *essential* to salvation, for I would not turn my own thoughts, or call the attention of Christians, to anything but the *one thing* needful.'

By the 'one thing needful' Law of course meant the reviving and cherishing the Divine life in the soul. This, he contended, could only be effected by the immediate, continual inspiration of God's Holy Spirit—a doctrine which was branded as enthusiasm by the 'rational' divines of the eighteenth century, but which was in Law's view the very pith and marrow of Christianity. Dr. Warburton had made the following extraordinary assertion : ' By the writings of the New Testament the prophetic promise of our Saviour that the 'Comforter should abide for ever,' was eminently fulfilled. For though his ordinary influence occasionally assists the faithful, yet his constant abode and supreme illumination is in the Sacred Scriptures.' It was not difficult for Law to show that 'this middle way had neither Scripture nor sense in it, for (he argued) an *occasional* influence is as absurd as an occasional God, and necessarily supposes such a God. Nothing godly can be alive in us but what has *all its* life from the Spirit of God living and breathing in us.'

This last sentence contains the gist of the whole address. It was a last solemn warning to those who, from various causes, were neglecting this inner spiritual life. Some were doing so by a perverse use of those very Scriptures which were their best guide to such a life. 'I exceedingly love,' writes Law, 'and highly reverence the divine authority of the sacred writings of apostles and evangelists, and would gladly persuade every one to be as deeply affected with them, and pay as profound a regard to them, as they would to an Elijah, a St. John the Baptist, or a Paul, whom they knew to be immediately sent from Heaven with God's message to them. I reverence them as a literal Truth of and from God;' but when it was argued that the Spirit's constant abode is in the Scriptures alone, this, he thought, was making positive nonsense of numerous statements in those very Scriptures themselves. There is a flash of the old humour which lighted up the controversy of nearly half a century before, between Law and another bishop, who, so far as belief was concerned,[1] occupied much the same ground as Warburton now did, in our author's exposure of this absurdity. 'Our Lord says,

[1] I say, 'so far as belief was concerned,' because on other matters, such as politics, &c., Bishop Warburton, of course, differed very widely indeed from Bishop Hoadly.

" It is expedient for you that I go away," or " the Comforter will not come unto you ; " that is, it is expedient for you that I leave off teaching you in words, that sound only into your outward ears, that you may have the same words in writing, for your outward eyes to look upon ; for if I do not depart from this vocal way of teaching you, the Comforter will not come ; that is, ye will not have the comfort of my words written on paper." Christ says, " If any man love Me, My Father will love him, and we will come unto him, and make our abode with him ; " that is, according to the Doctor's theology, certain books of Scripture will come to him and make their abode with him. Christ from Heaven says, " Behold, I stand at the door, and knock : if any man will hear My voice, and open unto Me, I will come in to him, and sup with him ; " according to the Doctor, we are to understand that not the heavenly Christ, but the New Testament continually stands and knocks at the door, wanting to enter into the heart and sup with it ; ' and so on with many other texts. In short, those who claimed for the Scriptures a function which could not be admitted without rendering ridiculous countless texts of those Scriptures themselves, were, in fact, making an idol-god of the Bible. ' I say an idol-god,' he repeats, ' for to those who rest in it as the " constant abode and supreme illumination of God with them," it can be nothing else. For, if nothing of Divine Faith, Love, Hope, or Goodness, can have the least birth or place in us but by Divine inspiration ' (and this was an axiom with Law), ' they who think these virtues may be sufficiently raised in us by the letter of Scripture, do in truth and reality make the letter of Scripture their *inspiring God.*'

Law, however, touches but lightly upon this part of his subject. It was not necessary to do more ; for the statement of Warburton could not bear a moment's discussion.

Its untenableness is manifest on the face of it, and as a matter of fact, it was superfluous to warn the clergy of the eighteenth century against Bibliolatry, for the very last thing of which they were in danger was a too superstitious regard for the Bible. The real peril to the spiritual life lay, in Law's view, in their setting too much stress upon their reasoning powers. And accordingly, Law devotes the greater part of this address to a final crusade against this 'letter-learned zeal.'

Again Dr. Warburton supplies the text for his sermon. The Doctor had owned that St. Paul 'sacrificed an extensive and intimate acquaintance with the classics to the glory of the everlasting Gospel.' 'If,' writes Law, in a passage of wonderful vigour, 'the everlasting Gospel is now as glorious a thing as it was in St. Paul's days; if the highest, most accomplished classic knowledge is so unsuitable to the Light and Spirit of the Gospel that it is fit for nothing but to be cast away, or, as the Doctor says, to be all sacrificed to the glory of the Gospel, how wonderful is it that this should never come into his head from the beginning to the end of his three long Legation-volumes, or that he should come piping hot with fresh and fresh classic beauties found out by himself in a Shakespeare, a Pope, &c., to preach from the pulpit the divine wisdom of a Paul in renouncing all his great classic attainments as mere loss and dung, that by so doing he might win Christ and be found in Him. Let it be supposed that our Lord was to come again for a while in the flesh, and that His coming was for this end, to do that for the Christian world *cumbered* with much learning, which he did to poor Martha, only *cumbered with much serving*, who thereby neglected that *Good Part* which Mary had chosen; must we suppose that the Doctor would hasten to meet Him with his sacred alliance, his bundles of pagan trash, and hieroglyphic pro-

fundities, as his full proof that Mary's good part, which
shall never be taken from her, had been chosen for himself
and all his readers ? '

And then comes Mr. Stinstra, with his pastoral letter
recommending ' that sound understanding and reason as
the means by which God principally operates.'   And then
comes Mr. Green, who ' wanting to write on Divine inspiration, runs from book to book, from country to country,
to pick up reports wherever he could find them concerning
Divine inspiration, from this and that *judicious* author, that
so he might be sure of compiling a *judicious* dissertation on
the subject.'

' O, vainest of all vain projects !   As soon as any man
trusts to natural abilities, skill in languages, and common-
place learning. . . . he has sold his birthright in the
Gospel-state of *Divine* illumination, to make a figure and
noise with the sounding brass and tinkling cymbals of the
natural man.   Parts and genius must go, as the blind, the
deaf, the dumb, and lepers formerly did, to be healed of
their *natural* disorders by the inspiration of that Oracle
which said " I am the Light of the world."   Every good
and perfect gift cometh from ABOVE.   He denies this who
seeks for the highest gifts of knowledge from BELOW, from
the poor contrivance of a common-place book.   Nothing
but light can manifest light.   The Gospel state has but
one light, and that is the Lamb of God ; it has but one
life, and that is by the Spirit of God.   Christendom now
glories in the light of Greek and Roman learning as a
light that has helped the Gospel to shine with a lustre that
it scarce ever had before.   In the first Gospel Church,
heathen light had no other name than heathen darkness.
In that new-born Church the Tree of Life, which grew in
the midst of Paradise, took root and grew up again.   In
the present church the Tree of Life is hissed at, as the

visionary food of deluded enthusiasts, and the Tree of Death, called the tree of knowledge of good and evil, has the eyes and hearts of priest and people, and is thought to do as much good to Christians as it did evil to the first inhabitants of Paradise. This tree, that brought death and corruption into human nature at first, is now called a tree of light, and is day and night well watered with every corrupt stream, however distant or muddy with earth, that can be drawn to it. The simplicity, indeed, of the Gospel letter and doctrine has the shine and polish of classic literature laid thick upon it. But, would you find a Gospel-Christian in all this mid-day glory of learning, you may light a candle, as the philosopher did in the mid-day sun to find an honest man. "Learn of me," said the Saviour, "for I am meek and lowly of heart." What a grossness of ignorance, both of man and his Saviour, to run to Greek and Roman schools to learn how to put off Adam and to put on Christ ! To drink at the fountains of pagan poets and orators, in order more divinely to drink of the cup that Christ drank of ! What can come of all this but that which is already too much come, a *Ciceronian*-Gospeller, instead of a *Gospel*-penitent. The classic scholar, full fraught with Pagan light and skill, comes forth to play the *critic* and *orator* with the simplicity of Salvation mysteries ; —mysteries which mean nothing else but the inward work of the Triune God in the soul of man. The ancient way of knowing the things of God, taught and practised by *fishermen*-apostles, is obsolete. *They* indeed wanted to have Divine knowledge from the immediate continual operation of the Holy Spirit, but this state was only for a time, till Genius and Learning entered into the pale of the Church ! Behold, if ever, the Abomination of Desolation standing in the Holy Place ! '

'From long labours in restoring the grammar and finding

out the hidden beauties of some vicious old book, men set
up for qualified artists to polish the Gospel pearl of great
price. A grave ecclesiastic, bringing forth out of his closet
skilful meditations on the commentaries of a murdering
Cæsar, or the sublime rhapsody of an old Homer, or the
astonishing beauties of a modern Dunciad, has as much
reason to think that he is walking in the Light of Christ
and led by the Spirit of God, as they have who are only
" eating and drinking, and rising up to play." Men called
to a resurrection of the first Divine life, where a new creature is taught by that same unction from above, whence all
the angels and principalities of Heaven have their light
and glory, set themselves down at the feet of a Master
Tully and a Master Aristotle, who only differ from the
meanest of all other corrupt men as the *Teaching Serpent*
differed from his fellow animals by being more subtle than
all the beasts of the field.'

In contrast to this 'eager searcher into words for
wisdom,' this 'book-devourer,' this 'opinion-broker,' this
'exalter of heathen reason,' this 'projecting builder of religious systems,' whose 'thirst and pride of being learnedly
wise in the things of God does no better work in the Church
of Christ than Eve's thirst after wisdom did in the Paradise
of God,' Law draws a very beautiful and touching picture
of the truly wise man and the source of his wisdom.
'" Speak, Lord, for thy servant heareth,"' he writes, 'is the
one only way by which any man ever did, or ever can
attain divine knowledge and divine goodness. To knock
at any other door but this, is but like asking life of that
which is itself dead, or praying to him for bread who has
nothing but stones to give. . . . Show me a man whose
heart has no desire or prayer in it but to love God with
his whole soul and spirit, and his neighbour as himself, and
then you have shown me the man who knows Christ, and

is known of him—the best and wisest man in the world.
Not a single precept in the Gospel but is the precept of his
own heart, and the joy of that new-born heavenly love
which is the life and light of his soul. In this man all that
came from the old Serpent is trod under his feet ; not a
spark of self, of pride, of wrath, of envy, of covetousness
or worldly wisdom can have the least abode in him, because that Love which fulfilleth the Law and the Prophets,
that Love which is God and Christ, both in angels and
man, is the Love that gives birth, and life, and growth to
everything that is either thought, or word, or action in
him ; and if he has no share or part with foolish errors,
cannot be tossed about with every wind of doctrine, it is
because to be always governed by this Love is to be always
taught of God.'

In this Address, which was intended to deal only with
the one thing needful, there is not one word of Behmenism,
as distinguished from mysticism generally—a striking proof
of what has been asserted above, that Law did not consider
the peculiarities of Behmenism as belonging to the essence
of Christianity, But of mysticism, that is of ' such mystic
absurdity as St. Paul fell into when he enthusiastically said,
" Yet not I, but Christ that liveth in me," ' Law does treat
largely ; for this was, in his view, not merely of the *bene
esse*, but of the *esse*, of religion. ' Look where you will,' he
says, 'through all the whole nature of things, no Divine
wisdom, knowledge, goodness, and deliverance from sin
are anywhere to be found for fallen man but in these
two points : (1) a total, entire entrance into the *whole
process* of Christ ; (2) a total resignation to, and sole
dependence upon, the continual operation of the Holy
Ghost, or Christ come again in the Spirit, to be our
never-ceasing Light, Teacher, and Guide into all those
ways of virtue in which He Himself walked in the flesh.

And here let it be well observed that in these two points consists the whole of that *mystic* divinity to which a *Jewish*[1] orthodoxy, at this day, is so great an enemy; for nothing else is meant or taught by it but a total dying to *self* (called the Process, or Cross of Christ), that a new creature (called Christ in us, or Christ come in the Spirit) may be begotten in the purity and perfection of the first man's union with God.'

It was, Law contended, the departure from 'this one mystic way of salvation' which was the cause of that sad anomaly which, before the Evangelical movement had leavened the land, was bewailed by all good men, and which Law describes as 'a Christian kingdom of Pagan vices, along with a mouth-belief of an Holy Catholic Church, and Communion of Saints.' This description very accurately pourtrayed the state of England. It was a Christian kingdom, inasmuch as it had certainly not rejected Christianity as an historical faith; on the contrary, I imagine that at few periods has belief, in one sense, been more general than it was at this time, just after the utter collapse of Deism. But it was full of Pagan vices. Law hardly drew too dark a picture when he said, 'There is not a corruption or depravity of human nature, no kinds of pride, wrath, envy, malice, and self-love, no sorts of hypocrisy and cheating, no wantonness of lust in every kind of debauchery, but are as common, all over Christendom, as towns and villages.'[2]

Instead, however, of dwelling on these more glaring abominations, Law—feeling, perhaps, that the class whom

---

[1] By 'Jewish' Law means such an orthodoxy as that of the Jews who opposed Christ in the flesh; the same spirit (as he frequently contends) was now opposing the spiritual Christ. See this 'Address' *passim.*

[2] As a proof of this, see Rapin, Smollett, Horace Walpole, Secker's Charges, Wesley's *Journals*, &c. &c. *passim.* In fact, the almost unanimous voice of all contemporary writers echoes the dreary wail.

he was especially addressing were not as a body addicted
to them (for the clergy, as a rule, were certainly not immoral)—specifies these particulars, which, 'though little
observed and less condemned,' were, in his eyes, equally
unchristian.

These were (1) *Mammon worship.*—'Though figured idol-
gods of gold are not now worshipped, yet silver and gold,
with that which belongs to them, is the mammon-god that
sits in the hearts of Christians. How else could there be that
universal strife who should stand in the richest and highest
place to preach up the humility of Christ and offer spiritual
sacrifices unto God? What god, but mammon, could put
into the hearts of Christ's ambassadors to make, or want to
make, a gain of that Gospel which, from the beginning to
the end, means nothing else but death to self and separation from every view, temper, and affection that has any
connection with the lusts of the flesh, the lusts of the eyes,
and the pride of life? Our blessed Lord told the Jews
they had made His Father's house a den of thieves, because
sheep and oxen were sold, and money-changers sitting in
the outer court of the Temple. Our Church sale is not
oxen and sheep, but holy things, cures of souls, parsonages,
vicarages, &c. ; and our money-changers, our buyers and
sellers, are chiefly consecrated persons.'

(2.) *Oaths.*—Law, as we have often remarked, took the
Sermon on the Mount quite literally, and had therefore, of
course, his text ready on this point. Before we accuse him
of fanaticism, let us remember that the multiplication of
oaths on all sorts of subjects really had brought it about
that many men avowedly and unblushingly took them, not
only without thinking of the solemnity of the act, but with
a positive intention of breaking them. Law really does
not exaggerate the matter when he says, 'Through town
and country, in all ignorant villages, in all learned colleges,

in all courts, spiritual and temporal, what with law oaths, corporation oaths, office oaths, trade oaths, qualification oaths, simony oaths, bribery oaths, election oaths, &c., &c., &c., there is more swearing and forswearing than all history reports of any idol-worshipping nations. It was said of old, " Because of swearing the land mourneth ; " it is full as true to say now, " Because of swearing the land rejoiceth in iniquity, is full of prophaneness, and without any fear of the Divine Majesty ; daily swallowing down all manner of oaths, in the same good state of mind, and with as much serious reflection, as pot-companions swallow down their liquor." Instead of saying what He did say, it might have been thought that Christ had said, " Let not a simple yea and nay be of any avail in all your communications, but let oaths be required of all that bear My name, for whatsoever is less than this cometh of evil." ' Though he never refers to it, the old man's mind must have wandered back nearly half a century, to the time when he sacrificed all his earthly prospects by refusing to take the oath which, as he must have known, others who had expressed themselves in language as diametrically opposite to the meaning of that oath as himself, had not scrupled to take.

(3.) *The love of war*, ' in full contrariety to the nature and spirit of Christ.'—' Fancy to yourself,' he says, ' Christ, the Lamb of God, after His divine Sermon on the Mount, putting Himself at the head of a blood-thirsty army, or St. Paul going forth with a squadron of fire and brimstone to make more havoc in human lives than a devouring earthquake!' Here, again, it must be remembered that when Law wrote war was regarded, not as a necessary evil, but almost as the normal state of nations. It was the time when the ' Protestant Hero,' whom so many Englishmen admired, was sacrificing thousands upon thousands of lives in the most glaringly unjust cause, and on the flimsiest pretences.[1] The very name, 'The Seven Years War,' shows the horrible duration of the scourge. Still, I must not disguise the fact that Law certainly would not have approved even of the milder views at present current respecting war. I doubt whether he would have even considered it a necessary evil; I am sure if there had been a 'peace at any price' party in his day, he would have been very loth to condemn it. With his intensely earnest Christian convictions, he looked at every question simply from the Gospel point of view. Realising with extraordinary vividness the boundless love of God for His fallen creatures, he could not understand the enmity of those creatures one to another, if they still professed to be Christians, and therefore to aim at being like God. 'Jesus Christ, God and Man, the only begotten Son of this infinite Love, came into the world in the name and under the character of infinite pity, boundless compassion, inexpressible meekness, bleeding love, nameless humility, &c. Now, from this view of God's infinite love and mercy in Christ Jesus, willing nothing, seeking nothing through all the regions of His Providence but that sinners of all kinds, the boldest rebels against all His goodness, may have their proper remedy, their necessary means of being fully delivered from all that hurt, mischief, and destruction, which, in full opposition to their God and Creator, they had brought upon themselves,—from this view, I say, of God and Christ, using every miracle of Love and Wisdom to give recovery of life, health, and salvation to all that have rebelled against Him, look at the murdering monster of War.' Then, after having vividly described the temporal miseries of war, he goes on : ' But there is still an evil of war much greater,

though less regarded. Who reflects what nameless numbers of young men are robbed of God's precious gift of life
to them, before they have known the one sole benefit of
living ? How many unconverted sinners fall, murdering
and murdered among flashes of fire, with the wrath and
swiftness of lightning, into a fire infinitely worse than that
in which they died ? O sad subject for Thanksgiving Days !
For, if there is a joy of all the angels in heaven for one
sinner that repents, what a joy there must be in hell over
such multitudes of sinners not suffered to repent ? This is
the pious prayer that those who pray " for the glory of His
Majesty's arms " must offer : " O blessed Jesus, dear redeeming Lamb of God, who camest down from heaven to save
men's lives and not destroy them, go along, we humbly
pray Thee, with our bomb-vessels and fire-ships ; suffer
not our thundering cannon to roar in vain, but let Thy
tender hand of love and mercy direct their balls to more
heads and hearts of Thine own redeemed creatures than
the poor skill of man is able of itself to do." '

The lust for foreign dominion, contrasted with the
apathy about foreign missions, which was one of the
darkest features of the eighteenth century, supplies Law
with another painful reflection. ' To this day, what wars
of Christians against Christians, blended with scalping
heathens, still keep staining the earth and the seas with
human blood for a miserable share in the spoils of a
plundered heathen world !—a world which should have
heard, or seen, or felt nothing from the followers of Christ
but a Divine love, that had forced them from distant lands,
and through the perils of long seas, to visit strangers with
those glad tidings of peace and salvation to all the world
which angels from heaven, and shepherds on earth, proclaimed at the birth of Christ.'

After this digression, Law returns to the main subject

of the address, 'the inward work of God in the soul, and
the inward work of the soul in God.' 'This,' he says, 'is
that *mystic* religion which, though it has nothing in it but
that same Spirit, that same Truth, and that same Life,
which always was, and always must be, the religion of all
God's holy Angels and Saints in heaven, is by the wisdom
of this world accounted to be madness.' It would transcend the limits of this work to follow him further ; it must
suffice to quote his last words. 'All that Christ was, did,
suffered, dying in the flesh, and ascending into heaven, was
for this sole end : to purchase for all his followers a new
Birth, new Life, and new Light, in and by the Spirit of
God restored to them, and living in them, as their Support,
Comforter, and Guide into all truth. And this was his
"LO, I AM WITH YOU ALWAY, EVEN UNTO THE END OF
THE WORLD."'

The writer never lived to see these words in print.
Almost before the ink in which he wrote them was dry,
the saint had gone to his everlasting rest. Whether he
intended to add more, we cannot tell ; but certainly no
words could have been better chosen to convey to the
minds of his readers the very lesson of life which he
desired to teach them. 'Our departed friend,' wrote Miss
Gibbon, 'ended his process with the words in which our
Divine Master and Saviour, Jesus Christ, ended His. And
they may well be called his farewell speech to the world,
calling all men to repent and believe the Gospel ; for these
words were written but a few days before his death, and
the last time his blessed hand was capable of holding
a pen.' [1]

One of the most remarkable points about this last
'Address' is the vigour which pervades it. No one would
have thought that it was the work of an old and dying

[1] See Walton's *Notes, &c., for an adequate biography of William Law.*

man. Never in his prime had Law written with more fire, energy, and raciness. But, in point of fact, though he was on the brink of the grave, Law *was* in his prime still. He was an old man in years ; but in nothing else. There was never the slightest trace of senility either in his mind or body. To quote Miss Gibbon again : ‘ Mr. Law lived to the age of seventy-five without the infirmities of age ; for, though the age of man is said to be threescore years and ten, and after that but labour and sorrow, yet it could not be said so of Mr. Law, who retained the strength and vivacity, both in body and mind, of a man in the prime of life.’ ‘ His eye,’ she adds, ‘ was still piercing ; for it was the organ of his immortal soul filled with Divine light. His heart was filled with God, and therefore his voice was the sweet trumpeter of Divine love.’

But other and more mundane reasons might be given for this ‘ piercing eye,’ and clear voice, and all the other symptoms of youth in old age. All the conditions of Law's life had been favourable to such a result. He was distracted by no inward misgivings ; for ‘ he knew in whom he believed,’ and he had, if any man ever had, ‘ a conscience void of offence both towards God and towards man.’ He had always lived most temperately ; yet not so abstemiously as to injure health. He had always been, on principle, an early riser, and had had sufficient, but not too much, exercise, both of body and mind ; for it is as prejudicial to health for the mind to live without exercise as for the body. He had had few cares. His writings had exposed him to a good deal of adverse criticism ; but Law was the last man to be sensitive on such a point. He bore the abuse with which he was assailed, I will not say as a philosopher, but as a Christian ; he had not written for human applause, and it was a matter of perfect indifference to him whether he received it or not. He was not even troubled

at the thought that his views did not make much way in
the world ; for he felt it was his part to plant and water,
and leave it to God to give the increase ; and he had absolute confidence that God would, in His own good time,
make His Own truth to be accepted. His lines had fallen
in pleasant places. He was practically complete master
at the Hall Yard ; and that by the use of no sinister arts,
but simply from the force of a strong nature, which gave
him an ascendency, which he never abused, over his pious
fellow-inmates. No wonder then, that, to the last, 'his eye
was not dim, neither his natural force abated.' No wonder
that his biographer has none of that painful duty which
falls to the lot of most biographers—the duty of tracing
the gradual decay of the mental and bodily powers in the
course of nature, or of describing a life cut short before half
its natural course is run.

The end came rather suddenly at last. On Easter Day,
which fell that year (1761) on March 22, his friend Mr.
Langcake was with him on a visit. Law was then apparently in good health and spirits. 'After we had heard the
afternoon Easter Sunday's sermon,' writes Mr. Langcake,
'we took a walk through the town of King's Cliffe. He
then opened a gate into a field—it was a rising ground—
and then he began the discourse [on the restoration of all
things], and spoke like an angel upon this and other
matters, as if he was ready and ripe for glory, just to be
carried up into Heaven, and in the bosom of the Divine
Love be blessed to all eternity.' That blessed consum-
mation was nearer than either of the friends then suspected.
Easter week was the time for the annual audit of the school
accounts, when the trustees were always entertained at the
Hall Yard. On this occasion Law caught a cold, which
produced inflammation ; this flew to his kidneys, and after
a severe and painful illness, which lasted less than a fort-

night, Law breathed his last on Thursday morning, April 9, 1761. The death scene was what might have been ex- pected. Law had lived the life of the righteous, and he died the death of the righteous. His attack could not have come on before March 28, at the earliest; for on March 27 he wrote his last letter to Mr. Langcake, in which he makes no allusion to his illness. In fact, he must have written the last pages of his ' Address to the Clergy ' after this ; for he says, ' I intend to send you a parcel by the carrier next week, in which will be the remainder of the copy for Mr. Ward.' The letter concludes, ' We all say, God be with you. W. LAW.' This letter was endorsed by Mr. Langcake, ' The last letter I had from my most beloved friend.'

Miss Gibbon has left us some touching memorials of Law's last hours. ' This death-bed,' she writes, ' instead of being a state of affliction, was providentially a state of Divine transport. The gracious words that proceeded out of his mouth were all love, all joy, and all Divine transport. After taking leave of everybody in the most affecting manner, and declaring the opening of the Spirit of Love in the soul to be all in all, he expired in Divine raptures.' One of his last, if not his very last act, was, actually amid the throes of death, to sing, ' with a strong and very clear voice,' a hymn called ' The Angels' Hymn.' Almost immediately after this his soul was with the angels. His body was laid under the shadow of that church at which he had never missed a service for many years. It was a fitting time for his burial, when the Church of which he had been a faithful and distinguished member was still, as it were, ringing with the echo of the glorious and com- forting thoughts of Easter-tide, and when nature was silently uttering her yearly parable, which to Law was more than a parable—actually a representation, in a lower

form, of the great resurrection. Those who disagreed with
Law most would hardly doubt that, at the last Easter-tide,
his body would rise to everlasting glory.

His epitaph was the joint production of his friends
Langcake and Ward. They 'consulted,' Mr. Ward tells
us, 'to render it as perfect as possible ;' but they were
not quite equal to the task. It is as follows :—

'Here lyeth the body of the Rev. William Law, A.M.,
who died April 9th, 1761, aged 75 years. He was well
known to the world by a number of truly Christian, pious
writings, exemplified by a life spent in a manner suitable
to a worthy and true disciple of his Heavenly, Divine,
Crucified Master and Saviour, Jesus Christ, who lived and
spoke in him and by him. In his younger days, he
sufficiently distinguished himself by his parts and progress
in human literature. Afterwards, taking the advice of our
Saviour to the rich young man, he totally renounced the
world, and followed Christ in meekness, humility, and self-
denial. And, in his last years, he was wholly absorbed in
his love to God and mankind, so that virtue in him was
nothing but heavenly love and heavenly flame.

> In parts and sense, inferior to none ;
> With wit most amiable, with learning stored,
> His talents great and high, were quite sublimed,
> In loving God with all his heart and mind.
> His time was all employed in things divine,
> By s٠rving God, in goodness to mankind.
> The poor, the maim'd, the blind, have lost in him
> The kind protector and the ready friend.'

The tomb was 'erected to his memory by a *particular
and dear friend,* who lived many years with him, and therefore, had long known, and highly and justly esteemed, his
singular worth.' The friend, of course, was Miss Gibbon,
who was the sole executrix of his will. He had originally
left all his little property to her ; but he afterwards, very

properly, added a codicil, by which he 'devised all his
estates to Hester Gibbon, her heirs and assigns, to be by
her or them disposed and given to, and amongst, the
descendants of my late brother George Law, in such shares
and proportions, and at such time and times as the said
Hester Gibbon shall direct, limit, and appoint.'

The inscription on the tomb was inserted, under the
heading of 'A Character of the Rev. William Law, M.A.,'
in several newspapers, having been sent to them by Mr.
Ward, who apparently managed most of the business
arrangements. Writing to Miss Gibbon, Mr. Ward speaks
of Law as 'our dear and most invaluable friend, in whom
I seem to have lost the best, the noblest, and most valuable part of myself.' About ten years later, Mr. Clarke, a
clergyman who had sat at the feet of Mr. Law, printed
anonymously fifty lines ' To the memory of that excellent
man, and truly illuminated divine, the late Rev. William
Law, A.M.' They commence—

> Farewell, good man ! whose great and heavenly mind,
> In love embrac'd the whole of human kind.

They are full of the most enthusiastic praise of Mr. Law ;
but as they are not very remarkable either for poetical
merit or depth of thought, and as they convey no special
information respecting Law, it would be cruel to inflict
them upon the reader.

The few who knew Law intimately all speak of him
with the same reverence, admiration, and love as Mr. Ward
and Mr. Clarke ; but they were very few. Nor will it be
difficult for the reader of the preceding pages to understand
why so powerful a writer and so saintly a character was
not better known and appreciated. In the first place, his
position as a nonjuror was against him. He belonged to
the wrong generation of nonjurors. If it had been the
oath of 1688, instead of the oath of 1716, that Law had

scrupled to take, he could not have failed to have met
with many sympathising spirits ; for not only was the first
generation of nonjurors deservedly esteemed more highly
than the second, but they also banded together in a small,
though compact and united, phalanx, which their successors
did not, at any rate to the same extent. Law was quite isolated *quà* nonjuror. Then, again, even his earlier writings
were not of the character to make him popular in the
eighteenth century. His contribution to the Bangorian
controversy, able and telling as it was, was on what was,
for the time being, the losing side. The three famous
letters expressed exactly the sentiments of numberless
churchmen of the seventeenth century, and of numberless churchmen of the nineteenth—that is, after the
Oxford movement ; but they would not find many sympathisers in the eighteenth century. So, again, his ' Christian
Perfection ' and ' Serious Call,' the most popular of all his
works, were so written as to find disfavour in two diametrically opposite quarters. They were vehemently accused,
on the one hand, as encouraging enthusiasm ; and, on the
other hand, they were denounced by the enthusiasts themselves as encouraging ' legalism.' Again, if enthusiasm was
the bugbear of the eighteenth century, reason may almost
be called its idol. As Law, in his ' Serious Call,' was the
stimulator of enthusiasm, so, in his answer to Tindal, he
was the depreciator of reason ; and hence, though in this
work he was on the popular side (for public feeling was
strong against the Deists), yet he did not advocate it in
the popular way. Again, if Law was out of harmony with
the *general* feeling of the eighteenth century, he was still
more so with that of the clergy in particular. This does
not appear upon the surface of his writings, because he was
particularly careful never to abuse personally his clerical
brethren. Such abuse was only too common among many

whose spiritual earnestness was aroused by the Evangelical revival. The Wesleys were honourable exceptions, but Whitefield was a sad offender, and, among inferior men, depreciation of the clergy was a stock subject ; but it found no place in the writings of William Law. And yet there were few men, if any, to whom the general habit both of thought and life among the typical eighteenth century clergy was more antagonistic than to Law. Their good points were just those which he would be least likely to appreciate, and their bad points were just those which he would be most likely to deplore. Much has been said and written concerning the shortcomings of the eighteenth century clergy, and, it must be confessed, not without reason ; but they had distinctly their good points as well as their bad ones. If they lived and dressed too much like laymen, by so doing they were able to mix with the laity on equal terms, to enter into their feelings, and to come at their real mind. And if the clerical standard of religion and morality was not a very high one, it was, at any rate, higher than that of the average layman, over whom their influence was on the whole, I believe, decidedly good. But Law was not at all the sort of man to appreciate the good side of their character. This vague and indirect, though, in my opinion, very real influence in the direction of religion, would count for nothing in the eyes of one who took the standard of the ' Serious Call ' as the lowest standard at which a Christian should aim. On the other hand, their faults were just those which would seem most glaring in the eyes of Law. They entered freely into the popular amusements. No Puritan held straiter views on the subject of amusements than the High Church William Law. They took a keen interest in the politics of the day, which, of course, involved those very points on which Law was, practically, a Quaker. On week-days they were more like laymen than clergymen. Law was always emphatically the priest, in his dress, in his conversation, in every habit of his life. They were, many of them, good scholars, and prided themselves considerably on their scholarship, and on the tradition of a learned clergy, which had always belonged to the Church of England. In Law's view, 'pagan learning' was a positive hindrance to the Christian, and 'scholastic divinity' not much better. We have already noticed the fundamental difference between Law's and Warburton's theories of the nature of the Holy Spirit's influence; it may be added that the majority of the clergy were decidedly on the side of Warburton, and perhaps they liked Law none the better because he could, and did, point out how diametrically the Church prayers, which they were bound to read, were opposed to the limited and somewhat grovelling views of spiritual influence which they held.

It will thus be seen that, quite apart from Law's mysticism, there is sufficient in his life and sentiments to account for the comparative obscurity of so great and good a man. His mysticism in general, and Behmenism in particular, rendered him, of course, still more out of sympathy with his age. So far as it was the object of his later works to recommend Behmenism, they must be regarded as a failure. Not because they were unpopular, and called forth violent opposition—many works have done this, and yet have been eminently successful in effecting the object they had in view. For instance, every one whose memory can carry him back some forty years will remember the storm of unpopularity with which the 'Tracts for the Times' were received on their first appearance; and yet perhaps no writings of modern times have produced such an immense effect, and won more people over to the views which they advocated. This cannot be said of Law's mystic writings. They have now been before the world for nearly a century

and a half, and the world does not appear to be at all
more inclined to Behmenism than it was when they were
first issued.   This is not what Law expected.   'All pretences,' he said to a friend, 'and endeavours to hinder
the opening of the mystery revealed by God to Jacob
Behmen, and its bearing down all before it, will be as vain
as so many attempts to prevent or retard the coming of
the last day.'   The prophecy has not so far been fulfilled ;
nor does it seem in the way of fulfilment.   Possibly one
cause of Law's complete failure, so far as this part of his
work was concerned, is that, to all intents and purposes, he
stood quite alone in his advocacy of the Theosopher ; for
it must be confessed that the other Behmenist writers have
made so little mark upon the world as practically to count
for nothing.

In fact, so far from ' bearing down all before it,'
Behmenism has acted as a sort of dead weight to Law's
own fame.   One of the writers of his memoirs has remarked
with perfect truth that, 'by drawing attention to Jacob
Behmen, Law has in too many instances only been preparing a tomb for his own works.'[1]   Some people will, no
doubt, think that it is a pity that they should ever be
disinterred.   Whether it be so or not, at any rate the
memory of the writer ought not to be allowed to die away.
Really great and good men are not so common that we
can afford to let one be forgotten ; and Law deserves both
epithets, if ever man did.   He was one of the greatest and
best of his day.   There were others of as original a genius,
others of as brilliant talents, others of as self-denying,
Christ-like lives ; but few of his contemporaries *combined*
all these excellences to the same extent that William
Law did.

---

[1] *Spiritual Fragments selected from the Works of William Law, with a brief
Memoir of his Life,* by Mary Ann Kelty.   ' Memoir,' p. xvii.

NOTE.

I HAVE not noticed in the text the part which Mr. Law is said to have taken in the dispute which divided the Nonjurors respecting what were termed the 'Usages.'[1] Carte, the historian, relates that when an attempt was made in 1731 to unite the two parties, 'those of their presbyters that opposed it drew up a representation against it—a very pompous, empty declamation— the penman supposed to be Mr. William Law.'[2] Mr. Lathbury states, but evidently on the authority of Carte only, that 'Law was among the opponents of the union.'[3] It seems right that I should state my reasons for believing that Law took no part whatever in the dispute. They are as follows :—

(1) At the time in question (1731) we have ample information respecting Law's sayings and doings. He was the most outspoken of men. How is it that he never referred, either in his printed works or in his reported conversations, to the interest he took in this subject of the 'Usages'?

(2) After the death of that very able man, Mr. Charles Leslie, in 1722, Mr. Blackburn became the leader of the 'Non-usagers.' Now, if Law had taken so prominent a part as Carte supposes against the 'Usagers,' he must, one would have thought, have been brought into contact with Mr. Blackburn ; and yet we have not the slightest hint that he had any acquaintance with him, though we have the fullest account of Law's friends and acquaintances at this period.

(3) I have shown in the text that Law always held the highest views of the Christian sacraments. Now, the 'Usagers' repre-

---

[1] For a full account of the 'Usages,' and the controversy between the 'Usagers' and 'Non-usagers,' see Lathbury's very interesting *History of the Nonjurors*, pp. 276-303, ch. vii.

[2] Nichols' *Illustrations*, v. 155.

[3] *History of the Nonjurors*, ch. ix. p. 371.

sented, broadly speaking, the higher sacramentarians, the 'Non-usagers' the comparatively lower. I cannot believe without strong evidence (of which there is absolutely none beyond the supposition referred to by Carte) that Law would have taken the part of the latter against the former.

(4) Prominent among the Usagers was the Hon. Archibald Campbell, for some time Bishop of Edinburgh, a friend of Mr. Law and a near relation of his disciple Mrs. Hutcheson. Is it not strange that if on this point Mr. Law had been opposed to his friend, no intimation should be given of their difference? But there is a strong presumptive proof that they agreed; for in the King's Cliffe Library, among the 'books of piety to be lent to the neighbouring clergy,' is the very book in which Mr. (in later life he dropped the title of bishop) Campbell expressed fully his sentiments on the 'Usages.' It is entitled the 'Doctrine of a Middle State between Death and the Resurrection; of Prayer for the Dead, and the Necessity of Purification proved from Scripture and the Fathers; some Primitive Doctrines restored: by the Hon. Archibald Campbell.' Now, of course Mr. Law might have had his friend's book without agreeing with it, but is it conceivable that in that case he would have helped to propagate the obnoxious doctrines by placing the work among those by which he desired to edify his brother clergy?

(5) Mr. Law never took part in controversy except when he considered the issue to be of vital importance. With regard to one of the Usages he has himself distinctly told us that he did not consider it of vital importance,[1] and the general tenour of his writings shows us that he would certainly think the same of the rest.

(6) I can scarcely conceive a competent judge (as Carte undoubtedly was) characterising any composition that was really Law's as 'a pompous and empty declamation.' Carte's words seem further to imply that he did not accept the alleged hypothesis as to its authorship.

(7) The last reason I shall adduce is mainly inferential and conjectural, but practically, in my opinion, a very strong one. Among John Wesley's memoranda are found the following rules : (1) To baptise by immersion; (2) to use the mixed chalice; (3)

---

[1] See p. 315 of this work.

to pray for the faithful departed. Now, it is clear that Wesley made one at least of these rules in the early part of his life, when Law was 'a sort of oracle with him ;' for the attempt to carry out the first of them was one of the causes of his troubles in Georgia. Law has expressed himself strongly against 'the Scripture baptism of the whole body under water being only, as it were, mimicked by scattering a few drops of water on a new-born child's face.' [1] It seems to me highly probable that the three rules came from the same source, viz. Mr. Law ; and, if so, then we see that Mr. Law agreed with the 'Usagers' in two out of the four points for which they contended.

Two or three other points may here be conveniently noted :—

(1) My attention has been called by a friend to the fact that in referring to Gay's pastorals in p. 62 I have not mentioned that they were burlesques. I was aware of the fact, but did not notice it because it did not affect the main point—viz., Gay's talents for that species of composition.

(2) An absurd erratum occurs in the note to p. 137. For 'never' read 'much.'

(3) Another point has occurred to me which seems to be a presumptive proof that Mr. Law entered Mr. Gibbon's family as tutor to his son earlier than the date commonly given (1727). Why did Mr. Gibbon, a High Churchman, and all but a Jacobite, send his son to Emmanuel, a Puritan foundation? If Law, the quondam fellow of Emmanuel, was the 'much-honoured friend of the family' *before* Mr. Gibbon's son was entered at Emmanuel, nothing is more natural than that, in spite of his predilections, he should have chosen, perhaps on Law's recommendation, a college which had trained so worthy a man.

(4) As an amusing illustration of the sway which Law exercised over his friends at Cliffe, I may mention a tradition that during Law's lifetime the ladies dressed in the severely simple style recommended in the 'Serious Call,' but that after his death the feminine love of finery broke out. Miss Gibbon appeared resplendent in yellow stockings, and Miss Mary Law (Law's favourite niece) had a new dress every month.

---

[1] See Law's *Letters*, No. II. in the printed collection.

457

INDEX.

Spottiswoode & Co., Printers, New-street Square, London.

THE ENGLISH CHURCH IN THE EIGHTEENTH CENTURY.

By C. J. ABBEY and J. H. OVERTON.

Two vols. 8vo. 1,172 pages. Price 36s.

— -

OPINIONS OF THE PRESS.

'No other period of the history of our Church has been so well and so fully illustrated as the eighteenth century is in this book. The Authors have rendered a great service to students by making accessible to all that knowledge of the eighteenth century without which any adequate understanding of the nineteenth is impossible.' CONTEMPORARY REVIEW.

' A critic cannot but be conscious of a certain presumption in attempting, in such brief space and time as are at his command, to estimate the result of labours that have evidently been a constant occupation through many years. . . . The work contains, among other things, what we are inclined to consider the best account of John Wesley that has yet been given to the world. . . . We take leave of these volumes, which are as agreeable as they are learned, with a hearty commendation of them to our readers.'

SPECTATOR.

' A work which is manifestly an important and much-needed contribution to English Church History ; . . . which bears evidence of many years of reading and thought before the task of writing began. . . . If we may hazard the conjecture, we should trace the origin of this valuable book to the abiding memories which associate the foundation of Bishop Fleming with John Wesley, of whose life, character, and work, an admirable sketch has been drawn by Mr. OVERTON. . . . We commend these instructive volumes to the attention of theological students.' SATURDAY REVIEW.

' We have in these volumes a contribution of substantial and permanent value to our ecclesiastical history. The subject has been dealt with of late by Mr. Hunt and Mr. Leslie Stephen. But there is certainly room for a treatment of it from the point of view of those who write "as Churchmen, taking, however, no narrower basis than that of the National Church itself." That position is most worthily filled by these volumes. They show very considerable thought and reading, a spirit of thorough fairness and historical insight, a tone of gravity and earnestness, and a style, scholarly, clear, and readable. We shall be greatly surprised if they do not take permanent rank as one of the books necessary for every student who desires to understand the history of our English Church. . . . We trust we have said enough to commend these volumes heartily to the attention of our readers. They cover much ground, and cover it well.' GUARDIAN.

'We desire to express our own satisfaction in the reading of these volumes, and our gratitude to the writers for this noble contribution to our historical knowledge of the Church of England. It may be supplemented, but is not likely to be superseded by the labours of any future historian.'

JOHN BULL.

'A work which is not likely for many years to be superseded as a text-book or as a work of reference.'

ATHENÆUM.

'They are evidently well acquainted with the past history of the Church; they have obviously studied the lives of its chief divines with care, and traced with acuteness the varying principles which influenced its rulers.'

ACADEMY.

'We are grateful to Messrs. ABBEY and OVERTON for their valuable contribution to ecclesiastical history.'

CHURCH TIMES.

'The Authors have given us an invaluable book, which must have absorbed the study of many years. Hardly a page of it is dull, and its anecdotal richness will make it a mine of suggestion and illustration to its possessor.'

ENGLISH CHURCHMAN.

'No similar work of at all equal mark has of late years appeared. The work deserves very high praise.'

LITERARY CHURCHMAN.

'They are full of interest, and we can cordially recommend them as exhibiting much research, and a strong desire to perform the duties of candid and impartial historians. . . . There are many points on which we should differ in opinion.'

RECORD.

'We have here a perfect thesaurus of the ecclesiastical, theological, and religious history of the last century; and, high-sounding as the pretensions of such a work undoubtedly are, they will be found fully sustained and vindicated by the manner in which the Authors have executed their task.'

WATCHMAN.

'They are only heavy in the sense of being big books; while the skilful blending of lighter touches with the deeper views of religious thought which they contain results in a graceful and fascinating story. . . . One of the most noteworthy books of the season; a book to be read with pleasure, and consulted over and over again.'

THE WEEK.

'The book has the merit of real ability, the attraction of novelty, the value which must always attach to the honest investigation of important questions by men who are desirous of setting forth the truth.'

ENGLISH INDEPENDENT.

'If the narrative before us should not interest the reader it must be the reader's own fault.'

NONCONFORMIST.

'A picture replete with life-like portraiture of the English Church in the eighteenth century.'

MORNING POST.

'It was a great undertaking, and it has been ably carried out.'

LEEDS MERCURY.

'A monument of very great industry and care.'   LITERARY WORLD.

GENERAL LISTS OF WORKS

MESSRS. LONGMANS, GREEN & CO.

———◦◦⁑◦◦———

HISTORY, POLITICS, HISTORICAL MEMOIRS, &c.

Russia Before and After the War. By the Author of 'Society in St. Petersburg' &c. Translated from the German (with later Additions by the Author) by EDWARD FAIRFAX TAYLOR. Second Edition. 8vo. 14s.

Russia and England from 1876 to 1880; a Protest and an Appeal. By O. K. Author of 'Is Russia Wrong?' With a Preface by J. A. FROUDE, M.A. Portrait and Maps. 8vo. 14s.

History of England from the Conclusion of the Great War in 1815. By SPENCER WALPOLE. 8vo. VOLS. I. & II. 1815–1832 (Second Edition, revised) price 36s. VOL. III. 1832 1841, price 18s.

History of England in the 18th Century. By W. E. H. LECKY, M.A VOLS. I. & II. 1700–1760. Second Edition. 2 vols. 8vo. 36s.

The History of England from the Accession of James II. By the Right Hon. Lord MACAULAY.

STUDENT'S EDITION, 2 vols. cr. 8vo. 12s.
PEOPLE'S EDITION, 4 vols. cr. 8vo. 16s.
CABINET EDITION, 8 vols. post 8vo. 48s.
LIBRARY EDITION, 5 vols. 8vo. £4.

Lord Macaulay's Works. Complete and uniform Library Edition. Edited by his Sister, Lady TREVELYAN. 8 vols. 8vo. with Portrait, £5. 5s.

Critical and Historical Essays contributed to the Edinburgh Review. By the Right Hon. Lord MACAULAY.

CHEAP EDITION, crown 8vo. 3s. 6d.
STUDENT'S EDITION, crown 8vo. 6s.
PEOPLE'S EDITION, 2 vols. crown 8vo. 8s.
CABINET EDITION, 4 vols. 24s.
LIBRARY EDITION, 3 vols. 8vo. 36s.

The History of England from the Fall of Wolsey to the Defeat of the Spanish Armada. By J. A. FROUDE, M.A.

CABINET EDITION, 12 vols. crown, £3. 12s.
LIBRARY EDITION, 12 vols. demy, £8. 18s.

The English in Ireland in the Eighteenth Century. By J. A. FROUDE, M.A. 3 vols. 8vo. £2. 8s.

Journal of the Reigns of King George IV. and King William IV. By the late C. C. F. GREVILLE, Esq. Edited by H. REEVE, Esq. Fifth Edition. 3 vols. 8vo. price 36s.

The Life of Napoleon III. derived from State Records, Unpublished Family Correspondence, and Personal Testimony. By BLANCHARD JERROLD. In Four Volumes, 8vo. with numerous Portraits and Facsimiles. VOLS. I. to III. price 18s. each.

A

The Constitutional History of England since the Accession of George III. 1760-1870. By Sir THOMAS ERSKINE MAY, K.C.B. D.C.L. Sixth Edition. 3 vols. crown 8vo. 18s.

Democracy in Europe; a History. By Sir THOMAS ERSKINE MAY, K.C.B. D.C.L. 2 vols. 8vo. 32s.

Introductory Lectures on Modern History delivered in 1841 and 1842. By the late THOMAS ARNOLD, D.D. 8vo. 7s. 6d.

On Parliamentary Government in England; its Origin, Development, and Practical Operation. By ALPHEUS TODD. 2 vols. 8vo. 37s.

History of Civilisation in England and France, Spain and Scotland. By HENRY THOMAS BUCKLE. 3 vols. crown 8vo. 24s.

Lectures on the History of England from the Earliest Times to the Death of King Edward II. By W. LONGMAN, F.S.A. Maps and Illustrations. 8vo. 15s.

History of the Life & Times of Edward III. By W. LONGMAN, F.S.A. With 9 Maps, 8 Plates, and 16 Woodcuts. 2 vols. 8vo. 28s.

History of the Life and Reign of Richard III. Including the Story of PERKIN WARBECK. By JAMES GAIRDNER. Second Edition. Portrait and Map. Crown 8vo. 10s. 6d.

Memoirs of the Civil War in Wales and the Marches, 1642-1649. By JOHN ROLAND PHILLIPS, of Lincoln's Inn, Barrister-at-Law. 8vo. 16s.

History of England under the Duke of Buckingham and Charles I. 1624-1628. By S. R. GARDINER. 2 vols. 8vo. Maps, 24s.

The Personal Government of Charles I. from the Death of Buckingham to the Declaration in favour of Ship Money, 1628-1637. By S. R. GARDINER. 2 vols. 8vo. 24s.

Memorials of the Civil War between King Charles I. and the Parliament of England as it affected Herefordshire and the Adjacent Counties. By the Rev. J. WEBB, M.A. Edited and completed by the Rev. T. W. WEBB, M.A. 2 vols. 8vo. Illustrations, 42s.

Popular History of France, from the Earliest Times to the Death of Louis XIV. By Miss SEWELL. Crown 8vo. Maps, 7s. 6d.

A Student's Manual of the History of India from the Earliest Period to the Present. By Col. MEADOWS TAYLOR, M.R.A.S. Third Thousand. Crown 8vo. Maps, 7s. 6d.

Lord Minto in India; Correspondence of the First Earl of Minto, while Governor-General of India, from 1807 to 1814. Edited by his Great-Niece, the COUNTESS of MINTO. Completing Lord Minto's Life and Letters published in 1874 by the Countess of Minto, in Three Volumes. Post 8vo. Maps, 12s.

Indian Polity; a View of the System of Administration in India. By Lieut.-Col. G. CHESNEY. 8vo. 21s.

Waterloo Lectures; a Study of the Campaign of 1815. By Col. C. C. CHESNEY, R.E. 8vo. 10s. 6d.

The Oxford Reformers— John Colet, Erasmus, and Thomas More; a History of their Fellow-Work. By F. SEEBOHM. 8vo. 14s.

History of the Romans under the Empire. By Dean MERIVALE, D.D. 8 vols. post 8vo. 48s.

General History of Rome from B.C. 753 to A.D. 476. By Dean MERIVALE, D.D. Crown 8vo. Maps, price 7s. 6d.

The Fall of the Roman Republic; a Short History of the Last Century of the Commonwealth. By Dean MERIVALE, D.D. 12mo. 7s. 6d.

The History of Rome.
By WILHELM IHNE. VOLS. I. to III.
8vo. price 45s.

Carthage and the Carthaginians.
By R. BOSWORTH SMITH,
M.A. Second Edition. Maps, Plans,
&c. Crown 8vo. 10s. 6d.

The Sixth Oriental Monarchy;
or, the Geography, History,
and Antiquities of Parthia. By G.
RAWLINSON, M.A. With Maps and
Illustrations. 8vo. 16s.

The Seventh Great Oriental Monarchy;
or, a History of
the Sassanians. By G. RAWLINSON,
M.A. With Map and 95 Illustrations.
8vo. 28s.

The History of European
Morals from Augustus to Charlemagne. By W. E. H. LECKY, M.A.
2 vols. crown 8vo. 16s.

History of the Rise and
Influence of the Spirit of Rationalism in Europe. By W. E. H. LECKY,
M.A. 2 vols. crown 8vo. 16s.

The History of Philosophy,
from Thales to Comte. By
GEORGE HENRY LEWES. Fifth
Edition. 2 vols. 8vo. 32s.

A History of Classical
Greek Literature. By the Rev. J. P.
MAHAFFY, M.A. Trin. Coll. Dublin.
2 vols. crown 8vo. price 7s. 6d. each.

Zeller's Stoics, Epicureans, and Sceptics.
Translated by
the Rev. O. J. REICHEL, M.A. New
Edition revised. Crown 8vo. 15s.

Zeller's Socrates & the
Socratic Schools. Translated by the
Rev. O. J. REICHEL, M.A. Second
Edition. Crown 8vo. 10s. 6d.

Zeller's Plato & the Older
Academy. Translated by S. FRANCES
ALLEYNE and ALFRED GOODWIN,
B.A. Crown 8vo. 18s.

'Aristotle and the Elder Peripatetics' and 'The
Præ-Socratic Schools,' completing the English
Edition of ZELLER'S Work on Ancient Greek
Philosophy, are preparing for publication.

Epochs of Modern History.
Edited by C. COLBECK, M.A.

Church's Beginning of the Middle
Ages, 2s. 6d.
Cox's Crusades, 2s. 6d.
Creighton's Age of Elizabeth, 2s. 6d.
Gairdner's Houses of Lancaster and
York, 2s. 6d.
Gardiner's Puritan Revolution, 2s. 6d.
— Thirty Years' War, 2s. 6d.
Hale's Fall of the Stuarts, 2s. 6d.
Johnson's Normans in Europe, 2s. 6d.
Ludlow's War of American Independence, 2s. 6d.
Morris's Age of Anne, 2s. 6d.
Seebohm's Protestant Revolution, 2 6.
Stubbs's Early Plantagenets, 2s. 6d.
Warburton's Edward III. 2s. 6d.

Epochs of Ancient History.
Edited by the Rev. Sir G. W.
COX, Bart. M.A. & C. SANKEY, M.A.

Beesly's Gracchi, Marius & Sulla, 2s. 6d.
Capes's Age of the Antonines, 2s. 6d.
— Early Roman Empire, 2s. 6d.
Cox's Athenian Empire, 2s. 6d.
— Greeks & Persians, 2s. 6d.
Curteis's Macedonian Empire, 2s. 6d.
Ihne's Rome to its Capture by the
Gauls, 2s. 6d.
Merivale's Roman Triumvirates, 2s. 6d.
Sankey's Spartan & Theban Supremacies, 2s. 6d.

Creighton's Shilling History
of England, introductory to
'Epochs of English History.' Fcp.
8vo. 1s.

Epochs of English History.
Edited by the Rev. MANDELL
CREIGHTON, M.A. Fcp. 8vo. 5s.

Browning's Modern England, 1820-
1874, 9d.
Cordery's Struggle against Absolute
Monarchy, 1603-1688, 9d.
Creighton's (Mrs.) England a Continental Power, 1066-1216, 9d.
Creighton's (Rev. M.) Tudors and the
Reformation, 1485-1603, 9d.
Rowley's Rise of the People, 1215-1485,
price 9d.
Rowley's Settlement of the Constitution, 1688-1778, 9d.
Tancock's England during the American & European Wars, 1778-1820, 9d
York-Powell's Early England to the
Conquest, 1s.

The Student's Manual of

Ancient History; the Political History, Geography and Social State of the Principal Nations of Antiquity. By W. COOKE TAYLOR, LL.D. Cr. 8vo. 7s. 6d.

The Student's Manual of

Modern History; the Rise and Progress of the Principal European Nations. By W. COOKE TAYLOR, LL.D. Crown 8vo. 7s. 6d.

BIOGRAPHICAL WORKS.

The Life of Henry Venn,

B.D. Prebendary of St. Paul's, and Hon. Sec. of the Church Missionary Society; with Extracts from his Letters and Papers. By the Rev. W. KNIGHT, M.A. With an Introduction by the Rev. J. VENN, M.A. [*Just ready.*

Memoirs of the Life of

Anna Jameson, Author of 'Sacred and Legendary Art' &c. By her Niece, GERARDINE MACPHERSON. 8vo. with Portrait, 12s. 6d.

Isaac Casaubon, 1559-

1614. By MARK PATTISON, Rector of Lincoln College, Oxford. 8vo. 18s.

The Life and Letters of

Lord Macaulay. By his Nephew, G. OTTO TREVELYAN, M.P.

CABINET EDITION, 2 vols. crown 8vo. 12s.
LIBRARY EDITION, 2 vols. 8vo. 36s.

The Life of Sir Martin

Frobisher, Knt. containing a Narrative of the Spanish Armada. By the Rev. FRANK JONES, B.A. Portrait, Maps, and Facsimile. Crown 8vo. 6s.

The Life, Works, and

Opinions of Heinrich Heine. By WILLIAM STIGAND. 2 vols. 8vo. Portrait, 28s.

The Life of Mozart.

Translated from the German Work of Dr. LUDWIG NOHL by Lady WALLACE. 2 vols. crown 8vo. Portraits, 21s.

The Life of Simon de

Montfort, Earl of Leicester, with special reference to the Parliamentary History of his time. By G. W. PROTHERO. Crown 8vo. Maps, 9s.

Felix Mendelssohn's Let-

ters, translated by Lady WALLACE. 2 vols. crown 8vo. 5s. each.

Autobiography. By JOHN

STUART MILL. 8vo. 7s. 6d.

Apologia pro Vitâ Suâ;

Being a History of his Religious Opinions by JOHN HENRY NEWMAN, D.D. Crown 8vo. 6s.

Leaders of Public Opi-

nion in Ireland; Swift, Flood, Grattan, O'Connell. By W. E. H. LECKY, M.A. Crown 8vo. 7s. 6d.

Essays in Ecclesiastical

Biography. By the Right Hon. Sir J. STEPHEN, LL.D. Crown 8vo. 7s. 6d.

Cæsar; a Sketch. By JAMES

ANTHONY FROUDE, M.A. formerly Fellow of Exeter College, Oxford. With Portrait and Map. 8vo. 16s.

Life of the Duke of Wel-

lington. By the Rev. G. R. GLEIG, M.A. Crown 8vo. Portrait, 6s.

Memoirs of Sir Henry

Havelock, K.C.B. By JOHN CLARK MARSHMAN. Crown 8vo. 3s. 6d.

Vicissitudes of Families.

By Sir BERNARD BURKE, C.B. Two vols. crown 8vo. 21s.

Maunder's Treasury of

Biography, reconstructed and in great part re-written, with above 1,600 additional Memoirs by W. L. R. CATES. Fcp. 8vo. 6s.

MENTAL and POLITICAL PHILOSOPHY.

Comte's System of Positive Polity, or Treatise upon Sociology :—

VOL. I. **General View of Positivism** and Introductory Principles. Translated by J. H. BRIDGES, M.B. 8vo. 21s.

VOL. II. **The Social Statics,** or the Abstract Laws of Human Order. Translated by F. HARRISON, M.A. 8vo. 14s.

VOL. III. **The Social Dynamics,** or the General Laws of Human Progress (the Philosophy of History). Translated by E. S. BEESLY, M.A. 8vo. 21s.

VOL. IV. **The Theory of the Future of Man ;** with COMTE's Early Essays on Social Philosophy. Translated by R. CONGREVE, M.D. and H. D. HUTTON, B.A. 8vo. 24s.

De Tocqueville's Democracy in America, translated by H. REEVE. 2 vols. crown 8vo. 16s.

Analysis of the Phenomena of the Human Mind. By JAMES MILL. With Notes, Illustrative and Critical. 2 vols. 8vo. 28s.

On Representative Government. By JOHN STUART MILL. Crown 8vo. 2s.

On Liberty. By JOHN STUART MILL. Post 8vo. 7s. 6d. crown 8vo. 1s. 4d.

Principles of Political Economy. By JOHN STUART MILL. 2 vols. 8vo. 30s. or 1 vol. crown 8vo. 5s.

Essays on some Unsettled Questions of Political Economy. By JOHN STUART MILL. 8vo. 6s. 6d.

Utilitarianism. By JOHN STUART MILL. 8vo. 5s.

The Subjection of Women. By JOHN STUART MILL. Fourth Edition. Crown 8vo. 6s.

Examination of Sir William Hamilton's Philosophy. By JOHN STUART MILL. 8vo. 16s.

A System of Logic, Ratiocinative and Inductive. By JOHN STUART MILL. 2 vols. 8vo. 25s.

Dissertations and Discussions. By JOHN STUART MILL. 4 vols. 8vo. £2. 7s.

The A B C of Philosophy ;
a Text-Book for Students. By the Rev. T. GRIFFITH, M.A. Prebendary of St. Paul's. Crown 8vo. 5s.

Philosophical Fragments
written during intervals of Business. By J. D. MORELL, LL.D. Crown 8vo. 5s.

Path and Goal ; a Discussion on the Elements of Civilisation and the Conditions of Happiness. By M. M. KALISCH, Ph.D. M.A. 8vo. price 12s. 6d.

The Law of Nations considered as Independent Political Communities. By Sir TRAVERS TWISS, D.C.L. 2 vols. 8vo. £1. 13s.

A Systematic View of the Science of Jurisprudence. By SHELDON AMOS, M.A. 8vo. 18s.

A Primer of the English Constitution and Government. By S. AMOS, M.A. Crown 8vo. 6s.

Fifty Years of the English Constitution, 1830-1880. By SHELDON AMOS, M.A. Crown 8vo. 10s. 6d.

Principles of Economical Philosophy. By H. D. MACLEOD, M.A. Second Edition in 2 vols. VOL. I. 8vo. 15s. VOL. II. PART 1. 12s.

Lord Bacon's Works, collected & edited by R. L. ELLIS, M.A. J. SPEDDING, M.A. and D. D. HEATH. 7 vols. 8vo. £3. 13s. 6d.

Letters and Life of Francis Bacon, including all his Occasional Works. Collected and edited, with a Commentary, by J. SPEDDING. 7 vols. 8vo. £4. 4s.

The Institutes of Justinian;
with English Introduction, Translation, and Notes. By T. C. SANDARS, M.A. 8vo. 18s.

The Nicomachean Ethics
of Aristotle, translated into English by R. WILLIAMS, B.A. Crown 8vo. price 7s. 6d.

Aristotle's Politics, Books
I. III. IV. (VII.) Greek Text, with an English Translation by W. E. BOLLAND, M.A. and Short Essays by A. LANG, M.A. Crown 8vo. 7s. 6d.

The Politics of Aristotle;
Greek Text, with English Notes. By RICHARD CONGREVE, M.A. 8vo. 18s.

The Ethics of Aristotle;
with Essays and Notes. By Sir A. GRANT, Bart. LL.D. 2 vols. 8vo. 32s.

Bacon's Essays, with Annotations.
By R. WHATELY, D.D. 8vo. 10s. 6d.

Picture Logic; an Attempt
to Popularise the Science of Reasoning. By A. SWINBOURNE, B.A. Post 8vo. 5s.

Elements of Logic. By
R. WHATELY, D.D. 8vo. 10s. 6d. Crown 8vo. 4s. 6d.

Elements of Rhetoric.
By R. WHATELY, D.D. 8vo. 10s. 6d. Crown 8vo. 4s. 6d.

On the Influence of Authority in Matters of Opinion.
By the late Sir. G. C. LEWIS, Bart. 8vo. 14s.

The Senses and the Intellect.
By A. BAIN, LL.D. 8vo. 15s.

The Emotions and the Will.
By A. BAIN, LL.D. 8vo. 15s.

Mental and Moral Science;
a Compendium of Psychology and Ethics. By A. BAIN, LL.D. Crown 8vo. 10s. 6d.

An Outline of the Necessary Laws of Thought;
a Treatise on Pure and Applied Logic. By W. THOMSON, D.D. Crown 8vo. 6s.

Essays in Political and Moral Philosophy.
By T. E. CLIFFE LESLIE, Hon. LL.D. Dubl. of Lincoln's Inn, Barrister-at-Law. 8vo. 10s. 6d.

Hume's Philosophical Works.
Edited, with Notes, &c. by T. H. GREEN, M.A. and the Rev. T. H. GROSE, M.A. 4 vols. 8vo. 56s. Or separately, Essays, 2 vols. 28s. Treatise on Human Nature, 2 vols. 28s.

Lectures on German Thought.
Six Lectures on the History and Prominent Features of German Thought during the last Two Hundred Years, delivered at the Royal Institution of Great Britain. By KARL HILLEBRAND. Rewritten and enlarged. Crown 8vo. 7s. 6d. ·

MISCELLANEOUS & CRITICAL WORKS.

Selected Essays, chiefly
from Contributions to the Edinburgh and Quarterly Reviews. By A. HAYWARD, Q.C. 2 vols. crown 8vo. 12s.

Miscellaneous Writings
of J. Conington, M.A. Edited by J. A. SYMONDS, M.A. 2 vols. 8vo. 28s.

Short Studies on Great
Subjects. By J. A. FROUDE, M.A. 3 vols. crown 8vo. 18s.

Literary Studies. By the
late WALTER BAGEHOT, M.A. Fellow of University College, London. Edited, with a Prefatory Memoir, by R. H. HUTTON. Second Edition. 2 vols. 8vo. with Portrait, 28s.

Manual of English Literature, Historical and Critical.
By T. ARNOLD, M.A. Crown 8vo. 7s. 6d.

The Wit and Wisdom of
the Rev. Sydney Smith. Crown 8vo. 3s. 6d.

Lord Macaulay's Miscellaneous Writings : -

LIBRARY EDITION, 2 vols. 8vo. 21s.
PEOPLE'S EDITION, 1 vol. cr. 8vo. 4s. 6d.

Lord Macaulay's Miscellaneous Writings and Speeches.

Student's Edition. Crown 8vo. 6s.

Speeches of the Right

Hon. Lord Macaulay, corrected by Himself. Crown 8vo. 3s. 6d.

Selections from the Writings of Lord Macaulay.

Edited, with Notes, by G. O. TREVELYAN, M.P. Crown. 8vo. 6s.

Miscellaneous and Posthumous Works of the late Henry Thomas Buckle.

Edited by HELEN TAYLOR. 3 vols. 8vo. 52s. 6d.

Miscellaneous Works of

Thomas Arnold, D.D. late Head Master of Rugby School. 8vo. 7s. 6d.

The Pastor's Narrative ;

or, before and after the Battle of Wörth, 1870. By Pastor KLEIN. Translated by Mrs. F. E. MARSHALL. Crown 8vo. Map, 6s.

German Home Life ; a

Series of Essays on the Domestic Life of Germany. Crown 8vo. 6s.

Realities of Irish Life.

By W. STEUART TRENCH. Crown 8vo. 2s. 6d. boards, or 3s. 6d. cloth.

Two Lectures on South

Africa delivered before the Philosophical Institute, Edinburgh, Jan. 6 & 9, 1880. By JAMES ANTHONY FROUDE, M.A. 8vo. 5s.

Cetshwayo's Dutchman ;

the Private Journal of a White Trader in Zululand during the British Invasion. By CORNELIUS VIJN. Translated and edited with Preface and Notes by the Right Rev. J. W. COLENSO, D.D. Bishop of Natal. Crown 8vo. Portrait, 5s.

Apparitions; a Narrative

of Facts. By the Rev. B. W. SAVILE, M.A. Second Edition. Crown 8vo. price 5s.

Max Muller and the

Philosophy of Language. By LUDWIG NOIRÉ. 8vo. 6s.

Lectures on the Science

of Language. By F. MAX MÜLLER, M.A. 2 vols. crown 8vo. 16s.

Chips from a German

Workshop ; Essays on the Science of Religion, and on Mythology, Traditions & Customs. By F. MAX MÜLLER, M.A. 4 vols. 8vo. £2. 18s.

Language & Languages.

A Revised Edition of Chapters on Language and Families of Speech. By F. W. FARRAR, D.D. F.R.S. Crown 8vo. 6s.

The Essays and Contributions of A. K. H. B.

Uniform Cabinet Editions in crown 8vo.

Recreations of a Country Parson, Three Series, 3s. 6d. each.

Landscapes, Churches, and Moralities, price 3s. 6d.

Seaside Musings, 3s. 6d.

Changed Aspects of Unchanged Truths, 3s. 6d.

Counsel and Comfort from a City Pulpit, 3s. 6d.

Lessons of Middle Age, 3s. 6d.

Leisure Hours in Town, 3s. 6d.

Autumn Holidays of a Country Parson, price 3s. 6d.

Sunday Afternoons at the Parish Church of a University City, 3s. 6d.

The Commonplace Philosopher in Town and Country, 3s. 6d.

Present-Day Thoughts, 3s. 6d.

Critical Essays of a Country Parson, price 3s. 6d.

The Graver Thoughts of a Country Parson, Three Series, 3s. 6d. each.

DICTIONARIES and OTHER BOOKS of REFERENCE.

One-Volume Dictionary
of the English Language. By R.
G. LATHAM, M.A. M.D.   Medium
8vo. 24s.

Larger Dictionary of
the English Language. By R. G.
LATHAM, M.A. M.D. Founded on
Johnson's English Dictionary as edited
by the Rev. H. J. TODD. 4 vols. 4to. £7.

Roget's Thesaurus of
English Words and Phrases, classi-
fied and arranged so as to facilitate the
expression of Ideas, and assist in
Literary Composition. Revised and
enlarged by the Author's Son, J. L.
ROGET. Crown 8vo. 10s. 6d.

English Synonymes. By
E. J. WHATELY.   Edited by R.
WHATELY, D.D. Fcp. 8vo. 3s.

Handbook of the English
Language. By R. G. LATHAM, M.A.
M.D. Crown 8vo. 6s.

Contanseau's Practical
Dictionary of the French and English
Languages. Post 8vo. price 7s. 6d.

Contanseau's Pocket
Dictionary, French and English,
abridged from the Practical Dictionary
by the Author. Square 18mo. 3s. 6d.

A Practical Dictionary
of the German and English Languages. By Rev. W. L. BLACKLEY,
M.A. & Dr. C. M. FRIEDLÄNDER.
Post 8vo. 7s. 6d.

A New Pocket Diction-
ary of the German and English
Languages. By F. W. LONGMAN,
Ball. Coll. Oxford. Square 18mo. 5s.

Becker's Gallus ; Roman
Scenes of the Time of Augustus.
Translated by the Rev. F. METCALFE,
M.A. Post 8vo. 7s. 6d.

Becker's Charicles;
Illustrations of the Private Life of
the Ancient Greeks. Translated by
the Rev. F. METCALFE, M.A.   Post
8vo. 7s. 6d.

A Dictionary of Roman
and Greek Antiquities. With 2,000
Woodcuts illustrative of the Arts and
Life of the Greeks and Romans. By
A. RICH, B.A. Crown 8vo. 7s. 6d.

A Greek-English Lexi-
con. By H. G. LIDDELL, D.D. Dean
of Christchurch, and R. SCOTT, D.D.
Dean of Rochester. Crown 4to. 36s.

Liddell & Scott's Lexi-
con, Greek and English, abridged for
Schools. Square 12mo. 7s. 6d.

An English-Greek Lexi-
con, containing all the Greek Words
used by Writers of good authority. By
C. D. YONGE, M.A. 4to. 21s. School
Abridgment, square 12mo. 8s. 6d.

A Latin-English Diction-
ary. By JOHN T. WHITE, D.D.
Oxon. and J. E. RIDDLE, M.A. Oxon.
Sixth Edition, revised. Quarto 21s.

White's College Latin-
English Dictionary, for the use of
University Students. Royal 8vo. 12s.

M'Culloch's Dictionary
of Commerce and Commercial Navigation. Re-edited, with a Supplement
shewing the Progress of British Commercial Legislation to the Year 1880,
by HUGH G. REID.   With 11 Maps
and 30 Charts. 8vo. 63s. The SUPPLE-
MENT separately, price 5s.

Keith Johnston's General
Dictionary of Geography, Descriptive,
Physical, Statistical, and Historical ;
a complete Gazetteer of the World.
Medium 8vo. 42s.

The Public Schools Atlas
of Ancient Geography, in 28 entirely
new Coloured Maps. Edited by the
Rev. G. BUTLER, M.A. Imperial 8vo.
or imperial 4to. 7s. 6d.

The Public Schools Atlas
of Modern Geography, in 31 entirely
new Coloured Maps. Edited by the
Rev. G. BUTLER, M.A. Uniform, 5s.

ASTRONOMY and METEOROLOGY.

Outlines of Astronomy.
By Sir J. F. W. HERSCHEL, Bart. M.A. Latest Edition, with Plates and Diagrams. Square crown 8vo. 12*s*.

Essays on Astronomy.
A Series of Papers on Planets and Meteors, the Sun and Sun-surrounding Space, Stars and Star Cloudlets. By R. A. PROCTOR, B.A. With 10 Plates and 24 Woodcuts. 8vo. 12*s*.

The Moon; her Motions,
Aspects, Scenery, and Physical Condition. By R. A. PROCTOR, B.A. With Plates, Charts, Woodcuts, and Lunar Photographs. Crown 8vo. 10*s*.6*d*.

The Sun ; Ruler, Light, Fire,
and Life of the Planetary System. By R. A. PROCTOR, B.A. With Plates & Woodcuts. Crown 8vo. 14*s*.

The Orbs Around Us ;
a Series of Essays on the Moon & Planets, Meteors & Comets, the Sun & Coloured Pairs of Suns. By R. A. PROCTOR, B.A. With Chart and Diagrams. Crown 8vo. 7*s*. 6*d*.

Other Worlds than Ours ;
The Plurality of Worlds Studied under the Light of Recent Scientific Researches. By R. A. PROCTOR, B.A. With 14 Illustrations. Cr. 8vo. 10*s*. 6*d*.

The Universe of Stars ;
Presenting Researches into and New Views respecting the Constitution of the Heavens. By R. A. PROCTOR, B.A. Second Edition, with 22 Charts (4 Coloured) and 22 Diagrams. 8vo. price 10*s*. 6*d*.

The Transits of Venus ;
A Popular Account of Past and Coming Transits. By R. A. PROCTOR, B.A. 20 Plates (12 Coloured) and 27 Woodcuts. Crown 8vo. 8*s*. 6*d*.

Saturn and its System.
By R. A. PROCTOR, B.A. 8vo. with 14 Plates, 14*s*.

The Moon, and the Con-
dition and Configurations of its Surface. By E. NEISON, F.R.A.S. With 26 Maps & 5 Plates. Medium 8vo. 31*s*. 6*d*.

A New Star Atlas, for the
Library, the School, and the Observatory, in 12 Circular Maps (with 2 Index Plates). By R. A. PROCTOR, B.A. Crown 8vo. 5*s*.

Larger Star Atlas, for the
Library, in Twelve Circular Maps, with Introduction and 2 Index Plates. By R. A. PROCTOR, B.A. Folio, 15*s*. or Maps only, 12*s*. 6*d*.

A Treatise on the Cy-
cloid, and on all forms of Cycloidal Curves, and on the use of Cycloidal Curves in dealing with the Motions of Planets, Comets, &c. and of Matter projected from the Sun. By R. A. PROCTOR, B.A. With 161 Diagrams. Crown 8vo. 10*s*. 6*d*.

Dove's Law of Storms,
considered in connexion with the Ordinary Movements of the Atmosphere. Translated by R. H. SCOTT, M.A. 8vo. 10*s*. 6*d*.

Air and Rain ; the Begin-
nings of a Chemical Climatology. By R. A. SMITH, F.R.S. 8vo. 24*s*.

Schellen's Spectrum
Analysis, in its Application to Terrestrial Substances and the Physical Constitution of the Heavenly Bodies. Translated by JANE and C. LASSELL, with Notes by W. HUGGINS, LL.D. F.R.S. 8vo. Plates and Woodcuts, 28*s*.

B

NATURAL HISTORY and PHYSICAL SCIENCE.

Professor Helmholtz'
Popular Lectures on Scientific Subjects. Translated by E. ATKINSON, F.C.S. With numerous Wood Engravings. 8vo. 12*s*. 6*d*.

Professor Helmholtz on
the Sensations of Tone, as a Physiological Basis for the Theory of Music. Translated by A. J. ELLIS, F.R.S. 8vo. 36*s*.

Ganot's Natural Philo-
sophy for General Readers and Young Persons; a Course of Physics divested of Mathematical Formulæ and expressed in the language of daily life. Translated by E. ATKINSON, F.C.S. Third Edition. Plates and Woodcuts. Crown 8vo. 7*s*. 6*d*.

Ganot's Elementary
Treatise on Physics, Experimental and Applied, for the use of Colleges and Schools. Translated by E. ATKINSON, F.C.S. Ninth Edition. Plates and Woodcuts. Large crown 8vo. 15*s*.

Arnott's Elements of Phy-
sics or Natural Philosophy. Seventh Edition, edited by A. BAIN, LL.D. and A. S. TAYLOR, M.D. F.R.S. Crown 8vo. Woodcuts, 12*s*. 6*d*.

The Correlation of Phy-
sical Forces. By the Hon. Sir W. R. GROVE, F.R.S. &c. Sixth Edition, revised and augmented. 8vo. 15*s*.

Weinhold's Introduction
to Experimental Physics; including Directions for Constructing Physical Apparatus and for Making Experiments. Translated by B. LOEWY, F.R.A.S. 8vo. Plates & Woodcuts 31*s*. 6*d*.

A Treatise on Magnet-
ism, General and Terrestrial. By H. LLOYD, D.D. D.C.L. 8vo. 10*s*. 6*d*.

Elementary Treatise on
the Wave-Theory of Light. By H. LLOYD, D.D. D.C.L. 8vo. 10*s*. 6*d*.

Fragments of Science.
By JOHN TYNDALL, F.R.S. Sixth Edition, revised and augmented. 2 vols. crown 8vo. 16*s*.

Heat a Mode of Motion.
By JOHN TYNDALL, F.R.S. Fifth Edition in preparation.

Sound. By JOHN TYNDALL,
F.R.S. Third Edition, including Recent Researches on Fog-Signalling. Crown 8vo. price 10*s*. 6*d*.

Contributions to Mole-
cular Physics in the domain of Radiant Heat. By JOHN TYNDALL, F.R.S. Plates and Woodcuts. 8vo. 16*s*.

Professor Tyndall's Re-
searches on Diamagnetism and Magne-Crystallic Action; including Diamagnetic Polarity. New Edition in preparation.

Professor Tyndall's Lec-
tures on Light, delivered in America in 1872 and 1873. With Portrait, Plate & Diagrams. Crown 8vo. 7*s*. 6*d*.

Professor Tyndall's Les-
sons in Electricity at the Royal Institution, 1875-6. With 58 Woodcuts. Crown 8vo. 2*s*. 6*d*.

Professor Tyndall's Notes
of a Course of Seven Lectures on Electrical Phenomena and Theories, delivered at the Royal Institution. Crown 8vo. 1*s*. sewed, 1*s*. 6*d*. cloth.

Professor Tyndall's Notes
of a Course of Nine Lectures on Light, delivered at the Royal Institution. Crown 8vo. 1*s*. swd., 1*s*. 6*d*. cloth.

Principles of Animal Me-
chanics. By the Rev. S. HAUGHTON, F.R.S. Second Edition. 8vo. 21*s*.

Text-Books of Science,

Mechanical and Physical, adapted for the use of Artisans and of Students in Public and Science Schools. Small 8vo. with Woodcuts, &c.

Abney's Photography, 3s. 6d.

Anderson's (Sir John) Strength of Materials, 3s. 6d.

Armstrong's Organic Chemistry, 3s. 6d.

Barry's Railway Appliances, 3s. 6d.

Bloxam's Metals, 3s. 6d.

Goodeve's Mechanics, 3s. 6d.

—— Mechanism, 3s. 6d.

Gore's Electro-Metallurgy, 6s.

Griffin's Algebra & Trigonometry, 3/6.

Jenkin's Electricity & Magnetism, 3/6.

Maxwell's Theory of Heat, 3s. 6d.

Merrifield's Technical Arithmetic, 3s. 6d.

Miller's Inorganic Chemistry, 3s. 6d.

Preece & Sivewright's Telegraphy, 3/6.

Rutley's Study of Rocks, 4s. 6d.

Shelley's Workshop Appliances, 3s. 6d.

Thomé's Structural and Physiological Botany, 6s.

Thorpe's Quantitative Analysis, 4s. 6d.

Thorpe & Muir's Qualitative Analysis, price 3s. 6d.

Tilden's Chemical Philosophy, 3s. 6d.

Unwin's Machine Design, 3s. 6d.

Watson's Plane & Solid Geometry, 3/6.

Light Science for Leisure

Hours; Familiar Essays on Scientific Subjects, Natural Phenomena, &c. By R. A. PROCTOR, B.A. 2 vols. crown 8vo. 7s. 6d. each.

An Introduction to the

Systematic Zoology and Morphology of Vertebrate Animals. By A. MACALISTER, M.D. With 28 Diagrams. 8vo. 10s. 6d.

The Comparative Ana-

tomy and Physiology of the Vertebrate Animals. By RICHARD OWEN, F.R.S. With 1,472 Woodcuts. 3 vols. 8vo. £3. 13s. 6d.

Homes without Hands;

a Description of the Habitations of Animals, classed according to their Principle of Construction. By the Rev. J. G. WOOD, M.A. With about 140 Vignettes on Wood. 8vo. 14s.

Wood's Strange Dwell-

ings; a Description of the Habitations of Animals, abridged from 'Homes without Hands.' With Frontispiece and 60 Woodcuts. Crown 8vo. 7. 6d.

Wood's Insects at Home;

a Popular Account of British Insects, their Structure, Habits, and Transformations. 8vo. Woodcuts, 14s.

Wood's Insects Abroad;

a Popular Account of Foreign Insects, their Structure, Habits, and Transformations. 8vo. Woodcuts, 14s.

Wood's Out of Doors; a

Selection of Original Articles on Practical Natural History. With 6 Illustrations. Crown 8vo. 7s. 6d.

Wood's Bible Animals; a

description of every Living Creature mentioned in the Scriptures, from the Ape to the Coral. With 112 Vignettes. 8vo. 14s.

The Sea and its Living

Wonders. By Dr. G. HARTWIG. 8vo. with many Illustrations, 10s. 6d.

Hartwig's Tropical

World. With about 200 Illustrations. 8vo. 10s. 6d.

Hartwig's Polar World;

a Description of Man and Nature in the Arctic and Antarctic Regions of the Globe. Maps, Plates & Woodcuts. 8vo. 10s. 6d.

Hartwig's Subterranean

World. With Maps and Woodcuts. 8vo. 10s. 6d.

Hartwig's Aerial World;

a Popular Account of the Phenomena and Life of the Atmosphere. Map, Plates, Woodcuts. 8vo. 10s. 6d.

Kirby and Spence's Introduction to Entomology, or Elements of the Natural History of Insects. Crown 8vo, 5s.

A Familiar History of Birds. By E. STANLEY, D.D. Fcp. 8vo. with Woodcuts, 3s. 6d.

Rural Bird Life ; Essays on Ornithology, with Instructions for Preserving Objects relating to that Science. By CHARLES DIXON. With Coloured Frontispiece and 44 Woodcuts by G. Pearson. Crown 8vo. 7s. 6d. cloth extra, gilt edges.

Rocks Classified and Described. By BERNHARD VON COTTA. An English Translation, by P. H. LAWRENCE, with English, German, and French Synonymes. Post 8vo. 14s.

The Geology of England and Wales; a Concise Account of the Lithological Characters, Leading Fossils, and Economic Products of the Rocks. By H. B. WOODWARD, F.G.S. Crown 8vo. Map & Woodcuts, 14s.

Keller's Lake Dwellings of Switzerland, and other Parts of Europe. Translated by JOHN E. LEE, F.S.A. F.G.S. With 206 Illustrations. 2 vols. royal 8vo. 42s.

Heer's Primæval World of Switzerland. Edited by JAMES HEYWOOD, M.A. F.R.S. With Map, 19 Plates, & 372 Woodcuts. 2 vols. 8vo. 16s.

The Puzzle of Life and How it Has Been Put Together ; a Short History of Praehistoric Vegetable and Animal Life on the Earth. By A. NICOLS, F.R.G.S. With 12 Illustrations. Crown 8vo. 3s. 6d.

The Origin of Civilisation, and the Primitive Condition of Man ; Mental and Social Condition of Savages. By Sir J. LUBBOCK, Bart. M.P. F.R.S. 8vo. Woodcuts, 18s.

A Dictionary of Science, Literature, and Art. Re-edited by the late W. T. BRANDE (the Author) and the Rev. Sir G. W. COX, Bart. M.A. 3 vols. medium 8vo. 63s.

Hullah's Course of Lectures on the History of Modern Music. 8vo. 8s. 6d.

Hullah's Second Course of Lectures on the Transition Period of Musical History. 8vo. 10s. 6d.

Loudon's Encyclopædia of Plants ; comprising the Specific Character, Description, Culture, History, &c. of all the Plants found in Great Britain. With upwards of 12,000 Woodcuts. 8vo. 42s.

De Caisne & Le Maout's Descriptive and Analytical Botany. Translated by Mrs. HOOKER ; edited and arranged by J. D. HOOKER, M.D. With 5,500 Woodcuts. Imperial 8vo. price 31s. 6d.

Rivers's Orchard-House; or, the Cultivation of Fruit Trees under Glass. Sixteenth Edition, re-edited by T. F. RIVERS. Crown 8vo. with 25 Woodcuts, 5s.

The Rose Amateur's Guide. By THOMAS RIVERS. Latest Edition. Fcp. 8vo. 4s. 6d.

Town and Window Gardening, including the Structure, Habits and Uses of Plants. By Mrs. BUCKTON With 127 Woodcuts. Crown 8vo. 2s.

CHEMISTRY and PHYSIOLOGY.

Practical Chemistry; the
Principles of Qualitative Analysis. By W. A. TILDEN, D.Sc. Lond. F.C.S. Professor of Chemistry in Mason's College, Birmingham. Fcp. 8vo. 1s. 6d.

Miller's Elements of Chemistry,
Theoretical and Practical. Re-edited, with Additions, by H. MACLEOD, F.C.S. 3 vols. 8vo.

PART I. CHEMICAL PHYSICS. 16s.
PART II. INORGANIC CHEMISTRY, 24s.
PART III. ORGANIC CHEMISTRY, 31s. 6d.

Annals of Chemical Medicine;
including the Application of Chemistry to Physiology, Pathology, Therapeutics, Pharmacy, Toxicology, and Hygiene. Edited by J. L. W. THUDICHUM, M.D. Vol. I. 8vo. 14s.

Health in the House:
Twenty-five Lectures on Elementary Physiology in its Application to the Daily Wants of Man and Animals. By Mrs. BUCKTON. Crown 8vo. Woodcuts, 2s.

A Dictionary of Chemistry and the Allied Branches of other
Sciences. By HENRY WATTS, F.C.S. assisted by eminent Scientific and Practical Chemists. 7 vols. medium 8vo. £10. 16s. 6d.

Third Supplement, completing the Record of Chemical Discovery to the year 1877. PART I. 8vo. 36s. PART II. completion, in the press.

Select Methods in Chemical Analysis,
chiefly Inorganic. By WM. CROOKES, F.R.S. With 22 Woodcuts. Crown 8vo. 12s. 6d.

The History, Products, and Processes of the Alkali Trade,
including the most recent Improvements. By CHARLES T. KINGZETT, F.C.S. With 32 Woodcuts. 8vo. 12s.

Animal Chemistry, or the
Relations of Chemistry to Physiology and Pathology: a Manual for Medical Men and Scientific Chemists. By CHARLES T. KINGZETT, F.C.S. 8vo. price 18s.

The FINE ARTS and ILLUSTRATED EDITIONS.

In Fairyland; Pictures
from the Elf-World. By RICHARD DOYLE. With 16 coloured Plates, containing 36 Designs. Folio, 15s.

Lord Macaulay's Lays of
Ancient Rome. With Ninety Illustrations on Wood from Drawings by G. SCHARF. Fcp. 4to. 21s.

Miniature Edition of
Macaulay's Lays of Ancient Rome, with Scharf's 90 Illustrations reduced in Lithography. Imp. 16mo. 10s. 6d.

Moore's Lalla Rookh.
TENNIEL'S Edition, with 68 Woodcut Illustrations. Crown 8vo. 10s. 6d.

Moore's Irish Melodies,
MACLISE'S Edition, with 161 Steel Plates. Super-royal 8vo. 21s.

Lectures on Harmony,
delivered at the Royal Institution. By G. A. MACFARREN. 8vo. 12s.

Sacred and Legendary
Art. By Mrs. JAMESON. 6 vols. square crown 8vo. £5. 15s. 6d.

Jameson's Legends of the
Saints and Martyrs. With 19 Etchings and 187 Woodcuts. 2 vols. 31s. 6d.

Jameson's Legends of the
Monastic Orders. With 11 Etchings and 88 Woodcuts. 1 vol. 21s.

Jameson's Legends of the
Madonna. With 27 Etchings and 165 Woodcuts. 1 vol. 21s.

Jameson's History of the
Saviour, His Types and Precursors. Completed by Lady EASTLAKE. With 13 Etchings and 281 Woodcuts. 2 vols. 42s.

The Three Cathedrals
dedicated to St. Paul in London. By W. LONGMAN, F.S.A. With numerous Illustrations. Square crown 8vo. 21s.

The USEFUL ARTS, MANUFACTURES, &c.

The Art of Scientific Discovery.
By G. GORE, LL.D. F.R.S. Crown 8vo. 15s.

The Amateur Mechanics' Practical Handbook;
describing the different Tools required in the Workshop. By A. H. G. HOBSON. With 33 Woodcuts. Crown 8vo. 2s. 6d.

The Engineer's Valuing Assistant.
By H. D. HOSKOLD, Civil and Mining Engineer. 8vo. price 31s. 6d.

Industrial Chemistry; a
Manual for Manufacturers and for Colleges or Technical Schools; a Translation (by Dr. T. H. BARRY) of Stohmann and Engler's German Edition of PAYEN's 'Précis de Chimie Industrielle;' with Chapters on the Chemistry of the Metals, &c. by B. H. PAUL, Ph.D. With 698 Woodcuts. Medium 8vo. 42s.

Gwilt's Encyclopædia of Architecture,
with above 1,600 Woodcuts. Revised and extended by W. PAPWORTH. 8vo. 52s. 6d.

Lathes and Turning, Simple,
Mechanical, and Ornamental. By W. H. NORTHCOTT. Second Edition, with 338 Illustrations. 8vo. 18s.

The Theory of Strains in Girders and similar Structures,
with Observations on the application of Theory to Practice, and Tables of the Strength and other Properties of Materials. By B. B. STONEY, M.A. M. Inst. C.E. Royal 8vo. with 5 Plates and 123 Woodcuts, 36s.

A Treatise on Mills and Millwork.
By the late Sir W. FAIRBAIRN, Bart. C.E. Fourth Edition, with 18 Plates and 333 Woodcuts. 1 vol. 8vo. 25s.

Useful Information for Engineers.
By the late Sir W. FAIRBAIRN, Bart. C.E. With many Plates and Woodcuts. 3 vols. crown 8vo. 31s. 6d.

The Application of Cast and Wrought Iron to Building
Purposes. By the late Sir W. FAIRBAIRN, Bart. C.E. With 6 Plates and 118 Woodcuts. 8vo. 16s.

Hints on Household Taste
in Furniture, Upholstery, and other Details. By C. L. EASTLAKE. Fourth Edition, with 100 Illustrations. Square crown 8vo. 14s.

Handbook of Practical Telegraphy.
By R. S. CULLEY, Memb. Inst. C.E. Seventh Edition. Plates & Woodcuts. 8vo. 16s.

A Treatise on the Steam Engine,
in its various applications to Mines, Mills, Steam Navigation, Railways and Agriculture. By J. BOURNE, C.E. With Portrait, 37 Plates, and 546 Woodcuts. 4to. 42s.

Recent Improvements in the Steam Engine.
By J. BOURNE, C.E. Fcp. 8vo. Woodcuts, 6s.

Catechism of the Steam Engine,
in its various Applications. By JOHN BOURNE, C.E. Fcp. 8vo. Woodcuts, 6s.

Handbook of the Steam Engine,
a Key to the Author's Catechism of the Steam Engine. By J. BOURNE, C.E. Fcp. 8vo. Woodcuts, 9s.

Examples of Steam and Gas Engines
of the most recent Approved Types as employed in Mines, Factories, Steam Navigation, Railways and Agriculture, practically described. By JOHN BOURNE, C.E. With 54 Plates and 356 Woodcuts. 4to. 70s.

Cresy's Encyclopædia of Civil Engineering,
Historical, Theoretical, and Practical. With above 3,000 Woodcuts. 8vo. 42s.

Ure's Dictionary of Arts, Manufactures, and Mines.
Seventh Edition, re-written and enlarged by R. HUNT, F.R.S. assisted by numerous contributors. With 2,604 Woodcuts. 4 vols. medium 8vo. £7. 7s.

Practical Treatise on Metallurgy.
Adapted from the last German Edition of Professor KERL'S Metallurgy by W. CROOKES, F.R.S. &c. and E. RÖHRIG, Ph.D. 3 vols. 8vo. with 625 Woodcuts. £4. 19s.

Anthracen; its Constitution,
Properties, Manufacture, and Derivatives, including Artificial Alizarin, Anthrapurpurin, &c. with their Applications in Dyeing and Printing. By G. AUERBACH. Translated by W. CROOKES, F.R.S. 8vo. 12s.

On Artificial Manures,
their Chemical Selection and Scientific Application to Agriculture ; a Series of Lectures given at the Experimental Farm at Vincennes in 1867 and 1874-75. By M. GEORGES VILLE. Translated and edited by W. CROOKES, F.R.S. With 31 Plates. 8vo. 21s.

Practical Handbook of
Dyeing and Calico-Printing. By W. CROOKES, F.R.S. &c. With numerous Illustrations and specimens of Dyed Textile Fabrics. 8vo. 42s.

The Art of Perfumery,
and the Methods of Obtaining the Odours of Plants ; the Growth and general Flower Farm System of Raising Fragrant Herbs ; with Instructions for the Manufacture of Perfumes for the Handkerchief, Scented Powders, Odorous Vinegars and Salts, Snuff, Dentifrices, Cosmetics, Perfumed Soap, &c. By G. W. S. PIESSE, Ph.D. F.C.S. Fourth Edition, with 96 Woodcuts. Square crown 8vo. 21s.

Mitchell's Manual of
Practical Assaying. Fourth Edition, revised, with the Recent Discoveries incorporated, by W. CROOKES, F.R.S. Crown 8vo. Woodcuts, 31s. 6d.

Loudon's Encyclopædia
of Gardening ; the Theory and Practice of Horticulture, Floriculture, Arboriculture & Landscape Gardening. With 1,000 Woodcuts. 8vo. 21s.

Loudon's Encyclopædia
of Agriculture ; the Laying-out, Improvement, and Management of Landed Property ; the Cultivation and Economy of the Productions of Agriculture. With 1,100 Woodcuts. 8vo. 21s.

RELIGIOUS and MORAL WORKS.

A Handbook to the Bible,
or, Guide to the Study of the Holy Scriptures derived from Ancient Monuments and Modern Exploration. By F. R. CONDER, and Lieut. C. R. CONDER, R.E. late Commanding the Survey of Palestine. Second Edition ; Maps, Plates of Coins, &c. Post 8vo. price 7s. 6d.

Four Lectures on some
Epochs of Early Church History. By the Very Rev. C. MERIVALE, D.D. Dean of Ely. Crown 8vo. 5s.

A History of the Church
of England ; Pre-Reformation Period. By the Rev. T. P. BOULTBEE, LL.D. 8vo. 15s.

Sketch of the History of
the Church of England to the Revolution of 1688. By T. V. SHORT, D.D. Crown 8vo. 7s. 6d.

The English Church in
the Eighteenth Century. By CHARLES J. ABBEY, late Fellow of University College, Oxford ; and JOHN H. OVERTON, late Scholar of Lincoln College, Oxford. 2 vols. 8vo. 36s.

An Exposition of the 39
Articles, Historical and Doctrinal. By E. H. BROWNE, D.D. Bishop of Winchester. Eleventh Edition. 8vo. 16s.

A Commentary on the
39 Articles, forming an Introduction to the Theology of the Church of England. By the Rev. T. P. BOULTBEE, LL.D. New Edition. Crown 8vo. 6s.

Sermons preached mostly
in the Chapel of Rugby School by the late T. ARNOLD, D.D. Collective Edition, revised by the Author's Daughter, Mrs. W. E. FORSTER. 6 vols. crown 8vo. 30s. or separately, 5s. each.

Historical Lectures on
the Life of Our Lord Jesus Christ.
By C. J. ELLICOTT, D.D. 8vo. 12s.

The Eclipse of Faith ; or
a Visit to a Religious Sceptic. By
HENRY ROGERS. Fcp. 8vo. 5s.

Defence of the Eclipse of
Faith. By H. ROGERS. Fcp. 8vo. 3s. 6d.

Nature, the Utility of
Religion and Theism. Three Essays
by JOHN STUART MILL. 8vo. 10s. 6d.

A Critical and Gram-
matical Commentary on St. Paul's
Epistles. By C. J. ELLICOTT, D.D.
8vo. Galatians, 8s. 6d. Ephesians,
8s. 6d. Pastoral Epistles, 10s. 6d.
Philippians, Colossians, & Philemon,
10s. 6d. Thessalonians, 7s. 6d.

Conybeare & Howson's
Life and Epistles of St. Paul.
Three Editions, copiously illustrated.

Library Edition, with all the Original
Illustrations, Maps, Landscapes on
Steel, Woodcuts, &c. 2 vols. 4to. 42s.

Intermediate Edition, with a Selection
of Maps, Plates, and Woodcuts. 2 vols.
square crown 8vo. 21s.

Student's Edition, revised and con-
densed, with 46 Illustrations and Maps.
1 vol. crown 8vo. 9s.

The Jewish Messiah ;
Critical History of the Messianic Idea
among the Jews, from the Rise of the
Maccabees to the Closing of the Talmud.
By J. DRUMMOND, B.A. 8vo. 15s.

Bible Studies. By M. M.
KALISCH, Ph.D. PART I. *The Prophecies of Balaam.* 8vo. 10s. 6d.
PART II. *The Book of Jonah.* 8vo.
price 10s. 6d.

Historical and Critical
Commentary on the Old Testament;
with a New Translation. By M. M.
KALISCH, Ph.D. Vol. I. Genesis,
8vo. 18s. or adapted for the General
Reader, 12s. Vol. II. Exodus, 15s. or
adapted for the General Reader, 12s.
Vol. III. Leviticus, Part I. 15s. or
adapted for the General Reader, 8s.
Vol. IV. Leviticus, Part II. 15s. or
adapted for the General Reader, 8s.

Ewald's History of Israel.
Translated from the German by J. E.
CARPENTER, M.A. with Preface by R.
MARTINEAU, M.A. 5 vols. 8vo. 63s.

Ewald's Antiquities of
Israel. Translated from the German
by H. S. SOLLY, M.A. 8vo. 12s. 6d.

The Types of Genesis,
briefly considered as revealing the
Development of Human Nature. By
A. JUKES. Crown 8vo. 7s. 6d.

The Second Death and
the Restitution of all Things; with
some Preliminary Remarks on the
Nature and Inspiration of Holy Scripture. By A. JUKES. Crown 8vo. 3s. 6d.

The Gospel for the Nine-
teenth Century. Third Edition.
8vo. price 10s. 6d.

Supernatural Religion ;
an Inquiry into the Reality of Divine Revelation. Complete Edition,
thoroughly revised. 3 vols. 8vo. 36s.

Lectures on the Origin
and Growth of Religion, as illustrated by the Religions of India ;
being the Hibbert Lectures, delivered
at the Chapter House, Westminster
Abbey, in 1878, by F. MAX MÜLLER,
M.A. 8vo. 10s. 6d.

Introduction to the Sci-
ence of Religion, Four Lectures de-
livered at the Royal Institution ; with
Essays on False Analogies and the
Philosophy of Mythology. By F. MAX
MÜLLER, M.A. Crown 8vo. 10s. 6d.

The Four Gospels in
Greek, with Greek-English Lexicon.
By JOHN T. WHITE, D.D. Oxon.
Square 32mo. 5s.

Passing Thoughts on
Religion. By Miss SEWELL. Fcp. 8vo.
price 3s. 6d.

Thoughts for the Age.
By Miss SEWELL. Fcp. 8vo. 3s. 6d.

Preparation for the Holy
Communion ; the Devotions chiefly
from the works of Jeremy Taylor. By
Miss SEWELL. 32mo. 3s.

Bishop Jeremy Taylor's

Entire Works; with Life by Bishop Heber. Revised and corrected by the Rev. C. P. EDEN. 10 vols. £5. 5s.

Hymns of Praise and

Prayer. Corrected and edited by Rev. JOHN MARTINEAU, LL.D. Crown 8vo. 4s. 6d. 32mo, 1s. 6d.

Spiritual Songs for the

Sundays and Holidays throughout the Year. By J. S. B. MONSELL, LL.D. Fcp. 8vo. 5s. 18mo, 2s.

Christ the Consoler; a

Book of Comfort for the Sick. By ELLICE HOPKINS. Second Edition. Fcp. 8vo. 2s. 6d.

Lyra Germanica; Hymns

translated from the German by Miss C. WINKWORTH. Fcp. 8vo. 5s.

The Temporal Mission

of the Holy Ghost; or, Reason and Revelation. By HENRY EDWARD MANNING, D.D. Crown 8vo. 8s. 6d.

Hours of Thought on

Sacred Things; Two Volumes of Sermons. By JAMES MARTINEAU, D.D. LL.D. 2 vols. crown 8vo. 7s. 6d. each.

Endeavours after the

Christian Life; Discourses. By JAMES MARTINEAU, D.D. LL.D. Fifth Edition. Crown 8vo. 7s. 6d.

The Pentateuch & Book

of Joshua Critically Examined. By J. W. COLENSO, D.D. Bishop of Natal. Crown 8vo. 6s.

Lectures on the Penta-

teuch and the Moabite Stone; with Appendices. By J. W. COLENSO, D.D. Bishop of Natal. 8vo. 12s.

TRAVELS, VOYAGES, &c.

Sunshine and Storm in

the East, or Cruises to Cyprus and Constantinople. By Mrs. BRASSEY. With 2 Maps and 114 Illustrations engraved on Wood by G. Pearson, chiefly from Drawings by the Hon. A. Y. Bingham; the Cover from an Original Design by Gustave Doré. 8vo. 21s.

A Voyage in the 'Sun-

beam,' our Home on the Ocean for Eleven Months. By Mrs. BRASSEY. Cheaper Edition, with Map and 65 Wood Engravings. Crown 8vo. 7s. 6d.

One Thousand Miles up

the Nile; a Journey through Egypt and Nubia to the Second Cataract. By Miss AMELIA B. EDWARDS, Author of 'Untrodden Peaks and Unfrequented Valleys,' 'Barbara's History,' &c. With Facsimiles of Inscriptions, Ground Plans, Two Coloured Maps of the Nile from Alexandria to Dongola, and 80 Illustrations engraved on Wood from Drawings by the Author; bound in ornamental covers designed also by the Author. Imperial 8vo. 42s.

Wintering in the Ri-

viera; with Notes of Travel in Italy and France, and Practical Hints to Travellers. By WILLIAM MILLER, S.S.C. Edinburgh. With 12 Illustrations. Post 8vo. 12s. 6d.

San Remo and the Wes-

tern Riviera; comprising Bordighera, Mentone, Monaco, Beaulieu, Villefranche, Nice, Cannes, Porto Maurizio, Marina, Alassio, Verezzi, Noli, Monte Grosso, Pegli, Cornigliano, Genoa, and other Towns—climatically and medically considered. By A. HILL HASSALL, M.D. Map and Woodcuts. Crown 8vo. 10s. 6d.

Eight Years in Ceylon.

By Sir SAMUEL W. BAKER, M.A. Crown 8vo. Woodcuts, 7s. 6d.

The Rifle and the Hound

in Ceylon. By Sir SAMUEL W. BAKER, M.A. Crown 8vo. Woodcuts, 7s. 6d.

Himalayan and Sub-

Himalayan Districts of British India, their Climate, Medical Topography, and Disease Distribution; with reasons for assigning a Malarious Origin to Goitre and some other Diseases. By F. N. MACNAMARA, M.D. F.R.G.S. Surgeon-Major (retired) Indian Medical Service, late Professor of Chemistry, Calcutta Medical College, and Medical Inspector of Inland Labour Transport, Calcutta. 8vo.   [*In the press.*]

The Alpine Club Map of

Switzerland, with parts of the Neighbouring Countries, on the scale of Four Miles to an Inch. Edited by R. C. NICHOLS, F.R.G.S. 4 Sheets in Portfolio, 42*s.* coloured, or 34*s.* uncoloured.

The Alpine Guide. By

JOHN BALL, M.R.I.A. Post 8vo. with Maps and other Illustrations : --

The Eastern Alps, 10*s.* 6*d.*

Central Alps, including all

the Oberland District, 7*s.* 6*d.*

Western Alps, including

Mont Blanc, Monte Rosa, Zermatt, &c. Price 6*s.* 6*d.*

On Alpine Travelling and

the Geology of the Alps. Price 1*s.* Either of the Three Volumes or Parts of the 'Alpine Guide' may be had with this Introduction prefixed, 1*s.* extra.

WORKS of FICTION.

Novels and Tales. By the

Right Hon. the EARL of BEACONSFIELD, K.G. Cabinet Editions, complete in Ten Volumes, crown 8vo. 6*s.* each.

Lothair, 6*s.*	Venetia, 6*s.*
Coningsby, 6*s.*	Alroy, Ixion, &c. 6*s.*
Sybil, 6*s.*	Young Duke &c. 6*s.*
Tancred, 6*s.*	Vivian Grey, 6*s.*
Henrietta Temple, 6*s.*	
Contarini Fleming, &c. 6*s.*	

Tales from Euripides;

Iphigenia, Alcestis, Hecuba, Helen, Medea. By VINCENT K. COOPER, M.A. late Scholar of Brasenose College, Oxford. Fcp. 8vo. 3*s.* 6*d.*

Whispers from Fairy-

land. By the Right Hon. E. H. KNATCHBULL-HUGESSEN, M.P. With 9 Illustrations. Crown 8vo. 3*s.* 6*d.*

Higgledy-Piggledy; or,

Stories for Everybody and Everybody's Children. By the Right Hon. E. H. KNATCHBULL-HUGESSEN, M.P. With 9 Illustrations. Cr. 8vo. 3*s.* 6*d.*

Stories and Tales. By

ELIZABETH M. SEWELL. Cabinet Edition, in Ten Volumes, each containing a complete Tale or Story :—

Amy Herbert, 2*s.* 6*d.*   Gertrude, 2*s.* 6*d.* The Earl's Daughter, 2*s.* 6*d.*   The Experience of Life, 2*s.* 6*d.*   Cleve Hall, 2*s.* 6*d.*   Ivors, 2*s.* 6*d.*   Katharine Ashton, 2*s.* 6*d.*   Margaret Percival, 3*s.* 6*d.*   Laneton Parsonage, 3*s.* 6*d.* Ursula, 3*s.* 6*d.*

The Modern Novelist's

Library. Each work complete in itself, price 2*s.* boards, or 2*s.* 6*d.* cloth :—

By Lord BEACONSFIELD.

Lothair.	Henrietta Temple.
Coningsby.	Contarini Fleming.
Sybil.	Alroy, Ixion, &c.
Tancred.	The Young Duke, &c.
Venetia.	Vivian Grey.

By ANTHONY TROLLOPE.
    Barchester Towers.
    The Warden.

THE MODERN NOVELIST'S LIBRARY *continued.*

By Major WHYTE-MELVILLE.

Digby Grand. | Good for Nothing.
General Bounce. | Holmby House.
Kate Coventry. | The Interpreter.
The Gladiators. | Queen's Maries.

By the Author of 'The Rose Garden.'

Unawares.

By the Author of 'Mlle. Mori.'

The Atelier du Lys.
Mademoiselle Mori.

By Various Writers.

Atherstone Priory.
The Burgomaster's Family.
Elsa and her Vulture.
The Six Sisters of the Valleys.

The Novels and Tales of the Right Honourable

the Earl of Beaconsfield, K.G. Complete in Ten Volumes, crown 8vo. cloth extra, gilt edges, 30*s*.

POETRY and THE DRAMA.

Lays of Ancient Rome;

with Ivry and the Armada. By LORD MACAULAY. 16mo. 3*s*. 6*d*.

Horatii Opera. Library

Edition, with English Notes, Marginal References & various Readings. Edited by Rev. J. E. YONGE, M.A. 8vo. 21*s*.

Poetical Works of Jean

Ingelow. New Edition, reprinted, with Additional Matter, from the 23rd and 6th Editions of the two volumes respectively; with 2 Vignettes. 2 vols. fcp. 8vo. 12*s*.

Poems by Jean Ingelow.

FIRST SERIES, with nearly 100 Woodcut Illustrations. Fcp. 4to. 21*s*.

The Poem of the Cid: a

Translation from the Spanish, with Introduction and Notes. By JOHN ORMSBY. Crown 8vo. 5*s*.

Festus, a Poem. By

PHILIP JAMES BAILEY. 10th Edition, enlarged & revised. Crown 8vo. 12*s*. 6*d*.

The Iliad of Homer, Ho-

mometrically translated by C. B. CAYLEY. 8vo. 12*s*. 6*d*.

The Æneid of Virgil.

Translated into English Verse. By J. CONINGTON, M.A. Crown 8vo. 9*s*.

Bowdler's Family Shak-

speare. Genuine Edition, in 1 vol. medium 8vo. large type, with 36 Woodcuts, 14*s*. or in 6 vols. fcp. 8vo. 21*s*.

Southey's Poetical

Works, with the Author's last Corrections and Additions. Medium 8vo. with Portrait, 14*s*.

RURAL SPORTS, HORSE and CATTLE MANAGEMENT, &c.

Annals of the Road; or,

Notes on Mail and Stage-Coaching in Great Britain. By Captain MALET. With 3 Woodcuts and 10 Coloured Illustrations. Medium 8vo. 21*s*.

Down the Road; or, Re-

miniscences of a Gentleman Coachman. By C. T. S. BIRCH REYNARDSON. Second Edition, with 12 Coloured Illustrations. Medium 8vo. 21*s*.

Blaine's Encyclopædia of

Rural Sports; Complete Accounts, Historical, Practical, and Descriptive, of Hunting, Shooting, Fishing, Racing, &c. With 600 Woodcuts. 8vo. 21*s.*

A Book on Angling ; or,

Treatise on the Art of Fishing in every branch ; including full Illustrated Lists of Salmon Flies. By FRANCIS FRANCIS. Post 8vo. Portrait and Plates, 15*s.*

Wilcocks's Sea-Fisher-

man : comprising the Chief Methods of Hook and Line Fishing, a glance at Nets, and remarks on Boats and Boating. Post 8vo. Woodcuts, 12*s. 6d.*

The Fly-Fisher's Ento-

mology. By ALFRED RONALDS. With 20 Coloured Plates. 8vo. 14*s.*

Horses and Riding. By

GEORGE NEVILE, M.A. With 31 Illustrations. Crown 8vo. 6*s.*

Youatt on the Horse.

Revised and enlarged by W. WATSON, M.R.C.V.S. 8vo. Woodcuts, 12*s. 6d.*

Youatt's Work on the

Dog. Revised and enlarged. 8vo. Woodcuts, 6*s.*

The Dog in Health and

Disease. By STONEHENGE. Third Edition, with 78 Wood Engravings. Square crown 8vo. 7*s. 6d.*

The Greyhound. By

STONEHENGE. Revised Edition, with 25 Portraits of Greyhounds, &c. Square crown 8vo. 15*s.*

Stables and Stable Fit-

tings. By W. MILES. Imp. 8vo. with 13 Plates, 15*s.*

The Horse's Foot, and

How to keep it Sound. By W. MILES. Imp. 8vo. Woodcuts, 12*s. 6d.*

A Plain Treatise on

Horse-shoeing. By W. MILES. Post 8vo. Woodcuts, 2*s. 6d.*

Remarks on Horses'

Teeth, addressed to Purchasers. By W. MILES. Post 8vo, 1*s. 6d.*

The Ox, his Diseases and

their Treatment ; with an Essay on Parturition in the Cow. By J. R. DOBSON, M.R.C.V.S. Crown 8vo. Illustrations, 7*s. 6d.*

WORKS of UTILITY and GENERAL INFORMATION.

Maunder's Treasury of

Knowledge and Library of Reference ; comprising an English Dictionary and Grammar, Universal Gazetteer, Classical Dictionary, Chronology, Law Dictionary, Synopsis of the Peerage, Useful Tables, &c. Fcp. 8vo. 6*s.*

Maunder's Biographical

Treasury. Latest Edition, reconstructed and partly re-written, with above 1,600 additional Memoirs, by W. L. R. CATES. Fcp. 8vo. 6*s.*

Maunder's Treasury of

Natural History ; or, Popular Dictionary of Zoology. Revised and corrected Edition. Fcp. 8vo. with 900 Woodcuts, 6*s.*

Maunder's Scientific and

Literary Treasury ; a Popular Encyclopædia of Science, Literature, and Art. Latest Edition, partly re-written, with above 1,000 New Articles, by J. Y. JOHNSON. Fcp. 8vo. 6*s.*

Maunder's Treasury of

Geography, Physical, Historical, Descriptive, and Political. Edited by W. HUGHES, F.R.G.S. With 7 Maps and 16 Plates. Fcp. 8vo. 6*s.*

Maunder's Historical

Treasury ; Introductory Outlines of Universal History, and Separate Histories of all Nations. Revised by the Rev. Sir G. W. COX, Bart. M.A. Fcp. 8vo. 6*s.*

The Treasury of Botany,

or Popular Dictionary of the Vegetable Kingdom ; with which is incorporated a Glossary of Botanical Terms. Edited by J. LINDLEY, F.R.S. and T. MOORE, F.L.S. With 274 Woodcuts and 20 Steel Plates. Two Parts, fcp. 8vo. 12s.

The Treasury of Bible

Knowledge ; being a Dictionary of the Books, Persons, Places, Events, and other Matters of which mention is made in Holy Scripture. By the Rev. J. AYRE, M.A. Maps, Plates & Woodcuts. Fcp. 8vo. 6s.

A Practical Treatise on

Brewing ; with Formulæ for Public Brewers & Instructions for Private Families. By W. BLACK. 8vo. 10s. 6d.

The Theory of the Mo-

dern Scientific Game of Whist. By W. POLE, F.R.S. Tenth Edition. Fcp. 8vo. 2s. 6d.

The Correct Card ; or,

How to Play at Whist ; a Whist Catechism. By Major A. CAMPBELL-WALKER, F.R.G.S. Latest Edition. Fcp. 8vo. 2s. 6d.

The Cabinet Lawyer ; a

Popular Digest of the Laws of England, Civil, Criminal, and Constitutional. Twenty-Fifth Edition, corrected and extended. Fcp. 8vo. 9s.

Chess Openings. By F.W.

LONGMAN, Balliol College, Oxford. New Edition. Fcp. 8vo. 2s. 6d.

Pewtner's Compre-

hensive Specifier; a Guide to the Practical Specification of every kind of Building-Artificer's Work. Edited by W. YOUNG. Crown 8vo. 6s.

Modern Cookery for Pri-

vate Families, reduced to a System of Easy Practice in a Series of carefully-tested Receipts. By ELIZA ACTON. With 8 Plates and 150 Woodcuts. Fcp. 8vo. 6s.

Food and Home Cookery.

A Course of Instruction in Practical Cookery and Cleaning, for Children in Elementary Schools. By Mrs. BUCKTON. Woodcuts. Crown 8vo. 2s.

Hints to Mothers on the

Management of their Health during the Period of Pregnancy and in the Lying-in Room. By THOMAS BULL, M.D. Fcp. 8vo. 2s. 6d.

The Maternal Manage-

ment of Children in Health and Disease. By THOMAS BULL, M.D. Fcp. 8vo. 2s. 6d.

The Farm Valuer. By

JOHN SCOTT, Land Valuer. Crown 8vo. 5s.

Rents and Purchases ; or,

the Valuation of Landed Property. Woods, Minerals, Buildings, &c. By JOHN SCOTT. Crown 8vo. 6s.

Economic Studies. By

the late WALTER BAGEHOT, M.A. Fellow of University College, London. Edited by RICHARD HOLT HUTTON. 8vo. 10s. 6d.

Economics for Beginners

By H. D. MACLEOD, M.A. Small crown 8vo. 2s. 6d.

The Elements of Bank-

ing. By H. D. MACLEOD, M.A. Fourth Edition. Crown 8vo. 5s.

The Theory and Practice

of Banking. By H. D. MACLEOD, M.A. 2 vols. 8vo. 26s.

The Resources of Mod-

ern Countries ; Essays towards an Estimate of the Economic Position of Nations and British Trade Prospects. By ALEX. WILSON. 2 vols. 8vo. 24s.

The Patentee's Manual ;

a Treatise on the Law and Practice of Letters Patent, for the use of Patentees and Inventors. By J. JOHNSON, Barrister-at-Law ; and J. H. JOHNSON, Assoc. Inst. C.E. Solicitor and Patent Agent, Lincoln's Inn Fields and Glasgow. Fourth Edition, enlarged. 8vo. price 10s. 6d.

INDEX.

Spottiswoode & Co. Printers, New-street Square, London.